OBSESSION

Every day he studied the scrapbook. Faithfully. To keep alive the memories. And the
hatred. In each of the hundreds of clippings
the name Kathryn Townsend was underlined in red ink which bled through the thin
newsprint, leaving small marks, like wounds.
Every article focused on her and her hotels.
Elegant, Fashionable, Sumptuous—the words
jumped out. Taunting him. She had stolen
the success that was meant to be his. . . .

With a sudden jolt of excitement, his eyes
took fire at a memory. A blade slashing
through silk . . . plunging into the softness
of the pillow . . . the thin steel blade of the
knife he used to destroy . . .

DARE TO DREAM

LINDA PRICE

AVON BOOKS ◆ NEW YORK

AVON BOOKS
A division of
The Hearst Corporation
105 Madison Avenue
New York, New York 10016

First Avon Books Printing: July 1989

AVON TRADEMARK REG. U.S. PAT. OFF. AND IN OTHER COUNTRIES, MARCA REGISTRADA, HECHO EN U.S.A.

Printed in the U.S.A.

K-R 10 9 8 7 6 5 4 3 2 1

Book One

Chapter One

Lowell, Massachusetts
September 1906

It was a Victorian monstrosity. Dark, cumbersome and sinuous, it dominated the front hallway. A carved lion's head snarled out from each corner of the mirror. At night Kathryn was afraid to walk past it, but now, with the morning sunshine pouring into the hall, it didn't seem nearly as frightening, and the four bowler hats hanging from their hooks above the mirror made the hat stand look like a familiar old friend—almost. Three of the hats belonged to the boarders. The fourth was Edward's. She sneaked a glance up the wide staircase that curved up to the second floor to reassure herself that he wasn't standing there, staring down at her. But she knew that Edward always had breakfast in his room. She was safe.

Kathryn sniffed at the air—bacon and coffee. She pictured her mother standing over the big black stove wrapped in a blue-and-white apron and enveloped in a cloud of steam, stirring oatmeal and frying eggs and definitely too busy to wander into the front hall. That left the boarders, but from the sounds of clipped, early morning conversations coming from the dining room she suspected they were all at the table.

Reassured, Kathryn turned toward the mirror. Edward wouldn't let her have a mirror in her own room; he said she was already vain enough for three little girls. But this morning was important. She really did have to see if her dress was pressed, her pinafore spotless and that her hair hadn't escaped from the tightly plaited braids. It was important. Im-

3

portant enough for her to sneak down into the front hall, where she didn't belong.

Today was the day her real life would begin. It was her first day of school and she'd been marking the days off on the drugstore calendar in the kitchen all summer long. Her eyes fell to her high, shiny black boots, carefully polished the night before, then slowly traveled up to the hem of her navy blue dress, to her white cotton pinafore and finally to her dark, shiny hair. Slowly she twirled in the mirror, making her skirt swing out from her twiglike, dark stockinged legs. It was only then she saw it—a great gaping hole in the back of her skirt. Like a tongue, the flap of material hung down, exposing the white of her petticoat.

She knew exactly how it had happened. But she could never admit she'd torn it climbing in the apple tree when she was lookout on a pirate ship. Edward said nice little girls didn't climb trees and they certainly weren't pirates. Well, she couldn't appear on the first day of school with a hole in her skirt either. Her mother would have to sew it up. She straightened her shoulders and marched into the kitchen.

"No, Kathryn, I cannot stop this moment to do your mending. How would the boarders like half-cooked eggs and raw bacon? They'd soon enough find another boardinghouse, and then where would we be? Then you'd be thankful for any dress, even one with a little hole in it."

"But, Momma, it's not a little hole at all. Look at it." Kathryn turned around and wiggled two of her fingers through the hole, but her mother wasn't even looking.

Kathryn tugged at her sleeve. She responded without taking her eyes off the eggs. "Kathryn, wait until after I've finished with breakfast, then I'll fix it."

Kathryn sighed. Her mother didn't understand at all. "But I'll be late for school. And Edward says they beat you if you're late. Even a minute. Honestly, he told me so."

Looking down at her daughter's pleading eyes, Lily was tempted to let the hired girl take over, but Bridget wasn't much of a cook and one of the boarders was bound to complain. "Well, Kathryn, you'll have to decide which you want to do—be late or stop being so vain and wear the dress, hole and all."

It was useless to argue with her mother when she was like

this. Sometimes her mother was so kind and gentle. She loved her when she was like that. It was harder to love her when she was strict and cross. Kathryn wondered why her mother couldn't be nice all the time. She bit her lip to keep from crying; girls who were big enough to go to school didn't cry. She was halfway up the narrow servants' staircase when Bridget caught up with her.

"Miss Kathryn, wait a minute. Wouldn't be right to go traipsin' off for your first day of school lookin' like that, would it? 'Tis an important day." A broad, sympathetic smile spread over Bridget's red-cheeked Irish face. "Don't fret. I'll fetch my sewing basket."

Suddenly lighthearted—her first day of school would be perfect after all—Kathryn scampered up the stairs. But at the sound of his voice her feet froze to the treads.

"What are you doing here? Why, aren't you in the kitchen? I was under the impression that was what we paid you for." Edward stood at the top of the stairs, his tall, cranelike figure looming over them, his shadow spilling down the stairs, engulfing them. His eyes were fixed on Bridget.

Whenever Kathryn heard about God in Sunday school, a God who made commandments and punished sinners, she thought of Edward. God also looked down on the world through half-hooded eyes, jabbing a bony finger at those poor souls below him. And it would only seem right that God's voice, coming from up in the sky just like snow, would sound cold, like Edward's. She never dared mention it to her Sunday school teacher. Somehow she didn't think Miss Fox would approve. She never told Edward either.

Confronted with silence and downcast eyes, Edward icily repeated his question. Finally Bridget stammered, "Miss Kathryn, you see, she has a tear in her dress. I was going to fix it. Wouldn't take me but a minute. 'Tis her first day of school. . . ."

"I am well aware that it is her first day of school. Just as I am well aware that you belong in the kitchen, and if you value your job you will return there. Immediately."

Kathryn spoke up. "Don't blame her. It was my fault. I can't go to school like this, and Momma . . ."

Edward never raised his voice. No matter how angry he was, he spoke in a low tone, but his quiet voice carried with it a sinister suggestion of barely restrained violence. "I will not listen to any excuses. You, Kathryn, will go to school. And you will go immediately. Without whining." As he turned on his heel and retreated to his room, quietly closing the door behind him, Kathryn and Bridget each gave an unconscious sigh of relief and scurried back to the kitchen.

Kathryn knew the way to school by heart. Go to the corner by the white house with the big pillars and turn right. Walk three blocks to the corner with the yappy dog that always sat on the front porch and turn right. Then go one block more past the little gray church with the colored windows. She must have walked past it a hundred times during the summer. She couldn't wait to walk up those steep front steps and through the door with the word "Girls" cut in big letters in the stone above it and into a new world. A world where all sorts of mysteries would suddenly become clear to her—reading and writing and sums and something she didn't quite understand called geography.

It was early and the school yard was deserted. Without a moment's hesitation she crossed the asphalt and hurried up the stairs. It was only when she reached the top and stared upward at the massive red brick building that she saw to her horror the letters above the door: "Boys." Would they punish her for going to the wrong door? Maybe they'd think she was stupid and couldn't read. Well, she could, if the words were short. What if going through the wrong door turned her into a boy? No, that was silly, but if she stood here or changed her mind and walked all the way down again and up the right steps, somebody might see her. Taking a deep breath and unconsciously straightening her thin shoulders, she pulled at the door. It barely moved. She gave it a stronger tug. Finally it opened about a foot and she slipped in.

On either side of her loomed a long hallway. It seemed to stretch on and on forever. Along the hallway were ranged doors—all forbiddingly closed. There must be hundreds of them. How would she ever find the right one? Behind her the heavy door gave a loud thump as it closed. She turned and resisted a temptation to flee. No, she'd been waiting too long for this day. She'd find the right classroom and no one would ever know about her dress.

She cocked her ear. There was a rattling coming from one end of the hall. Maybe it meant somebody was down there. She walked slowly, studying the class photographs on the walls so she wouldn't have to listen to the eerie echo of her boots tapping against the tiles. The hall was endless. Finally she peered around a corner. A man was mopping the floor. She tiptoed across the wet floor toward him. "Excuse me, could you please tell me where the first-grade classroom is?"

He looked up, surprised to see her. He spoke with a guttural accent. "Early, why here so early?"

Kathryn stared down at her boots. She couldn't explain to a stranger, but he didn't seem to need an answer. Sloshing his mop back into the bucket, he merely said, "You please follow me, miss."

He led her down to the end of the hall and then opened a door. "Here, first grade. Miss Hamilton." He nodded his head at her and backed out. Kathryn wondered if he was Greek. Her mother said all the Greeks who came to town to work in the cotton mills were dirty and lazy. But he seemed nice. She liked his white mustache and the way it bobbed up and down when he spoke.

The problem was where to sit. She didn't want to sit up front near the teacher, not if the teacher liked to beat students. She decided on the desk farthest away, in the back corner near the window. As she sank down into the well-worn seat, she finally felt safe and allowed herself to study her first classroom.

The front wall was covered with blackboards. Black. Untouched. Over the boards were cards with all the letters, big letters and little letters and numbers. She looked down at her desk; someone had carved his initials on it: "C.C." She wondered who "C.C." was. It must be a boy; girls never carried pen knives, although she thought it might be fun to have one. Boys seemed to find so many things to do with theirs—sharpening pencils, whittling twigs, carving soap boats . . .

"My, what have we here, an early bird?"

When she heard the voice, Kathryn turned toward the door and saw her. She looked like an angel. Not, of course, exactly like the ones in the Christmas carol books with their long white gowns and golden wings, but Kathryn would not

have been surprised to see a halo floating above her head.
She wore a white blouse with a high lace collar fastened with
a gold brooch set with purple stones. The purple matched
her skirt, which looked dark and shiny, just like the eggplants
in the garden. It was beautiful. She was beautiful.

As soon as Miss Hamilton walked into the classroom,
Kathryn knew she would love school. Her blond hair was
piled high on top of her head, and although little curls escaped from the pins, they looked soft and pretty. Not at all
like when my hair escapes from the braids, Kathryn thought
enviously. Her eyes were blue and sparkling and her complexion was soft and pink, like a kitten's nose, Kathryn decided. But the best thing was her smile. It was soft and gentle,
and Kathryn couldn't ever imagine her new teacher not smiling.

The morning flew by like a wonderful dream. Miss Hamilton didn't send her back out into the school yard, and when
the rest of the students filed in, she let Kathryn keep the seat
she had chosen. And as she wrote letters and numbers on the
blackboard, Kathryn was able to recognize them all and she
even forgot her shameful secret.

Until the lunch bell rang and the other students rushed off.
Only Kathryn stayed in her seat. Suddenly she felt the hole;
it burned into her body like a glowing coal. Everybody would
see it; the boys would tease her and the girls would never
want to be friends and, worst of all, she'd never be allowed
to come back here, into the warm circle of Miss Hamilton's
smile, into the sunny room that smelled of chalk dust and
freshly sharpened pencils and new paper.

"You may go now, too, Kathryn," Miss Hamilton repeated.

Finally Kathryn stammered, "I—I can't."

"Why not? Don't you want your lunch?"

Kathryn felt a hollow in her stomach and remembered she'd
left home without eating breakfast. Still she shook her head.
But looking into Miss Hamilton's soft blue eyes, she felt the
tears start streaming out of her own. They wouldn't stop.
"There's a . . . a hole . . . in my dress. I can't get up."

Miss Hamilton's lips smiled, looked for a moment as if
they were turning up into a laugh, then abruptly froze.

"That's not a big problem, is it? I have a sewing basket right here in my desk. Shall I mend your skirt for you?"

"Oh, yes, yes, please." Kathryn exhaled in relief.

As she walked home for lunch Kathryn decided this was the most wonderful day of her life. And that Miss Hamilton was the most wonderful person in the whole wide world.

"Kathryn, Kathryn." The querulous voice rose up the stairwell. She stopped. She wanted to be by herself in her own room this afternoon. To think about Miss Hamilton, her smile and her sparkly purple brooch. To remember how she, Kathryn Abigail Townsend, had stood up in front of the whole class and recited the alphabet without one mistake. She'd been the only one who could do it and she hadn't even been scared. She knew her mother wouldn't have time to hear about it. And Edward, Edward would only spoil everything. He always did.

The voice rose again. This time it sounded worried. Momma said she must be nice to her father. Slowly and reluctantly, she turned around and went downstairs.

She paused in the doorway of the library. This was her father's world. It had been ever since Kathryn could remember. Here he sat, winter and summer, in a worn old wing chair, a faded comforter wrapped around his legs. A book rested on his knees, but now he seldom even turned its pages. He stared out into the backyard. Kathryn sometimes wondered what he watched. The chickens scratching in the grass. The old black-and-white tomcat lazily stalking a bird. The leaves falling. The snow drifting.

She hated this room. It was hot. There was no air. And it smelled funny, sort of sweetish. Like when you raked up leaves in the spring and they were all wet and slimy underneath.

"Kathryn, there you are, my dear. Tell me, how . . ." He paused, his entire body caught up in a spasm of coughing. Finally it stopped, and he pulled a handkerchief from his sleeve and wiped his lips. "How was school? Your first day. An important day in your young life, wasn't it?"

"Yes, Papa," Kathryn said, solemnly nodding her head and hoping he wouldn't expect her to kiss him. His skin felt so warm and dry. Like paper in an old book that would crackle and break. She hated to touch him. But she knew she must never let him know that.

"Come here," he said, patting the stool at his feet. He was glad to have something to talk about. "Tell me all about it. Do you have a nice teacher?"

The floodgates opened. "Oh, yes, she is so wonderful. Her name is Miss Hamilton and she looks just like an angel in the Christmas carol book, honestly, she does. And she has the most beautiful purple brooch. When I grow up I am going to have one just like it." For some reason Kathryn didn't want to tell her father about the hole in her dress. She supposed because it would be like tattling on her mother. "Tomorrow we are going to start doing sums—arithmetic." She wrapped her tongue around the new word and then smiled because she knew she'd gotten it right.

Robert Townsend smiled down fondly at his daughter. It sometimes seemed impossible that he could have had any part in producing such a beautiful creature. No, she wasn't beautiful. Not yet. Now she was just pretty. But she would be a beauty. His artist's eyes analyzed his daughter's face. Her hair was dark—a rich mingling of colors from deepest black to reddish mahogany to golden brown—like the mellow colors of a fine old violin. Her cheekbones were exotically high. And her eyes were chameleonlike, constantly changing. Sometimes hazel. At other times green or golden. And they were framed by exquisite dark lashes. What an irresistible flirt she would be one day. But he doubted she would ever want to be. Even at the age of six his daughter was serious, far too serious for her age. It was as if she had a mission in life, although he certainly had no idea what it would be and was sure Kathryn didn't either.

As she sat caught in the late afternoon sunshine pouring in through the window, her hair glinted red and golden. Her features were delicate. All except her chin, which was strong and determined and would always keep her from being a doll-like beauty. How he wished he could paint her portrait. He looked down at his crippled fingers, the joints shiny red and swollen. Perhaps he would never have been able to capture her spirit on canvas.

He knew she didn't love him. How could she? The night she was born he'd driven all night through a blizzard to be with his wife. Before Kathryn could walk he had set her on his shoulders and galloped through the garden pretending to be a pony while she'd gurgled in delight and grabbed fistfuls of his hair. But she would remember none of that. All she knew of her father was that he was a sick old man, barely able to walk, confined to one room, living on the charity of a man he'd grown to hate.

"And what will you do when you learn all about arithmetic? Help your mother do the accounts?" he asked, eager to share in her excitement.

She stared up at him for a moment as if making an important decision. "No," she finally said, slowly and deliberately. "No, I am going to have my own money. Lots and lots of it."

"And what will you do with all this money?" he asked, forcing himself not to smile.

"I'll use some of it to make you well," she said, "and . . . and with the rest I'll buy a really big house and then the boarders will give me more money. And I'll buy another house."

Robert felt a little flame suddenly burst into being in his heart. Perhaps his daughter did feel some fondness for him. She certainly seemed to have a good grasp of how to make money. Begrudgingly he realized he had Edward to thank for that. Lord knew, it was a skill he had never mastered.

"Kathryn, you know who you remind me of? Your great-grandmother Abigail. Did I ever tell you about her?"

He had. So often, Kathryn knew the story by heart, but he loved to tell it, so she shook her head.

"Once upon a time in England there was a duke. He had six handsome sons. And when they were young men, almost grown, two of them fell in love with the same woman. She was beautiful and neither brother wanted to give her up. So they decided to have a duel to decide who would marry her. Because dueling was against the law, they met very early in the morning in a field next to the family chapel. The brothers were close and they really couldn't bear the thought of hurting each other. But a pistol misfired and the younger was killed. According to the story, the survivor carried his brother's body into the chapel. But he was so horrified by what he

had done that he ran away. He took a new name and came
to Boston. He never saw his family again.

"It was his son, Charles Townsend, who was given all this
land by the king," Robert said, stretching his crippled hand
toward the window. "Two square miles, it was. Then came
the American Revolution, and Charles' family were loyal to
the king. They were Tories." He paused. "Do you know
what that means?" Kathryn nodded. "It doesn't mean they
were bad people. They just thought differently, as people have
a right to do. But their neighbors didn't believe they had that
right, so Abigail Townsend—who was a little girl just about
your age—and her parents ran away, to Canada. Abigail grew
up and got married. Her husband was a merchant and she
worked right beside him. Even went on trading voyages with
him—to India and China. But she wanted to come back to
the house where she'd been born. And they did, with a big
bag of gold, and bought this house."

Kathryn knew all about her brave ancestor. After all, wasn't
she named after her? Kathryn Abigail Townsend. "What happened to the land?" she prompted.

"Well, that belonged to the neighbors. They'd stolen it
when they ran the family off."

"But she got our house back, didn't she? And our garden
and everything. And she made a famous inn out of it."

"That's right. I think you've heard this story before."

"And now Momma and Edward have the boarders, don't
they?" she said, satisfied that the story seemed to have come
full circle.

"Yes, that's right," he said sadly. "They have the boarders." Looking down at Kathryn, he resisted the temptation
to pat the little white hands that lay so still in her lap. But he
knew she didn't like being touched. At least not by him.

Kathryn dug her bare toes into the soft, sun-warmed earth
and lay her head back in the grass. It was long and it tickled
her cheeks. She was supposed to be weeding the kitchen
garden, but the weather was too warm. Too warm even for
her to climb the apple tree, although that abandoned birds'
nest was tempting. If Edward weren't home she could sneak
away and go swimming, but Edward said it wasn't ladylike.

It was as if summer, reluctant to leave, were making one

more spectacular appearance. Even the insects were fooled, buzzing around the garden on their earnest errands. Squinting into the sun, she stared up at the row of bean poles. The plants, long past bearing, were putting the last remains of their energy into growing up toward the sky. They looked as if they would go onward, up and up forever, if only summer would stay.

Just like Jack and his magic beanstalk, Kathryn thought. It was one of her favorite stories. The way Miss Hamilton told it, you could almost see the giant's big, black, shiny boots and hear his voice booming out, "Fee, fi, fo, fum, I smell the blood of an Englishman." It made the hairs on the back of her neck stand up every time she heard it, even though she knew Jack would be safe.

At first she was surprised that most of the other children, even Billy Mulligan, already knew these stories. Samantha Brewster, who sat next to her and who was her best friend, explained that her mother always told her a story before bedtime. She fastened her big dark eyes on Kathryn and asked, "You mean your mother doesn't tell you a story every night when she tucks you into bed?" Kathryn shook her head, ashamed to admit that she put herself to bed. Before that, Bridget had helped her get out of her clothes and reminded her to brush her teeth and say her prayers. Her mother was too busy, she said. But Kathryn's absolute favorite story—the one about Cinderella, the prince and the glass slipper— sounded familiar. Maybe her mother had told it to her once upon a time when she was a very little girl.

Kathryn's eyes turned from the beanstalks in the clouds back to the garden, where the pumpkins were just ripening. She could imagine them turning into golden coaches. It was harder to imagine rats becoming beautiful prancing horses, but if she shut her eyes and tried really hard . . .

The vision disappeared. A big black shape was blocking her sunlight, and she was suddenly cold. She opened her eyes to see her mother standing above her, and she remembered that she'd promised to weed at least three rows before lunch. Before she could scramble to her feet, her mother, gracefully wrapping her long skirt around her, sat down beside her on the grass.

"Lovely, isn't it?" Lily asked, inclining her head to include the lush green vegetable garden, the expansive lawn, the orchard and the cloudless cerulean sky.

"Mmm," Kathryn murmured, afraid to break the spell. She looked at her mother, who had closed her eyes and was tilting her face gratefully toward the sun. Kathryn had no idea of her mother's age. She only knew she must be old; one had to, to be a mother. But suddenly Lily's face looked younger, softer, as if she were a young girl again. The hardness of the years dropped away. Momma is beautiful, Kathryn thought in amazement. Not a golden angel like Miss Hamilton. But a dark angel. She supposed angels *could* have black hair and brown eyes.

Excited by her discovery, Kathryn asked, "Momma, do you know any fairy tales? And will you tell me one? Please."

Without opening her eyes, Lily smiled. Of course she knew fairy stories. Every Irish child grew up on them. Not only fairy stories but tales of leprechauns and hidden treasures, of long-ago knights and their ladies, of legendary kings, and big dogs that howled in the night when someone was going to die. Her uncle had told these stories better than anyone, especially when he'd been at the poteen. Then he would swear that he'd met with the little people and they'd shared their secrets with him. One day, he said, he'd go looking for their golden treasures, and then they'd all be rich and live in a castle. He'd promised.

Lily had a sudden urge to share these magical stories with her daughter—an urge that cut across her chest like a fierce pain. Then the memory of the dark and filthy tenement across the river flashed into her mind. Wasn't it better that her daughter continue to live the lie she had created? Edward had his place on the hill now; he'd forgotten that other world. She must, too.

"Fairy tales, no, I don't know any," Lily snapped.

Trying to ignore the all-too-familiar tone of voice, Kathryn said, "I do. Shall I tell you one? Miss Hamilton has told us lots of them."

But her mother didn't answer. "I know, I'll tell you all about Cinderella. She was . . ."

Lily looked down at her daughter. She was young and vulnerable. Something no woman could afford to be. "Kathryn," she said, placing her hand over her daughter's, "I know the story. It's a fine one. But you know it's only a story, don't you? Things don't happen like that. You can't depend on anyone else to change your life in some miraculous way. Your life is what you make it.''

''But, Momma, look at that pumpkin over there,'' she said, pointing to an enormously rotund one. ''Doesn't that look just like a coach?'' She gestured with her left hand, not wanting to pull away the one that rested so comfortably under the warmth of her mother's.

At times my daughter seems so mature, Lily thought. At other times, like now, she's a child. I suppose she's too young to understand. When she's a little older . . . I can't let her go into the world thinking everything will have a happy ending like a fairy tale.

As she rose and carefully brushed off her skirt, Lily scanned the garden. ''You have two more rows to weed before lunch.'' But her tone was gentle.

Kathryn attacked the weeds with a fury. Not one weed was to be tolerated amidst the rows of pumpkins and squash. Every last dandelion and chickweed uprooted, she kept hoping that her mother would return. To admire and praise. But she didn't. Not that it really mattered. Her mother was beautiful and she loved her. That was what was important.

Chapter Two

At the end of October, when the leaves were beginning to turn and the early morning air had a chill to it, a new boarder arrived. Mr. Walsh, after forty-seven years in the accounting department of the Appleton Mill, had retired. Now he sat, smug and self-satisfied, at the Townsend table for the last time. Occasionally his plump white hand would reach down to pat the new gold pocket watch that had been a retirement gift. He was somewhat disappointed that his fellow boarders had all been at the table when he'd shown it. Now there was no excuse to bring it out again. Unless perhaps the child—he glanced over at Kathryn—asked to see it once more.

Silly old fool, Edward thought, watching the hand disappear beneath the table once again. Wouldn't catch me working my heart out for half a century and then grinning myself silly when I got a handshake and a watch. No, there were better ways to make money. He frowned, remembering that Walsh had been paying him rent faithfully. He looked over at the new boarder. A Mr. Jamison. He was a traveling salesman. Everybody knew what they were like. Edward just hoped he'd pay his rent promptly. One lapse and he'd be out on the street. The man looked young, too young and handsome to be responsible. Soon as you knew it, he'd get some girl in the family way and there'd be an empty room again.

Lily Townsend was pleased. Mr. Walsh was a very demanding man. Took advantage of his seniority and demanded everything done the way he liked it. Never mind that she had five other guests to cater to. Then she looked over at Edward, who was frowning at the new boarder. Perhaps she shouldn't be so pleased after all.

Kathryn couldn't keep her eyes off Mr. Jamison. He was so handsome with his bright red hair and blue eyes. And unlike Mr. Walsh, who always looked as if he had a sour ball in his mouth, Mr. Jamison had a smile that stretched all the way across his face. Once when he caught her staring he winked. Hoping that no one else had seen him, she fixed her eyes on her plate as she felt her face turn red.

Mr. Jamison sold "notions"—she wasn't quite sure what they were—and he said he'd been everywhere. "Yes, I've seen just about every place in this country of ours—New York, Chicago, Washington, D.C., Charleston, Mobile, New Orleans, St. Louis. Why, I've even been to California." Kathryn's eyes widened in amazement. She'd never known anybody who'd actually been there, but she knew it was very far away and that they didn't have winters.

"Strange place, California," he said. "Lots of funny-looking trees—skinny with round tops. People speaking Spanish, too. Sun's always shining and there are miles and miles of beautiful beaches, the most beautiful you could ever imagine."

"Harrumph," Edward said, pushing away his plate. "What the shrewd businessman"—he looked disdainfully at David Jamison, making it clear that he was not included in that category—"is doing is not raving over some palm trees and beaches, but investing. Investing in California's future. Someday people will rediscover California. It will be the gold rush all over again. People will stream in from all over the country just for those beaches and warm weather. A man investing now stands to make millions of dollars. Millions." His voice took on that dreamy, faraway tone it always did when he spoke of making money.

To Kathryn, hanging onto every word, it sounded like a magical place. She knew she had to ask a question, although Edward had warned her to eat in silence and not bother the paying boarders. "Please," she piped up, "can you tell me how I get to California?" Mr. Jamison smiled, a smile so warm that Kathryn failed to notice Edward's threatening scowl.

"Why, by train. I'll bet there's a train you could catch right here in Lowell, go to Boston and then all the way to Los Angeles. Of course, you'd have to change in Chicago and maybe a few other places. But you could sleep and eat right on the train.''

Kathryn's mind was alight with the idea even as she tried to figure out where on a train they could hide the beds. ''When I grow up I am going to make a million dollars and then go to California and make a million more,'' she announced smugly, beaming at all the faces around the table.

Edward laughed, exposing too many yellow teeth in his gaunt white face. ''You mean you are going to marry a rich man? An admirable plan.''

''No,'' she said unhesitatingly, giving a determined shake to her braids. ''I am going to make a million dollars all by myself.''

As the boarders joined in the laughter, Edward felt a growing sense of embarrassment. She was making a fool of herself—and him. Spouting off all these childish little dreams. Why, she'd be lucky to find a man who could keep her fed adequately and had enough self-control not to saddle her with a new baby every year.

''I think we've heard quite enough of your infantile nonsense, Kathryn. Women cannot and do not make their own fortunes. That is men's work.''

''I already have four dollars in my coin bank. And I am going to California.'' She hesitated. Mr. Jamison said that people spoke Spanish in California. . . . ''Do they take American money in California?''

The friendly smile on Mr. Jamison's lips suddenly broke into a broad grin which turned into a loud laugh. Soon everyone at the table was laughing. Even Mr. Walsh. Kathryn looked around in horror, unable to understand what she had said that was making everyone laugh at her. She could feel her face redden and wished with all her heart she could disappear under the table.

The laughter abruptly halted when Edward spoke. ''You stupid child. Don't you even know that California is part of the United States? Are you so lazy that you don't try to learn anything that precious Miss Hamilton of yours tries to teach you? Or maybe you can't learn. I've always believed that educating women is like throwing money down a well. Women can't think the way men do. The good Lord didn't see fit to make their minds the same way.

"Maybe I shouldn't even bother sending you to school. It's time you started earning money for this family. Perhaps I should send you into the mills. There you'd have to work twelve hours a day. Do you know what happens to the mill girls when they don't pay attention?" He paused ominously. Scared, Kathryn shook her head.

Edward's eyelids dropped, and with the tip of his tongue he licked his thin pale lips as if he were relishing the warning. "They have their hands cut off. Or sometimes their whole arms. If they are careless for a second, their bodies get pulled into the machinery." He watched Kathryn's face grow paler, her eyes widen in fear. "Or worse, they get scalped. Like the Indians used to do. Their hair gets caught in the belts and is pulled out. By the roots. How would you like it if your beautiful hair were pulled out?"

Kathryn knew she must respond, but she was afraid to speak. Afraid she might cry. And tears only made Edward angrier. Without looking up, she nodded.

"Well," Edward said, staring at her, "I'll be lenient with you this time. You won't go into the mills. Not now. But you must be punished for your stupidity, mustn't you? Tonight you will do the dishes all by yourself. It's time you grew up."

Lily looked at him with surprise. How could he expect . . . ? Those iron cooking pots were heavy and unwieldy. Too small to reach the stove, Kathryn could easily scald herself. Lily opened her mouth to protest and found Edward's half-hooded eyes penetrating into hers; they seemed to control her whole body. No, she couldn't go against Edward. He knew what was best.

Nothing was said for the rest of the meal. The boarders ate in embarrassed silence. Although Edward made a feeble joke about sensitive little girls taking everything far too seriously, no one listened.

The pot wouldn't budge. Kathryn grasped the potholders and put her hands around it and tried to maneuver it toward the edge of the stove. She tugged until her fingers ached. Finally she dragged a chair over to the black range. Balancing on it, she carefully grasped the handle of the pot with both hands and pulled. The steam hit her in the face, making her drop the handle in surprise and pain. Wiping the moisture off her face, she rewrapped her hands in the potholders and tried again. Slowly she lowered the pot to the floor. With her feet she pushed the pot along the worn linoleum floor to the sink. Then she moved the chair. She hoisted the pot with a grunt and, standing on tiptoe, poured the steaming water over the pile of dirty dishes in the sink.

She picked up a bar of yellow soap and a brush and started scrubbing the way she'd seen her mother do. The plates were slippery and she didn't dare think what would happen if she broke one. Carefully she dipped each one in cold water to rinse it. Then she dried them, stacking them on the oilcloth-covered table. Just as she finished the last cup, the kitchen door opened. She hoped it would be her mother; Kathryn wanted her to see what a fine job she'd done.

But it was Edward. He said nothing as his eyes darted around the kitchen, searching for something undone or out of place.

Terrified, Kathryn shifted her gaze to the narrow dark door next to the chimney. Behind it lay a creaky flight of stairs and then—the cellar. It was dark down there, like a dungeon, and the earth floor made it cold and damp and smelly. The whitewashed walls were covered with mold. And even when you were carrying a lantern, you never could be sure what was hiding behind the bushels of apples and cabbages, sacks of potatoes and old cider barrels. Last winter Bridget had found an ugly black snake hanging from the rafters. She said she'd seen its eyes first, little yellow slits. It blinked at her, then slithered away, but was it still down there? Kathryn held her breath. If Edward found anything wrong, he might lock her up in the cellar.

Finally Edward turned to her. "Well, you seem to have escaped this time, didn't you? No spills. No broken dishes. Perhaps you will turn out to be useful." His eyes narrowed and his thin lips twitched. "But you are never, never to embarrass me with your stupidity again. If you can't keep silent during meals in the future, you shall eat in the barn with the rest of the dumb animals. Is that understood?" He disappeared without waiting for an answer.

Kathryn's pride in a grown-up job well done evaporated. Maybe she was dumb, just like Edward said. Angrily she tore off her mother's apron, which she'd folded over several times to fit her own small frame, and tossed it toward the table. The moment it left her hand she realized her mistake. It struck the handle of a teacup and fell to the floor. In powerless horror she watched as the blue-and-white flowered cup tumbled after it. She was sure everyone in the whole house must have heard the crash. But even when the door opened she could do nothing but stare down in shame. If only she hadn't . . .

"What happened?" her mother demanded. Then her eyes went from her daughter's pale face to the shattered cup. It was all Edward's fault, Lily thought bitterly. Luckily he'd gone to his room. She got a dustpan and a broom and swept up the pieces. When she'd carefully hidden the remains, she faced Kathryn.

"Off to bed now. You've had a long day," was all she could say. Anything else would be disloyal to Edward. And the love she felt for him was too strong to permit the slightest disloyalty. She had lived her life for him for too many years to break his hold now.

Chapter Three

Edward was a bastard born to Lily Margaret Mary O'Donnell when she was sixteen years old and entirely alone in the world.

The O'Donnells came from the west country of Ireland, the barren hills of Connemara. For centuries they had farmed the same plot of stony land; raised sad-looking, black-faced sheep; kept a fat pig to be butchered each fall and a handful of chickens which scratched a meager subsistence out of the farmyard, faring no better or no worse than their owners.

Occasionally a wise son or a foolish daughter left the land to find fortune elsewhere. Few found it. In 1878 Jack O'Donnell decided his fortune lay anywhere but in Ireland. He sold everything worth selling—which was little—and with his wife and his fourteen-year-old daughter, Lily, he headed south to Cork and a ship to America. The voyage was so terrible—the stench of unwashed bodies crowded together almost unbearable; the food, what there was of it, inedible; the constant pitching and rolling of the ship in the winter waters so sickeningly terrifying—that once she reached land Lily never spoke of it again.

Jack had a distant cousin who worked on the canals in Lowell, Massachusetts. So that was where the O'Donnells, sick, tired and weighed down with all they owned, headed. Where Lowell was or why there were canals there, they weren't sure. But it was the beacon that kept them going. If fortunes were to be made in the United States of America, theirs would surely be made in Lowell.

From the moment their train pulled into the city, Lily hated it. She found herself surrounded by mill buildings, massive red brick structures that stretched for blocks and looked alarmingly like prisons. Three stories high, they were bigger than any building she'd ever seen in her life. Dark, dank canals crept through the city like tentacles carrying power to the mills. The sky was completely obscured by the giant clouds of smoke pouring out of the stacks that sprouted up all over the city like evil mushrooms. Lily wrinkled her nose in disgust; the smell was nothing like the rich peat fires of home.

The cousin, surprised by their arrival but obliging, found them two rooms on the ground floor of a wooden tenement that leaned from the weight of time like an old man. When she saw the tiny kitchen and closetlike bedroom, Katharine Claire Costello O'Donnell, for the first time in her life, thanked the Lord for seeing fit to give her only one living child.

"The pigs at home smell better, even in the summer," Lily announced when she saw the open sewer in the street. Rotting vegetables lay in the gutter until they turned to pulp or were gratefully eaten by the packs of thin and hungry dogs that prowled the streets. She saw a bundle of rags lying there but was afraid to consider what it might be. "Welcome to The Acre," a neighbor said warmly, but all Lily could think of was their spotless little cottage nestled in the green hills. This filthy Irish ghetto would never be her home.

They arrived in Lowell on a Tuesday, and on Thursday Lily went to work in the Appleton cotton mill as a spinner. At six o'clock in the morning she filed through the mill gates with hundreds of other men, women and children and up two flights to the spinning floor, where she would spend the next twelve hours. Despite the cold outside, the temperature reached one hundred degrees inside. Hot, damp air was good for the cotton fibers. No one cared what it did for the workers. The filthy windows that let in their only light—because of the ever-present danger of fire, lamps were forbidden—had been nailed shut, and the suffocating air was thick with lint. It settled in her hair, made her dress white, irritated her nose and occasionally caught in her throat, causing dry coughing spasms. But it was the noise—the awful noise—which Lily found the hardest to endure. Hundreds of machines clickety-clacked continually, making such a racket that it was impossible to hear over them. Not that there was anyone to talk to.

Once she was trained, Lily was given a machine next to a
French Canadian girl who spoke no English and an olive-
skinned woman whose only words seemed to be "Hello, good
morning." It was, Lily learned, carefully arranged this way.
The owners didn't want the workers to waste time or foster
dissension by talking to one another.

As Lily stood day after day in front of the noisy machine,
wondering if she would faint from the heat or go deaf from
the racket, and feeling her feet grow numb from the constant
vibrating of the floorboards beneath them, she wondered if
she'd really died and gone to hell. Maybe hell was not devils
and pitchforks and eternal flames after all. Maybe this was
the American version of hell.

After two months in the mill, Lily found someone who
hated the life as much as she did. Someone who wasn't pitifully grateful for the small wages to feed a family. Someone
determined to get out. His name was Marcel Lacasse and he
was one of the French Canadians who, like the Irish, had
come to Lowell in search of a better life. Marcel was one of
twelve children for whom his father had tried to eke out a
living from twelve acres of worn-out land near Quebec. Only
Marcel had recognized the hopelessness and futility. At the
age of fifteen he'd walked three hundred miles across the
border, to a new country and a new life.

Like many immigrants before him, he didn't find it. But
by the time he was eighteen he thought he'd found the solution. "Unions—we workers must unite," he told Lily. "It's
the only way we can get anything from those bloodsucking
mill owners."

Lily was converted. It didn't matter that she was attracted
to his dark, curly hair, his blue eyes that blazed with an angry
fire when he spoke of injustice, and his strong, broad, manly
body; she was also seduced by his words. Her parents, scared
like most of the mill workers of losing their precious jobs,
feared him. "A confounded agitator," her father claimed.
Besides, he was a Frenchy, and the Irish hated them all.
There was nothing a gang of Irish schoolboys liked better
than throwing stones at a French Canadian victim. And so
Jack O'Donnell forbade his daughter to see Marcel. But by
then she was caught up in his spell, the spell woven by his
charismatic personality, his arresting good looks and his fiery

idealism. By the spring they had become lovers, and Lily discovered that he put as much passion into his lovemaking as into his speeches. She couldn't get enough of it.

By the summer Lily knew she was pregnant. At first fearful, she found herself cherishing the fact, imagining the life she and Marcel would share. But Marcel was frantic as he saw his glorious plans for the future vanish. With a wife and child, he too would become a prisoner of the mills. "Please, please try to understand," he begged her. "It's something I must do. Not for me, but for thousands of other people." Lily was smart enough to know she could force him into marriage. Or her father could. But she was wise enough to know that wasn't what she wanted.

When she told her parents, her mother cried, long keening cries, like an old Irishwoman mourning her dead. Her father looked like a volcano ready to erupt; then he cursed and threatened with all the force of his Irish temper. Finally they went off to consult with the priest. Father Carmichael, who had a fervent belief in the Old Testament God of wrath and vengeance, informed them their daughter had twice sinned. Once by fornicating—and with a Frenchy at that—and worse, by refusing to marry the man and give the baby a father. The church had no choice but to disown her, and neither did they.

From the moment she left her parents' two grim tenement rooms, Lily's whole life was focused on the baby. It was as if her family and Marcel had ceased to exist, as if this were to be a virgin birth. Everything she did was for the baby. Since she had no family, no friends, no church, a job she could barely tolerate, the baby became the sole reason for her existence. If her own clothes were becoming worn and frayed, she still spent her evenings lovingly embroidering tiny garments by lamplight. And if she went without coal for the stove or those little extras like tea and jam, it was to save money for the baby.

In one respect fate smiled on her, and she was able to conceal her condition until four weeks before she was due. Over and over she'd made her calculations: she could afford to be unemployed for only six weeks. Once the baby was born, she'd have to return to the mills or find other work. But the opportunities for a young immigrant girl with an illegitimate baby were few.

Chapter Four

Watching the dark, curly head poised above his chest, feeling the warm tongue tease his nipples into tight little buds and at last experiencing the delicious pain of sharp white teeth sinking into his flesh, Edward decided it was time to take a wife. Emperors need heirs. If he was to build a great financial empire, he needed sons—strong, clever sons to stand at his side and to carry his empire to even greater heights after he was gone.

The head rose and Edward closed his eyes. He didn't want to see it. Over the years the face had become repugnant to him. Once upon a time she had been beautiful, but whores age quickly. Especially the foreign ones. Their buxom figures turn to fat; their sensuous features become fleshy; their olive skin looks like old cheese. Only her mouth remained the same—full and ripe and red. And so creative. What she could do with her tongue. . . . Sometimes he wondered why he had chosen this Greek whore and why he kept returning to her sour-smelling room above the drugstore. Yet if anyone had pointed out that she had soulful eyes like Lily's, he would have been stunned.

To Edward, at the age of twenty-seven, looking for a wife was a new experience and he didn't know where to start. Lowell was teeming with women, young women of all sizes, shapes and colors, but they were mill girls, foreigners suitable for relieving the occasional physical need. Certainly not proper stock from which to breed emperors.

Emperor. Empire. They were not words he'd ever voice to another human being. But as he planned and schemed, he saw himself as a Julius Caesar, fighting, winning, consolidating his power, and most important, becoming richer and richer.

The boardinghouse was profitable, under his regime. So profitable that he wanted to acquire another one. He'd already found the right one. He had tried to buy the house, but the old widow who lived there all alone in her decaying old age had emphatically refused his offer. He'd have to either make his offer more generous—an unpleasant thought—or wait until she died and hope her heirs were more sensible than sentimental.

But someone would have to run the place, so he was looking for a wife. According to his calculations, it would, in the long run, cost less than hiring a housekeeper.

"Seventeen cents." Kathryn couldn't keep the pride out of her voice as she answered the question. Nobody else in the class knew the answer. Not even the boys.

Jessica Hamilton tried not to nod her head too enthusiastically. Little Kathryn Townsend never ceased to amaze her. The child's mind soaked up information like a sponge. She raced ahead of her classmates in her desires and abilities. While the rest of the class was still struggling with simple sums, Kathryn was begging to be taught the mysteries of multiplication. Was this the one brilliant student every teacher was supposedly blessed with once in a lifetime? No, Jessica decided. Kathryn Townsend was smart, but not brilliant. It was her determination that set her apart. The way she relished any challenge. In her mind nothing was too big, too difficult, too complicated. Every challenge could be met—and won.

She looked across the room at Billy Mulligan, who sat in apparent fascination contemplating his ten grubby fingernails. Life could play cruel tricks. How much better Kathryn's determination would be suited to a boy, even a boy like Billy Mulligan. To a girl, spirit was a hindrance, making life more difficult. But perhaps Kathryn would be different.

She remembered what a little lost soul Kathryn had been that first day of school, huddled in the back of the room like a timid little rabbit threatening to skitter off if anyone made a move in her direction. It hadn't taken the child long to blossom, which made Jessica wonder about Kathryn's family. Why didn't they give her the love and encouragement she so

desperately needed? Sending a child off to school like that
with a big hole in her dress . . . what had her mother been
thinking of? How could they be so blind? At least Jessica
hoped it was blindness, not calculated cruelty.

Kathryn looked around and saw Miss Hamilton staring at
Billy Mulligan. She didn't like Billy Mulligan. His hands
were always so dirty, which was surprising because they were
so often in his mouth. Perhaps he never washed. Her mother
said that the Irish seldom did. "Pigs," her mother called
them, but under her breath, and Kathryn knew she wasn't
supposed to hear. But even if they were pigs, the Mulligans
had invited Miss Hamilton to their home. And she had gone.
Other students had bragged about having teacher to dinner.
If only *she* dared ask. If only her mother would say yes. She
stubbed her toes on the floor. She knew exactly what she'd
say: "You will have to ask Edward." And Edward would say
no. And if he didn't . . . What if he sent her away from the
table in shame right in front of Miss Hamilton? She could
feel the flame of humiliation creep up her face.

But it was such a beautiful sunny afternoon—unseasonably
warm for early May—that as she walked home under an arch
of budding sycamores, her fears began to recede. How could
anything go wrong on a day like this? Even the hollow clip-
pety-clop of horses' hooves against the cobblestones had a
happy ring to it.

If Lily hadn't been feeling guilty, she never would have
said yes, and the tragic chain of events would never have been
set in motion. But she'd just come from visiting Robert. Her
visits were infrequent; the hired girl saw to his needs—fed
him, bathed his emaciated body, changed his bed linens,
fetched his medicine. Now Lily was overwhelmed by her
emotions. It happened every time. Either she pitied him, seeing in his pale, shrunken face the handsome man she had
married, or she hated him for failing her. Hating him made
her feel guilty. He was a good man. The illness wasn't his
fault. They were both victims. That was what she kept telling
herself.

"Please, Momma, may we invite Miss Hamilton to dinner? Everyone else in the class has. Please say yes."

She looked down into Kathryn's pleading eyes. Robert
loved his daughter so much. Perhaps if she said yes, she

could rid herself of these terrible feelings of guilt, at least for a little while.

Kneeling on the window seat, her nose pressed against the cool glass, Kathryn was dying a death of a thousand little agonies. If thoughts and wishes had power, Jessica Hamilton would have materialized right in the middle of the sidewalk. But the sidewalk remained deserted except for a small yellow dog sniffing along the gutter. Would she really come? What if she were late? Would the boarders wait? What would she wear? Kathryn hoped with all her heart that she would wear her beautiful purple brooch. A clock chimed and Kathryn's head swiveled toward it before she realized it was only the grandfather clock in the corner; it hadn't told the proper time, ever. Her father said it was a family heirloom, so it didn't matter.

The parlor, which no one had ever thought to modernize, was the prettiest room in the house. It was out of the eighteenth century, filled with polished mahogany in the manner of Thomas Chippendale, much as it had been when Benjamin Townsend and his family were driven out of town—under a threat of tar and feathers—with only their clothes on their backs. The walls were a faded Wedgwood blue highlighted with white molding. The wide oak floorboards showing the heelmarks of seven generations were covered with worn, though still richly colored, Turkish carpets.

Blue-and-white Delft tiles showing Bible scenes surrounded the elegant little fireplace; they had been imported by an earlier Townsend. Perhaps, Kathryn thought, the stern ancestor who stared out from over the mantel. Red-faced, hook-nosed and with a sour smile, he stood piously, Bible in hand. On the other side of the room his sharp-featured wife held a round-faced infant who looked like a caricature of its father. It was quite the funniest-looking baby Kathryn had ever seen.

She turned from the portrait when she heard footsteps in the hall. Her heart sank. Would nothing go right? Edward was home. Please, God, she prayed silently, don't let him be mean tonight. Sometimes he just sat there without saying a word. If only her mother would smile and talk and look happy. This evening had to be perfect.

When Miss Hamilton arrived, exactly on time, she was wearing her purple brooch and a mauve dress and looked more like an angel than ever. Kathryn proudly led her into the dining room and recited her introductions as she had been taught. "Miss Hamilton, this is my mother." The two women nodded politely to each other. Kathryn turned to Edward. "And this is—"

"And this must be your father," Jessica Hamilton smoothly interrupted.

Edward, pretending not to hear, announced in a nervous tone, "I am her brother, Edward, and I am delighted that you could join us this evening." Lily blushed self-consciously yet proudly, like a young girl, as she always did when people made this mistake, which they often did. Edward's gaunt face and sharp features and the way he stooped slightly made people think he was well into middle age. And since no one ever saw Lily with Robert . . .

Very graciously Edward pulled out Jessica's chair. As the guest of honor, she was seated on his right. His introductions to the boarders were perfunctory, although all six men appeared to be fascinated by her. Kathryn was so excited she could barely sit still; even Edward liked Miss Hamilton. Her heart almost burst with joy as she saw a smile on Edward's pale face as he turned to her and said, "I am pleased to meet you. Kathryn has told us so much about her teacher. I understand you are newly arrived from Boston."

"Yes, I was born and grew up there, but I decided I wanted to see a little more of the world and came to Lowell to live with an aunt. Not," she said, laughing at herself, "that this is so far away from Boston or really another part of the world."

"In spirit, perhaps," Edward said. "The mills. All the foreigners. Different languages. Unusual customs. Although I must say we are rather isolated from all that up here on the other side of the river."

"Yes, I find that a little disappointing. What fascinating stories those people must have to tell. How I would love—"

"Their stories would definitely not be for a woman of your background, I fear," Edward said. But he was relieved when Bridget entered bearing the soup tureen. He worried that his words had been harsh. To compensate, he smiled and asked,

"Tell me, how do you find teaching? I've always thought it a most worthwhile occupation for a woman."

"Oh, I love it. I can't imagine ever doing anything else. Molding young minds is thrilling. Especially when I have a student as bright as your sister, Kathryn," she said, smiling down the table at her beaming pupil.

"Is that so?" Edward said, not bothering to hide his surprise. "I'm afraid I . . ."

Kathryn knew it. He was going to say something dreadful about her—about how she was a vain little girl, a useless child who climbed trees and didn't know her place—and Miss Hamilton would hate her.

As if he understood her fears, Mr. Jamison came to her rescue. "I'm pleased, Miss Hamilton, that you came to Lowell, but I don't understand how the men of Boston ever let you escape." He grinned. "I bet you left a string of broken hearts behind you."

Miss Hamilton returned his smile and with no trace of coyness or malice said, "Some hearts deserve to be broken."

Kathryn's eyes lit up with excitement. So Miss Hamilton had a romantic past. She bet nobody else in class knew that. Wait until she told Samantha Brewster! She wondered if any of these men ever fought a duel over her, like the men in her father's story.

Now that he had Miss Hamilton's attention, Mr. Jamison was determined to monopolize it. She was impressed to hear he'd been to California. Her grandfather had almost joined the gold rush. "Only a sudden case of gout stopped me from being born a Californian," she said with a gentle laugh. "By the time he'd recovered from the gout he decided to go to sea, and he made his fortune in the Orient trade instead."

Cutting off Mr. Anderson, who was trying to initiate a discussion about the unseasonable weather, Edward turned to her and said, "Yours sounds like an adventurous family."

"I'm afraid that streak was short-lived. My father continues to run the shipping business, but he sits at a desk and, according to him, gets seasick on a ferryboat."

Only Lily, who was watching him closely from the other end of the table, noticed it—a sudden flicker of attention in Edward's eyes at the mention of business interests. Something went cold in her heart. Her son had never before shown any serious interest in another woman. She had foolishly allowed herself to relax, to think it might never happen. But of course Edward would want a wife, and considering how charming and solicitous he was being tonight, he must consider this woman a suitable candidate. Family money—that was what would make Jessica Hamilton attractive to Edward.

It wasn't fair, Kathryn thought crossly. Miss Hamilton was her guest; she should be sitting next to her. Instead Edward's sleek, dark head was poised close to Miss Hamilton's golden one, and they were talking so quietly that all Kathryn could hear was old Mr. Cranshaw's false teeth as he chewed on the grisly pot roast. She looked at her mother, whose lips were pinched into a thin white line as she stared down at her plate. Was her mother mad because she couldn't hear either? Angrily Kathryn poked at her meat and planned what she would say to Miss Hamilton after dinner.

But staring at Miss Hamilton as she sat in the parlor balancing a coffee cup in her lap, Kathryn found herself tongue-tied. She so much wanted to say something interesting or clever, but her mind had suddenly stalled. Instead she took the excuse to run upstairs and get her wrap so she and Edward could walk Miss Hamilton home. Edward was in the front hall when she came down. "Where do you think you are going?" he asked.

"With Miss Hamilton and you," she said.

"I do not recall anyone inviting you," he said, coldness chilling every word.

"But—but she is my guest," Kathryn said as she felt her lower lip tremble.

"You are just a child. Whatever makes you think she would enjoy your company? I'm sure she gets enough of little brats during the day." Edward watched her eyes fill with tears and marveled how women, of any and every age, were always so emotional.

Kathryn stared up at him, forcing herself not to cry. This time he would not spoil everything. Her jaw took on the stubborn set that in later years would be a warning signal. "Miss Hamilton is my teacher and I won't let you be mean— not tonight." She accompanied her words with a stamp of her small foot.

"You will go up to bed now. Without another word. You'll pay for defying me, you little—"

He stopped as the parlor door opened and Miss Hamilton appeared. "I see I'm going to have two escorts," she said, looking at Kathryn, whose heart leapt for joy.

"I am afraid my sister is tired and overly excited. I have suggested that she go to bed early. I am sorry," Edward said with an oily sincerity.

The way Miss Hamilton looked at her almost made up for Kathryn's disappointment. Her eyes were so soft and her voice was so warm when she said, "Well, I'm sorry, too. But off you go to bed. And thank you for the invitation. This was the nicest evening I've spent in a very long time." She bent down and kissed Kathryn on the cheek, enveloping her in the sweet scent of lavender. I bet she didn't do that to Billy Mulligan, the dazed Kathryn thought as she drifted off to sleep, her hand pressed against her unwashed cheek.

Lily couldn't sleep. As she lay alone in her bed, her mind kept returning to Edward. Finally she fell asleep remembering the tender touch of his lips as he suckled at her overflowing breasts.

Chapter Five

Edward's birth had been an easy one, a fact which convinced Lily that hers was the most wonderful baby ever. "You're all I have in the world," she crooned to him as soon as the midwife placed him in her arms. "And I promise I'll do anything in the world for you." She didn't name him after Marcel, whom she had not thought of in months. Instead she chose to name him after a favorite uncle, an exuberant, laughter-loving man. When she went to register his birth, she put down—with no regrets—"Father Unknown."

She decided not to return to the mill. The money would be less, but she could spend all her time with Edward if she took in laundry. Her dawn-to-dusk days were spent over a steaming washtub or bending over the kitchen table ironing the fine linens of the gentry up on the hill. She always took Edward when she went to deliver the laundry. She thought it important that he see where the gentry lived, because one day her son would live up on the hill with them.

When Edward was three, Lily sold her old copper laundry tub and began to call herself a seamstress. By the time Edward was four, the women from the fine houses were allowing Lily O'Donnell to make their lacy petticoats and camisoles, long cotton nightdresses and occasionally a plain lawn blouse. Her tiny stitching and innate sense of style impressed them, and soon she was permitted to make their day dresses, walking outfits and riding habits.

Once a week Lily still crossed the river and went up the hill to where the gentry lived, but now she could afford to make the trip on the trolley. Edward accompanied her and they always played the same game: if I could have any house

I wanted, which would I choose? Edward chose a rambling Victorian with turrets; he called it a castle. Lily's favorite was a big white clapboard with a fanlight over the front door, black shutters and two tall brick chimneys. To Lily that house symbolized Yankee wealth, tradition and respectability. A dream to be aspired to.

Lily Margaret Mary O'Donnell no longer believed in God. Along with Sunday mass, Hail Marys and confessionals, He was relegated to her past life, a life which she seldom, if ever, thought about. So when she joined a church it was not out of a spiritual need, but because the church was the only place where an Irish immigrant girl could rub elbows with the gentry. As soon as Edward could be trusted to behave himself, Lily took him to services at the Episcopal church. She chose the church carefully. It had been established by one of the most important mill owners and numbered among its congregation the majority of the wealthy and influential Protestants in the city.

To anyone observing Lily, she was a beautiful young woman completely caught up in the religious rituals. No one had any reason to suspect the real motive for her attendance: to study them—their clothes, their speech, their manners. While everyone bowed in prayer, Lily's eyes swept the room, studying the ladies' hats, noting what was in style and which hats were most becoming.

Every Sunday morning Lily's mind churned with information, and she spent the next week putting to use what she'd learned. Within a year there wasn't a trace of a brogue in Lily's speech—except when she was angry, and then she could sound like a Dublin fishwife.

When Edward was old enough to start school, Lily had to accept the fact that no matter how much in demand her work became and how many hours a day she worked, she could never make enough money to send her son to private school. She only hoped that he would choose his friends from his little Sunday school class rather than from the social undesirables of the first grade. The first friend Edward made was Sean, the red-haired, freckled son of an Irish canal worker. An aghast Lily told him he must never speak to the boy again. After several more false starts he finally brought home for Lily's inspection the eldest son of a haberdasher and the

grandson of a local doctor. Occasionally Edward would look
wistfully across the school yard where Sean was leading his
friends in a loud game of snap-the-whip or cowboys and Indians and think that perhaps his two new friends were a bit
dull, but he'd been taught not to question his mother's de-
crees. Much to Lily's regret, no one in his Sunday school
class ever showed any interest in befriending him.

If her son had new friends, Lily felt no need for female
companions and no desire for a man. After all, she had Edward. Although men considered her beautiful, they knew by
her manner that they could look but never, never touch. Lily
went everywhere with her son.

They attended lectures on spiritualism and temperance; saw
magic lantern slides of the Holy Land and the Amazon jun-
gles; listened to readings of Shakespeare and Dickens. In the
summer they took the trolley to the end of the line and went
hiking and blueberry picking in the country. In the winter
they walked in the park and, when it was cold, watched the
ice skaters. Edward begged his mother for a pair of skates,
but she, seeing how easy it would be to break through the
ice and drown, refused. Boys had to be protected from themselves.

When Edward was old enough to be taught gentlemanly
manners, it was his mother's arm he took when crossing the
street and whose chair he pulled out when, once a month,
they dined out in a restaurant. It was expensive, but not a
self-indulgent treat; Edward had to learn how to behave in
the world outside the Irish ghetto.

At the age of seventeen Edward had sprung up to well over
six feet tall. He'd never be handsome—his nose was too
hawklike, his chin too pointed, his cheekbones too prominent—even his mother had to admit that. But he was distin-
guished-looking. She almost burst with pride when she
walked into church on his arm and saw all the other women
stare enviously and the young girls sneak sly glances.

At the same time, the adolescent Edward was undergoing
a subtle—but dangerous—change. He was realizing how much
power he wielded over his mother. In his hands her love for
him was a weapon. The discovery was to change the course
of both their lives.

At first he was surprised to see how she blushed like a

young girl when he complimented her on a new outfit. How he could make her pretty pink mouth harden into a thin ugly line when he said he wouldn't be coming right home to her after school, that he was meeting friends. It didn't take him long to learn how to use this knowledge to his advantage. If she refused to increase his allowance, he would talk about some pretty classmate until he could see the tears welling up in her eyes. Then she'd promise him the extra money and he'd reassure her that the girl was not nearly as pretty as she was—that she was his best and most beautiful girl. Sometimes he did it just for fun. It was like pulling the wings off a fly and watching it struggle, and he enjoyed it.

Lily's client list continued to expand. More and more frequently she was summoned to the fine houses up on the hill and she savored each excursion into the world of the rich, memorizing every detail of the houses and their inhabitants, storing away descriptions of the antique furniture, the fine paintings, the crystal chandeliers, the richly colored Oriental carpets, the silver tea services, to tell Edward. She studied how the servants performed and how their employers treated them. When the time came, she would be ready.

In the spring of 1898 her time finally came. Calling on a new client, Lily was delighted to discover that the house was the big white one she had labeled hers in that long-ago game with Edward.

Burning with curiosity, she trotted up the wide brick steps and dropped the lion's-head knocker against the shiny blue door. No one came. She waited, staring at the brass lion. Its smirk seemed to dare her to give in to curiosity. If no one was at home, she rationalized, no one could possibly see her walking in the garden.

As she came through the lush flower garden into the orchard, she spotted a man sitting at an easel. She almost fled, but once again curiosity outweighed caution. His canvas was filled with bright, shimmering colors. Puzzled, she looked at the subject in front of him—a tumbledown old shed surrounded by a thicket of dead weeds—and thought what a miracle the artist's eye must be.

"Do you approve?" he asked without even turning around.

Lily forgot she was a trespasser. "Oh, yes. It's beautiful. It's the most beautiful thing I've ever seen."

And when Robert Townsend turned around, he decided that Lily Margaret Mary O'Donnell, with her sparkling eyes, cap of dark hair and generously molded figure, was the most beautiful thing he'd ever seen.

The customer she'd come to see was his mother, who had been called away, but he volunteered to bring out some lemonade. It was the first excuse he could think of to keep the enchanting creature at his side. And so Lily perched on his artist's stool, sipped lemonade and told him her life story: how she was left a widow with a young son to raise after her husband had been killed at sea.

Robert Townsend was thirty-seven years old and obsessed with his painting. This was the first time he'd ever been in love. His mother had no choice but to accept, albeit reluctantly, the idea of a former seamstress joining the family. Robert was her only son; if he didn't marry, the Townsend name, one of the oldest and proudest names in Lowell, would die out. This girl was a bit old, but she could be expected, with a little luck, to produce one or two children and preserve the line.

Four months later Lily walked down the aisle of St. Anne's Church on Edward's arm. As she looked up toward the altar, the wedding guests noted the smile on her lips and assumed it was directed at Robert, who was gazing at his bride with awe and adoration. They would have been surprised—shocked—to know she was seeing a big white house up on the hill.

On her wedding night Lily endured Robert's lovemaking—which bore little resemblance to the youthful, uninhibited passion of Marcel—and wished with all her heart that she could love her new husband. But that really didn't matter. She had arrived. She and Edward now lived up on the hill.

They were still newlyweds when Robert's mother died. She went to her reward peacefully, knowing that there would soon be another Townsend entering the world. Lily genuinely mourned her mother-in-law, but it was the revelation that came after the woman's death that caused her to cry out in pain and agony.

There was no money. It was as simple as that, the lawyer said. The family fortune had been waning for years—there had been a series of bad investments—and Mrs. Townsend senior had been living off her capital. The house, of course, was theirs, as were the contents. Perhaps some of the land could be sold off. . . . Robert, existing in an unreal world of shock and grief, was no help.

Two days later Lily came up with an idea. By the time she finished outlining her plan, Robert was perfectly agreeable that his family home become an inn once again.

Of course, she never used the word "boardinghouse," which was what she really had in mind. There were six extra bedrooms, and she knew that single gentlemen in the city had trouble finding accommodations. Within the week all six rooms were rented, and if it was painful to Robert to see strange faces seated around the family dining table, he adored his wife too much to complain.

Chapter Six

Edward knew what he wanted. So did David Jamison. As carefully as generals at war, the two men, inspired by visions of golden curls and a peachlike complexion, planned their campaigns to win the hand of Jessica Hamilton.

On Sunday Edward accompanied Jessica to church, walking down the aisle proudly bearing the prize on his arm. Lily trailed behind him, impatiently tugging at Kathryn's hand. Kathryn was so delighted she sang the hymns with an unaccustomed zeal that made Lily look down at her in surprise. Usually Edward would have given her a sharp rap across the knuckles "for making a spectacle of yourself," but he was oblivious of everything but the tiny mauve-gloved hand clutching their shared hymnal.

Not to be outdone, David Jamison invited Jessica to a church picnic the following Saturday. In return, Edward escorted her to a lecture. "The Call of Christianity in Africa" was the subject, and Edward heard not one word. Two nights later David, who hated classical music, accompanied her to a chamber music recital.

Flattered, Jessica enjoyed the company of both men, and when she found herself mentally comparing them, she realized she didn't know which one she liked better. David laughed a lot and called her Jessie, which she said reminded her of an Irish kitchen maid; this made them both laugh, because Jessica Hamilton with her delicate, classical features and soft, cultured Boston voice was as far from an Irish immigrant as . . . "as a mule from a Thoroughbred," David declared. And his eyes lit up when he looked at her.

Edward . . . well, Edward was different. Very polite. Very

attentive. His eyes seemed to consume her with—she was almost afraid to think the word—passion. He did not tease her and laugh the way David did, but his seriousness was what attracted her. He was a man of ambitions. He had plans—plans to buy another boardinghouse, plans to open up a hotel, plans that didn't stop at Lowell but extended to Boston "and all over the East, and even into California. That area is expanding. They'll require hotels. It could be extremely profitable." Edward's enthusiasm stirred her. She was thrilled to imagine herself a part of that dream, standing behind him as he built his empire. Few women had the opportunity to make their mark in the world; their success came through the husbands they chose. Choosing a husband was very important. It was the only chance a woman got.

Not that either man had asked Jessica to become his wife, but Jessica knew that they would. Deep in her heart she knew.

Bridget's broad, work-reddened hand carefully smoothed out the fresh sheet. Working for the Townsends wasn't easy. Edward was too stingy to pay for proper help, and she and poor Mrs. Townsend were kept running all day long. Upstairs, downstairs, cooking, cleaning, ironing—there was always something to do from six o'clock in the morning, when she lit the kitchen stove, until ten o'clock at night, when she fell into bed. Still, there were nice things about the job. Taking care of Mr. Townsend was one of them. Kind, gentle, and he always seemed to know what you were thinking. Her grandmother back in Galway had been like that; everyone said she had special powers. It was a pity that he was so sick. Still, maybe it was better. He couldn't see how shamefully Mrs. Townsend doted on her son. Something not right about that. Bridget's brow furrowed. It was almost as if he were her husband. Always Edward this, Edward that, and "I'll wear this dress because it's Edward's favorite," and then she'd be heartbroken like some lovesick girl if Edward didn't notice.

What Edward needed was a wife, but Bridget couldn't find it in her heart to wish that that nice Miss Hamilton would accept him. Edward did seem smitten with her. It wasn't like him at all. If it were anyone but Edward, she'd hope that love might bring some warmth to his cold voice and those dark, icy eyes that could send a chill right down into your soul.

"You're looking very serious this morning, Bridget." Bridget was Robert Townsend's lifeline to the world. It was Bridget who cheered him up and kept him informed about the happenings in his house and the world outside.

"Am I?" He was, after all, her employer, and she was never sure how much she should say to him. If she said too much it might catch up with her. But it was his house and he did have a right to know, at least about some of it.

So she told him all about Miss Hamilton. "It would be nice for Miss Kathryn if they were to marry. For her, doesn't the sun rise and set on that woman?"

"Sounds as if you aren't entirely happy about it."

"Can't keep any secrets from you, can I, sir? No, I'm afraid Miss Hamilton, God help her, may be too . . . too fragile a creature for this house." There, she'd said it, and she hoped he wouldn't be angry.

He sat staring out the window and Bridget was certain she'd offended him. When at last he spoke, his voice was weaker than usual. "Yes, once upon a time this was a happy house. My mother—you never met her, did you?—a very warm, loving woman, and my father, my father was a true gentleman. Not like . . ." He paused, embarrassed. "Still, I don't suppose there's anything we can do about it. One invalid without the strength to leave his room and one overworked housemaid. I worry about Kathryn. I have a feeling she'll grow up to be a very strong woman, but she's still young and vulnerable. I want to keep her from being hurt, but . . ."

Bridget nodded her head in agreement as she punched the feather pillows into place. What could either of them do? The pity was that Kathryn was probably a little afraid of her father, scared and uncomfortable like most children when faced with sickness they didn't understand. And Mr. Townsend was in awe of his beautiful daughter. Sad thing was they needed each other. Kathryn was a little girl desperate for love and he adored her. If only one of them could reach out. A well-timed prayer was generally the answer, and Bridget resolved to say one that night and every night until they were answered.

* * *

The battle turned in David's favor the night he escorted Jessica to a moving-picture show. They sat on the hard chairs in the darkened nickelodeon which had once been Cabot's Hardware Store, listening to the tinny piano playing, watching the figures move jerkily across the screen, and were enthralled. And if, in the thrilling chase scene, his fingers sought out hers and were rewarded with a squeeze, it all seemed very right and natural. Afterward neither of them could not contain their enthusiasm; they talked fast, their words overlapping, until they realized they didn't have to talk at all, that they both felt the same way about this amazing new invention.

The next night they returned to see the same pictures. It was just as wonderful. The only thing different was that David held her hand throughout the whole show. Then, sitting in the back of the dark and almost empty streetcar, he asked her to marry him.

Although her heart was bursting to say yes, she was enough her mother's daughter to know that she shouldn't give him an answer immediately.

"Time, yes, if you insist, my Jessie." He hadn't been prepared to propose and he wasn't prepared for her answer, but he knew without a doubt that she loved him the way he loved her. "I have to go to Albany tomorrow morning," he explained, for the first time regretting his traveling life. "It'll only be for three days. If you need time to play coy maiden," he said, giving her hand an understanding squeeze, "I think I can wait that long."

Once she said yes there would be, Jessica realized, one difficult task to be faced—telling Edward.

But as it happened, the task fell to David. He couldn't resist the urge to wipe the self-satisfied look off Edward's face, let him know the better man had won. "I'll be back on Friday," he said jauntily the next morning. "To make an announcement."

He watched Edward's pale face; it betrayed no interest, no emotion. Damn cold man, David thought, pleased to be saving the woman he adored from such a chilly fate. To think that such a lively, warm, loving woman . . .

But Kathryn was excited. "What is it? Can't you tell us now?" She looked imploringly up at him. "Please. Just a hint." David knew how fond she was of Jessica and was tempted, when Edward interrupted.

"How many times have I told you that if you are allowed at this table you are to remain quiet. No one wants to hear a small child's chattering throughout the meal. You will ruin everyone's digestion."

Kathryn's eager face suddenly deflated. The corners of her mouth turned down and her eyes lost their sparkle of enthusiasm. Even her braids seemed to droop. Damn him, David thought. How can he do that to a child? She's bright and enthusiastic. Not naughty. No one else minds if she talks. No one except Edward. He just likes to torment her. What makes his life so miserable he can't bear to see anyone else—particularly his little sister—happy? The pity he felt for Kathryn was suddenly overwhelmed by anger when he thought of the child he and Jessica would have one day and the awful possibility that someone could be cruel to her. He wanted to lash out at Edward, to watch his face twist in pain. All he could think of was getting revenge. The consequences be damned.

"Don't worry," David said, forcing his salesman's smile to his tensed lips and staring at Edward's pale, hawklike face. "We'll send you an invitation to the wedding."

Kathryn, still not sure what he meant, watched in disappointment as he disappeared into the front hall. A moment later the door closed with an angry thump. In the dining room, where everyone sat in nervous silence, it sounded twice as loud. The boarders understood and were afraid to look at Edward. As was Lily, but only because she was fighting the smile which was threatening to break out all over her face.

Edward hated losing—anything. Once he'd had a mangy old cur, too lazy and stupid to learn any commands. Edward tried to beat obedience into him, but Brutus just got more stubborn and stupid. Edward complained bitterly about the useless dog and kicked it whenever his boot got within range of its lumpy, sleeping body. But one day the dog disappeared and Edward was furious. Mad as if the dog had been his best friend. So angry he took out an ad in the newspaper, offering a reward for its return. But the dog, perhaps with more cunning than Edward gave it credit for, was gone for good.

The thought that he might lose Jessica Hamilton gnawed

at him all day. Gone in a flash of anger was the vision of her angelic loveliness, the memory of her soft voice. All he knew was that Jessica was his, and that, like Brutus, she was being taken from him. Stolen.

By evening he had a plan.

The next morning when Kathryn left for school, she found Edward waiting for her, pacing back and forth outside the kitchen door. In his hand was an envelope addressed to Jessica.

Kathryn was surprised to see that Miss Hamilton didn't look happy to see the letter. She stared at it for a moment and then shoved it into her desk drawer. Just as she did when she'd taken the dead frog away from Billy Mulligan.

Edward waited until he heard the parlor door close and light footsteps in the front hall before he looked around at the boarders and said in a voice rather louder than usual, "I wonder whether we shall see Mr. Jamison again."

Mr. Dougherty puffed on his large cigar. "Don't see why not. Only going to Albany, he said. Goes at least once a month."

"Yes, I know that," Edward said, affecting a worried tone of voice. "Except for the letter . . ."

Mr. Anderson was always eager for a vicarious peek into someone else's life. His bald head popped up and he demanded, "Letter? What letter?"

"Not that I am in the habit of supervising the lives of my guests, but the day before he left, our Mr. Jamison received a letter. It was in a pale blue envelope. And it looked very much like a woman's handwriting. Flowery. Of course, I could be in error."

"Never know about traveling salesmen, do you?" Mr. Anderson piped up, hoping to hear more.

Edward smiled benevolently. Just as he had predicted, his guests were playing their roles perfectly.

Mr. Dougherty, who liked to be thought of as wise in the ways of the world, although he had lived his entire life in Lowell, said, "Once knew a traveling salesman had three wives and nine children. None of them knew anything about the others, of course. Worked out a clever schedule so he could spend four, five days with each every month. Always looked tired," he said with a knowledgeable wink in Edward's direction.

Edward resisted the temptation to deliver a moralistic frown. "Well, we don't know that Mr. Jamison is like that, do we? I'm afraid I didn't even ask him if he was married when he came here. Although he certainly hasn't been acting like a married man or even a man with commitments, has he?"

"Wonder why he goes to Albany so often," Mr. Anderson pondered.

"String of girls," Mr. Dougherty said disjointedly, as if contemplating the possibility, "all around the country."

Edward rose. "Well, gentlemen, I must join my mother and Miss Hamilton in the parlor now. And I am sure that you all have your own activities planned for this evening." He made his speech loudly enough so that Jessica would have time to disappear. He only hoped she'd noticed the blue envelope addressed to David Jamison in a feminine hand. He'd left it out on the table where she couldn't miss it. He thought he'd done the flowery script rather well.

As Bridget was bundling up the dirty linens, there was a knock at the door. Her eyes met Robert's in surprise. Kathryn was in school. Edward hadn't visited the sickroom in years, and Lily came only rarely.

Lily's brow was etched with deep furrows, there were dark circles under her eyes and her lips were set in a hard white line. Reluctantly Bridget picked up the laundry. Mr. Townsend was a saint, even if he wasn't a proper Catholic. She just hoped Mrs. Townsend wouldn't take out her anger on the poor, patient man.

But Lily forced a smile. "Good morning, Robert. How are you feeling?"

"Better, today," he replied. It was the answer he always gave, no matter how much his stiff joints protested in pain.

Nervously Lily circled the room. Straightening a picture frame here, flicking an imaginary speck of dust there. Her back was toward him when she said, "I think Edward is . . . he wants to get married. We must discuss it."

As she slowly turned toward him, Robert could feel her pain settling into his own heart. She had the broken look of a mother fighting for her child. He fought down his sympathetic instincts that made him want to take her in his arms and tell her it would be all right. But she had to learn to be sensible about her son.

"What wonderful news," he said with a smile. Then, to soften the blow, he added gently, "It's time he married. He is a grown man."

Lily's face wilted until she looked like a beaten puppy. Her eyes threatened to brim over with tears. "You mean you don't object? He might want to bring her here to live with us, you know." The possibility, her voice said, was certain and intolerable.

Object? How can I object? You've seen to that, Robert thought. The time is long past. My stepson is too firmly ensconced as master of this house.

To Edward his stepfather's illness had been a heaven-sent opportunity. The chance he had been waiting for. Edward had been employed as a bookkeeper for a gentlemen's clothing store. He did his job well, but the columns of dollars and cents were meaningless to him, as if he were adding and subtracting turnips or bicycle tires. The essential fact remained: the money wasn't his. Whether his employers made money or lost it was immaterial. He stood to make not one penny more or less. With each passing week and each identical paycheck the injustice ate deeper and deeper into his psyche. And he planned and schemed and vowed that someday it would be different.

When Robert fell sick, Edward quit his job and informed his mother that he would be taking charge. "Only until your husband recovers from his unfortunate illness, of course." He began by increasing the charges for room and board, evicting a tenant who was two months behind in his payments and decreeing that cheaper food and smaller portions be served. This was only the beginning, Edward vowed. If the changes upset Robert or his mother, it was not important. He had begun to build his empire. And empires, as historians will testify, are always built on a foundation of the fallen.

"No," Robert said. "How can I object?"

Lily stared across the empty bed at her husband huddled in his chair. Why couldn't he stand up for her? This was his house. His poor, crooked body. His sad, watery blue eyes.

He looked like an old man and smelled like a dying man. At moments like these she couldn't remember the strong, handsome man she had married. And she hated him for being ill and weak. Yet she'd made her bargain with the devil and lost. Oh, yes, she had the fine white house for Edward. But nothing more. Only empty coffers and a sickly husband.

"It . . . it isn't certain yet," she mumbled. "It may never happen."

Lily clenched her hands until her knuckles whitened. Robert knew what she was praying for. "Marriage may be good for him," he said, his eyes drifting to the charcoal sketches and oil portraits that lined the walls. He would never regret his marriage: it had given him Kathryn. The paintings were of her as a baby, but the chronicle stopped abruptly when Kathryn was three years old. The doctors said that if he expected to recover, he required complete rest. After the first year of consuming weakness and then bone-wracking pain, Robert resigned himself to the fact that his fingers would never hold a paintbrush again.

"Lily, we have to let our children grow up. They will, no matter what we do. We may as well accept it gracefully." Why couldn't Lily channel some of her overwhelming love toward Kathryn? He'd learned to live without her love, but Kathryn . . . a little girl needed her mother's love. That Lily felt some emotion for her daughter he never doubted, but she was afraid to show it, afraid to anger Edward, who demanded all her love and used it so ruthlessly against them all.

That's fine for you to say, Lily thought bitterly. You're not a mother.

As Lily stalked out of the room, Robert lowered his eyes in a prayer, that God would grant him a few more years on earth to protect his daughter. Only until she could take care of herself, that was all he asked.

Chapter Seven

Timing was important, and he'd chosen the Friday dinner hour. Once again Edward reviewed his strategy. He studied the faces of those who would be most affected by his announcement. At the other end of the white-clothed, gravy-stained table sat Lily. With distaste he noticed how sallow her skin had become and how much gray now marred her sleek black cap of hair. Her drab, mustard-colored dress stretched too tightly across her sagging breasts and accentuated her unfortunate coloring. She'll never accept my wife, he thought with satisfaction, but would she treat her new daughter-in-law with cold hostility or with a heady dose of the Irish temper which still lurked beneath her cool Yankee exterior? The situation would be interesting.

He turned his narrowed eyes on Kathryn. She would be torn, wouldn't she? How she would adore the idea of her precious teacher living with them. Yet her happiness would always be blighted by the knowledge that Jessica belonged to him. Kathryn despised him. He knew that. The fact neither pleased nor displeased him.

Kathryn Abigail Townsend. He remembered the day she was born. How he'd stood at the foot of the four-poster bed watching Lily cradle the baby. Lily was staring at it with a silly expression on her face. Robert, with his ridiculously sensitive artist's temperament, looked ready to cry.

"What a funny little face," Edward exclaimed. "Like a little monkey. No, maybe more like a wizened old man."

He saw Lily's arm tighten automatically, protectively, around the child, but when she looked up at Edward, she had to agree with him. "She does a bit, doesn't she? But I suppose all babies do."

No, it didn't bother him that his half sister hated him.

The best he had saved till last, and now he swiveled his gimlet eyes toward David Jamison. Jamison, acting his intolerably cheerful self, still obviously cherished the thought of leading the lovely Miss Hamilton off to his own bed. The idea angered Edward, and his long, bony fingers clutched spasmodically at his knife. Then for a moment he allowed his mind to play with a delightful fantasy: Jamison staying on to see his adored one become another man's bride. Living under the same roof. Tortured by the sight of her every day. No, David Jamison was too much of a man for that. It was unfortunate.

Like an actor stepping onstage, Edward affixed a smile on his lips, impatiently pushed his half-empty soup bowl out of the way and said, "Now, if you will be quiet, I have an announcement." All eyes turned toward him. "I am sure you will all agree that the presence of a beautiful young woman would add a great deal to this house. Therefore I know you will greet my news with enthusiasm." Out of the corner of his eye he could see Jamison's face freeze. With a sense of timing that would do credit to any actor, he paused. Let them guess.

Lily's fingers nervously picked at the frayed hem of her napkin. Kathryn's eyes widened in anticipation, and he could tell she wanted to ask questions but was afraid. Edward picked up his water tumbler and took a long, slow sip. Careful to replace it within the confines of the already wet ring on the tablecloth, he wiped his lips with an exaggerated delicacy. "Hmph . . . therefore it is my great pleasure to tell you, my family and friends," he said with an amicable nod at the surprised boarders, who knew he certainly did not consider them friends, "that Miss Jessica Hamilton has done me the enormous honor of consenting to be my wife." There was a sharp intake of breath. He knew it could only be Lily, but he refused to meet her eyes. "The wedding will be four weeks from tomorrow. I know that you will all," he said, giving undue stress to the last word, "wish us well."

Edward sat in his spacious second-floor bedroom—the best in the house—and stared into the empty fireplace grate, waiting. He knew she would come and he was eagerly anticipating the scene, but when the door opened he didn't bother to turn around.

She was no longer the cool and proper Yankee matron. The anger and ferocity of a thousand years of Irish warriors lit Lily's voice. "How could you do this to me?" she demanded as she slammed the door behind her. "I've devoted my life to you, and this is the gratitude I get? Ever since you were a baby, ever since before you were born, everything I've done has been for you. You have been my whole world. Every dream I had was for you. I went without so you could have. And now you blithely announce that you are getting married. Announce it to me, your mother, in front of strangers. And expect me to be happy about it."

Edward turned slowly and fixed her with his dark, half-hooded eyes. "Your whole world," he said with a scornful laugh. "Do you have any idea how tired I am—sick and tired—of that particular phrase? You trotted it out at every opportunity all through my childhood. I wasn't allowed to go ice skating because if I fell through the ice and drowned, you would lose everything. 'You're everything I have in the world,' " he said, mimicking her voice and giving it a slight trace of the brogue he knew she hated. "That's what you told me when I wanted to be with my friends instead of traipsing off to another damned concert or lecture with you. And when I insisted on going with my friends anyway, you put on that poor broken-martyr look and told me how you sacrificed everything for me."

"And what if I'd never allowed you to be born?" Lily asked, her eyes glinting with triumph. "There were women who . . . there were ways. Don't think it wouldn't have made my life easier."

"Do you expect me to get down on my knees and thank you for the favor, Mother?"

"Don't call me that," she screamed. "Don't ever call me that."

"Why not? You are my mother, aren't you?"

"Of course," she said, her anger momentarily defused. "It's just that you haven't called me that since you were a little boy." A distant, softer light lit her eyes.

"And you'd like me to stay a little boy, your little boy, forever, wouldn't you? That would suit your plans perfectly, because little boys don't get married. Did you think I'd be content to have only one woman in my life, that woman my mother, forever?"

Lily stared down at the floor uncomfortably, and when she spoke, her voice was a whisper. "But it had been so long and you'd never seemed to . . . never shown an interest."

"So you assumed what, Mother? That I didn't have needs like every other man? Is that what you would have wished on me just to keep me by your side?"

He waited for Lily to speak, but her only reply was the tears that ran like rivers down her cheeks.

"You must think your son is stupid, that I don't understand what you really want. I see how you smile and simper every time some fool mistakes us for husband and wife. You love it, don't you? And that's the dream world you'd like to live in; you'd like us to be husband and wife. And would you want to be a wife to me in every way? Answer me, will you?" Edward reached out and tried to grab her arm, but Lily slipped away and with a sob rushed to the other side of the room. Edward's bed stood between them—wide and protective—and she felt safer. She had sewn the comforter herself. Her eyes were clouded with tears, but she didn't dare turn her back on him.

"It's no wonder, is it, that you want another husband, married to that eunuch down there." Edward inclined his head toward the library. "That you want a real man." His lips twisted into a cruel smile. His pulse began to race and he could feel the pressure building in his groin.

Lunging across the bed at her, he grabbed out, but his hand caught only her shawl, which slipped off her shoulders and fell onto the bed in a golden heap. She retreated, pressing her body against the far wall, willing herself to disappear into the cabbage rose wallpaper.

For a long moment he stared at her. His eyes, narrowed into mere slits, were impenetrable. Lily waited. Then he started across the room toward her. She pressed herself tighter and tighter against the wall until she thought her spine would crack. She'd seen hundreds of battered women, knocked about when their husbands lost their jobs or had too much to drink. Black eyes and bruised cheeks were common enough to be ignored in The Acre. But Edward had never laid a hand on her. Now, even as he came toward her, raking her body with his eyes, she refused to believe what was happening.

He grabbed her arms and pulled her body to him. For a moment he held her in his iron grip, so close she could hear his heart pound and smell the sweet, musky scent of his hair pomade. He looked down at her, reading the fear in her eyes and relishing it. He was a stranger. She stared up at him, trying to penetrate the darkness of his eyes. Neither moved. It was as if they were locked together by some lethal emotion. Finally Edward broke the spell, propelling her roughly around the bed to the other side of the room. He pulled her to an abrupt stop by his marble-topped dresser, where his silver-backed brushes were laid out in perfect precision on the runner she had crocheted. His hand reached up to her neck and his fingers, like steel instruments, forced her head up.

"There, look. Look into the mirror," he said. "What do you see? Tell me, do you see a beautiful young woman who could attract a man? Do you?" His fingers tightened on her neck.

Lily closed her eyes.

"Answer me. Open your eyes, woman, and tell me what you see, what image of loveliness." He shook her head the way a dog shakes the rat in its teeth, but still she refused to open her eyes and confront her image. She knew what she would see.

"Then I'll tell you. You'll see an old woman. An old woman with yellowing skin. An old woman with wrinkles. An old woman whose hair is starting to turn white. A fat old woman. Did you really think I'd be content with you, pretending to be your husband? Can you honestly believe I don't desire a young and beautiful woman, a real woman, to warm my bed and take care of those needs you would prefer to think I don't have?" Edward could feel her body heaving with each sob, and he relaxed his grasp.

"Tell me, was my father a real man? Or was he a pitifully poor specimen like Townsend?"

"He was . . ." Lily sobbed.

"I know, he was a fine and handsome sailor and, poor man, he was drowned at sea," he said, mimicking her. "Do you think I believe that old story? I haven't believed it since I was ten years old and found out, from some helpful playmates, what a bastard was. That's what I am, Mother, isn't it? A bastard. Say it. Say the word,'' he demanded.

As he watched her face in the mirror, he saw her eyes open. They were clear, no longer wet with tears, and there was a fire raging in them, a determination Edward had never seen before. For a moment he wondered if his mother had gone over the brink into madness.

But her voice was cool and controlled. "Yes, Edward, you are a bastard. And your father was no common sailor drowned at sea. No, he was a compassionate man, a man who believed in something bigger than himself. A better man, God help you, than you'll ever be.'' It was as if she had become the old Lily, the Lily who had borne a child alone and fought her way out of the tenements. And as she spoke, her Irish brogue returned, strong and pure.

Edward watched in amazement as his mother scooped up her shawl from the bed and wrapped it around her shoulders. Then she turned toward the mirror and, staring into it, carefully rearranged some of the tendrils of hair that had come loose. In silence, her head held high, she walked out the door and disappeared into the darkened hallway.

Chapter Eight

The farewell committee for David Jamison consisted of one. He found her perched on the little side chair opposite the hideous Victorian hatstand in the front hall. She looked nervous. *Probably scared someone will see her there, where Edward had decreed little girls didn't belong,* he thought. *What,* he wondered, *were the odds that those two would crush Kathryn's spirit before she was old enough to escape this damned house?*

When she saw him she didn't even smile. "Why so glum?" he asked as he walked down the stairs, a battered leather valise in either hand, his panama hat at a jaunty angle.

She shook her head, as if ashamed to admit her sadness; then all of a sudden she burst out, "Do you have to go? I'll miss you."

He knelt down and took her little hands in his and looked into her hazel eyes and thought about the heartbreaker she'd be someday. "I'm afraid I have to, Kathryn."

"But why? Why do you have to go? I don't understand."

"I'm afraid it isn't always easy to explain why we adults do the things we do. You'll understand when you're grown up."

"Pooh. That's what Edward says. I'm sure I could understand right now. I can already read books and do sums."

"Maybe you could, little Kathryn. But I have a train to catch and I don't have time to explain."

Her eyes lit up. "Are you going to California? Oh, please say you're going there and that you'll send me a card with palm trees on it."

"No, not this time. This trip it's Baltimore." Seeing her

frown, he added quickly, "But someday soon I'll go back to California."

"Someday I'll go there, too. Even if Edward says I can't because I'm a girl."

"That's the spirit." He paused. "Kathryn, you are a very bright and very beautiful young lady. There are times when you shouldn't listen to what other people say you can and can't do. Sometimes you have to follow your own heart and your own dream, if you want it badly enough." He looked at the spark of determination in her eyes and the serious set of her little chin and said more to himself than to her, "And I think that you will get what you want. Everything you want. Because you will want it badly enough."

She looked at him with a seriousness way beyond her six years and announced, "Then I want to make a million dollars and go to California."

"Well, Miss Kathryn Townsend, let me have the privilege of starting you on your fortune." He reached into his trouser pocket and came up with a clenched fist. "Now, hold out your hand and close your eyes."

When she opened her eyes and saw the ten-dollar gold piece shining up from the middle of her palm, an enormous golden smile broke over her face. "Is it mine, really? All mine?" Without waiting for his answer, she squealed, "Thank you, oh, thank you. I will never, ever spend it."

David laughed. "You know that you have to spend money to make money, don't you?"

"Oh, yes. But not this," she said, her fingers closing around it.

"I believe you will do it, Kathryn. No matter what Edward says. You just have to dare to dream."

Kathryn watched David as he walked down the block and wondered how he had managed to put everything he owned into two small valises.

He resisted the urge to look back and wave; he found the tenderness Kathryn aroused in him difficult to understand. If things had been different he could have kept an eye on her. But things weren't different, he thought, fighting down the memory, trying not to imagine Jessica with Edward, his bony hands touching her, his bony arms wrapped around her. He'd been so sure of her affection. What had happened?

Kathryn watched until his hat disappeared around the corner and then looked down at her gold piece. She wouldn't tell anybody about it; it was her secret. If Edward knew, he'd make her put it in the bank and she'd never see it again. Carefully she wrapped it up in a clean white handkerchief and dropped it into her pocket. It was nice to feel its weight and know it was there. It was even nicer to know somebody believed in her and her dream.

A jaunty whistled tune arose from the garden, and Robert Townsend turned to the window in time to see a stocky figure round the corner, looking uncomfortable in a black suit and a stiff white collar. It was Bridget's new beau. Robert smiled. Bridget deserved something better than this dismal house; instead of ministering to a cranky old invalid, she should be taking care of a passel of rosy-cheeked children.

Duff McDermott had escorted her home from church three Sundays in a row. The fourth Sunday she'd shyly requested permission to bring "her friend" in to meet him, and Robert knew it was serious. Poor Duff had stood awkwardly with his shiny black bowler in his work-scarred hands and acted as if he were being introduced to the lord of the manor. He'd explained that he worked with an uncle "in construction" but didn't intend to stop there: he "had plans." And Robert, seeing the adoring way he looked at Bridget, knew what his plans were.

"And did you like him?" she asked anxiously as soon as Duff had been fed a cup of tea and ushered out the kitchen door with a chaste kiss. "I thought it would be all right to bring him in, what with Mr. Edward not being here."

"Fine, Bridget. I was glad to meet him." Darn Edward, why must we always tiptoe around him? If only I had the strength. . . . "Seems like a very nice man. Are his intentions honorable?" Robert watched the blush rise over Bridget's face.

"Oh, sir, we've never discussed anything like that. After all"—the normally unflappable Bridget seemed flustered—"it's only been four weeks."

"He seems like a good, solid man, and I'm sure his intentions are honorable," Robert said solemnly.

Bridget shone with happiness for the rest of the day. The fifth week Duff came to call on Friday, her half day off. It was his bad luck that he arrived at the back door as Edward walked into the kitchen.

"Is Bridget . . . I mean . . . Miss Costelloe here?" He blushed and stared down at his boot tips.

"Whatever you are selling, we are not interested," Edward replied.

"No, sir, you see, I'm not selling anything. I've come, uh . . . to call on Miss Costelloe."

"Gentlemen callers," Edward said carefully, eyeing Duff's dirty and frayed work clothes to show that the word "gentlemen" was one of derision, "are not permitted. Bridget is here to work."

"But surely this is her afternoon off, isn't it?" Duff asked, the servility in his tone giving way to annoyance.

"Yes," he snapped, "but that's no excuse for all sorts of men to come sniffing around. This is a moral, Christian household and I will not permit—"

"Permit what?" Bridget demanded, her ample bulk filling the doorway, her hands set defiantly on her hips. Something had snapped. For years she had tolerated his bullying, but she would not allow him to talk to Duff that way. Edward stared at her in amazement. For a moment he was stunned speechless, and Bridget stepped deftly into the silent gap. "This is my friend, my good friend Mr. Duff McDermott, and we are going out." Crossing the kitchen in three easy strides, she put her arm through Duff's and they sailed out the door.

That night Edward was lying in wait for her. A book was spread out in front of him on the kitchen table, but his eyes were fixed on the back door. The lamplight illuminated the prominent bones of his face, making him look like a massive bird of prey, waiting, half hidden in the dark.

"Well, Miss Costelloe, how nice of you to come home. I trust you had a pleasant afternoon." His tone was oily smooth. It surprised Bridget, but not enough to relax her guard. He couldn't be trusted. She nodded, waiting for him to show a sign. She was prepared for a fight, but clever enough not to start it herself.

"Now, Bridget, you have worked in this house a long time,

haven't you? Let's see, how many years?—seven, I think. I appreciate your fondness for Mr. Townsend senior and little Kathryn. And I'm certain you would not want to desert them.''

''I like them very much, yes.'' She felt like a little mouse being toyed with by the sly old tomcat. Which way would he pounce next?

''And,'' he said, finally oiling his way around to his objective, ''after you have been accepted as one of the family in such a genteel home as this, I cannot see you throwing away your life on a . . .'' He paused as if searching for the right word. ''A working person such as Mr. McDermott.'' He pronounced the words ''working person'' with as much horror and disdain as if he'd called him a bigamist, robber or murderer.

''Mr. Edward,'' she said, taking a deep breath and squaring her shoulders, ''I love Mr. McDermott.'' Even as she said the words she asked herself, Am I crazy? Why am I confessing this to him? She'd never admitted it even to herself.

Edward ran his palm over his sleek pomaded head as if he were thinking and trying to come to a decision. ''I am sorry to hear that, because I am afraid that you will have to make a choice. A choice between Mr. McDermott and the life he could offer you—which I am certain would not be a pleasant one; I have seen how the Irish live down there,'' he said, nodding in the direction of the river and the city beyond —''and the life you lead here. In a beautiful old house. With paintings, antiques, books and cultured people. A place with running water and good food and . . .'' And a place with no love, Bridget thought, biting her tongue to keep from spitting the words out.

''And everything a young woman could want.'' He stared at Bridget, trying to gauge the effect of his argument. ''Think about it. Because I am afraid that I can no longer permit Mr. McDermott to visit here. For your own sake and the sake of the women in my family, who lead rather sheltered lives. If you want to remain in your employment in this house, you must . . . relinquish him.''

Without a moment's hesitation she plunged in. ''And do you think I'd stay in this house a day longer? Even with its

indoor plumbing. Even if you were to get down on your high-
and-mighty knees and beg me. 'Tis an unhappy house. And
you are the one who makes it that way. You are an evil man,
Edward Townsend. Controlling people. Torturing them.
Treating them as if they were little ants crawling across your
tabletop. Money and power. That's all you ever think about.
Someday when you're down there burning in hell—and sure
as my name is Bridget Anne Costelloe, that's where you're
going—you'll realize it all counts for nothing—nothing.''

"I've heard enough. You will leave this house in the morning. And you will never again communicate with my sister
or stepfather. I will not allow them to be exposed to your
immoral influence.''

Edward's tone was low and glacial. His control was almost
supernatural, she thought with a shiver, as if he were not
human at all. She refused to be defeated. Staring at him,
daring him to meet her eyes, she said, "Then I'll expect my
week's wages in the morning." She had no idea what lay
dark and impenetrable in his sunken, half-hooded eyes as he
turned on his heel and stalked out of the kitchen.

Afraid of waking Kathryn, who slept in the attic room next
to hers, Bridget crept quietly into bed. There would be time
enough to tell the poor child in the morning.

Kathryn knew something was wrong as soon as Bridget appeared at her bedside early in the morning wearing her blue
coat and the straw hat with the big pink roses when she should
have been downstairs helping with breakfast.

Bridget took her in her arms and tried to explain, being
very careful not to blame everything on Edward. She knew
that Kathryn didn't like her brother, but it would be years
before Kathryn could pack her bags and escape. No sense
stirring up any more hatred.

But Kathryn knew: Edward was making Bridget leave. It
was always Edward's fault. When Bridget finally kissed her
for the last time, reminding her to be good to her father, and
disappeared down the stairs, a carpetbag in each hand, Kathryn knew what she had to do. She had to warn Miss Hamilton. Tell her she couldn't marry Edward.

Kathryn wasn't sure what marriage meant. Except she knew
men kissed their wives and sometimes slept in the same bed-

room with them, although her mother and father never did. But when she imagined Edward's hard white lips meeting Miss Hamilton's soft pink ones, she felt sick to her stomach, like when she ate too many green apples. She must make Miss Hamilton understand. Edward was always so nice when she was around; he never said anything mean then. She had to do it right now. Even if it meant Miss Hamilton wouldn't be coming to live with them. Kathryn felt a sharp pain of loss. First nice Mr. Jamison. Then Bridget. Now Miss Hamilton.

If only it weren't Saturday. She wasn't exactly sure where her teacher lived, except that she took the trolley right in front of the school and that her aunt's house was white with a big weeping willow tree hanging down all over the front yard. Miss Hamilton had told her that. It wouldn't be hard to find. All she had to do was get on the trolley; when she saw the house, she would get off.

Kathryn had never been on a trolley all by herself, but she clutched her pennies tightly and tried to pretend she did it every day. The car was open on both sides and she carefully positioned herself in the middle of an empty seat, as far away from the edges as possible. Wide-eyed with fascination, she swiveled her head from side to side, looking for a white house with a willow tree. When they reached the working-class section of small attached houses along the river, she still hadn't seen it. The streetcar clanked across the bridge and she squeezed her eyes shut so she couldn't look down.

Once into the maze of the city with its huge red-brick mill buildings that seemed to stretch upward and onward forever, she realized there would never be a willow tree. Everything was streets and sidewalks. They passed shops, all sorts of shops, some with funny names on the doors—there was O'Leary's Alehouse, James O'Leary, prop.; Kanakaris' Coffee House; Pelletier, Grocer. Kathryn slowly spelled out the unfamiliar names to herself. The shops were small, their windows crowded with boots and lamps and cheeses and sausages and shovels, and the streets were dirty. Occasionally a group of ragged children scattered in front of the streetcar as it broke up their games. She stared down at them, amazed that their mothers would let them out when their hands and faces were so filthy. They laughed and shouted, but she

couldn't understand what they were saying. Gradually the
dark, narrow little shops gave way to bigger shops on a
broader, cleaner street. Their glass windows were immaculate and the names over the doors were in gold letters. She
saw the milliner's where her mother bought her hats and the
drugstore where, as a special treat, she was taken for polar
sherbets. Kathryn's mouth watered. Unclutching her fist, she
looked down at her remaining pennies and wondered how
much a polar sherbet cost. She swallowed. Today she had
something more important to do. Something very grown up.

"End of the line," the conductor finally shouted, and Kathryn knew she had no choice. Wherever she was, it didn't
seem a likely spot for a white house with a willow tree. The
other passengers melted away and the streetcar clanked its
way back up the street, leaving her alone. She looked up and
found herself staring at the gates of a mill. The mill buildings
were so enormous—bigger than anything she'd ever seen before. They stretched on forever, forcing her eyes to dart back
and forth, here and there, trying to take it all in. Before her
a planked bridge spanned the narrow, dark canal. The bridge
ended abruptly with an iron gate. Peering through the gate,
she could see a huge courtyard surrounded on all four sides
by the massive mill buildings. They rose three stories high
with turrets rising even higher in each corner. Row after row
of tall, closely set windows stared out at her like dark, ominous eyes. Like Edward's eyes. From within came a thumping, as if giants were pacing around and around, making the
whole building shake. Kathryn shivered at the power of her
own imagination and wondered what to do next.

Suddenly there was a series of shrill whistles, followed by
silence. The giants had quieted. Within moments there came
a rushing sound, like a strong winter wind, and the babble
of voices. People poured forth from every door, all rushing
toward the gate. The men in front of the pack grasped the
iron rails and shook them, shouting angrily. Finally a voice
rose above them: "Patience. Patience. I'm coming. Can't you
wait a minute?" A black-suited figure with long white whiskers pushed his way through the crowd, slowly dug a big iron
key out of his waistcoat and inserted it into the lock. He
barely had time to back out of the way before the crowd

pushed open the gate and surged forward. If Kathryn hadn't stepped aside quickly, she would have been caught up and carried along.

The surge was endless. Boys in blue overalls, their shirt-sleeves rolled up on sinewy arms. Men in black suits and bowler hats or shapeless cloth caps. Women and girls, their hair swept up, wearing aprons over their dresses. They were all in a hurry. Some stalked along silently. Others walked in large groups, chattering in languages Kathryn didn't under-stand.

It took Kathryn a moment to realize these were the mill girls Edward talked about. Her eyes were irresistibly drawn to searching for missing fingers, dreading the sight of bloody stumps. Then a moment's inattention of her own and she was swept up in the crowd and forced to scurry along to avoid being trampled. No one noticed her. She was too small. Knees bumped her. Feet trod on hers. Swinging arms clipped her head. All too soon she was out of breath trying to keep pace with longer legs and brisker strides. She tried inching her way toward one edge of the crowd but was blocked on one side by an enormously fat woman who was crowding the man ahead of her. On the other side three girls, arm in arm, formed an impenetrable barrier. She had no choice but to keep her feet moving and hope she didn't fall. If only these people spoke English, she could ask them to let her out, but she didn't recognize a single word. And their smells assaulted her—unwashed bodies, damp clothes, foreign foods.

Just as she thought she couldn't keep up any longer, the crowd thinned out. There was a gap in front of her and she could see they had reached a corner. Instinctively she darted through the gap and pressed herself into a doorway. Like an endless wave, the crowd continued to surge past. Their shouts and laughter and odors filled the air like a palpable barrier, forcing her back into her shelter.

When at last there were only a few stragglers, she cau-tiously peered around the corner. She was met by a broad freckled face peering back at her, its nose almost touching hers. "Who're you?" it demanded.

"I'm Kathryn Townsend," she said, annoyed.

"Now don't get mad. What you doin' out here anyway?" The boy rubbed at his nose with a grubby sleeve and stared at her. He'd never seen anything quite so pretty; it was clear she didn't belong here.

"I was looking for my teacher's house. It's white and it has a willow tree in the front yard. Do you know if it's near here? Please," she added, slightly ashamed of her belligerence.

"Naw, nothin' like that around here. Nothin' so fancy. Sounds like the other side of the river."

"But that's where I came from," she protested.

The boy picked up the pile of newspapers that lay at his feet. For the first time in his young life he felt the ancient male urge to protect the weaker sex. He hefted his papers. Not many left; it had been a good day. He could afford to lose a few pennies, he supposed. Couldn't let this pretty little girl stay here all by herself. "Come on. I'll take you home."

To his surprise, Kathryn didn't jump at his offer. "No, thanks. I must find Miss Hamilton's house. It is really very important."

He didn't pry. People were entitled to their secrets. But when she smiled at him he knew he'd do anything in the world she asked. The next trolley car clanked in and he pulled her aboard. "I'm Alfred," he said. "but my friends call me Alfie. I sell newspapers," he added unnecessarily, self-importantly patting the papers in his lap. When the conductor come to collect their money, he insisted on paying her fare, even though she produced her own handful of pennies.

As he dropped his coins into the conductor's hand, Kathryn saw with horror that he was missing a finger. "Did you get your finger cut off in the mill?" she asked excitedly.

"Yep," he said. "But you should see my sister. She lost three of hers," he announced proudly. "That's when my mother made us stop working there."

Kathryn was enchanted with her new friend. It didn't matter that his remaining fingernails looked as if they'd never been cleaned and that his hair had been hacked off at uneven lengths; he was fascinating. She bombarded him with questions as the trolley made its laborious way through the city, across the river and up the hill. So intrigued was she that she didn't realize they had passed the school. Suddenly, out of the corner of her eye, she caught sight of a big tree in a front yard—it was a willow. And the house was white.

"This is it, this is it!" Alfie looked surprised as she dragged him across the seat and down onto the sidewalk.

"You sure this is the right place, miss? Don't want you gettin' lost again. You go find out. I'll wait here."

But Kathryn wanted to show off her new friend. "No, come with me. I want you to meet Miss Hamilton."

Five minutes later the three were ensconced in Jessica's aunt's kitchen drinking milk and eating gingerbread, of which Alfie finished three pieces, pausing only to grunt approval. Jessica packed up three more pieces for him and then, with more thanks and good-byes "and trolley fare, plus a little extra for you," sent him off.

"Now," she said sternly, seating herself back down at the table, "are you going to tell me what was so important that you had to set out on this hairbrained adventure to find me? It was a very stupid and dangerous thing to do, Kathryn, and I want you to promise never to do it again."

Solemnly Kathryn nodded. She'd never heard Miss Hamilton speak like that before, even to Billy Mulligan when she caught him with the frog.

"Well?"

Kathryn merely looked dumbfounded and said nothing.

"Well," she tried again, "why did you have to see me?"

"I had to tell you." She paused.

"Tell me what? Kathryn Abigail Townsend, I am beginning to lose patience."

Kathryn swallowed. This wasn't as easy as she thought it would be. She'd expected Miss Hamilton to understand and make everything all right again. Just like she had with the hole in her dress. "I had to tell you . . . that you shouldn't marry Edward," she blurted out. "He's mean and nasty."

To her surprise, Miss Hamilton laughed. A clear, bell-like peal that Kathryn usually adored hearing. Now it made her angry.

"Honestly, he is," she said through clenched teeth.

"Poor Kathryn. Did he scold you, is that why you are mad? You know Edward says that you are too sensitive. Sometimes little girls have to be scolded, even punished. And you know big brothers just love to tease their little sisters. I'm sure he didn't intend to be mean."

Kathryn didn't say a word, just stared down imagining patterns in the red-and-white tablecloth. This whole crazy journey was so unlike the usually sensible Kathryn that Jessica asked gently, for some reason fearing the answer, "Edward didn't hurt you, did he?"

If she said yes, would that save Miss Hamilton from Edward? she wondered. She paused. She knew telling a lie was almost the worst thing you could do. "No," she said sadly. "He fired B—Br—Bridget." The words cascaded out amidst tears.

A flood of relief washed over Jessica and she couldn't help laughing. "Is that all? Are you crying because he fired a servant? Kathryn, sweetheart, people do that all the time. For all sorts of reasons. It's nothing to cry about. I'm sure he had a perfectly good reason. Did he tell you why?"

Kathryn shook her head. "Bridget didn't say."

Edward had probably caught the woman stealing, Jessica decided, although Bridget had seemed so nice. . . . Edward was right: Kathryn was entirely too sensitive. But once she married Edward, she could help her new little sister-in-law.

When Edward heard the story of Kathryn's escapade, laughingly related by Jessica, he found it hard to hide his anger. That interfering brat had nearly ruined all his plans. She was entirely too independent for a child of six. He'd have to keep a close eye on her. In the meantime, to keep the peace, he rehired Bridget on the condition that her suitor never again be seen on Townsend premises. He could always fire her later, after he married Jessica.

Chapter Nine

Edward and Jessica were married in Boston on a Saturday afternoon early in September. The sun streaming in through the windows and bathing the white walls a pale gold seemed to Jessica a good omen. It almost helped her to overcome her anxieties, the anxieties her hovering mother assured her were entirely normal. But the fears followed her down the red-carpeted aisle under the sky-blue vaulted ceiling, up to the altar massed with yellow chrysanthemums, and by the time the minister declared solemnly, "I now pronounce you man and wife," she was silently praying that she wouldn't faint.

Edward stood at the altar feeling cheated. The first in a series of unpleasant shocks had come when the hired carriage had pulled up in front of the Hamiltons' home. It was not nearly as grand as he had expected. Narrow, three-storied, like hundreds of others in the city. As he mounted the steps he consoled himself with the hope that they did not believe in an ostentatious show of their wealth. Once inside, he discovered that the furniture was neither new nor opulent. Although the carpet in the parlor was Chinese, there were worn spots. There was a chip in the gold rim of his soup plate, and when he spooned up the last of his onion soup, he found a hairline crack in the bottom.

He had also realized with a shock that John Hamilton, despite his paunch and thinning hair, was a much younger man than Jessica had led him to believe. Certainly not a man in need of heirs at any time in the near future. Even more disturbing were Hamilton's frequent references to a nephew who was his "right-hand man." Edward's plan to add shipping to his financial empire sank abruptly.

Somewhat to his annoyance, Edward found his disappointment blunted every time he looked at Jessica. She was so lovely, her blond curls swept up on her head, her lips pink and provocative, her figure temptingly ripe, her voice delicate, angelic. And after all, there was perhaps more in the Hamilton family coffers than met the eye.

When he saw Jessica gliding down the aisle toward him, looking heavenly in pale violet silk and carrying an armful of pink roses, he felt a genuine glow. His thin chest puffed out with pride as he placed the ring on his bride's finger. A small, round opal surrounded by diamonds, it had belonged to Robert Townsend's mother. If his stepfather had any objections, Edward didn't know that. He had removed the ring from the wall safe in the library without telling him. Robert wouldn't live to discover his loss, and Lily, he knew how to deal with Lily.

The reception was, much to Edward's disappointment, a modest one at the Hamilton home. He was anxious to depart for his honeymoon, not so much for the thought of what was to come, but to escape the threadbare Chinese carpet that had become the symbol of his dashed hopes.

Jessica had some idea of what would happen on her wedding night, and once she and Edward were alone in their hotel room, her curiosity outweighed her fear. She was surprised that Edward seemed in no hurry. They talked awkwardly of inconsequential matters until Jessica's mind was frazzled by doubts. What if he doesn't find me attractive? What if he regrets our marriage? Finally the bells of a nearby church struck twelve. Edward rose from his chair, held out his arm stiffly to her and asked, "Shall we retire?"

The act didn't even really hurt. Afterward Jessica wished it had, wished she could have felt something.

Only occasionally had Edward permitted himself to contemplate the moment when Jessica finally became his—physically. It didn't seem proper to anticipate the act. Not with Jessica. Now as he looked down at her angelically delicate face he found it difficult to make his body respond. With a sigh he shut his eyes and concentrated on his Greek whore and her caressing tongue.

Early the next morning Edward, pleading a business appointment, left his bride and took a cab to one of Boston's most exclusive milliners. There he bought a frothy blue hat with long white plumes. He knew she'd adore it. The fact that he'd purchased it on his honeymoon would make it irresistible. The night he'd announced his marriage Lily had made the end of that scene so terribly unpleasant, stalking out the door, pretending she didn't care. But he knew she did, she always would. A gift like this would restore her humor. He'd fuss over her, tell her how young and beautiful the hat made her look.

If Jessica was disappointed in marriage, she took great care not to show it. Perhaps this is the way all women feel, she thought. Edward's behavior confused her. In public he made a great show of kindliness, always solicitous, overly solicitous. Was she too hot? Too cold? Would she like another cup of tea? Could he fetch her book? Especially when his mother was within hearing, his behavior was lovingly servile. When they were alone he ignored his bride, and when Kathryn was with them his words were sharp, his comments cruelly barbed. How Jessica hated to see Kathryn's thin, pained little face when she heard him. It was almost as if Edward enjoyed hurting his sister, but no, he couldn't be so cruel. He was her husband.

Even more puzzling was the way he looked at her when he thought her attention was occupied elsewhere—his eyes bright, his face flushed; she could have sworn it was a look of genuine passion.

Although Jessica had married Edward with the desire of being a helpmate as he made his fortune, he seldom spoke of business and then only to proclaim it unsuitable for women. "You would not understand, so why try? It is beyond your charming capacities, I'm afraid."

They'd been married for several months before her husband said the words she'd prayed for. Awakened at dawn to the chatter of songbirds, Edward lay watching his bride's face bathed in the golden light of morning and felt something rising in his chest. A sensation of happiness that suffused his body and threatened to explode. Jessica looked so lovely that he was afraid to touch her. He had no desire to make love to her; he merely wanted to study her delicate, golden features. Tentatively, to ensure that his vision was real, he touched her sleep-pinkened cheek with his fingertips. Watching her wide blue eyes gaze up at him with surprise, he could not control himself. "Jessica, I love you. I love you more than any other man has ever loved a woman."

It was the last time he ever mentioned love. Love was not part of his plan. It could only lead to weakness. A shameful feeling, to be uprooted. Destroyed.

After months of wondering about the complex nature of her marriage, Jessica abandoned the effort. Everything had changed. She had something new to think about: her baby. Edward was ecstatic and had his heart set on a boy. Every night she prayed for a son. Maybe that would make her husband happy.

Chapter Ten

It was the last week of school and unseasonably hot and humid. The windows were open as wide as they could go, but the morning sun pouring into the room made it feel like an oven. The air was heavy; not a breeze stirred. The only movement came from a fly buzzing around the wilted philodendron sitting dry and forlorn on a windowsill. Even the most unruly students had lost the desire to squirm. They sat quietly staring out the windows, trying to will a cool breeze into the room.

Mrs. Hastings didn't blame them. Weighed down by that hot air, they found it hard to concentrate. Only little Kathryn Townsend had forced her mind to overcome the heat. Her arithmetic book was propped up on her desk and her head was bowed down over a piece of yellow lined paper. Occasionally she would write something and her whole body wriggled in triumph. In the row behind her Samantha Brewster sat, trying to copy her friend's dedication, but failing as her eyes kept straying longingly to the windows.

All eyes turned eagerly when the door opened and there was a sudden rush of cooler air. The tall girl with corkscrew curls marched self-importantly to Mrs. Hastings' desk and handed her a note. She did her best to read the message over Mrs. Hastings' shoulder, but failing, turned her eyes toward the windows. She was a fifth grader and couldn't be bothered looking at a roomful of baby second graders.

"That will be all," Mrs. Hastings announced in a not-to-be-argued-with tone of voice, and the girl reluctantly shuffled out the door. "Kathryn Townsend and Samantha Brewster, would you please step up here to my desk. I want a word with both of you."

Noting the scared look on Samantha's face, Mrs. Hastings knew she was worrying she'd done something wrong. Kathryn's face was calm; she knew she hadn't broken any rules.

Mrs. Hastings looked at the note in her hand and then stared over the top rim of her glasses at the two girls. "I have a message that you are to go home with Samantha today, Kathryn, and are to stay there until your mother sends for you."

For a second Kathryn looked puzzled, and then her face gave way to a grin. "I know. I know. It's time, isn't it? Jessica's having her baby." Her braids bobbed up and down as she nodded, encouraging Mrs. Hastings to say yes.

Emily Hastings shuddered. One did not discuss such matters in public, particularly in front of seven-year-old children. "That may be, my dear," she whispered. "You'll find out soon enough. Now just do as your mother asks."

"No, I can't. I want to be there. Jessica promised that I'd see the baby right away." She flung the last words over her shoulder as she rushed out the door.

She couldn't wait to see the baby. She and Jessica had been counting the days. But there were still fifteen left. What had happened? At first Kathryn couldn't believe that there was going to be a baby. She'd watched Jessica's figure swell up and was afraid that Jessica was sick. Tight-lipped, her mother had said, "No, she's not sick. But there are some things it's not proper for little girls to talk about." So she went to Jessica, who explained that the baby was growing inside her. She even let Kathryn rest her hand on her stomach and feel the baby kick. It was, Kathryn decided, the most exciting thing that had ever happened in her whole life.

Kathryn stopped risking Edward's displeasure by climbing trees and started learning how to make baby clothes. If her stitches were crooked and the seams puckered, she still couldn't wait to see little Eleanor wearing them. Kathryn just knew in her bones that it would be a girl, even though Edward wanted a boy.

The thought that she would actually see Eleanor in a few minutes drove her legs faster. Forgetting her mother's rule that young ladies never ran in public, she dashed across the street, forcing a delivery boy to squeal his bicycle to a halt amidst fallen boxes. The little black dog saw her and dashed from his porch, nipping at her heels and yapping his excitement. At the corner he abandoned his pursuit and slunk home panting. Kathryn was panting, too, and didn't even have enough breath to answer Mr. Carlotti, the iceman, who was walking by leading his patient old white horse. "Where you going in such a hurry, Miss Kathryn?" he called out. She waved in his direction. He'd know what was so important when he heard about the baby. When she reached home one braid had come undone; her throat ached; there was a sharp pain in her side and she forgot she was supposed to use the kitchen door. She threw her weight against the big, heavy front door and it squeaked open.

As she stepped into the hall a scream rang out. A scream so unearthly that it stopped her in her tracks. It sounded like a dog she'd heard once; its foot was caught in a trap and it was wailing out its desperate agony. Then there was silence. Such a deep, quavering silence that she could hear the erratic ticktock of the grandfather clock in the parlor and the sound of blood rushing in her ears. Afraid to move, she stood rooted to the floorboards. Gradually she forced herself to look around. Everything seemed normal. The carved lions on the hatstand stared out at her, and for a second she wondered if the shriek had come from their snarling mouths.

When she could hear above the pounding of her heart, she decided she'd been wrong. The message was about something else. Perhaps her father had been taken sick. Perhaps . . . Her mind stopped. All she knew was that she wanted more than anything to be in the safety of her own little attic bedroom with its sloping ceiling and rose wallpaper.

When she was halfway up the stairs, the scream cut through the silent air. Again and again. Then she heard a voice wailing, "Please, make it stop hurting. Please. . . ." The voice was so strangled with pain Kathryn barely recognized it. When she did she felt the power return to her legs. They couldn't hurt Jessica. She'd make them stop.

Another anguished cry split the air, but the words were agonized gibberish. Kathryn raced down the corridor and flung open the door to Edward's room.

The hot, heavy air smelling of sweat and blood hit her with

the strength of a solid object, almost forcing her back into
the coolness of the hallway. Facing the bed, their backs to
her, stood her mother and Bridget. At first they didn't hear
her, but then, as if they felt her terrified presence, they turned
in unison. And as they turned, Kathryn saw the body on the
bed beyond. It could have been a ghost. Her face was as pale
as the sheet which was wrapped around her, except for the
inky circles under her eyes. And her blue eyes, even they had
lost their color; the pupils stood out big and black. Her hair
hung down in tangled strands. Against the white face her lips
were unnaturally, brilliantly red. It took a moment for Kathryn to realize that they were bitten raw and bloody. Horrified,
she forced her eyes to travel to the sheet where Jessica's hands
grasped the cloth so hard her knuckles were shiny white
against the bloodstains.

"She's dead, she's dead," Kathryn wailed. Then the body
moved. Jessica's bloated, tortured body heaved and twisted
under the sheet, trying to escape the agonizing pain which
cut through her insides. Bridget grabbed her ankles and tried
to force her to be still, crooning softly, telling her to rest "for
the sake of the babe."

But Jessica heard nothing, saw nothing, knew nothing except that pain was consuming her body and she wanted to
die, wanted it to end. And when it finally ended, she shuddered and closed her dark, unseeing eyes.

Remembering Kathryn, Lily turned on her with a snap.
"Get out. This is no place for a little girl." She raised her
hand and brought it down across Kathryn's cheek. "Do you
hear me? Get out."

Too numb to feel the pain of the blow, Kathryn stood transfixed. "Is she going to die? Please don't let her die." There
was a hardness in Lily's eyes as they met hers, and Kathryn
realized she didn't care. Instinctively she turned to Bridget.
"Save her. Oh, please save her. I love her. Don't let her
die."

Bridget knelt and put her strong arms around her, and as
Kathryn nestled up to her soft, cushiony breasts she whispered, "Hush, we're doing everything we can. And Mr.
Edward's gone to fetch the doctor. Don't worry, little one,
don't worry."

Her words were drowned out by a cry and then sharp little

whimpers, like a puppy in pain. Bridget released Kathryn's trembling body and her mother grabbed her by the arm and pushed her roughly through the door. Too stunned to protest, Kathryn tried to open the door again and heard the sound of a key clicking in the lock. Her knees were too weak to support her and she sank to the floor.

That was where they found her, lying crumpled like a bundle of rags in front of the door, exhausted from pounding on the stolid mahogany and begging to be let in. Edward and the doctor merely stepped over her. It was the sound of the door slamming shut which woke her.

She listened. There were voices, but so hushed they were only a tantalizing murmur on the other side of the door. Then silence. She was afraid to breathe. Afraid to break the spell. Afraid to unleash the chilling screams. Suddenly the silence was broken—three thudding gongs that shook the house. The clock in the parlor announcing the hour as if everything were normal.

A buzz of a conversation crept out from under the door. Gradually Kathryn could distinguish one voice above the others. Familiar, but . . . Finally she realized whose it was—Dr. Morrow's. He came to see her father, and when she'd had whooping cough he'd come, brusquely poked and prodded and given her a sickening brown syrup. But Kathryn also knew that doctors had something to do with the coming of babies. That was a good sign. She strained, waiting to hear the wail of an infant. Jessica and Eleanor were going to be fine. Just fine. She started to get to her feet. Eleanor would need the little flannel gown which was now wrapped in tissue paper and lying in the bottom drawer of her dresser.

She stopped when she heard the doctor's voice. This time his every word was clear, distinct and angry. "You blasted idiot. You waited too long. What the hell do you expect me to do now?"

There was an apologetic murmur which sounded like Edward's voice.

"No excuses. Don't you think I know the real reason? Can't pull the wool over my eyes." His gruff voice grew louder. "You were afraid to spend the extra money. Afraid I'd charge you more if you called me too early and I had to sit around waiting for the girl to give birth. You're as bad as all those bloody ignorant immigrants. Men never think of their women. They want their pleasure, whatever the consequences. Won't call the doctor until the poor women are half dead from trying to force another child into the world.''

There was no reply, only a deep and deafening silence, and then a small, startled cry.

Kathryn rose stiffly from the hard floor and reached up toward the doorknob. She turned it slowly; it was unlocked. She cracked the door open.

The doctor's words stopped her. ''Well, you've paid the price. Your wife is dead, the baby, too—it was a girl, if you care, which I doubt. Bloody awful death. Nothing more I can do here.'' There was a metallic clink as he dropped his unused instruments back into his bag.

He nearly knocked Kathryn over as he flung open the door. His bushy black eyebrows were hunched down over his eyes, and his lips were set in a firm, disapproving line. He glared at Kathryn as if she were part of the guilty plot and then stomped through the hall, down the stairs and out the front door.

Miss Hamilton was dead and it was Edward's fault. Kathryn forced herself to imagine what it would be like never to hear Jessica's bell-like laugh or see her walking through the flower garden with her white skirt swirling or smell the lavender scent that surrounded her. Kathryn's heart dropped. Eleanor. There was no Eleanor to wear the gown she'd made.

When Lily opened the door she did not see her daughter, a scared sentinel, standing in the hallway. Kathryn couldn't even look at her mother.

Walking down the stairs, Lily tried to fight the feelings that rose in her breast. It wasn't right, she couldn't . . . she was not an evil person, so how could she welcome the death of another human being, especially such an agonizing, tortured death? She'd never wished death on her daughter-in-law. Never, even at night when she'd envisioned Edward and his bride lying together across the hall, would she have given in to such wickedness. Even when her heart had felt close to breaking as she watched Edward pamper his bride as once he had pampered her. No, Lily had not wished her dead, but she couldn't pretend to be sorry. She had her son back. Fortunately, the child had not survived. Now they could resume their old life and forget this unpleasantness had ever happened.

"Sittin' outside that door just like a little lost soul. So small. So scared. I thought my heart was like to break when I saw her." Bridget's hands expertly plumped up the pillows and Robert Townsend lay back, exhausted, closing his eyes gratefully. "She wouldn't cry. Lord knows, it might help her if she could. It's not natural," Bridget said indignantly, covertly wiping away a tear from her own red cheek.

With an effort Robert raised his head slightly and spoke. "What a ghastly scene for a child to see. I'd hoped that after I was gone, Jessica would look out for Kathryn. Now she has no one . . . no one," he repeated, sinking back into the pillows.

Bridget fussed with the blankets, reluctant to leave, wondering if her news would bring him any comfort. "Sir, I just walked past Mr. Edward's room . . . and do you know what he was doing?"

"What?" he said, not really wanting to know. Singing, dancing, laughing, drinking—nothing the new widower was doing would surprise him.

"I heard him crying." Seeing the surprised look on Robert's face, she said, "On my mother's grave I swear it." She did not explain that she had stood outside his door for a long time, unable to believe her own ears. Perhaps they had all been wrong and Edward was capable of love. In Bridget's rigid book people were either black or white, good or bad, condemned eternally to the flames of hell or destined to sit with the angels. It was almost inconceivable that Edward, whose streak of cruelty was as wide as the river and in whose veins she would have sworn by all her saints flowed nothing but ice water, cold as the river in winter, that a man such as he could be capable of love. But the sobs were those of a man whose heart was breaking.

"Crying? Edward? That I find hard to believe," Robert said, his voice husky with illness and exhaustion. "However, I pray that he feels one decent emotion before the end of his miserable life. Feels some love besides the love of the al-

mighty dollar. Perhaps there is hope for him yet. Perhaps he
will," he said as his eyes slowly closed, "change."

But that night at dinner Edward showed no signs of recent
grief. He accepted with polite disinterest the pious expressions of grief from the boarders, interrupting Mr. Anderson's
carefully composed condolence speech with a request to pass
the gravy.

As she served, Bridget watched Edward carefully. His eyes
were dry and clear, and she began to wonder if she'd imagined the tears. It wasn't until the next afternoon that she knew
the truth.

The next day, Bridget took Kathryn to school. In the school
yard, Bridget knelt down to give Kathryn a kiss.

Eye to eye, Kathryn stared at her. Her eyes were the color
of gold in the morning light, but had the hardness of steel.
"I hate him," she said, yet her voice betrayed a terrifying
lack of emotion. "I hate Edward. He killed Jessica. I'll never
let him forget." With an impassive face she continued to
stare at Bridget, although she seemed to expect no response.
Then, her sentence pronounced, she turned, trooped up the
long flight of red brick steps and disappeared through the
school doors.

Kathryn's steps were lighter and less labored on the way
home from school. The little black dog was content to yap
at her from the safety of its own front porch, and when she
saw Mr. Carlotti, he merely nodded his head sympathetically; his long black mustache seemed to droop more than
ever. Angelo knew he would miss the lovely blond-haired
lady; she always had a cheerful word for him and sometimes
an apple or a carrot for Bianca. He flicked the whip over the
horse's broad white back and she trudged on.

The closer she got to home, the more Kathryn's footsteps
dragged. She didn't want to go home. Not without Jessica.
As she turned the corner her feet suddenly dug into the pavement. Her eyes grew wide with disbelief: a thin column of
smoke was rising from one side of the house, and as she
watched, an occasional orange tongue of flame lapped around
the far corner of the house. Realizing it was coming from her
father's room, she began running. Panting with fear and desperation, she fought her way through the tangle of overgrown
rhododendrons at the side of the house and into the backyard.

What she saw was not what she'd expected, but it was as horrifying.

Although the leaping flames obscured his body, she knew it was Edward. Like a great stone statue, he stood unmoving, staring into the fire. The flames threatened to engulf him, but if he felt the scorching heat, he gave no indication. His pale face glowed red in the fire. A shock of his slick pomaded hair cut across his brow like a black scar. His prominent nose appeared even more beaklike as the flames danced over his face, creating macabre shadows. The narrow slits of his eyes were dark and dead. They were fixed on the blaze. He was a man mesmerized. With a sudden flash of insight Kathryn realized she was watching a tortured demon in hell. At that instant hell became more real in her mind than any preacher could ever have made it.

Like a creature in a trance, Edward raised the rake he held and thrust it into the bonfire, whipping it up so that the flames doubled, rising upward against the sky to ignite the clouds. The flames soared so high Kathryn could no longer see her brother. But she did see what his rake had inadvertently dislodged—a flash of mauve that was immediately consumed by the greedy fire.

Afraid to be seen, Kathryn turned and forced her way out through the dense shubbery, ignoring the branches that bounced back and scratched her arms. Trying to forget the hellish images, she let herself in through the front door and instinctively made her way to her father's room. She wanted to know that he was safe.

The next morning Kathryn rose early and, still in her nightdress, stole out into the garden. The air was cool and the grass was dew-covered under her bare feet. Only the birds challenged her privacy. All that remained of the fire was a circle of ashes and burned, blackened grass. There was no trace of the horror. As if to prove the ordinariness of it all, she touched the ashes with her foot and traced dusty gray circles. In the softness her foot touched something sharp.

She bent down, dug her fingers into the ashes and picked it up, rubbing the blackened object on her nightdress. The heat of the fire had melted some of the metal filigree into an ugly lump, but she knew immediately what it was: Jessica's purple brooch. Wrapping it carefully in a handkerchief, she put it in her pocket. In later years she would have diamonds and emeralds, pearls and rubies and sapphires, but the purple brooch would always remain in her jewel box, treasured as if it were the most precious.

Chapter Eleven

As Lily wished, their lives returned to normal. But in her absence Jessica loomed larger and more threatening than ever. In the depth of the night Lily lay sleepless, remembering. Remembering every kind word Edward spoke to Jessica. Grieving over the memory of the little gallantries. Tortured by his concern for his wife's every comfort. And she imagined her son lying in his lonely bed remembering. Jealousy gnawed at her and the wound festered, swelling to such terrifying proportions that she had to bite her lips to keep from screaming out in rage. When she could stand it no longer, Lily confronted her son.

They had gone back to their old habits and were sitting in the parlor after supper. Wordlessly, like an old husband and wife, they sat, she occupied with her needlework, he absorbed in the newspaper. Without looking up or losing a stitch, Lily asked, "Do you miss her?"

As much as she dreaded his answer, the silence was even worse. Her words hovered in the air. The ticking of the grandfather clock beat like a drum. Finally he said, "Do I miss who?"

"Jessica." Lily felt a sense of relief as soon as the word was out of her mouth, as if the taboo had been broken. She looked up, praying that she wouldn't see the raw pain etched on his face. But his mouth was twisted and bitter.

"I spent a great deal of money on that woman. She died. It was a bad investment." Silently he added, One I won't make again.

Conflicting emotions fought within Lily—happiness that she no longer had a rival, horror that her son could be so unfeeling. From the moment he was born she had surrounded him with love, enough love so that he would never feel deprived of a father's love or miss the love of grandparents and brothers and sisters. She'd filled the gap with her own great, overwhelming love. But Edward had never learned to love. Of course, when he was a little boy he'd loved her; she was the center of his world. But now she wondered. . . . Had he ever loved? Was he even capable of feeling that emotion? But it was too late for her to stop loving him.

Like a wounded animal, Kathryn endured her hurt in dumb silence. With no one to share her sorrow, she too fell into the habit of remembering. Every night as she lay in her narrow iron bed she would relive the months she'd had with Jessica. She chose only the absolute best times: the first day in class; the moment she discovered that Jessica was coming to live with them; the evening Jessica returned from her honeymoon. When she'd relived all these—re-creating every detail, resurrecting each scrap of conversation—she turned to the less important moments. Gradually she began talking to Jessica, carrying home to her the details of her school day, just as she had when Jessica was alive. When she won the class spelling bee, it was Jessica she told, not her mother. And when Billy Mulligan called her a rude name, she cried to Jessica.

After three months Kathryn stopped talking to Jessica and made a decision. Loving hurt. She refused to fall into that trap again. She would never allow herself to love.

Despite the setback of a bad investment, Edward prospered. He bought another boardinghouse, but with no wife to run it he was forced to hire a housekeeper. Because she came without references and could be gotten for his miserly wages, he hired a slovenly German with a thick accent and, Edward suspected, a fondness for schnapps. When he discovered she was padding the grocery bill, he replaced her with an attractive young woman. Kathleen Corrigan claimed to be a widow, but Edward suspected that her young son was illegitimate. He hinted that he would be willing to overlook her "peculiar situation" if she were willing to accept the wages he offered. But every week when he paid her he thought of Jessica. She'd failed him; she should have been there doing this work, helping him build his empire.

* * *

"Kathryn, I can't possibly go. I have five bushels of tomatoes to can today." Exasperated, Lily gestured to the mason jars that covered every flat surface in the kitchen. "The tomatoes are too ripe; they can't wait." Kathryn tried to understand, but with all her heart she wished her mother could go to the spelling bee. All the other mothers would be there. And she knew she'd win. Even if stuck-up Edgar Cabot bragged that he intended to take home the trophy.

As she grew older Kathryn stopped inviting her mother to school events. Eventually she even stopped mentioning her accomplishments. Her mother just didn't care.

But that didn't stop Kathryn. Every year without fail she stood at the top of her class. She won every spelling bee, captured the prize in every essay contest and took the honors for everything from arithmetic to deportment by working hard and welcoming each new challenge. Occasionally a more perceptive teacher wondered what drove her, but no one seemed to know. Teachers also noted sadly that Kathryn had no close friends and no need of them. If she had no friendly ear into which to whisper girlish confidences, it was unlikely that she had any to whisper: she seemed so serious, uninterested in the chatter about fashions and social events that consumed the other girls. Not that her seriousness made her unpopular. She was liked and admired, and any girl would have given her eyeteeth to be her best friend. And as she matured and gave signs of the beauty she was to become, any boy in the school would have been happy to carry her books, despite the fact that she was determined to beat him on every algebra exam or history paper. But she never gave any of them the chance.

At the end of her first year in high school, Kathryn was a finalist in a countywide essay contest. When she filed out on stage with six other students, she was dumbfounded to see her mother sitting in the middle of the first row. Kathryn turned away, then looked again to make sure her nervousness had not merely excited her imagination. No. There Lily sat, in a lacy white dress with a big yellow straw hat with pink roses. She looked beautiful. Hardly the mother Kathryn was accustomed to seeing, irritable and tired from the never-ending chores. Gradually her nervousness disappeared and was replaced by an expanding glow of pride; her mother had cared enough to come.

When it was Kathryn's turn, she approached the podium with poise and confidence, as if she knew she already had the audience on her side. Oblivious of all the hundreds of other faces in the auditorium, Kathryn focused on her mother's. Her speech, entitled "The Role of Women in America," was given to Lily and for Lily. And to Lily it seemed as if Kathryn's words not only were directed to her but were about her. As Kathryn spoke of women—how their courage, their stamina, their sacrifices, their achievements helped to make America a great nation—her words rekindled memories of the past. The struggle to survive. The struggle to raise a son. And the fulfillment of her dream. As Kathryn spoke enthusiastically of the future that lay ahead for women in the twentieth century, Lily couldn't help smiling. Kathryn would have opportunities she had never dreamed of. For a moment Lily also felt a glimmer of jealousy, but only for a moment, before it was overwhelmed by pride. This intelligent, articulate, beautiful young woman was her daughter.

The applause at the end of her performance was deafening. Kathryn automatically curtsied her acknowledgment to the audience and returned to her seat. She could only think of her mother. The applause of hundreds didn't matter; she wanted to bask in her mother's praise.

The reception afterward was noisy and crowded. Everyone wanted to stop Kathryn and offer congratulations, but she scarcely heard anyone's words. Her eyes were darting around the room, searching out her mother. When she finally caught sight of the big straw hat, the woman turned around but she wasn't Lily. It took a long time before Kathryn was willing to admit Lily was gone. To be polite, she forced down a tiny square of pound cake and a cup of sweet, lukewarm punch before escaping.

From the clattering sounds in the kitchen, Kathryn knew her mother was already back at work. Her buoyant mood of elation gone, Kathryn pushed open the door hesitantly. Lily was once again in her navy blue working dress, a worn apron tied around her waist, but she wasn't working. She was standing in front of the sink, staring out the window, a faraway look on her face, as if a better world lay beyond. Kathryn felt as if she were intruding on a private moment and hesitated, wondering if she could slip out unseen.

Her mother's face lit up with an unaccustomed warm smile when she turned around and saw Kathryn. "My dear, you were wonderful. I was very proud of you." If they had been almost any other mother and daughter, they would have fallen into each other's arms, but it was years since Lily had hugged Kathryn.

Kathryn's happiness lasted until dinner, when Edward mentioned that he had spent the day in Boston and she understood why her mother had come to see her: because Edward wasn't there to find out.

At the end of Kathryn's honor-filled sophomore year, Edward made his announcement.

His second boardinghouse was a financial success. Weekly the numbers in his bank accounts grew fatter, and he considered acquiring a third house, or perhaps a small hotel. But then Kathleen Corrigan announced smugly, happy to get out from under his threats, that she was getting married. Who would work for such a low wage? Perhaps he could find someone else with a guilty secret, someone who could be exploited. . . . He decided it was hopeless and saw the dream of a hotel fading.

Until he thought of Kathryn. She was old enough to leave school. There was no reason for a woman to be educated. She could run the boardinghouse, and best of all, she was family, which meant he wouldn't have to pay her anything. Oh, perhaps a little now and then for a hair ribbon or toilet water, those little bits of finery women seemed to thrive on. He thought of the little gifts to Lily over the years, given to soothe her imagined hurts. They always worked. Although Kathryn was much cleverer. He'd have to be careful with her.

"Kathryn, you look lovely this morning. Doesn't she, Lily?" he said as they were riding to church the following Sunday. Edward begrudged the cost of buying a carriage and feeding a horse, so they rode the trolley. The two women stared at him in surprise. Kathryn's look was immediately wary. Choosing to ignore her silence, he continued. "I suppose we shall soon be losing you to some young man. Per-

haps you already have one in mind," he said, knowing
perfectly well she didn't.

"No, I don't," she replied, surprised but determined not
to be bullied. What was Edward up to?

Edward smiled indulgently at her. "It's never too soon for
a woman to start thinking, you know. For some women, finding a suitable husband is more difficult than for others. Men
have very specific ideas about what they want in a wife. They
do not want one who is too intelligent. Or ambitious. Or
unladylike."

"Edward, Kathryn is still very young. Don't you think this
is all a bit . . . a bit premature?" Lily asked.

Don't want to admit to yourself you have a daughter old
enough for marriage, do you? Edward thought to himself as
he looked at Lily. He had to admit she was still attractive.
For her age. Big-bosomed. Small-waisted. And the silver
strands in her dark hair were flattering.

He fastened his eyes on Kathryn. "Don't worry about your
future. I am sure that everything will work out satisfactorily.
But in the meantime, I," he said, pulling himself up in his
seat and inflating his chest in an expansive gesture, "have
decided to make a provision for your future. It will give you
independence. You will have no need to depend on the bounty
of some husband you may or may not acquire. It's an opportunity not many girls your age are fortunate enough to have."

Oh, I hope, I hope he's going to say he's sending me to
college, Kathryn thought, crossing her fingers. Then reality
intruded. Spending money on a college education for a
woman was something Edward would never do.

"I have a responsibility toward my family and I have given
your future a great deal of thought," he continued, "and I
have decided to fire Mrs. Corrigan and allow you to run the
boardinghouse in her stead. It is an excellent opportunity for
you, one for which you should be grateful."

"Surely, Edward, you can't mean . . . a single young
woman running a boardinghouse full of men. It's not proper.
Why, it's . . . it's . . . scandalous," Lily gasped.

Kathryn could not believe her ears. She would have to give
up school, the best part of her life. There were so many more
wonderful things to learn. If she could just continue to learn,
the world would be hers and she could get out of that grim

house, away from Edward, his penny-pinching and his grandiose scheming, and do what she wanted to with her life. She had the awful feeling that if she gave in to him on this, she'd never escape. She'd become a prisoner like her poor mother.

She looked him straight in the eye. ''I refuse to quit school to become your unpaid servant.''

Edward watched in surprise as she calmly opened her prayer book and began to read. He cursed himself for approaching the situation in the wrong way. Too nicely. He could always force her to comply. He had the right legally, or at least Lily did. Kathryn was the perfect solution to his problem, and he would not give up.

Kathryn would not give up either. In a strange way she felt that she owed it to Jessica. If she fell into his trap—spending the rest of her days working for him, running his boarding-house, serving him uncomplainingly, as her mother did—she would be as dead as Jessica.

If he killed her dream she'd die. Once she escaped the house and Edward, the exciting possibilities for the rest of her life seemed endless, stretching on and on, each one rich and tempting, like the sumptuous dishes on a banquet table. Women could become doctors. They wrote novels and edited newspapers. They drove automobiles and ran shops; they went on the stage and painted portraits. Right now in the European war hundreds of brave English girls were nursing the never-ending stream of wounded soldiers, risking their own lives on the battlefields. She'd discover her own dream and she'd fulfill it. Deep down in her heart she had no doubts.

But first she had to deal with the problem of Edward. The idea plagued her, following her into bed that night. Fears and memories churned in her head. Hot, she kicked off her blankets, only to have her fevered body turn icy. Her cotton nightgown twisted uncomfortably around her legs. Her body craved sleep and her mind could no longer function rationally. The figure of Edward loomed above her. She was trapped. The thought kept pounding at her until she could think of nothing else. *Trapped.*

Yet in her feverish, half-formed thoughts one solution fought its way through. When she awoke heavy-headed and gritty-eyed the next morning, the tantalizing memory lin-

gered. The harder she tried to force the idea back into her
brain, the more fleeting it became.

Then, as if a door had suddenly opened, the idea came
slamming back into her brain. Her father! The memory was
disappointing. There was nothing her father could do; he
never stood up to Edward. Sometimes she almost hated him
for his weakness. He ignored or accepted Edward's behavior;
Kathryn was never sure which. Although she and her father
had grown closer over the years, they never spoke of the
things nearest to their hearts. It was as if Lily and Edward
and the exact nature of their unusual family were taboo—
never to be spoken of. As if they feared that this discussion,
like Pandora's box once opened, would let loose a flood of
carefully concealed emotions that could never again be controlled.

No; her father, much as he loved her, was not the solution.
Who was left? Her mother, she thought wryly. Over the years
the truth had painfully dawned on Kathryn: Edward would
always come first in her mother's heart. What had happened
in the past to forge such a bond between mother and son? At
times they almost acted like husband and wife, Kathryn realized with a flush of embarrassment.

What she needed was someone who had a hold over Edward. She stared at the crack running across the ceiling. How
many generations of Townsends—more likely their servants,
since this was the attic—had lain here, preoccupied with their
own problems, and stared at the same crack?

Then it came to her. The house. The Townsend house. It
belonged to her father. The house was legally Robert Townsend's. No matter how much Edward strutted around playing
man of the house, bragging of his blue-blooded ancestors, he
was walking on another man's carpets and sitting at the head
of another man's table. If she could persuade her father to
use this as a weapon against Edward . . . She knew she'd
have to approach him cautiously. He'd been passive for too
many years; fighting would not come easily. If only he loved
her enough to try.

Chapter Twelve

Robert's jaw was set, his lips pursed into a determined line. He had rehearsed the words often enough; he knew what he must say. He turned to his stepson. "I have heard all about your scheme and I will not allow you to exploit my daughter. She is a Townsend and she will be raised as is proper, as a lady—which, don't you forget, she is—not as your unpaid servant."

Edward smiled his condescending, toothy smile. "If that is what is worrying you, I'm sure that we can work out the proper remuneration for Kathryn's tasks."

"You don't understand at all, do you? In your little book-keeper's mind everything revolves around money." Robert bit his tongue. He was tempted to remind Edward that he might have no idea of what was proper for a lady. But there was no use antagonizing him; he could be a dangerous enemy. Perhaps this could be resolved without . . .

But it was not to be.

"My dear stepfather," Edward said without bothering to mask the contempt in his voice, "you pretend to be so far above all thoughts of money, but who do you think has been putting food on your table and clothes on the backs of your daughter and wife while you"—he gazed down at Robert's crooked, emaciated figure—"laze about?"

Robert's voice remained annoyingly calm. "It seems to me that it is my wife who runs this place. Not you."

"Then you perceive the situation wrongly. Now, if you've finished with your diatribe, I have more important concerns than listening to the whining of an . . . invalid."

"You think of me as a sick, weak old man, don't you? You

didn't expect me to interfere. Why should you? I never have before—a fact that now shames me. Things would have been different around here if I had. Very different.''

Without saying a word, Edward turned on his heel and stalked toward the door.

''You're probably saying to yourself, 'What can he do about it? Poor man can hardly move his body out of bed.' But what you forget—you're so busy playing the man of the house—is that this is my house. And I can force you to leave it anytime.''

''That I doubt, old man,'' Edward said, his voice oozing confidence; he sounded no more worried by the threats than a horse is by the buzzing of a small but persistent insect.

''Oh, no, not physically I couldn't, you're right,'' Robert said, his voice growing stronger. All of Edward's past cruelties were fueling the fires of his anger. ''No, my lawyers would handle it. An old firm that has served my family for generations and is quite devoted to my welfare.''

Edward's face paled imperceptibly and his voice lost a little of its cockiness. ''I don't think you'd do that.'' Then, like a man pulling the ace out of his sleeve, he added, ''Because there could be consequences.''

''Are you threatening me?'' Robert asked, his pale eyes fastening on Edward's dark ones. ''I misjudged you. I didn't think even you would stoop as low as to threaten me with physical violence.''

Ignoring Robert, Edward continued. ''I had hoped to avoid this unpleasant possibility—I didn't care to upset you—but have you considered your wife might choose to leave with me?''

Robert paused. The idea did not surprise or hurt him. ''That is a chance I am willing to take. To protect my daughter.'' He saw the quick flash of triumph on Edward's face and knew what he was thinking. ''And don't bother threatening to take Kathryn with you. I am her father. With legal rights, rights I would not hesitate to exercise. Kidnapping is a serious matter.''

''You are welcome to the brat. Very welcome.''

''Tell me, is there anyone in this world you care for?'' Robert asked with genuine concern ringing in his voice. Then, seeing the impassive look on Edward's face, he said sadly,

"No, I suppose there isn't. But just remember I'm not like you. I love my daughter and I'll fight for her."

"If you still can," Edward said.

"You mean that I'm dying. You don't have to pretend that you are not longing to have me out of your way. Your book-keeper's brain has it all figured out: Lily will inherit the house. You're right. That's how my will reads—now. But I'm warning you: it can be changed at any time. And I will change it, without a moment's hesitation. You won't get your hands on my property. I'll leave it to some worthy cause—like a society for lost dogs or unwed mothers or missionaries."

"I'd—we'd—contest the will. I'd see that your wife got her fair share."

Robert pounced on his answer. "Of course, that is exactly what my lawyers would expect you to do. The will would be drawn up to withstand your greedy efforts to overturn it."

"You're crazy. Definitely not of sound mind. The will wouldn't stand up." Edward's voice was low; only the quickness of his words betrayed his nervousness. Who could have believed his stepfather capable of such clever scheming? For a second he had a wild thought that perhaps Kathryn . . .

"I've thought of that, too," Robert said. "I will have a statement prepared by Dr. Morrow attesting to my sanity. The doctor would be only too pleased to do it. He's not one of your greatest admirers, you know. He sees through that polite facade right down to your selfish little soul. Although I doubt that you have one of those. A soul, I mean."

In the back of Edward's brain he saw the whole grisly scene and heard the doctor's words: *"You've paid the price. Your wife is dead, the baby, too. Bloody awful death."* Words he'd tried desperately to forget over the years.

"He blames you for Jessica's death. Luckily for you, he's too much of a professional to spread his accusations around town."

"You blasted idiot. You waited too long. What the hell do you expect me to do now?" The words hammered in Edward's brain. Echoing again and again. They were all he could hear. The room around him faded into nothingness. All he could see was Jessica. The image of her face. The blond hair piled on her head. Her peachlike complexion. The hurt look in her blue eyes. He knew he was guilty: he had killed her.

The facade of excuses he'd constructed was just that—excuses. The truth was staring him in the face. It was in her eyes. God, how he missed her. Still missed her. There was never a day when he didn't think of her.

Robert watched his stepson, and for a moment he felt sorry for him. Throwing the past in his face, digging up the painful memories, perhaps that had been cruel and unfair.

Bridget pressed her ear to the door. The silence scared her. What if Mr. Townsend was having an attack? Would Mr. Edward know where to find his medicine? Surely he wouldn't just stand by and watch his stepfather suffer. A dark thought hit her, a thought so black she shivered; it was as if someone were walking over her grave. Edward couldn't be *that* evil. She imagined Mr. Townsend, sick and vulnerable, a pillow pressed over his face, too weak to fight for his life.

To her relief, when she burst in she found the two men standing on opposite sides of the room, but the atmosphere was heavy with emotion as they glared at each other. Mr. Townsend's kindly blue eyes were transformed by a dark, steely hatred. And Edward's, Edward's were those of a man in hell.

"What are you doing here?" Edward snapped.

"It is time for Mr. Townsend's medicine," she said, daring him to object.

He seemed glad of an excuse to leave. As he opened the door Robert spoke up. "I'm delighted we had the chance for this talk. And pleased to know that you agree with me it's important Kathryn finish her education."

Robert gave an almost imperceptible nod and was gone.

"Weren't you wonderful?" Bridget said, looking at Robert's flushed but ecstatic face. "Finally giving Mr. Edward what he deserves."

He grinned like a little boy. "Yes, I was, wasn't I? But how do you know what happened?"

"How else? By listening at the door. I was ready to come in and give him a good pounding if need be."

Robert laughed. The good, solid laugh of a young, healthy man. "I believe you would have, too."

"And, Lord forgive me," she said, pounding her clenched fist into her palm, "I would have enjoyed every moment of it."

What they were afraid to say was that it was only a temporary victory.

The atmosphere in the house continued to be tense. Like the unseasonal heat and humidity that arrived in late May and lingered on till early June, it hung in the air. Edward felt betrayed. Robert, like a perfidious animal, had bitten the hand that fed him. A sick old man, he would have been out on the street, starving, years ago if Edward hadn't generously abandoned his own career to take on the running of the boardinghouse. And instead of getting down on his rickety knees in gratitude, the old man had threatened to kick him out. All because of that spoiled, rotten little . . . half sister of his. He consoled himself with the thought that Robert would soon die, but Kathryn . . . Kathryn would have to be coped with.

Kathryn had won, but she discovered there was a price to pay. Edward's hostility was like a newly sharpened knife, slashing at her, eager to prove its sharpness. She stayed out of his reach and when his words wounded her, she refused to let it show. But his hatred wore her down. For the first time the lines had been clearly drawn: he was her enemy. The hardest for Kathryn to bear was her mother's alliance with the enemy. At first Lily had tried to be, if not peacemaker, at least pacifier. Then Edward turned his hostility on her and she caved in.

Kathryn buried herself in her schoolwork, and when school was over for the summer, she did her chores without complaint and went out of her way to avoid Edward whenever possible. It hurt her to see how her mother scurried out of a room as soon as she entered it and couldn't bring herself to meet her daughter's eyes.

Even her little attic bedroom with its revolving bookcase and comforting rose wallpaper was no longer a haven. It was as if the tensions in the house rose up the back staircase and seeped in under her door. And so, since the summer was a dry, pleasant one, she took to the roads and spent most of her days out of doors. At first she walked; then, having exhausted the neighborhood, she rode the trolley into the country.

Lily knew perfectly well that respectable young girls of sixteen did not go wandering around the countryside by themselves—there were too many dangers lurking out there; men, waiting to take advantage—but Edward seemed happier when Kathryn wasn't around, so she said nothing.

He recognized her almost immediately. She was a young lady now, and what a beauty! The midday sun made her dark hair sparkle with red-and-gold highlights. She was still too young to wear her hair up, and it tumbled down her back in a cascade of curls. She hadn't grown much taller, he noticed; she was still a tiny figure. But curves were beginning to fill out the cornflower-blue dress she wore. Her feet planted on the bottom rung of the fence, she was leaning over and petting Bianca's big, shaggy white head. Angelo Carlotti smiled and started across the pasture.

She turned around in surprise. "Mr. Carlotti, what are you doing here? I haven't seen you in an awfully long time."

"Bianca and me. We retire. No more delivering ice for us. My sister, she is married to man who owns this farm."

Embarrassed to be caught in what Edward condemned as "unladylike behavior," she hopped down off the fence, scooped her straw hat off the ground and tied it neatly under her chin.

"Miss Kathryn, now you must—" All of a sudden a massive, fast-moving black-and-white shape emerged from a patch of woods on the other side of the road and hurled itself at them. "No, Cricket," Angelo shouted just as it launched itself at Kathryn. He caught it by the collar and forced it down to the ground, and Kathryn could see it was an enormous shaggy dog. Hair hung down over its eyes and a big pink tongue lolled from its mouth. She knelt and offered her hand for sniffing. The dog responded eagerly, licking it with his soft tongue.

"Stop, Cricket. You get Miss Kathryn all dirty. Be careful with her. She's tiny lady. You knock her down."

Kathryn's dark head was bent over the dog, who was taking eager swipes at her face with his tongue and sending her hat flying. Finally Angelo pulled him back. "Miss Kathryn, you come into house. Wash. Meet my little sister, Rosa."

They walked up through the pasture to a cluster of red barns and sheds surrounded by a low stone wall. In the center was a freshly painted white clapboard house. Angelo's "little sister" was not little. She looked as if her clothes had been stuffed with down pillows. A smile lit up her moon-shaped face as she welcomed Kathryn into her kitchen. She insisted on making Kathryn a cup of thick black coffee and serving spicy little cookies.

There was a warmth in the kitchen that didn't come from the heat of the day. Angelo and his brother-in-law, a rangy and weathered New Englander, seemed shy in front of Kathryn, but Rosa chattered on.

As she sat in the kitchen Kathryn felt as if she too were part of their warm world. Their love enveloped her. Is this what it feels like to be part of a family? she wondered. Reluctant to leave, she gave in easily to their pleas to have another cup of coffee, and another.

From then on, her walks ended up in Rosa's kitchen. She helped Rosa make her spinach pasta and took home fat eggplants and plum tomatoes from Angelo's garden. Ezra escorted her around his dairy barn, proudly telling her the name of every cow. Whenever Cricket saw her, he greeted her the same enthusiastic way, and she soon learned to grab a fence post or flatten herself against a wall for support when he jumped up and placed his huge paws on her shoulders. All of a sudden Kathryn found the prospect of a long summer stretching ahead of her a pleasant one full of possibilities.

Chapter Thirteen

The young man wiped his greasy hands on his trousers and then grasped the crank tightly in both hands, forcing it with all his wiry strength. The engine rewarded him with a weak cough before dying. He stared up at his automobile; he'd had it for less than a week. A red Stutz Bearcat with black upholstery and yellow wheels and he loved it—except for moments like these. He'd driven her all the way from Boston with only one tire change.

The day was warming up and steam was rising from the puddles on the deserted road. He pulled out his handkerchief to wipe his brow, then used it to flick off a few specks of dust that clung to the sparkling chrome radiator. At least it wasn't raining. They'd had a week of rain which had climaxed in a spectacular downpour yesterday. The city fathers had decided to hold the Fourth of July parade anyhow. Rain had pelted the marchers and even the music had sounded soggy. Seemed appropriate for a city like Lowell—all dreary and gray. Endless rows of big brick factories manned by endless streams of scared, gray-faced workers. A sky made eternally gray by the smoke of hundreds of smokestacks. He missed Boston already. What would he do in this city all summer long? It had all sounded like a grand adventure until he'd found himself a prisoner in this dreary place. The one bright spot was the car.

He turned once more to the crank and gave it one more enormous twist. Nothing. He'd noticed a farm farther back. Perhaps the farmer could lend him a carriage or even a wagon. All eyes had been on him when he chugga-chugged away in his shiny new automobile. How humiliating to return behind some broad-beamed plowhorse.

Faced with that possibility, he decided to give it one last try. As he reached for the crank he noticed someone coming toward him. A girl, and she was running. At her heels a big black-and-white dog loped slowly along so as not to get ahead of her. Her behavior was far from ladylike, but she didn't seem to care. As she came closer he could see that her long skirt was bouncing up and down, revealing high-buttoned shoes and an occasional glimpse of white-stockinged calf. Embarrassed, he turned his eyes toward her face. My God, she's pretty, he thought. Not artificially pretty like those white-faced china dolls, but genuinely pretty. Her dark hair, if it ever had been carefully combed, now surrounded her face in a wild tangle of curls that bounced as she ran. Her cheeks were attractively flushed. She was tiny with a trim figure; the big dog reached almost up to where her . . . uh . . . figure showed under the blue dress that molded her body. A farm girl, he decided, wondering if the stories he'd heard about their virtue were true: Would they do things proper young ladies in Boston weren't even permitted to think about?

She hadn't seen him; her eyes were on the dog. "Come on, Cricket. Let's go, boy," she shouted. "I'll race you to the pond." But the dog had caught sight of him, and with a resonant woof it charged. Adam Elliott didn't know what to expect. For a second he considered hopping into the car but then decided, when the dog turned out to be friendly, he'd look foolish. And if there was one thing he didn't want to appear in front of that beautiful girl, it was foolish.

The massive dog hurled toward him, its huge paws splashing into every puddle along the way. Too late did Adam realize the dog's intentions, and when he turned toward the car his effort was useless. A shaggy black-and-white face was staring into his, its heavy paws resting on his shoulders. If he'd stayed where he was, the accident wouldn't have happened, but he stepped backward to avoid Cricket's tongue. Thrown off balance, the dog scrambled to steady itself and pushed him over—right into the widest, deepest, muddiest puddle on the whole road. Adam could feel himself going down and there was nothing he could do to stop himself. He landed with a loud splash.

Kathryn arrived at the scene breathless. "Oh, I'm so terribly sorry. . . ." she managed to say before bursting into laughter. There he lay—a well-dressed young man in his black suit and starched white collar—smack in the middle of a mud puddle. Cricket stood over him, licking his mud-splattered face and looking delighted with himself for having found a new friend.

"I don't see what's so funny. Can't you keep your dog under control? Do you always let him hurtle around the countryside pushing people into puddles?"

He was mad. Kathryn could see how his deep blue eyes flashed with anger. She grabbed Cricket's collar and attempted to pull him away, but she was too small and he was too large and too intrigued with his new friend.

She was even prettier than Adam had first thought. Suddenly he saw himself the way she must see him. Unconsciously his hands went up to straighten his tie, leaving muddy fingerprints all over his white collar.

When Kathryn saw what he'd done she laughed even harder, but her laughter gave way to embarrassment. It was her fault, after all. If she'd had better control of Cricket . . . "I am sorry, I really am," she said, trying to sound contrite. "He's not even my dog. It's just that he loves people. Don't be scared, he's not dangerous."

"I am not scared, just wet," Adam said, sitting up. To Cricket this was a sign that his new friend was ready to play, and he began prancing and barking.

"Cricket, look what you've done to this poor man. Aren't you ashamed of yourself?"

The man was tall. Tall and very solid-looking as he rose from the puddle. His hair was somewhere between blond and brown, and it curled. His nose and lips were delicately chiseled, like those on a Greek statue. She had a fleeting thought that he was the sort of man the girls at school would swoon over. But she certainly wasn't about to swoon over a wet and muddy man.

"Well," she said, eyeing him, "you certainly can't drive home like that and get your beautiful new car all dirty. There's a farm down the road—where Cricket comes from—you can wash up there."

Later Adam would regret that they hadn't talked, that he

hadn't found out more about Cricket's companion, but they walked in awkward silence up to the farm. She directed him to an outside pump and then disappeared. A few minutes later she came out with a towel and told him to come into the house. "After all, it was Cricket's fault. This is the least we can do."

He was introduced to a round, smiling woman named Rosa. Rosa bustled around, fixing him a cup of coffee, cutting him a slice of cake, but still the girl did not talk. When Rosa's husband appeared he offered Adam a change of clothes and a ride into town. Adam accepted graciously, although he didn't really want to leave. The atmosphere in the kitchen was warm and intimate, filled with Rosa's love and motherly concern. And besides, he could look at the beautiful girl. Her dark head was bent over Cricket as she brushed him. She was completely absorbed in her task and Adam couldn't help staring at her. Crazy, he realized, but he felt a glimmer of jealousy. A dog, for heaven's sake. It was ridiculous, but he couldn't take his eyes off her long, slender white fingers fondling the dog. How would they feel touching him?

Driving back to the city with Ezra, Adam discovered that her name was Kathryn and that she was "a friend." But Ezra was a taciturn New Englander, and that was all he could find out.

Adam located a man who was a self-proclaimed "whiz with motors," and that evening they walked out to retrieve the car. The man did work miracles, and soon they were chugga-chugging back to Adam's hotel. The next day being Sunday, Adam decided it was only proper to call on Rosa and Ezra to thank them for their help. As he drove up the rutted lane to the farmhouse he couldn't help hoping that Kathryn would be there.

"Nice young man. Polite of him to come all the way out here to thank us," Ezra said after Adam had left.

"You men. Can't see nose on account of face," Rosa said, mutilating her English idioms as usual.

"What do you mean? It was nice, wasn't it?"

"He did not come to see us," Rosa said slowly and carefully, as if she were talking to a child. Ezra still looked puzzled. "He came to see Miss Kathryn."

"Nonsense. Barely said two words to each other yesterday," he said, burying himself in his newspaper.

"*Sí*. That is right." Rosa was beaming; his observation confirmed her belief that the seeds of love were sprouting. "They are only shy. He looked at her all the time."

It suddenly occurred to Ezra that his wife might know what she was talking about. "You may be right," he admitted. What did they know about this young man? Nothing. Dropped into their lives out of the blue. The gravity of the thought made him lay down his paper. "But let's hope not."

Rosa's moon face turned indignant. "Why not? Miss Kathryn so pretty. Age to settle down. And this Mr. Elliott is verry handsome." She rolled her *r*'s as if she were speaking her own language.

"Rosa, we can't let Miss Kathryn . . . We don't know one darned thing about him."

"Except that he is verry handsome. And rrich," she added.

"Rich? How do you know that?" Ezra looked at his wife more closely. Sometimes he wondered if she had gypsy blood.

"He has a new car, doesn't he? And"—she waved her hand triumphantly—"he has a big diamond. Don't you see stickpin?"

The thought failed to comfort Ezra. "There, I told you. We know nothing about the young man. What's he doing sporting a piece of jewelry like that anyway? Seems suspicious to me. Too smooth a character. Don't trust him." Much as Ezra would like to have the final word, with Rosa it was impossible. But he reopened his newspaper.

Silently Rosa chewed over her husband's objections. Finally she said, "Maybe he is salesman. A traveling salesman."

"That's worse," Ezra pronounced in a satisfied tone of voice. "Girl killed up in Manchester couple weeks ago. Traveling salesman did it, so they say. Never caught him. Slit her throat. Just like a pig."

Every afternoon for the next week Adam found some excuse to drive past Rosa and Ezra's farm. He peered ahead hoping to see Kathryn and Cricket. But the road was disappointingly empty except for an occasional small, tan boy trudging along with a fishing pole. He didn't even know her last name, and it was quite possible, he realized, that he might never see her again.

Why did that thought produce a great empty feeling in his chest?

Granted, she was pretty, but he knew plenty of pretty girls, girls who could chatter, make a man feel at ease and keep a conversation going. All a little contrived, he sometimes suspected, but at least there were none of those awkward silences. Kathryn hadn't seemed to mind the silences. What, he finally decided, impressed him the most was how capable she seemed. A tiny thing, she could have fluttered around helplessly, waiting for him to take charge. But she hadn't. With a start he realized that she had told him what to do.

A decisive woman. She'd give a husband a run for his money. A husband. The mysterious empty feeling gave way to jealousy. ''Ridiculous, absolutely ridiculous,'' he muttered to himself. It wasn't as if he wanted to get married. Too many wonderful possibilities lay ahead of him—if he could survive this summer in Lowell. But at the moment Lowell didn't seem nearly as grim.

''If thou must love me, let it be naught except for love's sake only. Do not say, 'I love her for her smile—her look—her way of speaking gently—for a trick of thought that falls in well with mine'. . . .'' Kathryn read the lines again, this time more softly. She wasn't sure why the poem appealed to her. Action and adventure—that was what she usually liked. Halfway through the second stanza the mood was broken by a knock at her bedroom door. Bridget's cheerful face appeared. ''There's a gentleman to see you, Miss Kathryn.'' She couldn't keep the pleasure out of her voice. It was high time Miss Kathryn started looking for a man to take her out of this place.

Kathryn's heart jumped. Rosa, bless her, had told Adam Elliott where she lived. Over the past week she'd found herself thinking often of Adam. Too often, she decided and resolved to stop. At times she knew she'd never see him again and was glad. He was a stranger. She didn't know one single thing about him—except that she liked the way his hair curled and his eyes sparkled. A proper young lady would never talk to a strange man. If her mother and Edward ever discovered her indiscretion . . . At other times she nurtured the slim hope that Adam would be interested enough to find her again. Why hadn't she said more to him when they were together? At least told him her name?

Seeing Kathryn's faraway expression, Bridget repeated the message. "He's waiting on the front steps. Very impatient, he is. And handsome," she couldn't resist adding.

"Thank you," Kathryn called. "I'll be down in a minute." As soon as Bridget left, Kathryn hurried over to her mirror. Her hair was a shameful tumbled mass of curls, and the sun had left a bloom of freckles across her nose. She brushed the curls into an orderly fashion, tied them with a pale yellow ribbon to make sure and decided she would have to live with the freckles. "Darn him," she muttered to herself. "Who does he think he is, appearing here like this? Doesn't he realize we haven't been properly introduced?" But there was a broad smile across her face as she ran down the stairs. As she hit the front hallway she forced herself into a more ladylike walk and tried not to grin with happiness. If only she'd had time to put on a prettier dress. Taking a deep breath and telling herself to be calm, she opened the front door.

"I apologize for intruding like this, but . . ."

Kathryn's face fell in disappointment.

"I'm sorry," he said. "Have I come at a bad time?"

"No, no," Kathryn insisted, trying hard to remember her manners. "Please come in." What was Jack Jordan doing here? He was a senior; he played on the football team and always had the lead in the drama society plays. Most of the girls thought he was the handsomest thing they'd ever seen, with his smooth dark hair and green eyes guaranteed to melt any female heart.

"I seem," he said, "to have your copy of *A Midsummer Night's Dream.* We must have gotten the books mixed up at rehearsal. I stopped by to find out if you have mine."

But why did he come all the way over here in the middle of summer vacation to find that out? Kathryn asked herself. "I'll see. Wait here for just a minute," she said, running up the stairs.

He was staring up at her, thinking what wonderful curves

her dress had, when behind him a door opened and a voice coldly demanded, "What are you doing on these premises?"

He turned around to face a pale, gaunt man. "I'm Jack Jordan, sir, and I'm here to see Miss Townsend." As Jack watched, emotion suffused the man's face, making his lips twist in distaste. Jack could have sworn that this man—whoever he was—was jealous. He felt the man's eyes traveling contemptuously up and down his body.

"I do not permit Miss Townsend gentlemen visitors, so I suggest that you leave. Immediately."

"Hey, exactly who are you to make such demands?" Jack asked, his temper rising.

"I am her brother. And I must ask you to respect my wishes. My sister is young and innocent. I will not permit any man . . ." He paused, searching for the right word. ". . . to take advantage of her."

The accusation caught Jack by surprise, and he found himself blushing in anger and confusion. "Hold on, you can't accuse me of anything like that. I am here to return this, that's all," he said, holding the book up for inspection. At the sound of footsteps on the landing, both men looked up. Kathryn stood at the head of the stairs. Jack couldn't help noticing how she drew back slightly at the sight of her brother.

"I did have your book. I'm sorry," she said. She looked so lovely and so tiny that Jack was overcome with a desire to protect her.

To his surprise, her brother said nothing. He merely flashed a hate-filled look at both of them and stalked off. Almost as if, Jack thought, he were annoyed to discover the visit was genuinely innocent.

"Thank you," Jack said. He stared down at her. Beautiful as she was, was it worth his taking on that perverse watchdog brother? After all, there were plenty of other pretty girls at school, lots of them. With families who'd be happy to let him court their daughters.

He turned and left, leaving Kathryn puzzled. Why, if he didn't intend to stay, had he come on such a silly errand? Could Edward have done something, said something, to drive Jack away?

* * *

The suspicion had been gnawing at Edward for weeks, the realization creeping up on him. Seeing how snugly her dresses fitted. Watching the new way she walked with her hips swaying. Suddenly her lips were fuller, riper, and the look in her eyes seemed more worldly, confident. Kathryn was grown up.

His little sister a woman. The thought horrified him—it meant he was getting older—and intrigued him. She was beautiful. The thought of this lovely creature living in his house and subject to his will made his mind prickle with delight.

Sometimes he woke up in the middle of the night and thought about her: the way her young breasts were swelling, her tiny wasp waist—he imagined spanning it with his hands—and the soft whiteness of her skin. At first these thoughts shocked him and filled him with guilt. Let it be any other woman but her. She was his sister, or at least his half sister, and she was still a child. To fight the fullness in his groin, he tried to remember her as a baby. How ugly she'd been, red-faced and squealing, like a funny little monkey. The image helped, but only for a little while. Then his body refused to allow his mind to connect the two images. Kathryn was a woman—a very desirable woman. Lust and guilt fought for possession of his body. Sometimes guilt won.

Chapter Fourteen

"I think Rosa was happy to get rid of us," Adam said as they crossed the dusty farmyard to the winding rutted path that led through Bianca's pasture down to the road. "She thinks she's a matchmaker." He grinned. "Actually, Cricket is the matchmaker. If he hadn't pushed me into that mud puddle . . ."

It never occurred to Kathryn that it was presumptuous of Adam to consider them a match already made. Something had drawn her to the farm that Sunday afternoon, and when she'd entered Rosa's sun-filled kitchen, she hadn't been surprised to find Adam sitting there. Everything had seemed so natural, so right. Rosa served them her delicious strong coffee, but she didn't offer them a second cup. Instead she shooed them off, insisting that it was a beautiful day, too beautiful to stay indoors, but refusing to go with them.

And it was a beautiful day. They would have sworn that it was, without a doubt, the most beautiful day of the summer. The fields and trees glimmered green and gold in the sun. Mountainous white clouds drifted overhead. It was warm, but not an oppressive heat. The warmth was pleasant, comforting, like a fire on a chilly night.

When they reached the road they walked for about a hundred yards. Then Kathryn, with Cricket at her heels, suddenly veered off into the woods. Adam could see no sign of a path, but she wove her way amongst the trees as if she knew the way. Adam followed without hesitation.

She pushed a branch out of the way and carefully skirted a patch of poison ivy. "This is one of my favorite places. I found it a few weeks ago and I keep coming back. My retreat from the world.''

Adam studied her closely. Most girls he knew couldn't wait to throw themselves into the world—parties, concerts, balls. He was right: Kathryn Townsend was different.

"Here it is," she announced triumphantly as they came out of the cool darkness of the woods into a patch of green with a sparkling blue pond. "Don't you love it? It's a kettle hole. A bit of glacier got stuck here and when it melted, there was the pond. I think this is what Paradise must have looked like."

"I agree," Adam said, but he wasn't looking at the pond with its cool fringe of trees, he was looking at her eyes—and the long dark lashes that fringed them. They sparkled gold with excitement, just as the water sparkled in the sunlight. His eyes traveled over her face, delighting in what he saw. He loved the scattering of freckles on her nose. Most girls he knew hated freckles, but he couldn't imagine Kathryn wasting time worrying about them. She looked like a child of the summer sun, all golden. No, not a child, definitely not a child. He had to control his thoughts; as a woman, she was entirely too tempting.

"Tell me, do you often lure men up here?" he asked.

Her eyes flashed. "I've never brought anyone here before. Never. And if you think that, then we'd better leave."

"Wait," he protested, grasping her arm. She could feel his fingers through the light fabric. Her flesh tingled. She looked up at him and suddenly felt guilty for the feelings running through her body. "I was only teasing you. I'm sorry."

It suddenly occurred to Kathryn with embarrassing clarity how brazen she'd been. "You must think I'm awful, dragging you out here into the woods." She flushed, Adam noted, an attractive shade of pink. "I just wasn't thinking. I know perfectly well that proper young ladies don't do things like this."

"You're not a proper young lady, are you?"

For a second Kathryn looked as if she were going to take offense; then she laughed. "No, I suppose I'm a failure at that. All those rules seem so . . . so pointless. All geared toward the most important thing in a woman's life: catching a husband.''

"You don't intend to catch a husband?" Adam asked in a teasing tone of voice.

"No, there are too many more exciting things to do." For a moment she thought about telling him of her vow never to love, but she barely knew him. She'd been improper and forward enough already.

Her voice sounded so determined and the strong line of her jaw was set so defiantly that for an instant Adam felt a pang of disappointment. It surprised him. It wasn't as if he wanted to marry this girl. He'd just met her, and although he felt a warm attraction to her . . . No, he was not ready to settle down. When he was, no doubt his mother would pick out a suitable young lady with proper bloodlines, one who wouldn't drag strange men off into the woods. And one who'd be a damned bore. Before he knew it, he found himself looking into Kathryn's eyes and saying, "I'll bet anything you'll change your mind."

"Fine. What do you want to bet?"

He was surprised that she'd called his bluff, but Kathryn Townsend, whatever she was—and he wasn't sure—was not predictable. "You're on." He cast about for a suitable stake. Definitely not money. Glancing down, he saw his diamond stickpin winking up at him. It had been a birthday gift from his father and out of habit he wore it, although he considered it ostentatious. "What about this?" he asked.

"Mr. Elliott, whatever you think, I am a proper enough lady to know that I can't accept valuable gifts like that from a total stranger." Even as she said the words she knew he wasn't a total stranger. At times she felt as if they'd known each other forever.

"It wouldn't be a gift. You'd win it—fair and square."

"And what do I pledge in return?" Kathryn asked. "I should warn you, my fortune doesn't run to diamonds."

Adam knew what he'd like to answer, but instead he replied, "A lock of your hair, my fair maiden. Would that be proper?"

"You're making a bad bargain, you know. What sort of businessman are you?"

Adam laughed. A rich, throaty laugh of sheer delight that brought an automatic smile to Kathryn's lips. "And what sort of businesswoman are you to point that out to me? If you were smart you'd take the offer and run, you know."

"I guess I'll have to learn to be shrewder, won't I?"

"You don't have to. Fortunately, women don't have to worry about all that. They don't have to succeed in the business world." They're lucky, Adam said to himself.

"But these days women can do so many things. New paths are opening up for us. I remember once when I was about five or six, I announced at the dinner table that I intended to make a million dollars—on my own—and everyone laughed. But now I really think it's possible for a woman to do it."

"You are so determined I pity anyone who gets between you and your ambitions."

It took only five minutes to circle the cool edges of the pond under the tall pines. Then they sat down on a flat boulder by the water's edge. Kathryn dipped her fingers into the still, cool water. Neither felt the necessity to talk. They basked in the sun and silence, finding joy in just being together.

Finally Kathryn broke the silence. "There is something important I have to ask you."

"You sound so serious. What do you want to find out? No, I am not married, and yes, I have all my own teeth. Anything else you want to know?"

"Yes," she said. "I want to know if you're a traveling salesman."

Adam howled so loudly with laughter that Cricket came running to find out what was happening. "Ezra asked me the same question. Some sort of local prejudice against them?"

"No, it's just . . ."

"It's just that your mother warned you against them. A menace to every female within fifty miles," he mimicked in a falsetto. "Right?"

"Wrong. My brother warned me."

"Protective toward his little sister. How nice." Adam was surprised to see her shudder slightly.

"Yes. At least lately. I'm not sure why. Usually he is too busy. Money is what he is most protective about."

"Sounds like my father." He made no effort to hide the bitterness of his tone."

"You don't like your father, do you?"

"Not any more than you like your brother."

"Actually, I hate my brother." There was steel in her voice. Adam was taken aback by her vehemence. Most people he knew went to great pains to cover socially unacceptable feelings.

"Do you want to tell me why?"

Kathryn paused for a moment. "There are many reasons. Sometime I'll tell you. Not now. I refuse to ruin this day."

"You're right. Someday we'll tell each other everything." His voice rang with such sincerity that Kathryn couldn't help staring at him. It was a feeling she couldn't explain, but she knew he was right.

"If you're not a traveling salesman, what are you?" Kathryn asked, trying to disperse the emotional intensity that suddenly surrounded them.

"I'm studying political history at Yale, and I'm in Lowell for the summer. At my father's insistence. Learning the business. 'Education's fine for a boy, not for a man. A man has to get out in the business world. That's where he proves himself. Not in some dusty old library.' End of quote." Adam's voice was deep and gruff. "That's the gospel according to my father, Adam Elliott The Second.

"My father is trying to make a businessman out of me this summer. He's got a large interest in—actually, he practically owns—one of the cotton mills here, and I'm spending the summer learning the business from the ground up. Well, not exactly from the ground. It's not as if I operate the spinning machines or looms. I pity all those poor creatures who do. The heat. The noise. It is intolerable.

"What I am doing is observing. Supposedly learning. But more than anything, scaring the wits out of everyone because I'm the owner's son. It's embarrassing how they bow and scrape every time they catch sight of me."

The memory brought Adam abruptly back to reality. He reached into his waistcoat and brought out a gold pocket watch. "It's five o'clock. I'd better get you back before Rosa thinks her matchmaking worked too well. You may run around country roads like a farm boy, but there are limits."

"Yes, I suppose so," Kathryn said with a reluctant laugh. She got up, wiped off the grass and bits of leaves that clung

to her white cotton dress and then led the way through the
trees back to the road.

"If I promise that my car won't break down again, may I
drive you home?"

For a moment Kathryn looked frightened, and Adam wondered again what she had yet to tell him about her family.
"No, thank you. It's not far to the trolley line. It would be
out of the way and . . ."

"And what?"

"It could cause problems." She brightened and added,
"But thank you for a wonderful afternoon."

"Thank you for sharing your secret place—and yourself.
I'll be here tomorrow evening," he added softly, fighting the
desire to kiss her.

"I'll be here, too," Kathryn said unnecessarily; they both
knew she would be.

Their lives settled into a pattern. Every evening Kathryn
arrived in Rosa's kitchen to find Adam waiting. Yet every
evening as she rode the trolley and walked the long road up
to the farm, she worried. What if he wasn't there? What if
all this was just a dream? But when she saw his red car
parked in the farmyard looking bright and modern and out
of place amidst the scratching chickens, she was not surprised, only relieved. She knew in her heart that he would
be there. She knew they would drink Rosa's coffee and Rosa
would chatter on and Ezra would read his newspaper and
Angelo would sit staring at her, his mustache drooping in
worry.

"He doesn't trust me yet," Adam said. "He's fond of
you and wants to protect you." But Angelo's protectiveness
was comforting and reassuring, not like Edward's. "They
don't know I would never let anything happen to you.
Never."

After coffee Adam and Kathryn and Cricket would go off
by themselves, usually to their pond. One day Adam took her
hand to help her over a fallen log and kept it in his for the
rest of the evening. After that, whenever they were alone,
their hands were joined. Kathryn was amazed to discover
simple human contact could feel so wonderful. With her hand
in Adam's the world, all of a sudden, became a safer, better

place. They talked about everything and anything, sharing secrets they'd never told anyone before and dreams they didn't even know they had. Greedily they wanted to know everything about each other.

For the first time Adam confessed his doubts about the future. "The world of business, finance, commerce, all that, it's what my father raised me for, but I'm not sure. My father lives to make money, which is ridiculous, because my grandfather made enough money in railroads and copper mining to keep the family in style for generations. But my father loves to brag that he's already doubled my grandfather's fortune. He seems to think it's up to me to triple it, but I'm afraid I just can't see the point. Especially when your gains are at the expense of the poor workers. How many houses, cars, diamond stickpins do I want, knowing that some of my employees can barely afford to eat?"

"Maybe that's not it," Kathryn said slowly. "Maybe it's the challenge. Like a game. To see how much money you can make. To come up with a better idea. To see into the future, predict what people will need or want. Anticipate. And do better. Always to do it better, faster, cheaper than your competitors."

There was no mistaking the fervor in her voice and the sparkle in her eyes as she spoke. "There's been a mistake here," Adam said. "You should be my father's son. You would take to business like a duck to water. How did you learn so much about the business world? Most women—"

"I know," Kathryn interrupted. "Most women don't consider it properly ladylike. Well, times are changing and I intend to change with them." She leaned back and stared up into the darkening sky. "I learned from listening to Edward. He may be . . . despicable in other ways, but he is determined to found his own financial empire. He thinks too small, though. He's never going to succeed the way he wants to."

"Whereas you could?" He smiled indulgently.

"I'm sorry, Adam. I'm just spinning dreams. Forgive me."

"No, I believe you. But you lack one thing, one essential qualification: you are not ruthless enough. My father is not an evil man, not deliberately cruel. Just single-minded. Like a horse with blinders. Heading straight for his goal, which is to make as much money as possible. If people are hurt in the process, well, that's the way of the business world. You can't change it, or so my father says. I'm not sure." He paused. "No, I'm not sure at all."

Chapter Fifteen

The August air was stifling, hot and humid. A ghostly greenish light illuminated the night sky. The feel of unpleasant expectation hung so heavily in the air that Cricket refused to leave the safety of Rosa's kitchen. Kathryn and Adam had just reached their pond when the first rain fell. A few fat raindrops hit the ground with loud plops. The sky had darkened and a wind had arisen out of nowhere. The trees swayed noisily, swishing their ominous warnings.

Without a word they turned and started running back toward the road. Suddenly it was as dark as night. They ran blindly through the trees until a flash of lightning illuminated their path. The dust on the road was rapidly turning to mud.

Hand in hand, they dodged ruts in the pasture path and came skidding into the farmyard just as the rain began in earnest, pelting them with icy force.

"Come on," Adam yelled over the wind as he grabbed her hand and pulled her toward the barn. For a second she looked longingly at the warm, welcoming light coming from the house, but the barn was nearer and the thunder was coming closer.

Adam threw open the barn door just as the sky lit up. Once they were inside, the storm outside became a magnificent entertainment. Jagged streaks of lightning zigzagged across the inky sky and fell to the distant earth.

"Like the Fourth of July," Kathryn murmured, entranced by the show.

Adam turned to her. Her eyes were dark and flashed with excitement like the lightning that crackled against the sky, creating a halo around her dark hair. Her delicate nose and

113

exotically high cheekbones stood out in the dramatically golden light while the rest of her face faded into shadows, like the face of an angel in an old painting. To Adam she had never looked so beautiful—or so wild. A creature of the storm. Never to be tamed. One might as well try to tame an eagle and expect it to live in a cage in the parlor like a canary. Her face was wet and glowing from the rain, and Adam longed to cover every inch with kisses. To hold her body against his until all the thunderstorms of summer had passed.

"I'm drenched," Kathryn said. "I hope the storm doesn't keep up all night."

"We'd better go further inside, where it's warmer." He took Kathryn's hand and led her into the darkness.

"On your right, along the wall, Ezra keeps a lantern hanging. There should be matches on the shelf above. Can you find them?" she asked.

With the lantern lit they sunk down into a pile of hay in the middle of a golden circle of light. From the surrounding darkness they could hear the gentle rustle of hay as the cows, unnerved by the storm, fidgeted in their stalls. Occasionally there was a gentle, low moo. Kathryn would call out soft, reassuring words and the cow would quiet. Like animals making nests, they settled themselves down in the straw.

"Now isn't this just as comfortable as a feather bed?" Adam asked as he looked down at Kathryn curled up by his side. "Your family won't worry, will they?"

"They don't even know I'm gone, and even if they did . . . Edward wouldn't care, unless he thought I might be doing something to discredit his name. Funny thing, the name isn't even his."

"Is now the time to tell me why you hate your brother? I'm a good listener."

She hesitated only a moment, then said, "Because he killed the only person in the world I ever loved." It was as if every word she spoke were a bullet, deadly, without emotion. Coldly she recited her story, as if it had happened to someone else, refusing to give in to the pain of memory. But as the memory of Jessica's agonized cries and bloodstained lips rose before her, she lost control. Time had not dulled the pain; it cut into her heart as deeply and painfully as ever.

Adam wrapped his arms around her and pulled her small body to his. There were no words he could offer to ease her pain; he could only rock her in his arms and let her cry her heart out. When her tears ran dry, then he would comfort her. He pulled her closer and felt her head rest on his shoulder. Her body trembled with each fresh sob and he wondered if his own heart would break.

Gradually the storm subsided, and for Adam, the outside world faded away. All that mattered was the beautiful girl sobbing in his arms and the small circle of golden light surrounding them. A circle within a circle. He was no longer aware of the cows mooing from their stalls. A plaintive meow from the barn cat coming in search of a friend in the storm went unnoticed. Rosa waiting and worrying in her warm, dry kitchen could have been on the other side of the world. The fear that Edward might discover Kathryn's absence no longer mattered. Suddenly Adam had no past, no future. All his awareness was focused on Kathryn, the softness of her body in his arms, the sound of her weakening sobs, the fresh, soapy smell of her hair as it lay like silk against his cheek.

A warm feeling was rising in his heart. Like a flame, it grew stronger and stronger, until it became a fire threatening to engulf his whole body. His heart ached for Kathryn. He wanted to protect her for the rest of his life, to shield her from the pain of the world. Suddenly it dawned on him that this all-encompassing feeling which was threatening to consume his body and soul was love. Love, he thought with amazement. I am in love. I love Kathryn Townsend. And whatever he'd felt for any woman in the past was suddenly reduced to nothing. So this was what it was really like. He knew he would never have this feeling for any other woman as long as he lived.

He felt Kathryn stir in his arms and wanted to share his discovery with her. They'd been so close, certainly she must be experiencing the same incredible emotions. She looked up at him with her tear-stained face, but to Adam she looked more lovely than ever. "I'm sorry," she said, her voice stronger. "I shouldn't have done that. It was childish."

"Shh, it doesn't matter," Adam said, gently brushing the tears off her cheeks with his thumb.

"But it does. I want to tell you the rest of the story. I

want you to know that I'll be fine, honestly, I will." And so she told him about how she had coped: first reliving her times with Jessica, then talking to her friend as if she were still alive. "It all sounds peculiar now," Kathryn said. "But at the time it seemed the thing to do. And it helped. Finally, a few months after the funeral, I made the decision that pulled me through. I'd learned my lesson and I was determined not to get hurt again. I knew that when you love you get hurt. So I vowed that I would never love again. You remember I told you that I didn't intend to get married?"

He was falling off the side of a very high mountain. He felt his heart plummeting downward, followed a moment later by his body. His senses were so finely attuned he felt each agonizing second of his fall. Faster and faster he plunged downward to almost certain death, and there seemed no way to stop it. The terrifying sensation of falling continued. Why didn't his body crash? Why didn't he feel the blessed relief of death?

Then he realized he wasn't falling, that he was still sitting in a pile of straw staring at the woman he'd just discovered he loved. The woman who had blithely announced that she would never love. He swallowed several times, hoping he could speak. When his voice finally came out, it was strangled. "The storm seems to be letting up. We'd better go." But Kathryn didn't notice.

For a moment they stood in the doorway watching the rain, which had subsided to a drizzle. Kathryn found herself growing cold again. And vulnerable, without Adam's arms around her. A lingering clap of thunder made her start. She wanted Adam to hold her.

Adam was wondering how long before he could escape, go home, go anywhere to nurse his wounds. Even the warm light from the house was no longer inviting. He had only just realized that he loved Kathryn. Certainly the love wouldn't be hard to rout out, to destroy. Wasn't a small sapling easier to kill than a mature tree? If he never had to see her again—to see her masses of dark curls; her eyes that changed color with her moods; the sprinkling of freckles across her nose—then he could forget her and the love that had suddenly filled his heart. There were other women, more beautiful women, more suitable women. He would find one and forget Kathryn Townsend. But he didn't think he could bear to have her standing beside him for another minute, knowing she didn't love him.

As they stepped out the door the sky lit up, and for a moment the whole farmyard was as bright as noon. Then there was a roar and a tremendous shattering sound. They turned and watched as the enormous old elm tree in the middle of the pasture sank to the ground. All that remained was six feet of the main trunk, gleaming white where the force of the lightning had stripped it bare.

They both stood frozen with surprise and fear. Finally Adam said, "We'd better stay here. At least the barn has lightning rods."

Kathryn settled back into the straw again and wished Adam were with her. She felt warm and safe in his arms. But he stood in the open doorway, his tall, broad body silhouetted against the sky as the lightning danced across it. Silent, unmoving. Remote and unapproachable. His attitude puzzled Kathryn. She thought they were close. All those evenings spent talking; she felt she could tell him anything and he would understand. Now she desperately wanted him back here with her, needed him, and she was afraid to ask. His dark back looked forbidding, like granite.

Something furry touched her ankle, startling her. She looked down and found Rusty, the orange-and-white barn cat, rubbing against her. When she put out her hand, he sniffed it cautiously, then rubbed his head against it gratefully. "What's the matter, boy? Were you afraid of the storm?" Hearing her words, he jumped up onto her lap and stood there purring until she petted him. "Are you lonesome, is that it? I guess we all need somebody. No matter how hard we try to be independent." Rusty settled down in her lap and Kathryn dared to look up at Adam. His back was still toward her, but his body moved slightly. It was a good sign. "Cats pride themselves on their independence, don't they, Rusty? Yet here you are sitting in my lap purring, wanting to be with me. I think you may even love me."

Quietly she picked the cat up and put him down at her feet; he continued to purr. She got up and moved toward

Adam. Still he didn't turn around. "Oh, Adam, I was wrong, so wrong. I want to love again. And I want to love you. Please turn around and say you love me and forgive me."

Chapter Sixteen

She was flying. It was the first time she'd ever ridden in an automobile and it went so fast, not at all like the lumbering old trolley. The scenery flashed by—pastures with black-and-white cows; the white-steepled Congregationalist church; the old elementary school; the drugstore; Dr. Morrow's house. She stared up at the dark bowl of sky; the stars were whizzing by.

"Adam, how fast do you think we're going? I feel as if I were flying. It's wonderful," she said, throwing her arms open wide like wings.

Adam looked over at her and couldn't help smiling. She was so full of life and enthusiasm—and love. "I'd say about twenty-five miles an hour. But that's not much. Do you know that someday automobiles will go eighty miles an hour? Think of it!"

"I can't. I like this just as it is: flying along at twenty-five miles an hour. But I don't think I'd need an automobile to fly tonight. I'm so happy, Adam. I didn't think it was possible to be this happy. I love you so much."

"I love you, too, and I'd kiss you right now if I didn't think I'd run this automobile into a tree."

Except for the rain-slicked streets and an occasional puddle, there was no sign of the storm. The clouds had passed and a pregnant moon was lighting their way. When Kathryn and Adam finally left the safety of the barn and the warm circle of their new love, it was already dark and Adam insisted upon driving her home. That Edward might discover her secret was unimportant; she didn't want to be separated from Adam. Every minute together was precious. Like explorers embarking on a great adventure in a foreign land, they couldn't wait to find out what was around the next corner. Kathryn wanted to know everything about Adam: what he ate for breakfast and when he went to bed; who his best friend was and the name of his first-grade teacher; what his mother looked like and whether he liked brussels sprouts. She snuggled closer to him.

As they neared home her mind jolted back to the practicalities. They couldn't very well drive brazenly up to the front door. Love made her feel euphoric enough to think that she could handle Edward, but if he were to discover her coming home at night alone with a man openly, for all the neighbors to see . . .

"Turn here," she told Adam. She had a plan. The neighbor who lived behind them was a widowed lady, and Kathryn knew that she was in Chicago visiting her daughter. Next door was a retired army man who was deaf as a post and went to bed early. All she'd have to do was cut through their gardens to her own back door.

Adam protested. "What sort of gentleman would I be if I didn't escort you to your door? You can't walk all that way by yourself in the dark."

"Remember, I'm not one of your pampered society ladies. Of course I can find my way through two backyards. I'll be perfectly safe. There hasn't been an Indian on the warpath around here for years."

"Fine, but what about your brother? Don't you think we should face up to him together?"

Adam was amazed to see the change that suddenly came over Kathryn. Her posture became rigid. Her lips tightened. Even her voice sounded different, as if she were forcing each word out. "No; you don't understand the situation. I'm not sure how my brother will react to our news. All I know is that . . . well, if he gets angry, I have the awful feeling he could be dangerous. Let's keep our secret until we can figure out how to handle him." She sounded so calculating, not like the girl who had raved about flying. He wondered if he'd ever truly understand this amazing woman/child.

The warmth of Adam's kiss still lingered on her lips as Kathryn set off.

She slipped into the kitchen and breathed a sigh of relief.

For a moment she stood still, adjusting to the darkness and trying to sort out the extraordinary events of the evening. One thought prevailed: Adam loved her and she loved him. She was going to be with him forever.

For the next few weeks Kathryn felt caught up in a whirlwind. Swept backward and forward, eddied to and fro by her emotions. Joy and fear; love for Adam and bewilderment at the sudden change in her life consumed her, confused her. At times nothing seemed real. It was as if she were trapped in Miss Hamilton's first-grade world of giants and glass slippers, worlds where handsome young men in shiny automobiles could rescue girls with dogs on country roads. Worlds where only love and joy were known and only happy endings were permitted. She fell asleep thinking of Adam and woke up to marvel that he wasn't merely a dream. The details of everyday life blended into a haze of unimportance. She did her chores mechanically and spoke seldom.

Occasionally, like a weakened, drowning swimmer, she thought she should fight back, pull herself out of this haze of fantasy, back to the real world where she felt in control. Then she would think of Adam and surrender herself to emotion, losing herself to love.

The slight shadow over her happiness was that she wanted to shout out her love for the world to see, but there was no one she could trust with her secret and so she tried to pretend that life was the same as it had always been, that joy wasn't bubbling up in her chest, threatening to explode like a bottle of champagne.

Had Adam seen the man watching him, he never would have gone into the store, but his attention was caught by the jewelry winking and blinking in the afternoon sun. He could imagine each necklace on Kathryn's lovely white neck; the little pearl eardrops peeking out from under her russet hair; the diamonds circling her fingers. He knew he should wait. Wait until he'd formally asked Robert Townsend for Kathryn's hand. Wait until he told his own parents. But then he pictured Kathryn's face, pink with enthusiasm, her eyes sparkling as she opened the box. It was undoubtedly some primitive instinct—men marking women as their own—but he wanted more than anything to see his ring on Kathryn's finger; to know that she belonged to him now and forever.

The ring was a dark blue sapphire, the color of their pond, and it glistened like the wavering reflections on the water on a sunny day. When they were old the ring would be a reminder of their first summer together. He smiled at the thought of himself and Kathryn, white-haired, surrounded by a flock of adoring grandchildren who never tried of hearing the story of how Grandmother and Grandfather had met and fallen in love. Perhaps they'd even take them to see their pond, a pilgrimage to the magical place where it all began.

As Adam came out of the jewelry store he patted the small box in his pocket and wondered when he should present it to Kathryn. Social niceties and tradition be damned. They loved each other and nothing in the world would stop them from getting married.

It was then he remembered the ring—the other ring. It had all been arranged, his mother had said: when he chose the girl he wanted to marry, he would give her his maternal grandmother's ring. A vague memory of the ring lingered, but his grandmother's hands had been so shriveled and crippled that to a child they had looked like claws. He shivered as he thought of her ring on Kathryn's strong yet delicately formed hand. Not that he would ever hurt his mother by telling her. "Tradition is one of the important things that sets a family like ours apart." It was a sentiment she frequently voiced and firmly believed in.

It was when he turned toward his hotel that his eyes met those of the man across the street. The man hastily and unconvincingly turned to stare into the window of a haberdashery. For a moment Adam was puzzled, and then a wave of anger and understanding washed over him. A spy—although his father preferred to refer to them as "my eyes" and insisted that loyal informers were a business fact of life. But why should his father pay a stranger to spy on him? Certainly anyone at the mill—a manager, a clerk, a supervisor—could have been asked by his all-powerful employer to report on the doings of the son, if that was what Adam's father wanted. It didn't make sense. What if the man reported to his father about the ring? Well, Adam decided, his family had to know sooner or later.

The next day Adam saw the same man loitering in the lobby of his hotel and he decided it must be a coincidence. If his father were to hire someone to spy on him, surely he'd hire someone more skillful. Someone who wouldn't be noticed, someone who could disappear into his surroundings. Not this tall, pale, gaunt figure who looked like the specter of death.

Chapter Seventeen

Edward clutched the arm of his chair until his knuckles turned white. He cursed fate. Of course, he knew it would happen someday. It was inevitable. But there was no way he could have prepared himself. His sweat-soaked body felt icy, yet when he tried to wipe the perspiration from his brow, his hand shook so violently that he had to grasp the chair again. He was scared. His body was running out of control. His stomach churned, making him weak and nauseous. It was all her fault. He tried to recall Kathryn as a baby, red-faced, squawking and ugly, but it didn't help. Lust and jealousy continued to gnaw away at him.

He'd found out by accident. Grimacing, he wondered whether the accident was fortuitous or not. He didn't see the man more than half a dozen times a year. Ralph Donaldson was the loan officer at his bank; they'd met in the barbershop one afternoon. "Pretty fancy car your sister travels in," Donaldson had said with a laugh, pleased that he had something to say. Edward Townsend was a stiff, silent man, hard to make conversation with. Yet he was a depositor, and the bank felt it was important to be amiable to good customers.

At first Edward didn't know what the man was talking about, but he hated to appear ignorant. Besides, instinct told him it might be important. He was glad he had played along when he realized how embarrassing it would have been to be unaware that his sister was gallivanting around town with some young man.

"Happened to see the same man coming out of the Beaufort Hotel the other day. Hope he isn't a traveling salesman," Donaldson said with another hearty laugh.

The news left Edward with a sinking feeling in his stomach, a feeling that he refused to admit had anything to do with jealousy. That night as he lay in bed, righteous indignation burned in his chest. How dare Kathryn do this to him? To her family? The scandal. She would have to be punished. And the man would be sent away. No matter who he was. Seducing a virtuous young woman. Vile. Filthy. No better than a mongrel pursuing some bitch in heat. He found his heart racing furiously at the thought. Imagining . . . imagining the act between that nameless man and his sister.

With the light of day, Edward's shrewdness returned. If he wanted to bring this affair to a successful conclusion, it would be wise to learn more about the man. Some men could be bought off; others, threatened. He imagined a Kathryn heartbroken by the sudden unexplained disappearance of her lover. It was what she deserved for bringing shame on her family. For carrying on behind his back while the whole town watched and gossiped.

He began his search at the Beaufort Hotel. The room clerk, overawed by the presence of Adam Elliott in the hotel, was only too anxious to confide. "His father owns the mill. Couple of railroads, too." But his explanation was unnecessary. Edward Townsend knew perfectly well who Adam Elliott senior was.

Bile rose in Kathryn's throat. She swallowed, trying to force it down. The sight and smell of the gray, gravy-soaked meat on her plate made her stomach churn. A fitting ending to a miserable day, she thought crossly. A day spent canning peaches, sweating in the steamy heat and up to her elbows in sticky syrup. The cloying smell still lingered, and she never wanted to see food again. She poked at the sickly-green cabbage, then put her fork down with a resigned sigh.

From across the table she felt Edward's eyes on her. She raised hers, determined not to let him bully her. Not tonight. If she didn't want to eat, she didn't have to. She wasn't a child, and the sooner Edward realized it . . .

His large yellow teeth were exposed in a grin. "I see that you are unable to finish your dinner, Kathryn. Perhaps you are not hungry, or perhaps you have someone more important on your mind."

No one else paid any attention, but to Kathryn his words were as lethal as a spike driven into her heart. "He knows," a little voice said. "He knows. He knows." It grew into a fearful roar. "He knows about Adam and me."

How had he found out? Should she deny it? Should she boldly acknowledge the truth? Or should she pretend she didn't understand? Fear drove all rational thought from her head. She sat mutely staring at him, knowing that guilt was written all over her face.

Edward was her enemy. If she was to fight him, she had to understand him. Over the years she'd peeled the layers of his character as if it were an onion—each layer revealing another, even more perplexing one—and she wondered if she'd ever reach the core. Perhaps Edward was a hollow man, a man with no soul. What she did know was that he had a deadly instinct for ferreting out a person's weakness and using that knowledge to cause pain. A pain that seemed to give him pleasure.

Her love for Adam was her weakness, the chink Edward would aim for. The nature of his attack would be a surprise. Edward was unpredictable. Sometimes Kathryn saw this as a symptom of an unbalanced mind, at other times as merely a sign of his shrewdness and cunning. If his victims didn't know what to expect, they couldn't protect themselves.

Edward expected his victims to cower—that was *his* fatal chink. Like any bully, he chose only those who wouldn't fight back. And so Kathryn had made a decision to give in on the little things and not to fight back unless it was important. Then she would have the advantage of surprise. But now she had to wait until Edward made *his* move. Then she could fight back.

She forced her eyes up to his face. He was staring at her, looking smug. Waiting like a cat to pounce on a mouse. Torturing her with his silence. Giving no indication of how or when he would commence the battle. . . .

"He looked like an evil, ugly old cat ready to pounce. I could practically see his whiskers twitching in anticipation," Kathryn said as she nestled into Adam's arms. "I hate him."

"My darling," he crooned and rocked her in his arms as if she were a tearful child. An unfamiliar feeling of anger and hatred rose in his chest. He wanted to kill Edward, to punish him, to protect Kathryn.

The thought had barely formed in his mind before the words were out of his mouth. "We'll get married right away. Then you'll be my wife and he can't hurt you." Silently he cursed himself. This wasn't the way he wanted it to happen. He'd wanted this to be a romantic moment they would remember always. He wanted to put into words that swelling feeling in his chest when he was with her and the hollowness he felt when they were apart. The way his body tingled when he heard her laugh. The way his flesh burned when it touched hers.

The idea of becoming Adam's wife made Kathryn's heart soar. Happiness bubbled up inside her. Her body felt light enough to float up to the clouds. Mrs. Adam Elliott—the name rang in her head like a million joyous church bells.

Kathryn raised her head and looked at Adam. Seeing the sadness and longing in his eyes, she thought that her heart would break for love of him. Marriage would be a sacrifice. The end of his college education. And although he said his parents would welcome her with open arms, they undoubtedly had a life all mapped out for their son—a life in which she, the daughter of a boardinghouse keeper, had no part.

She forced her heart to be still and slowly shook her head. "More than anything else on this earth I want to be your wife, but don't you see that running away to get married would just be playing into Edward's hands? I'm a minor. What if he had you arrested for kidnapping? You don't know him. He enjoys causing pain." She paused, and her next words were barely a whisper. "And I honestly think he's dangerous—capable of doing almost anything to get his own way."

Melodramatic as it sounded, Adam knew she was telling the truth. He tightened his grip on Kathryn, determined to protect her. "I suppose you're right, but don't forget I'm here for you. And that I will wait for you." He pulled his arm away from her and reached into his coat pocket.

Kathryn watched in fascination and delight as he drew out a small box wrapped in silver paper and handed it to her. "This comes with all my love—forever."

Wordlessly she opened it. Inside, lying on a bed of pristine white satin, was the most beautiful ring she'd ever seen—a sparkling blue sapphire surrounded by tiny white seed pearls set on a wide gold band.

Kathryn couldn't say anything. She just stared, overcome by the emotions flooding her body. Finally Adam said, "I've never known you to be speechless. Does this mean you like it?"

The trance was broken. "Of course it does. I love it. And I love you. Do you know what it reminds me of? Our pond on a sunny day."

Adam laughed, showing the trace of dimples that Kathryn loved. "Now we'll never forget our special place. But I also have something more practical for you." He handed her a slip of paper. "My phone numbers. Someone will always know where to reach me. I hate to think of you being in the same house with that . . . that fiend. Promise me you'll call if anything happens?"

"I didn't really mean to scare you. I think I can handle Edward. I know him and I know his weaknesses. If only he'd given some sign of which way he is going to jump."

But a week passed and Edward gave no sign. It became a war of nerves. All Kathryn could do was wait. She knew she had to play the game Edward's way if she hoped to win. And the stakes were so high—her future, her happiness, her life—that she had to win.

Dozens of times every day her fingers sought out the sapphire ring, hanging on a white satin ribbon around her neck and safely hidden under her dress. Touching it gave her strength. It became a talisman. With it, with Adam's love, she *would* win. *They* would win.

Chapter Eighteen

Outside, a steady drizzle fell from the twilight sky. Inside, an oil lamp cast a small yellow circle around the kitchen table. Rosa had badgered Ezra into going to bed early. In a far corner Angelo sat dozing. Kathryn and Adam faced each other across the table. The were arguing.

"Fine, if you want to be arrested," Kathryn said. "Because if I run off to Boston with you—even for a few hours and for the most innocent of reasons—Edward will have the police on us as soon as he finds out. He'd like nothing better than to have you arrested for kidnapping."

"My father would bail us out," Adam insisted.

"Yes, and wouldn't that be a terrific way for him to meet his future daughter-in-law." She refused to admit how much she'd enjoy being squired around the city by Adam. How proud she would be to let the world see they were in love. But that would have to wait. They had years in which to parade their love.

Watching the fire of enthusiasm light up in her eyes, Adam pushed harder. "I want you to meet my parents." His father had a keen appreciation of feminine beauty, and Adam could imagine his eyes bulging with surprise and admiration when he walked into the house with Kathryn on his arm.

"Adam, I don't think it's a good idea," she said softly.

"And why not?" he said, bringing his fist down on the table. "They'll love you. How can they help it?"

"In time, maybe. But don't forget, I come from a very different world. Will they be able to overlook that?"

"Of course," Adam protested, trying to sound hearty to mask his doubt. "Must you always be so practical?"

129

"Well, one of us has to be. You can't just spring me on them. They don't even know I exist, do they?" Adam shook his head sheepishly. "If you just appear with me out of the blue, announcing we are going to marry, I wouldn't blame them for hating me. Perhaps this trip you should just give them a hint."

Adam glanced quickly over at Angelo—he was snoring—and brought Kathryn's hand up to his lips and tenderly kissed each fingertip. "Do you know, I love you," he whispered, "even when you are being so infuriatingly practical. My father, by the way, will love that characteristic."

Kathryn laughed. "I'm glad I have one thing in common with the famous Adam Elliott of the Boston Elliotts. But why do you have to go to Boston at all?"

"The mill agent has asked me to take some money from some contract or other back to my father. It will be faster than a bank transfer."

"Lots of money? How exciting. Is that why you wanted me along—to ride shotgun?"

Adam's mouth twitched with amusement. "There doesn't seem to be any end to the surprises in store for me. Ride shotgun. Where in the world did you pick up that expression?"

"Bridget, our maid, is addicted to Western serials. She reads them to my father. Occasionally I listen." She paused and added, "Someday you'll know everything about me. We'll have no secrets from each other. Isn't that the way it is with lovers?" As she said the word "lovers" she could feel her face color.

"If they are lucky," Adam said, "and I think—I *know*—we are lucky." Kathryn looked so serious and appealing that he walked around the table and planted a kiss on the tip of her nose. And then on her lips, and on her throat. Without taking his lips off her, he sat down and pulled her onto his lap. She was so soft and responsive, and one kiss only left him longing for another and another. Twilight had turned to darkness when they finally came apart. Adam's breathing was ragged. He was scared when he realized how close they had come to giving themselves to each other completely. At another time, in another place . . . But she was the girl he was going to marry, and they would wait.

In silence they drove home under the stars. Strange, Kathryn mused, how I can still feel his arms around me even when he's not touching me.

Adam gave her only a quick kiss on her forehead before saying good night. "I'll miss you," he said. "But I'll see you the day after tomorrow." She nodded and then fled, a white streak across the lawn, before vanishing into the dark of the garden. To Adam it was as if his heart went with her.

The Persian carpet with its deep pile and rich tones of orange and blue. The gleaming mahogany paneling. The gilt-framed landscapes, small enough not to be ostentatious but all bearing the signatures of well-known artists. The Georgian silver tea service, resplendent in the late afternoon sunshine. All so expensive and so elegant. Adam looked around his father's office and inwardly cursed it all. And he cursed his father for keeping him waiting as if he were some minor and tedious business functionary to be put in his place.

Adam had entered the office brimming over with enthusiasm, eager to discuss his ideas for the mill, but his father hadn't even ventured out of his inner sanctum to greet him. Instead he'd sent Abbott, his assistant. A round man with a shining forehead and an oily manner, Abbott protected his employer from the world and, Adam reflected bitterly, from his own family. Abbott had taken the envelope of money from him as if he were a messenger boy instead of the heir and announced, "Mr. Elliott will be with you when he is free."

Adam sat in the slat-back chair—antique and priceless but uncomfortable—smoldering with anger, and tried to rationally plan his conversation with his father. There were two important matters to discuss. He resolved to tackle the hardest one first. Later he would tell his father about Kathryn—after they had dispensed with business. That was the way his father would do it.

He was glad Kathryn had not come with him. Now he could break the news to his parents gently. What a relief it would be to tell someone. For weeks he'd wanted to shout his joy to the world. As soon as they met Kathryn, his family couldn't help but share his happiness.

It all went wrong once he got into his father's office.

"I've learned a great deal during my month in the mills and I have all sorts of ideas, but the most important thing I've learned is that we can't continue treating the workers the way we do. Why, our . . . our carriage horses get better treatment than the mill workers. You can't imagine the conditions they work under. It's inhuman, working twelve, sixteen hours a day."

His father appeared to be listening carefully to every word—his narrow blue eyes were riveted on his face—and it encouraged Adam. He continued, recounting the cruelties and injustices he'd witnessed in the mills. Finally, when his outraged words were exhausted, he said, "Isn't there something we can do for them?"

Adam watched as his father prepared to speak. He seemed to be choosing his words carefully. Did he dare hope it could be this easy to make his father understand?

When his father finally spoke, the emotion in his voice was barely concealed. "I am thankful that my father is not alive to hear you. He worked hard all his life to build up the family fortune—to pass it on to future generations—as have I." He shook his silvery head. "And what is our reward? Our heir, our only heir, ungrateful. A . . . a . . . social reformer who doesn't appreciate his own birthright but whines about the plight of the poor workers."

Adam drew himself up in his chair. "Father, I do appreciate my birthright. And I appreciate all the hard work you and Grandfather have done to provide for the family, but don't you think we could live with smaller profits and provide for our workers a little better?"

Adam Elliott II stopped drumming his manicured fingers on the polished mahogany desk and tried to make his voice sound sympathetic. "Do you know, ever since the day you were born I've looked forward to having a son follow in my footsteps, to keep up the family tradition. I doubled the money I inherited from my father and I expected you to double my business."

"Family tradition," Adam sputtered. "What about the families of the workers? They have nothing to pass on to their sons. Except perhaps—if they are lucky—a job in the mill so they too can work sixteen hours a day, take home a pittance and consider themselves lucky."

"Don't you think I work as hard as any of my mill workers?"

"Yes, Father, but you don't do it in one-hundred-degree heat. Standing on your feet all day. Barely able to hear yourself think because of the racket of the machines. Barely able to breathe because of the lint in the air. I wonder how you would enjoy the rats and the filth."

"These people are foreigners and as such should consider themselves damned lucky to be here and be employed, not starving in a hovel in some uncivilized place. Trouble is they come here and expect the world. Certainly they'd like an office like this." He gestured expansively to the paneled walls and antique furniture. "And lily-hearted people like you would probably give it to them."

"You're wrong. I'm not asking for Persian carpets and Chippendale chairs. All I ask is for you to think about making their lives a bit more bearable."

"All you ask . . ." he said, his face growing redder by the moment, ". . . is that they should be pampered. That's not good business sense. I raised you to be a businessman and now you sound like some sort of Salvation Army preacher or one of those crazy Bolsheviks in Russia. They're going to make trouble, take my word for it. You'll never be a success if you insist on spouting these ridiculous notions. I trust you haven't been spreading them around the mill?" He gave Adam a long, hard, demanding stare, and when Adam shook his head, he said, "And I must have your word that you won't." Reluctantly Adam nodded.

"You will go back to Lowell this afternoon, and for God's sake, try to think like an Elliott and the businessman you were bred to be, not like some half-baked social reformer or trade unionist. I will inform your mother that you were called back to the mills. She was looking forward to seeing you at dinner, but in view of the . . . um . . . circumstances, I think it best you not come to the house. For the moment I will consider your notions as a childish aberration. One that will shortly disappear as you do some much-needed maturing. You are the grandson of one of the city's most successful businessmen, and I expect you to live up to his name. In every way."

"Yes, Father," Adam said, hoping his father couldn't sense

the defiance in his heart. It wasn't until the smug-looking
Abbott had ushered him out into the hallway and closed the
door firmly behind him that Adam realized he'd never mentioned Kathryn.

As the car chugged back to Lowell, Adam fought down
the memory of his father's heartlessness, trying to replace it
with the thought of Kathryn. She would be waiting for him.
And she would understand.

"Would you be willing to marry a pauper?" Adam asked,
sitting back and drinking in the sight of Kathryn. How could
she be more beautiful now then she had been forty-eight hours
ago? Her face was dappled by sunlight filtering through the
tracery of trees. Despite the heat, she looked cool and crisp
in her white cotton dress. The past two days without her had
seemed the longest in his life.

She flashed a smile at him. Her long dark lashes fluttered
slightly. "It would depend on who he was. Perhaps if he were
handsome and intelligent and kind enough, I would." Then,
seeing the downcast expression creeping over his face, she
experienced a feeling of fear that made her tongue stumble.
"Did you tell your parents about us? And . . . and . . . did
they disown you?"

"No, I didn't even mention you."

For a moment Kathryn's fear was tempered by hurt. "But
I thought . . ."

"I was going to, but first I had to let my father know
exactly what the conditions in the mills are. He's never been
there himself, never seen how intolerable things are. I thought
if he only knew . . . that I could convince him. I was wrong,"
he said sadly. "He's not willing to give up one cent of his
dirty profits to help them. Not one cent."

"I can understand your father," Kathryn said, reaching
out to touch him.

He jerked his arm away as if her fingers had scorched him.
"How can you say that? I thought you'd understand me. If
you could only see those mill girls . . ."

"Adam, be practical. Your father is in business to make
money. He has many, many competitors. And if he were to
pay his employees more or reduce their wages, he couldn't
compete. He would be out of business."

"Yes, but he'd hardly be in the poorhouse. He would never have to work another day in his life and we'd still be rich." Adam stared at the ground angrily. "My father says I'm no businessman. Maybe I shouldn't even try. There's no law that says I have to follow in his footsteps. There are other things I can do with my life."

"Like what?" Kathryn asked. "You have an opportunity most ambitious men would give their eyeteeth for. Don't be stupid and throw it away."

It was as if he weren't listening. "Some friends of mine from Yale enlisted."

"Enlisted? But President Wilson promised to keep us out of the war."

"They went to England. You have to admit that fighting the Germans is a damn sight more important than sitting behind some desk making money I don't need. Wilson's wrong. We've all got to take the responsibility for stopping the Germans."

"So you'd risk your life just to show your father? On some silly whim?"

"Fighting for freedom is hardly a whim. Besides, some people think the United States will have to get involved eventually, and I'd join up then anyway. Why wait? I'll leave it to my father to increase the family fortunes."

"Perhaps," Kathryn said slowly, "it isn't the money. Perhaps he enjoys being successful. Perhaps he likes the power. Likes taking risks and winning."

Adam watched the light dance in her eyes as she spoke, and for the first time since he'd met Kathryn he had doubts, doubts that they might really be right for each other. It made him angry. "Damn," he said as he leapt up. "Damn, why can't you understand? Why do you have to side with my father?"

"I'm not siding with your father. It's only that I can see both sides of the argument." She forced a smile to her lips. "This is our first argument, isn't it? Except for the first time we met. You were mad at me then, too. Remember?"

Adam had a sudden picture of himself floundering in the mud puddle, Cricket standing over him licking at his face. He loved Kathryn too much to let a silly argument come between them. He had days and weeks and years to prove to her the justness of his cause. Together they would convince his father.

Like a spider he sat, waiting for the prey to walk into his trap. The image pleased Edward.

For the past three nights he had waited patiently in the darkened front hall, listening for Kathryn to come home. He knew she always entered by the kitchen door shortly before eleven. Tonight he would be waiting. His web had been painstakingly spun out. There could be no mistakes. His sister was clever. Far more clever than any woman had a right to be. But he consoled himself that he had the element of surprise in his favor. She would be flushed with the ecstasy of love—his own face grew warm at the thought—confused and weak.

Darkness would be his ally. The kitchen was dark; only a few vague shapes emerged from the blackness. A lamp and a box of matches sat on the oilcloth in front of him, ready for the right moment.

The house was quiet. From the garden came the insistent chirp of crickets. If he strained his ears he could hear soft snores from Robert's room. This time his stepfather would not ruin his plans.

A sharp sound like a twig snapping broke the silence. He tensed. The door would be opening within seconds. He waited. Nothing happened. It was only some foraging night animal, he decided.

She came silently, without warning. All of a sudden the kitchen door was flung open. She was halfway across the room before his voice rose out of the darkness.

"I trust you had a pleasant evening."

Kathryn felt her heart leap into her throat and then heard it pound with fear. Her mind was still with Adam, remembering the warmth of his body, the strength of his arms. She'd crept back into the house safely for so many nights that she'd almost forgotten to worry. Her mind scrambled for an answer.

"Yes, thank you. I did." She forced her voice not to tremble. I must be strong, she told herself.

"You were with friends?"

His social chatter unnerved Kathryn. "I was," she acknowledged.

"Someone I might know?" he asked politely.

"No. I doubt it." He would never admit to even knowing the name of his former iceman.

"Please don't sound so defensive. Isn't it only proper that I take an interest in my sister's activities? A young lady must have a protector, and your father, your dear father, is not quite up to the task."

His voice had a sneer, and Kathryn had to bite her tongue to keep from lashing out at him. That's what he wants, she told herself. To make me mad. To make me lose control. "I appreciate your concern. Now I'd like to go to bed. If you will excuse me."

He allowed her to take several steps toward the door. Suddenly she felt his hard fingers grabbing her from out of the blackness and she stifled a scream.

"You and I have much to talk about." His voice had taken on a sharp and bitter edge.

"I know that you have a beau." As he said the word, Kathryn could feel his thumb begin to massage her wrist in small, nervous circles. Repulsed, she tried to pull away; his grasp tightened. "But I am unhappy, Kathryn, that you didn't tell me and your mother about him. I had to hear about it from a virtual stranger. It was embarrassing."

There was a pause. Kathryn was waiting, waiting for Edward to explode, hurl names at her, threaten to throw her out of the house, but nothing happened. All she heard was a strange scratching noise in the darkness, then saw a glaring, revealing flash of light as the oil lamp on the table blazed forth.

Edward stared at her. His hooded eyes seemed to scrutinize her face as if searching for the truth. She forced herself to meet the dark cavities of his eyes. Finally he dropped his stare. "I wanted to tell you that there is no need to sneak in and out of the house. You no longer have to hide your young man. In fact, you may feel free to bring him to the house to meet your family."

As relief flooded her body, Kathryn felt her knees go weak and she could only stammer a "Thank you" before disappearing up the stairs. Emotionally drained, she drifted off to sleep thinking of Adam. Now nothing would stand in their way. It wasn't until the next morning that she began wondering what was behind her brother's easy acceptance of Adam. Edward never did anything without a selfish motive.

Lily received the news in pinched-lip fashion. In the back of her mind was the hope that the man—whoever he was—would take Kathryn away, far away. It would be more peaceful in the house with Kathryn gone; she was always doing something to annoy Edward. The idea of losing her daughter shouldn't have pleased her, she knew, and she hated herself because it did.

Bridget threw open her arms and crushed Kathryn to her cushiony bosom. She brought the news to Robert immediately. It was an answer to their prayers. She only prayed that Edward would not ruin it. As he ruined everything else he touched.

Chapter Nineteen

Adam stubbed his toe into the dirt, raising a cloud of dust. "I don't understand," he said angrily. Why can't we get married right away? You said your father is happy about our plans and now we know that Edward won't stand in the way, so what is there to stop us?"

Kathryn was perched on a low branch of a wild cherry tree, her feet swinging in the air. She looked down at him. The idea was tempting: leave Lowell now and start fresh, free from Edward, her mother and all the bad memories. "No, we can't, you know that. You have to finish college first, that's what we decided."

"But that's a whole year away."

His eyes looked at her so pleadingly that she longed to give in and say she would marry him right away. But no, they could wait. She would have a whole lifetime to share with Adam. At the back of her head sprang up the frightening memory of Adam's prediction of war. But President Wilson had promised. No matter what Adam thought, it wasn't their fight. "Why are you in such a hurry? Are you afraid you won't still love me a year from now? That some new girl will have stolen your heart?" She laughed, sure of his answer.

"I could never not love you. You know that. It would be like stopping breathing—I'd die. And if it's possible, I think I'll love you even after I die."

"By then we'll have been married at least fifty years and you may have grown tired of me."

"Never. I'll still be discovering all the facets that make up the wonderful Kathryn Townsend. And I'll love them all equally." He reached up and gently lifted her down from the branch. Their bodies pressed together, and Kathryn knew she could never hold him close enough. She longed for their bodies to merge, to become one. Every fiber of her being yearned for him. Their lips came together, gently at first, then with all the hard, demanding force of their young bodies.

As Adam felt her soft breasts against his chest, he imagined what they would look like. He wanted to caress them, to touch them with his lips. To make love to every inch of her body.

His head was swimming with the heat of the moment. All he could think of was the soft, pliant and beautiful young body he held in his arms. He slipped his hand from her neck where it held her silky loose curls and around to the front of her dress. Slowly he began to undo the tiny buttons. As the vee dipped lower, revealing the pale roundness of her swelling breasts, he felt his excitement building.

A rush of fresh air cooled Kathryn's burning body for a moment; then she felt Adam's hand plunging like a flaming brand under the lace of her camisole. When he touched her nipple she wanted to cry out with relief. Then with desire for more. But his lips were clasped firmly over hers. She found her body moving instinctively as his hand gently kneaded her breasts. The feeling—an excitement, a yearning, a sense that she was poised on the brink of something unknown. It was like nothing she'd ever experienced before. And she knew she would never be able to get enough of him.

When his hand finally withdrew, she started to protest. "Shh," he said, touching her lips with her fingertips. "Wait, it will get even better." Gently he laid her on the ground and began unfastening the rest of her buttons. Entranced by the awakening feelings in her body, she didn't have the will or the desire to resist.

She was the most beautiful thing he'd ever seen as she lay there under the trees on a fragrant bed of pine needles, her dark hair spilling over the ground, wearing a lacy white camisole and managing to look both sensuous and innocent. "My beautiful temptress," he whispered. Although his body was burning with desire for her, he forced himself to undress her slowly and gently. It was like opening a gift. And when her layers of clothes were gone and she lay before him, he realized that he was the first man who'd ever seen her like this and he knew that he was receiving the most precious gift a woman could give to a man.

For several moments all he could do was stare at her soft alabaster body in awe. She was perfect. Petite. Exquisitely rounded. He had never known a woman could be so beautiful. Then slowly he began to remove his own clothes.

She watched him in fascination and with no embarrassment. Every detail of his strong white body was etched on her mind. When he was finally naked, she smiled up at him and opened her arms to receive him.

He fell into them and clutched at her as if he were a drowning swimmer and she his life raft. Then he could no longer control himself. Her frenzied body moved with his. Why, he wondered, were women said not to enjoy the physical side of marriage? Was this another wonderful way in which his Kathryn was different?

Their bodies were still locked together. She could feel his heart pounding against her chest. "I want to stay like this forever," Kathryn murmured.

Adam raised his head and looked down at her. They smiled sheepishly at each other, as if they'd just shared a miraculous new discovery, experienced a feeling no one else had ever felt. A feeling that could never be put into words.

Never before had Kathryn been so conscious of her body. Every inch of her flesh was alive and aware. It had cried out in desire, been filled, and now was suddenly blissfully content. As if she'd sunk, mindlessly, into a warm bath. The intensity of her physical delight was surprising and frightening. Nothing mattered; it was as if the world had come to a shuddering halt around her. She was aware only of her body and Adam's entwined gloriously together.

In silence they drove home. Wrapped in warm memories of lovemaking. Overwhelmed by new sensations and emotions. When Adam stopped in front of her house, he could say no more than "I love you." The thoughts and feelings revolving around in his head were too new, too confusing and too complex to be put into words, and he wondered if words could ever express his extraordinary love for this wonderful girl fate had joined him to.

"I love you, too," Kathryn whispered, making no move

to leave. She still needed to feel Adam's body next to hers—
warm and hard and reassuring. "I never thought it possible
to feel so close to another person." She looked up at the
house, dark and unwelcoming. "I hope we can always be
that close."

"We will be, my love, I promise you."

Reluctantly Kathryn opened the door, afraid if she lingered
Edward might come out. She barely remembered walking up
the steps and into the house. She wanted to be alone under
the sloping ceiling of her attic room, to relive this evening
and reflect on her new experiences and new emotions. Suddenly her body was a woman's body, capable of entirely new
sensations and acts. A body that had given itself willingly
and miraculously to the man she loved.

She had just pulled on her white cotton nightdress when
the door was flung open. She stared up in surprise. There
stood Edward, looking rigid in his black suit and starched
white collar.

"And when," he asked pleasantly as if there were nothing
unusual about barging into her bedroom, "are we going to
meet this young man of yours? Or do you have some reason
to hide him? Perhaps he has a club foot or crossed eyes. But
surely even you could do better than that."

"It may surprise you that he is quite handsome."

"And quite rich, too, I understand."

Kathryn felt a flash of anger. "How do you know that?"

"I was merely doing my duty. Finding out as much as I
can about the man who wants to marry my sister."

"Who says he intends to marry me?" she demanded.

"A gentleman does not go running around the countryside
with an unchaperoned young lady, keeping her out until all
hours of the night, unless his intentions are honorable."

"Adam is an honorable man," she said simply.

A toothy smile of triumph spread across Edward's face.
"Then he has asked you to marry him?"

Kathryn cast her eyes downward. "No," she whispered.
She was afraid to let Edward know the truth, afraid that he
still had some trick up his sleeve.

"Such a pity to let all that money get away. Adam Elliott
senior owns two railroads, three banks, the cotton mill, and
has controlling interest in a copper mine and an iron foundry,

you know. Conservative estimates are that he is worth over twelve million dollars. All in all, a perfect father-in-law for you."

Suddenly it all clicked into place. She knew why he hadn't objected to the match. "How dare you? Having Adam investigated like . . . like he's some property you want to invest in. Now get out of my bedroom. I won't listen to any more of this. You're disgusting. All you ever think of is money. Money, money, money. Get out. I want to go to sleep."

But Edward didn't move. He merely stood there staring. For a second Kathryn had the awful feeling his eyes were penetrating the thin cotton of her nightgown. "I am going to bed," she announced. She waited. He continued staring and reluctantly she climbed under the sheltering covers.

Instead of leaving, Edward came over and sat on the bed. She shuddered: he looked like a giant black insect waiting to pounce on her. "My dear sister," he said, reaching out to pat her leg under the comforter. When she quickly drew her leg away, he pretended not to notice. "Whatever happened to the girl who said she was going to make a million dollars? Now is your chance. Don't pretend money isn't important to you. That you wouldn't like to have all the pretty dresses and jewels your heart desired. Eat at the finest restaurants. Stay at the finest hotels. Have servants at your beck and call." He waited for her denial. She lay in stony silence. "Well, if you are so unnatural and do not desire that sort of life, think about your parents. How can you deny them the benefits of the Elliott fortune? Your mother has led a hard life; she deserves a little luxury. And your father . . . perhaps the Elliott money could provide the doctors to make him well."

Hatred burned in her eyes. "You are vile and cruel and selfish. You want the money yourself. Why don't you admit it? You know my father is never going to get well. And you really don't care what our mother wants. You just think that the Elliott connections and whatever of their money you could get your grasping hands on—as if I'd give you a penny— would help you build up your little financial empire, don't you? That's what's at stake."

Edward's reply was infuriatingly cool and unemotional. "I don't know why you hate me. But I am a compassionate man. I know that women in love sometimes act . . . strangely. We will discuss this matter later. When you are behaving more rationally.''

"I will not marry Adam Elliott for your sake—ever.''

"My dear, why are you so angry? Perhaps because the young gentleman has not yet asked you to marry him? Is that it? But there are ways, you know, ways women have employed successfully for centuries to trap men into marriage. And certainly worth the risk when the prize is so . . . so valuable.''

Kathryn listened in horror, knowing what he was going to suggest.

"I trust that Mr. Elliott is a healthy young man with . . . um . . . normal . . . um . . . desires.'' Kathryn felt his eyes focusing on her breasts. "Desires that a skillful woman could manipulate to her advantage. Perhaps he will then feel guilty enough to marry you. Or perhaps you will have to tell him that you are expecting his child. Certainly the Elliotts of Boston would not welcome the scandal of a bastard. And if your lover is not inclined to do the right thing by us, I am sure I could have a little talk with Mr. Elliott senior on your behalf.''

Kathryn's anger was defused. She no longer had the strength to protest. What had seemed like such a natural act of love hours before suddenly seemed dirty, defiled by her brother. Guilt, not ecstasy, flushed her face. She had done what no honorable woman would do: she had given her body to a man, a man who was not her lawful husband.

"I see that I have given you something to think about. Just remember the duty you owe your family, the family who has given you everything.'' Patting her leg again, he rose stiffly and walked out the door, shutting it quietly behind him.

Kathryn hid her head in her pillow, trying to stifle her sobs. "I hate him. I hate him,'' she moaned into her pillow. But she didn't know whether she meant Edward or Adam.

Chapter Twenty

Conflicting emotions waged their war within Kathryn. All through the next day the questions continued to pound at her brain.

One minute she didn't know how she would ever face Adam, the next she couldn't wait to lie in his arms again.

When at last she was on the road to the farm, her feet flew. Seeing her, Adam dashed down through the pasture. Kathryn flung herself into his arms, begging, "Hold me, please just hold me."

"My love, what's the matter?" He looked into her eyes, trying to understand. "You aren't upset about what happened yesterday, are you?"

Kathryn studied him, his tousled hair, the concern shining in his soft blue eyes, and wondered how she could have hated him even momentarily; how she could have allowed Edward to drive her to that.

"No, nothing's wrong, now that I'm with you," she said, nestling into his arms.

The summer, once an endless stream of glorious days to be shared, was ending. Now as they lay on the fragrant pine needles making love under the towering trees, the stars appeared in the sky earlier and earlier every evening.

"I'll love you for as many years as there are stars in the sky," Adam declared one night as they peered up at the sky though the dark lacework of pine boughs. She lay with her head resting on his shoulder, her hair streaming across his bare chest. His hand molded the smooth curve of her hip.

145

"And exactly how many stars are there?" Kathryn asked, nestling closer.

"Billions," Adam whispered into her ear. "Billions we can't even see. Promise that when you look up at the stars you'll think of me and remember how much I love you." Kathryn nodded silently. Summer was over and soon Adam would be gone.

When the day arrived, he came to the house to say good-bye. It was early and Kathryn rushed out as soon as she heard the car. As she climbed in beside him, something made her look back toward the house. There in an upstairs window stood Edward. His black suit and long, sallow face made him look like a figure of doom. She shuddered.

"What's the matter?" Adam asked.

"Edward is up there watching us." She hadn't told Adam about Edward's awful plan. How could she admit that her own brother was so heartless and scheming?

"Why don't you come with me right now? We could drive away from all this and then you'd be safe forever. I can't bear to think of you here with him."

"No," Kathryn said, praying that her willpower would survive the next few minutes. "We've discussed all this. We're going to wait until the time is right."

"My head knows you're right, but my heart . . . my heart feels like it's been chopped in two already. Kathryn, I'm going to miss you. You will write, won't you?"

"I promise. Every day."

"I'll write to you first. Tonight, as soon as I get home."

He put his arms around her and pulled her to him and dared Edward to protest. After all, he had a better claim on Kathryn than her stepbrother. He was going to be her husband.

"Ouch," she said, poking at his chest. "What do you have in your pocket?"

He opened his coat and pulled out a stiff, bulging envelope. "Money. We could take it and run away together. Five thousand dollars. We'd never have to worry about what our families thought if we were in Patagonia, would we?"

Kathryn laughed. "Just where is Patagonia, and why are you carrying all that money?"

"I think it's in South America and I'm taking the money

to Boston. Father has to trust me more than Wells, Fargo; I'm an Elliott.''

"And you'll be an Elliott who is late to work," Kathryn said. If he stayed a minute longer, she would break into tears.

"I love you," he said, his eyes hovering over her face, memorizing every detail for the long months ahead. "I'll talk to my parents. I'm sure they'll invite you to come for a visit at Christmas.''

"Maybe," she said, slowly getting out of the car. "I do love you. Don't forget me, will you?"

Adam forced a laugh. "As if I could forget my wife-to-be. Next time we're together you'll be wearing my ring on your finger, where it belongs. We'll tackle Edward together—he can't be as awful as you say—and everything will work out, you'll see.''

Seeing Kathryn's weak nod, he knew she was on the verge of tears. Gently he touched her fingers that lingered on the edge of the door. "Remember, as many years as there are stars in the sky.''

Kathryn nodded again and turned to the house so she wouldn't cry. Neither of them could bear to say the word. Good-bye. As he drove away, Adam looked back at the house. He saw Edward standing at the window and felt a shiver of cold run through his body.

Walking back to the house, her feet dragging heavily along the pavement, Kathryn felt Edward's eyes following her. And suddenly all the emotions seething within her—the love, the longing, the sadness—coalesced into one single feeling. Outrage. Outrage at her brother for his degrading suggestions. For feasting his dirty eyes on their private farewell.

By the time she reached his bedroom door her anger was threatening to boil over. It was Edward who stood between her and Adam. It was Edward who spoiled her every chance at happiness.

Without bothering to knock, she flung open the door. It hit the wall with a satisfying thud, and mentally she dared Edward to protest. But he was silent, standing black and rigid at the window. Finally he turned slowly and they looked at each other for a moment.

"I hope you enjoyed spying on me," she spat out.

"You can hardly accuse me of spying," he said coolly.

"Since when can a man not look out of his own bedroom window? And on such a beautiful morning, too. Although I hope that none of our neighbors shared my impulse. They might not take such a sympathetic view of your carrying on with a young man in public." He paused and said eagerly, "He removed something from his pocket. I trust it was a ring?"

Kathryn laughed. "You aren't a very good spy. It was an envelope with some money he was taking home to his father. And I was not carrying on. We were saying good-bye, that's all. Adam is driving back to Boston this afternoon. Perhaps you were here to wave good-bye to all that lovely Elliott money."

"You mean he's gone? Left you?" he asked, as if he couldn't believe his ears.

Kathryn could feel her anger dissipating. She had the power to hurt him the way he had hurt her. "What did you expect? Did you really think the heir to the Elliott fortune would want to marry the daughter of someone who runs a boarding-house? No, I was merely a . . . a summer diversion. He's returning to Boston to marry from his own class." Kathryn winced, afraid of jinxing their love with her lie. And they are lies, she told herself sternly. Adam loves me. It doesn't matter to him who I am.

Edward's face collapsed in disappointment. Even his head seemed to droop, as if the starched white collar could no longer hold it upright. His pale skin grew chalkier. His lips were bloodless and grim. The two lines that etched his cheeks seemed to bite even deeper into his flesh.

Kathryn watched the changes with satisfaction. "You're more interested in the money than in my happiness, aren't you? You don't care what I feel; you're just upset because you see all that lovely Elliott money slipping out of your grasp—permanently. Never to get your greedy fingers on all those stocks and bonds, all those railroads and banks and mines. Poof." She made a quick, exploding gesture with her hands. "Gone with your ridiculous little dreams of a financial empire. You'll never succeed, you know."

"Stop it." Edward's teeth were bared and he looked like a cornered animal. But Kathryn was giddy with the feeling of triumph and she couldn't stop. The wheel of destiny had been set in motion. She would have her revenge.

"Do you know why you'll never have the empire you dream of? Because you're not clever enough. You think too small. One little firetrap boardinghouse in the wrong part of town. One old hotel where even traveling salesmen won't stay. That's what you dream of. Petty little dreams for a petty little man. When I—"

Edward interrupted, ignoring her taunting words. "You threw away the opportunity of a lifetime, you realize that, don't you? What's left for you now? Marrying some little clerk from the mills who can barely support you and a brood of sniveling brats. He'll give you a new one each year. Of course, with a little luck some of them will die. Or perhaps you'll be an old maid. If you are nice I may let you live here with us. But you will have to be very nice. And make yourself useful."

His words bounced off Kathryn. Her future was secure. She would be Mrs. Adam Elliott III. "If you think—"

Her words were halted by the power of his eyes. They seemed to burn into her body, branding her with his hatred. "You, you let him escape. My little sister may win all the prizes at school and think she's so damned clever, but she can't catch a man. Even after I told her exactly how to do it."

He paused, and Kathryn watched as a pink sliver of tongue emerged to lick his lips. "What happened? Wouldn't you let him touch your precious lily-white virgin body? Or"—he glared at her triumphantly—"wasn't he man enough to want it? Was he a spoiled little rich boy, not red-blooded and man enough to take a woman?" He watched gleefully as a flush came over Kathryn's face. "Perhaps he did take you and then walked off, is that it? Perhaps you didn't let him enjoy it enough for him to want more."

No, Kathryn thought, I refuse to let him do it again. I won't let him degrade my love for Adam. She knew the chink in Edward's armor and she took deadly aim.

"What do you know about love? You killed the only woman you ever loved. Or said you did. You killed Jessica."

"That's . . ." Edward sputtered.

"A lie? No. I heard the doctor. He said you killed your

wife and child.'' Looking at the devastated expression on
Edward's face—the wounded animal that could no longer put
up a fight—she said, ''You can't even admit it to yourself,
can you? But you killed her, and I won't let you ruin my life
the way you ruined hers. I owe it to Jessica. I won't let you
take another victim. You ruined my mother's life, then my
father's, then Jessica's. But you won't ruin me, because I will
get away from you and your wickedness and greed and cruelty. I'll live a normal life, with a normal family, not one
tainted by your perversity.

''You love to have people in your power, don't you? To
make them do your bidding. It may work with my mother,
because for some strange, sick reason she loves you. And my
father, he's too weak and ill to protest. But I'm strong and
healthy and I hate you with every bone of my body and I'll
never give in to you. I've got a whole life ahead of me, and
you are not going to spoil it.''

How dare she speak to him this way? He couldn't take it
anymore. How dared this child defy him? He reached out his
hand to slap her across the face, but she was too quick and
caught his wrist. Her grip was surprisingly strong.

''If you ever touch me in any way, I'll ruin you. Remember
that. How would you, with all your pride and pretensions,
like to be known around town as the man who killed his
wife?''

With a quick turn she stalked out the door. Her heart was
pounding and she couldn't wait to get to her own room. The
strength which had been holding her up suddenly deserted
her, and she felt weak at the knees and at the same time dizzy
with her triumph. Edward would not try to interfere in her
life again. Of that she was certain.

The black mark stood out against the white baseboard. Edward took aim carefully and kicked the spot again, wishing
it were Kathryn's body.

Kathryn. His dear half sister. She was the cause of his
problems. Ever since she had come into the world looking
like a little monkey, she'd been a thorn in his flesh. Demanding Lily's attention. Embarrassing him with her childish nonsense. And bringing that woman into his life. That woman
to whom he'd given his name, his love, his child. She had

betrayed him: she had died. And now Kathryn said it was his fault. It was not his fault. It was God's will that women died in childbirth, part of His plan. Of course he hadn't killed Jessica.

The thought gave him momentary comfort, until he remembered. Kathryn had failed him again. He had been so close, so close to the railroads, the banks, the mines. It would have been right for Kathryn's father-in-law to admit him into those sacred portals. Perhaps a seat on the board of directors of one of his companies. And, of course, tips on the right investments to make. Then no more thin-walled boardinghouses reeking of cabbage or rickety old hotels where only the lowliest of traveling salesmen were willing to stay. He would have had his own railroads and banks and mines. Nothing would have stopped him. If only Kathryn hadn't failed. He gritted his teeth as he felt the anger building up in his chest. The pressure was so great it made him feel dizzy. Gone. All gone.

His fingers moved convulsively as if grasping for the money. It was then that the tiny ray of an idea penetrated into his frenzied mind. Gradually his hands stilled. His eyes lost their angry fire. And he started to plan.

Chapter Twenty-one

Years later Kathryn would remember that evening's dinner with perfect clarity: pot roast with gravy, boiled potatoes and brussels sprouts, the glutinous rice pudding. The boarders talked about the war. "I intend to vote for Wilson again. He won't let our boys get killed fighting someone else's battles." "I hear the Brits lost twelve thousand men last week trying to take ten yards of ground." "What happened to the good old-fashioned war? Cavalry charges and all that?" "Wonder if my boy will have to go. He's got a bad leg, you know, so maybe . . ."

Edward didn't join in the conversation; he seemed distracted. To Kathryn it was as if she were watching it all from a great distance, as if she were not a part of the scene. Is this the way God feels, sitting way up there, looking down at the world? she wondered. No, God would care. She didn't.

If her eyes registered the little things, her heart and mind were with Adam. Had he told his parents yet? Was he thinking of her right at this moment? She wouldn't receive his letter until Friday. Perhaps if she were lucky it would come Thursday, but she told herself not to count on it until Friday. She began counting the days.

Friday's mail brought a letter from Edward's bank, a postcard from Mr. Anderson's mother and a bill from the gas company. Kathryn examined the mail three times to make sure. Adam had promised to write as soon as he got home . . . perhaps he had been too busy. His family had social plans, she told herself on Saturday, when all that arrived was another manila envelope from Edward's bank.

The next week, in her desperation, she began playing

games. Staring out of her bedroom window, she decided that if a leaf fell off the yellowing maple tree in the front yard within the next ten seconds, there would definitely be a letter from Adam the next day. Sometimes the leaves fell. Sometimes they didn't.

She pushed her fears back into the recesses of her mind and tried to find excuses for his silence. Perhaps his father was ill. Perhaps his letters were lost in the mail. Perhaps . . . perhaps . . . perhaps. She tried until she ran out of perhapses.

Unable to face the possibility of his betrayal, she retreated—as she had after Jessica's death—into her memories. Reliving every detail: his teasing words, the jaunty way he walked, his crackling laugh. Every moment, no matter how small, was hoarded like a precious jewel, taken out, enjoyed and then hidden again, lest anyone spoil its luster.

It was as if her life had stopped when Adam left and could begin again only when she could hold his letter in her hands. When she returned to school she obediently did her lessons, but her heart was with Adam. She felt no connection with the school, with her family, with her world. The daily newspaper went unread. There were no more country walks.

"Do you ever hear from that rich beau of yours? Or did he find one of his own kind to marry?" It was the only time Edward mentioned Adam, but his words sent a sharp pain knifing through Kathryn's mind. Adam had promised to love her for as many years as there were stars in the sky and she believed him; she would always believe him, but, forcing a smile to her lips, she answered, "I don't know. Or care."

It became a ritual—looking for mail every morning—even when she knew there would never be a letter. She continued to wear his ring around her neck, but she never touched it anymore; it was too tangible a proof that Adam had been real. That he had once loved her and no longer did.

Christmas was different that year, and it was Edward who made it so. Kathryn couldn't help thinking of Ebenezer Scrooge in Charles Dickens' story *A Christmas Carol*. Strange as it seemed, Edward actually acted jolly and appeared to be enjoying the holiday. When Kathryn discovered that he had given her a complete set of Jane Austen's novels, all bound in calfskin and inscribed "From your loving

brother, Edward,'' she was speechless. Then she thought
about it and realized his joy was not at all seasonal but the
result of having recently purchased a small piece of property
which he had turned around and sold at a good profit.

That wasn't the end of Edward's surprises. On New Year's
Day he announced that she would begin the new school term
at Miss Fitch's Seminary for Young Ladies in Boston. From
the look in Lily's eyes, Kathryn knew that even her mother
had not been told. The old Kathryn would have protested,
insisting that she should be consulted about her future. But
the old Kathryn was gone and the new Kathryn didn't care.
Where her body was physically no longer seemed important.
It was only peculiar that Edward, who had never considered
women worth educating, would suddenly send her to an expensive school.

Peculiar until she realized why: he was sending her to Boston to have another chance at catching the brass ring—the
Elliott fortune. It made her want to yell and scream and tell
him that she refused to be manipulated. But at least it would
give her the chance to see Adam again. To find out why he
hadn't written. There had to be an explanation. But what if
she did see him—with another woman? Her heart ached with
jealousy. Adam was no longer a dream lover.

She wouldn't fight Edward's scheme. She'd go and she'd
find Adam. For her own peace of mind, she had to know.

The uncertainty was the worst. If she knew he was gone
for good, the hurting might stop—sometime.

Chapter Twenty-two

At Miss Fitch's Seminary for Young Ladies, she discovered how many levels there were in Boston society. Most of her fellow students belonged to upper-middle-class families that did not move in the same exalted circles as the Elliotts. Except for Amanda Wainwright. Kathryn heard her name mentioned constantly by awestruck students the first day. Why she, an heiress, was condescending to attend Miss Fitch's was a mystery to everyone except Miss Fitch. Perhaps she had done something awful, they speculated—awful enough that her family was disowning her by sending her to Miss Fitch's. So caught up were they in gossiping about Amanda Wainwright that scarcely anyone noticed the other new student who was much less interesting. Kathryn had never felt so alone in her life. Here no one knew that she was a whiz in algebra and won every essay contest. Here no one knew that her recitation of "When Lilacs Last in the Dooryard Bloom'd" could reduce the female half of the class to tears. Here no one knew her at all—or seemed to care.

Not wanting to seem unfriendly, Kathryn lingered on the fringes of the group stationed at the parlor window to catch a glimpse of the newest student. Finally an old-fashioned black carriage drew up, and a small woman in a plain dark suit and an unflattering hat got out. "Oh, look, she's brought her maid. Is that allowed?" one student demanded.

To their surprise, no one else emerged from the carriage. "Maybe she's changed her mind; she's not coming after all and she's sent her maid to tell Miss Fitch." They didn't linger by the window long enough to see a trunk and two small bags being unloaded, so their eyes bulged with astonishment when the small figure entered the dining room that evening and was introduced as Miss Wainwright. A collective sigh of disappointment hovered in the air. "She looks like a little brown mouse. How can she ever hope to find a husband looking like that?"

Kathryn's heart immediately reached out to her, but if Amanda Wainwright sensed their disappointment, she didn't seem to care. Girls soon gravitated to their own groups in the parlor, leaving the newcomers on their own, sitting awkwardly on the hard horsehair sofas at opposite ends of the overly decorated room. For a moment they stared at each other and then rose simultaneously.

"Since we seem to be outcasts, shall we be friends?" Amanda asked with a shy laugh. It was a laugh which made her entire face light up until she didn't look plain at all. A bond was immediately formed, and soon Kathryn found herself describing the scene in the parlor when Amanda had arrived.

"So that's why they seem so standoffish," Amanda said with a hearty laugh. "Did they really expect me to arrive decked out in furs and diamonds and trailing gold pieces?"

"Are you really as important as the girls say?"

"My parents are, I suppose. But I think it's all rather silly."

Every common like and dislike she and Amanda discovered drew them closer. Mathematics was much more exciting than needlework, and neither of them could understand why knowing how to warble sentimental songs to the tinny accompaniment of the parlor piano was a social asset. Instead, when Kathryn and Amanda were alone, their room would ring out with the risqué music-hall songs Amanda had learned from an Irish maid who worked for her family.

For the first time in years Kathryn enjoyed a real best friend. But she never told Amanda about Adam. Her new friend spoke so scornfully of men and what she called "the marriage market" that Kathryn knew she'd never understand. Nor did she talk of Edward. And for the first time in her life she felt free of the gaunt, godlike figure.

Amanda's family moved in the same circles as the Elliotts. A few words and Kathryn would know all about Adam. But what if she found out he was engaged or even married to someone else by now? Could she face the truth? No, not yet, she decided. Let time have a chance to heal the emotional wounds.

Chapter Twenty-three

But the wounds were slow to heal, and Kathryn kept postponing the question. Until it was too late.

"Promise to write at least once a week with all the gossip?" Amanda demanded as they said good-bye at the end of the school year. Amanda's parents had decided she wouldn't be returning to Miss Fitch's.

"How can they expect me to stay home and live my life for tea parties and ball gowns?" she fumed. "I feel like a prize pig being fattened up and groomed for the marriage market. But don't worry. I'll find a way to get back to Miss Fitch's before Thanksgiving."

But in November she wrote, "They're exiling me to a boarding school in Switzerland. Can you imagine anything worse than being cooped up with a lot of snobbish girls in the middle of the mountains? But Mama says I will, unlike at Miss Fitch's, be meeting the right sort of people there."

"Right sort of people." Kathryn chuckled. What would Mrs. Wainwright think if she could see me now? Up to my elbows in hot water, washing greasy dishes from the boarders' lunch. Her mother was ill with influenza and someone had to help Bridget. So Edward, rather than hire more help, had demanded she come home. Edward may pay the fees, but he'll never make one of Miss Fitch's ladies out of me.

A wave of loneliness swept over her. She missed the fun-loving, irreverent Amanda. She had made no new friends at Miss Fitch's.

The dishes done, she escaped to her room and began a long, gossip-filled letter to Amanda. Edward was out, so she knew she'd be safe stealing a stamp from his desk. Tomorrow she'd make an excuse to get out and mail the letter.

There were no stamps in the top drawer, so she began hunting through the other drawers.

The bottom drawer was locked, and Kathryn decided to snoop because she knew it would make Edward angry. Childish, she told herself, but she retrieved the key she'd seen in the top drawer and was pleased when it fitted the bottom one. The drawer slid open to reveal a large envelope labeled with her own name. Opening it, she found a dozen envelopes addressed in her hand to her father—the letters she had written him from Miss Fitch's. Why would Edward have locked them in his desk? Underneath was a small black ledger. Each page was written in Edward's precise accountant's hand. Recorded were the fees for Kathryn's schooling, her clothes, her books, her allowance: a scrupulous accounting of what Kathryn cost to keep. Seeing her life reduced to a series of black figures trapped between blue lines gave her an uncomfortable feeling, as if Edward were peering over her shoulder every moment. It also made her curious about what else the drawer might hold.

Beneath the ledger was a black metal box. The key sat temptingly in the lock, begging to be turned. When she lifted the lid she saw something she never expected to see again— Adam's diamond stickpin, blinking up at her as it had by the pond the day he'd wagered she would change her mind about marriage. A sinking feeling consumed her body; she fought against it. This was a coincidence. It had to be a coincidence. After all, what would Adam's stickpin be doing here in Edward's desk? She remembered that Adam had been wearing it the morning they said good-bye. For a moment she just stood there, staring down at the diamond, engulfed in painful memories.

Hesitantly she picked it up. Beneath it lay a white linen handkerchief. She touched it; it was wrapped around something hard and curved. Slowly she unfolded the handkerchief. A gold pocket watch. She recognized it immediately. Something was terribly wrong.

The brown envelope was there with only a few bills left. Adam's words echoed in her head: *Money. We could take it and run away together. Five thousand dollars. We'd never have to worry about what our families thought if we were in Patagonia, would we?* Oh, Adam, if only I hadn't been so practical. If only we'd run away. We'd be together now and none of this would have happened. In her heart she knew what had happened. Adam hadn't deserted her; Adam was dead.

The yellowed newsclipping lay on the bottom of the strongbox. "Boston and Lowell police are puzzled by the disappearance of Adam Elliott III, only son of railroad magnate and mill owner Adam Elliott. The heir to the Elliott fortune has not been seen since September 12, when he was allegedly returning to Boston from Lowell, where he had been employed in his father's cotton mill. According to Adam Elliott, his son was carrying a large sum of cash. 'I would not be surprised if he was set upon, robbed and murdered by someone who knew about the money,' " his father commented.

Anger surged through Kathryn. How could he sound so cold-blooded and rational about the death of his son? He was talking about Adam, her Adam, murdered. Murdered by— Kathryn had to force her brain to form the words—her brother. She was the one who had told Edward about the money. It was as if *she* had killed Adam. She clutched the edge of the desk to keep from fainting. Her body was weak and her head was buzzing. Nothing felt real.

"My brother killed Adam," she whispered to herself. If she said the words out loud, perhaps she could believe them. "My brother is a murderer." Was it greed that had driven him to kill? Would she ever know?

She must report Edward to the police. But would they believe her? A murder accusation against a respectable churchgoer, a successful local businessman? But she had the proof! If she could only reach Adam's father, he would listen to her. But the man didn't even know that she existed. What if Edward went to him first with his own explanation and lies?

She felt so desperately alone. There was no one to turn to. Even her mother wouldn't believe her. And if she confided in her father or Bridget, she'd put them in danger.

First she must get out of this house. She tried to force her mind from the horror. She must think clearly and plan. Trying to control her own ragged breathing, she listened. Bridget was in the kitchen; she could hear the rattle of pans. Her mother was resting.

Without considering the danger, she picked up the stickpin and watch and dropped them into her pocket. After a moment's hesitation she took the envelope and tiptoed to the door. She peered out. The hall was empty.

Scared that Edward would appear at any moment, she raced up the stairs. With the bedroom door closed behind her, she was safe. Now she could think.

It was so quiet that the old house seemed to be breathing. Kathryn thought of her ancestors who had fled this house in fear for their lives. And of Abigail Townsend, who had vowed to return. The memory of her courageous ancestor gave Kathryn strength. Abigail had managed to survive and prosper. And I will, too, Kathryn vowed. I will.

She would return to school as if nothing had happened, she decided. Once she was there, safe from Edward, she could make the decision about her future. Hoping that no one would notice she was leaving with one more valise than she had arrived with, she began choosing among her belongings—what to take and what to leave—as if she might never return. She packed all her treasures: Jessica's brooch, the gold piece Mr. Jamison had given her so long ago, her poetry books that held memories of Adam.

She had finished stuffing an extra pair of shoes into the bag when she heard the front door open. She recognized Edward's steps and quickly reminded herself that she had to pretend nothing was wrong.

As she listened to Edward's footstep clicking down the long, uncarpeted hallway, a sudden sinking fear hit her—had she left the desk drawer open? She couldn't remember. Her mind refused to answer the question. Mercifully it also balked at imagining what Edward would do if he found out.

There was a loud shriek from downstairs. Kathryn's heart stopped until she realized it was only Bridget letting fling at Edward with her Irish temper. Kathryn silently blessed her. Edward was distracted, giving her a chance to sneak downstairs and check the drawer. She'd reached the bottom step when she looked up and saw Edward storming out of the kitchen, a scowl on his face.

It was an unconscious reaction; she couldn't stop herself.

Before she knew it, Kathryn was staring through the open
door of the study. Her expression of fear gave her away. Edward immediately followed her gaze. There, in plain view,
was the drawer, open for all the world to see. Proving her
guilt and his. Without saying a word, he grabbed her arm
and propelled her up the stairs and into her bedroom. He
closed the door behind him and stood staring at her. It was
a long while before he spoke.

"So you were spying on me. Tell me, what dirty little
secrets did you hope to discover?"

"A stamp, actually. I was looking for a stamp," Kathryn
said, trying to sound innocent.

"Hidden in the bottom drawer?" he asked. "Surely you
can come up with a more imaginative tale than that, little
sister. You are generally so clever."

She looked at him long and hard. When she spoke, her
words were cool and controlled. "I found out that you killed
Adam. I found the evidence."

"And can you prove that that particular stickpin was his,
that that gold watch, of all the gold watches in the world,
belonged to him? There are no inscriptions, you know. I made
sure of that." Edward's voice was smug and there was a
sinister look of satisfaction on his face. "A young girl who
has been jilted by her lover can hardly be expected to behave
rationally, can she?"

It was the word "jilted" that broke Kathryn's control. "I
was not jilted. Adam didn't leave me. He never would. He
loved me. You killed him."

"Hush," Edward said, placing a white, bony finger up to
her lips. The feel of it made her flesh crawl and she pulled
away. "Do you want everyone to hear you?"

"Yes, I want everyone to hear. I intend to tell everyone. I
want to see you punished for your crime. I want to watch
you hang."

"And who do you think will believe this ridiculous accusation? The police? I'm sure they are wary of stories told by
hysterical women who have been sadly thwarted in love. Your
mother? You know that our mother would never take your
word against mine. Edward Townsend a murderer? Never.
They'd all laugh at you."

Kathryn stared at him, focusing her hatred on him, wishing

she had the power to kill him right now as he stood gloatingly before her. "The money. What about the money?"

"That would be an even more difficult task. Unless you have the serial numbers on the bills your young man was carrying." He looked hard at Kathryn, daring her to produce the proof. "Now you can see what an impossible situation you are in. May I suggest we just forget all about your theory?"

"Theory? Forget? How can you expect me to forget that you murdered the man I love! I'll never forget that. And I'll never stop hating you!"

Edward walked over to the wing chair and sat down, stretching his long legs out in front of him. "You deserve to know the truth, I suppose. I did not murder your beau. I admit that when I watched him leave that morning, I wanted to. Or perhaps I wanted to murder you—I honestly don't know. All that money, so close and then gone." His eyes took on a glazed expression. "You've no idea how important a connection with a family like the Elliotts could have been. For all of us. You failed to capture the prize. So I decided to try."

Kathryn marveled that her brother could make his confession with less emotion than if he were reading a grocery list. She stared at him, trying to detect some decent human feeling.

"I was waiting for him at the gate of the mill when the whistle blew. He appeared surprised to see me. I made the suggestion that we go somewhere to talk. In private."

"But why did he go? I'd warned him that you were dangerous."

"I'm sure you did, Kathryn. I'm sure you did. But when I told him I had a message from you, he seemed pathetically eager to accompany me. We drove out to a somewhat isolated area overlooking the river. You will understand that if there was to be a scene, I didn't want the embarrassment of witnesses. As it turned out, it was a lucky decision on my part. I told him that since he had ruined your reputation, it was his duty to marry you. Everyone in town had seen you riding around in his automobile at all hours of the night. You would never be able to find a suitable husband now. He owed it to us, and if he didn't see where his responsibility lay, I thought his father might. That scared him and he looked rather green around the gills, so I pressed my advantage. That's when I made my mistake. It was unfortunate, but how was I to know?

"I told him that people would think you a whore. The idea enraged him. For a man who had jilted you, he seemed strangely concerned with your reputation. He came after me. I was afraid he was going to strangle me. I put my arms out to defend myself; he was obviously off balance on the uneven ground and fell backward. I thought he was merely unconscious, lying with his head against the fender. But he didn't move for the longest time."

Edward was silent for a moment as if he were remembering the scene. When he spoke again, his voice had lost its sureness. "When I looked more closely he was dead. What could I do? What could you expect me to do, call the police and confess? That would have been stupid. I would have been proved innocent, but not before the scandal ruined our family. So I unlocked the brake and pushed the car with Mr. Elliott over the embankment into the river."

Kathryn's body was numb with shock, but she managed to make her lips work. "But . . . but you had to steal the money and his diamond and watch first, didn't you? That was your mistake."

He pretended not to hear her. "The river is deep there; they'll never find his body, and if they do, it will merely look like an inexperienced motorist drove off into the river. I doubt there is much left of the body now anyway."

"Stop it. Stop it! How can you calmly sit here telling me this? How can you?"

"I wanted you to know what happened. It isn't as if I murdered him. I merely coped with an accident, a tragic accident. Some would say a fortuitous accident." His cockiness had returned.

"It's always money with you, isn't it? A man died. My lover died, and all you can think of is the money you're getting out of it." Gradually the realization dawned on Kathryn. "So that's why you suddenly sent me to that fancy school, isn't it? I was being educated on blood money. Adam's blood. Tell me, did you do it to salve your conscience? Did making sure that I benefited from my lover's death make you feel better? Or did you just want to get me out of the house, afraid I'd find out? And that new boardinghouse you purchased . . .''

"It helped. Yes, the money helped," Edward said, his voice taking on the pleased, slightly smug tone it always did when he spoke of profits. He looked at Kathryn and then said sharply, "But don't expect you can prove anything."

Kathryn longed to yell and scream, rant and rave and threaten, but she couldn't. The horror of the last half hour had finally drained her of all emotion. She couldn't even raise her voice. But she could tell Edward the truth; he would find that painful enough.

"You may be right. The legal system may never catch you, but you'll have to live with a man's death on your conscience—if you even have one. Worse, you'll have to live with the knowledge that Adam's death was unnecessary, that you could have had everything if you'd only waited." She paused. "Waited until Adam and I got married. You see, we planned to."

Edward's features froze. He opened his mouth to speak. "But . . ." No further words came out.

"But I told you he'd left me. Yes, I lied. I lied to protect myself and Adam from you and your schemes. And because, foolishly, I didn't want to give you the satisfaction of knowing your fondest dream would come true. You were just too greedy. And you will pay for your mistake."

Edward's coolness quickly turned to outrage. "Don't threaten me. It's all your fault." His voice rose to an almost hysterical pitch. "If you hadn't lied to me, you'd be Mrs. Adam Elliott today and I'd be . . . I'd be just where I deserve to be."

He was right. If she hadn't gotten so angry at Edward and lied to him out of spite . . . Her brain kept pounding away at the thought: I killed Adam. I killed Adam. She threw herself down on the bed, burying her face in the pillow.

When Edward left, she didn't even notice until the click of the key in the lock snapped her back to reality. She couldn't dwell on her own inadvertent role in Adam's death. If she did she'd go crazy. And she had to have all her wits about her if she was to make sure that Edward paid for his crime.

All night long her mind careened back and forth. She thought and thought until she ached with fatigue and frustra-

tion and fear. If she could get out of her room and reach a
telephone . . . If only she had a weapon . . . She surveyed
the room—books, hairbrushes, coat hangers—nothing useful.
There was no doubt in her mind: she would not hesitate to
kill Edward and avenge Adam.

The front door slammed. A low murmur of voices rose
from the dining room. In the kitchen Bridget sneezed. Ordinary morning sounds. Familiar sounds she'd known all her
life, yet they made her feel alone and helpless. Her mother,
her father, Bridget, the boarders, they were all out there. She
could cry out for help whenever she wanted. They would hear
her, but she knew they wouldn't come. Edward would have
told one of his lies and no one would come. She could only
wait.

As soon as the boarders had all left for work, there was a
knock at her door and the key turned in the lock. "I trust
you slept well?" Edward said. Kathryn stood silently with
her back to him. "I'm glad to see that you have calmed down.
I was worried about you last night." His voice was soft,
almost sympathetic.

Kathryn forced herself to turn and face him. She was
shocked to see her mother standing at his side, wrapped in a
faded terry-cloth bathrobe and looking ill. Her face was pale,
her eyes red-rimmed. "Don't bother pretending to be nice,
Edward," Kathryn said.

"Try to behave yourself. I have come to tell you about the
arrangements I have made. It was difficult, but I've managed
to settle everything to our satisfaction. Yesterday I realized
just how disturbed you are. Obviously when your young man
left you . . . well, something happened. We need to find
someone who can help you through it. You'll understand that
I can't have you here, upsetting your mother and your poor
father, not to mention the boarders. We do depend on them
for our livelihood, you know. I worry about you, so I've gone
to a great deal of trouble and expense and arranged for a stay
at Brookville."

Kathryn gasped as a vision of Brookville rose before her.
An ugly blocklike building of red brick. Bars on every window. Engulfed by dark, straggly trees that looked like skel-
etons. Bound by a high wall of brick and barbed wire. Every
once in a while someone would escape, and there would be

rumors and fears. . . . "But Brookville is a mental asylum. I'm not . . . you don't really believe . . . ?" She turned to her mother, her eyes pleading. "Mother, stop him. You don't think I'm crazy, do you?" But Lily bit her lip and said nothing. "Please help me. Can't you see he's the one? Edward's the crazy one. He murdered Adam."

For a long moment Lily stared at her. Her thin white lips quivered. Her dark eyes brimmed with tears. "I'm sorry. But . . . but Edward is right. You must be sick. To . . . to make such accusations against your own brother." A lone tear escaped and ran down her cheek. She blinked back the rest and rushed out the door.

As the echoes of her footsteps died away, Edward said, "She's right. What choice do I have after the scene you created yesterday? Saying I had murdered your lover. Those are not the words of a sane person."

"You did kill Adam. You confessed everything to me."

"Now why would I do something like that? Kathryn, your mind, I'm afraid it's sadly disturbed."

"I can prove you killed him. The diamond, the watch, the money."

"Yes, you did find valuables in my desk. Surely no crime. Your mind is so distraught you just imagined they belonged to someone else."

"I'll tell everyone. You'll pay," Kathryn said. "I promise you that."

"And I promise that if you behave, you may come home from Brookville. Eventually." His tone suddenly became low and threatening. "But if I hear that you have made any accusations against me, you will never come home. Is that understood? And then you will be the one who pays. You'll die there. I won't even let them send your body home for burial."

Kathryn felt the strength drain out of her. She no longer had the courage to protest. Her mother had turned her back. Edward had won. She nodded her head in agreement.

"That's a good girl. A doctor will be arriving tomorrow morning to examine you and escort you to your new home, so perhaps you should occupy yourself packing, provided you feel up to it. I will bring up your meals. I think it is better if

you don't speak to anyone else. They might be upset by your
. . . state. I will tell them that you said good-bye.''

Kathryn lay down on the bed and drew herself into a protective ball. She was wearing the same clothes she had on
yesterday—it seemed like years ago—but it didn't matter.
Nothing mattered. Adam was dead.

When Edward brought her dinner, she ate it without thinking, without tasting. This might be the last dinner she ever
ate in her home. The last night she would sleep in her bed.
The thought angered her, and gradually she felt her numbness
give way to anger. Edward could not treat her this way. She
would fight. But how? He was bigger and stronger. What she
could do was escape. She stared at the small window. Her
room was on the third floor. No convenient tree stood outside, the way it always did in novels. If she could tie her
sheets and blankets together, would they stretch far enough?
What if the knots slipped? Then I'll fall, she decided; anything's better than not trying.

The hours dragged. She stared out of the window, trying
to see how frighteningly far below the ground lay. It was
dark. Clouds covered the quarter moon; not one single star
pierced the blackness. Occasionally Kathryn started as a gust
of autumn wind made the window chatter. The familiar sights
and sounds all concealed unimagined terrors.

At last the human noises died down, and all she could hear
was the wind and the creaking of the old house as it settled.
Moving quietly, she stripped the sheets and blankets off her
bed. She tied two sheets together and then pulled as hard as
she could. The knot slipped, and she could imagine her body
falling into the blackness. She kept tying the knot over and
over again until her clumsy fingers grew surer and it finally
held. The blankets were more difficult. She tied and tested
until her hands ached, and still she wasn't sure they would
hold. She was ready to cry with frustration when there was
a shuffling noise outside her door. She held her breath, praying that it wasn't Edward. There was no time to conceal her
escape preparations. She stared at the doorknob, waiting for
it to turn. All she could hear was the house creaking. Perhaps
her imagination had been playing cruel tricks.

She was tiptoeing toward the door when her foot touched
something. The silence was shattered by a metallic clink.

When she looked down she had to bite her lip to keep from screaming in joy. A key. The key. The key to her bedroom door and freedom.

She grabbed up the key and held it to her chest. Who had slipped it under the door? Bridget? Her mother? Surely her father didn't have the strength. She wanted with all her heart to believe it was her mother. That she did care and was willing to disobey Edward to protect her daughter. Kathryn felt a warm glow in her heart. It had to be her mother. She longed to see Lily and her father one more time. But there was no time, no time to make up for all the lost years.

Hastily pulling on her coat and grabbing her valises, she took a deep breath and cracked open the door. Dark shadows filled the hallway. She watched. Nothing moved, and after a minute she plunged into the darkness.

Afterward she couldn't remember breathing at all as she crept down the back stairs and into the front hall. Taking a last look at her small white shape in the blackened mirror, she bade silent farewell to the snarling lions. They no longer frightened her. Quietly she pushed open the front door.

The cold night air gave her new life. Appealing as it was to stand on the steps for a moment to savor her freedom, she didn't dare. She knew the way through the back garden by heart, and when she emerged on the next street she almost expected to see Adam sitting in his automobile, waiting to gather her into his arms. No, she told herself, he's gone. I'm on my own. From now on I have only myself to depend on. She had a sudden and vivid memory of her mother sitting in the garden and saying those words to her many years ago when she was a child and still believed in fairy tales.

As she hurried down the street, not knowing where she was going, just knowing she had to escape from Edward, something made her look up. The clouds had parted to reveal a mass of stars. *Remember, I'll love you for as many years as there are stars in the sky.* Whatever happened to her, wherever she went, something of Adam would always be with her.

Book Two

Chapter One

New York City
November 11, 1918

She thought the noise would drive her crazy. Church bells clanging, clashing. Automobile horns honking, braying. Streetcars clanging metallically, insistently. Above it all rose the high-pitched cries of the newsboys. Rachel Aarons tried to shut out the din. All of New York City had gone mad. Mad with joy.

"Huns surrender. We win the war." The newsboy's voice was hoarse from trying to make itself heard above the crowds of laughing, crying, singing people who thronged the streets.

The doorbell rang three times before Rachel heard it. Then she fretted because Elsie, the downstairs maid, didn't come running. She should ignore it; no doubt it was someone who had taken the end of the war as an excuse to drink and was now running wild up and down the streets. Or perhaps it was Mr. Grimes; he was always forgetting his key. Serve him right if he were locked out for the afternoon.

Curiosity got the better of her and she heaved her stout, top-heavy body out of the massive velvet chair and crossed to the bay window, which overlooked the street. If she drew the heavy drapes aside cautiously enough, she could see who was standing at the door without the person seeing her.

To her surprise, it wasn't a wild-eyed drunk or Mr. Grimes. It was a young girl. Too young, Mrs. Aarons decided, to be on her own. The thought annoyed her. What could the parents be thinking of, allowing her out by herself on a day like this? Her shrewd eye traveled over the girl's clothing. She

was wearing a tailored blue suit, obviously of good quality—
originally. Now it was creased and disheveled, as if it had
been worn for too many days under too trying conditions.
The girl's hair was piled up high on her head, but several
reddish-brown strands were escaping. Rachel's eyes traveled
downward. Two bulging valises rested at the girl's feet.

The sight brought memories flooding back. Rachel couldn't
help seeing herself, many years ago alone in a strange city,
carting about all her belongings. Not the slightest idea of
where to go. Would she have been better off if . . . ? No, it
was easier, Rachel Aarons had learned, if one accepted what
happened—whatever it was—as happening for the best.

Slowly she let the curtain drop. Emotions shouldn't get in
the way of business decisions. True, she did have a vacant
room to let. . . . "Well, Jacob, what shall we do? The girl
looks respectable enough. But too young." She clicked her
tongue. "Too young to have a job, and, I ask you, how does
she expect to pay the rent? After all, I can't afford to take in
charity cases. Anyone off the streets like this . . ."

She turned around. The air in the overfurnished, ornately
decorated Victorian parlor was heavy with silence. There was
a sinking feeling in her heart. Her Jacob had been dead for
seven years. Still, there was hardly a day when she didn't
find herself talking to him.

Jacob, bless him, had left her well provided for; he had
known his responsibilities. She'd taken in the lodgers to fill
the empty, echoing rooms, but they hadn't filled the emptiness in her heart. Why had he had to leave her? Influenza. If
he'd worn his coat the way she'd told him to . . . Stubborn.
A wonderful, kind man, but stubborn.

"So, Jacob, shall we take her in?"

When Rachel opened the door, she realized there was one
thing she hadn't seen when she peeked out at the girl—the
look of determination in her eyes. Despite her crumpled appearance, flyaway hair and pale complexion, there was a look
of strength in her eyes and in the line of her chin.

Yet the girl's voice was surprisingly weak when she asked,
"Do you have a room to rent?"

Rachel paused. This girl could be a runaway—a wife or
daughter—it was hard to tell. Sooner or later she would be
tracked down by father or husband or even the police and

forced to go home. That was probably why the poor girl looked so exhausted: she'd been turned down all over the city by respectable landladies afraid of just such trouble.

But Rachel had the feeling that if this girl were escaping something or someone, she'd be clever enough not to allow herself to be found. "Yes, I do have a room. How it would suit you, I don't know," she added brusquely.

"May I please see it?" Kathryn asked. It was the first time in two days anyone had even admitted to having a room available. Not that she would allow this stout woman with the piercing eyes to know, but she was ready to take almost anything.

Rachel looked her over carefully again and Kathryn could feel her eyes assessing every wrinkle in her travel-worn suit. Finally she gave a nod, said, "Follow me" and led the way up the red-carpeted mahogany staircase. The room was her second best and Rachel usually got six dollars a week for it; she suspected she could get seven if she dyed the faded drapes and replaced the worn bedspread, but she looked at Kathryn's eager face and said as she threw open the door, "Five dollars a week," then added, "Paid promptly Saturday afternoon, or you will find yourself sleeping in the park Saturday night."

Desperate as Kathryn was to find a place to spend the night, she looked the room over carefully, perching on the bed to test the mattress, drawing aside the heavy drapery and opening the window, unlocking the old-fashioned wardrobe and running her fingers over the chipped marble-topped dresser.

Rachel's eyes followed her. Young as this girl looked, she knew what she wanted. "If you intend to take the room, I'll need five dollars. Now."

With a last reluctant look Kathryn opened her purse. She pulled out a bill and handed it over wordlessly. The roll of bills was small and might have to last for a very long time.

"You'll want a receipt?" Rachel asked, tucking the money into the pocket of her billowing black serge skirt.

"A receipt, yes, thank you, Mrs. . . ."

"Mrs. Aarons, Rachel Aarons. And you are?"

"I'm Kathryn . . ." She paused and Rachel's suspicions were confirmed. She *was* a runaway. "Townsend." She said it defiantly, as if daring anyone to recognize the name. It would be too complicated, she decided, to live with a new name. And here in New York she would be safe. No one would recognize Kathryn Townsend. Not in a city of millions. She'd never seen so many people in all her life; it was overwhelming. The streets were crowded all day long. Where was everyone going, and why were they in such a hurry? By comparison, Boston seemed a quiet little town.

"Is there anything else you need?" Rachel asked.

Kathryn shook her head. She just wanted to be alone.

Obligingly, Mrs. Aarons left, carefully shutting the door behind her. Kathryn looked around, hoping that this room, so unlike her little attic bedroom at home, would be a refuge. Home, no, I mustn't think like that anymore, she told herself. This is home now. But it was hard to forget the cozy little room with the rose wallpaper.

Her new home was packed with dark, heavy, curlicued Victorian furniture, and every flat surface was littered with delicate china figurines. She wondered about Mrs. Aarons. There were still traces of an aristocratic beauty in her fleshy face. Who was the Mr. Aarons who had been captured by it? The trace of an accent in the woman's voice was also puzzling. Not that it was any of her business. She didn't have time to become involved.

So much furniture in such a tiny room made it hard to move around. The bed was huge; it would be like sleeping in an old-fashioned sleigh. The once lovely crocheted spread was yellowing with age. Heavy crimson drapes rose from the worn flowered carpet to the high white curved ceiling. The walls were so faded they gave no clue as to their original color. But, Kathryn consoled herself, it was sparkling clean. And for the next week at least it would be a roof over her head—home.

The night she ran away she would have been only too glad to find a refuge like this.

Chapter Two

At first she'd run mindlessly, driven by one desire: escape. If she wanted to reach Boston safely she'd have to find the railroad station. It was too late for the trolleys and she wasn't sure she could find it on her own. She had to avoid the main streets in case Edward discovered she was missing and tried to track her down. Fighting desperately to keep her sense of direction, she ran through the maze of back streets, slowing down only when her breath failed and the pain in her side became intolerable. At night everything looked different; the familiar suddenly became threatening. Although she'd passed the small graveyard hundreds of times before, now she saw Edward's face in every monument rising palely out of the blackness.

At last she came to the river; then she had no choice. She had to cross the bridge. There was no traffic. Deserted and flooded by moonlight, the bridge with its skeletonlike struts looked vast and endless. She'd never felt so scared and so defenseless in her life. If only there'd been a passing carriage or an automobile to break the silence. But nothing moved in the midnight stillness except the wind.

The streets, like the bridge, were eerily deserted. It was only when she came closer to the center of the city that she encountered a few late-night wanderers. As soon as she saw them she ducked into a doorway or flattened herself in the shadows. Perhaps they were merely respectable citizens, but they might ask questions. Once she was surprised when a drunk lurched out of a tenement doorway a few feet ahead of her. She froze. But he was too drunk to notice her. From inside the building she could hear raucous laughter and she prayed no one would follow him. When at last he collapsed and lay still in the gutter, she forced herself to move on.

It became the promise of shelter and warmth rather than safety that drove her onward. With the wind howling like a beast, rampaging through the streets, sweeping up debris in its path, it was growing colder by the minute. Her coat felt as thin as tissue paper against the wind, which forced its icy way down her collar and up her sleeves. She longed to warm her hands in her pockets for a moment but was afraid to let go of her valises, afraid she'd never be able to force her cold, cramped fingers to pick them up again.

Once or twice she was afraid she was lost. Finally she saw the familiar outline of the railroad station and forced her chilled body to run the last block. Her feet felt so cold as they hit the hard pavement she feared her frozen toes might snap off. But she couldn't stop. She had to get warm.

When she reached the corner it became obvious: the station was dark and locked tight. She dropped her bags and pounded her numb fists against the door, but no one came. The glass chattered under her hands, but the only other sound was the mocking howl of the wind. The lighted face of the City Hall clock said two. There would be no train until the morning. She had no choice but to wait. Even if she knew where to find a hotel, no respectable one would admit a single young lady in the middle of the night.

Perhaps there was an outbuilding that would provide shelter for a few hours, anything that would protect her from the bone-chilling wind. Her eyes strained in the darkness. Slowly she walked around the building, trying every door and window. Locked tight as a drum. Not even a woodshed or a coal bin.

But there was a car. It was an old, open model parked behind the station. She tried the door; it was unlocked and she climbed in.

Groping in the back seat, she found a blanket and gratefully wrapped herself in it. It wouldn't warm her up, but at least she was out of the biting wind and she couldn't get any colder. For warmth she thrust her hands deep into the pockets of her skirt, and as her fingers began to thaw, they felt the familiar smooth, round shape of Adam's watch. She fell asleep with it in her hand. . . .

How long had she been asleep? She had no idea—was it minutes or hours?—but she felt strangely rested. The sky was still dark. If the owner hadn't come for his car by now, she'd probably be safe until morning. She had to think. Concentrate on the future. Was there an early morning train? She thought she remembered one that passed through on the way to Boston around six o'clock. If she were lucky, Edward didn't even realize she was gone. If she could reach Boston safely, he'd never find her there.

The first thing she must do was find Adam's father and tell him the truth. He'd protect her against his son's murderer. But what would he think when a strange woman barged into his home announcing, "My brother killed your son"? If she showed him the watch and stickpin, he might think she'd been involved in his son's disappearance. *She* could go to jail.

Edward was clever, very clever. What if he reached Mr. Elliott first, with his lies—"My sister, I'm afraid, is sadly disturbed. I'm only sorry that she has distressed you." She'd be sent home and shipped off to Brookville. And she'd never get out.

Perhaps she should begin a new life, take a new name, find a job and cut all ties with her old life. But what could she do? All her essay contests and spelling bees had hardly prepared her to do anything useful. How did a young woman earn a living in a city like Lowell?

The answer came to her like a bolt of lightning—the mills. Thousands of women without any training earned their living there. Many of them could barely speak English. Certainly they'd have to hire her.

She'd change her name and blend into the throngs of faceless, interchangeable mill women. Edward would never find her. But she couldn't forget the tales Adam had told her of conditions in the mills—the heat, the humidity, the rats, the long backbreaking hours, the miserly wages. And she remembered the great thumping noise, the tired faces of the girls and the angry voices of the men as they streamed out of the mill. But then she thought of Brookville, the dark, barred windows, the terrifying rumors. At least someday she could save enough money and work her way out of the mills.

For the first time in two days she slept soundly. She had a

plan for the future. But she also dreamed. It was hot and she could barely breathe. Her body ached and beneath her the floor shook. She felt as if she were falling. As she reached out to steady herself, something grabbed her arm. She saw wheels and gears and belts and menacing metal teeth. They were devouring her arm. She felt herself being dragged closer and closer into the giant machine, but she couldn't scream. She tried again and again, but her throat was clogged. Something grabbed at her hair; she felt the pain as it was twisted tighter and tighter. And all of a sudden she knew. It was happening just as Edward had warned: she was being scalped by the machine.

When she awoke she knew it had all been a dream. Until she felt something dripping down her forehead. She was afraid to put her hand up, afraid to see that it was blood dripping from a raw scalp. Her heart was pounding so loudly she could barely think. Finally she forced her eyes open.

What she saw made her want to scream for joy. It was snowing; fat snowflakes were falling all over her face, all over her body, all over the car. She exhaled and felt the knot in her throat melt. Slowly she reached up to her head; it was there, all her hair. But she knew she'd never go into the mills.

Her body was painfully stiff as she unwrapped herself and sat up. In the east she could see a faint light and she decided she'd better get up before someone discovered her camped out in the automobile.

The stationmaster arrived at five forty-five, and if he was surprised to see a young lady standing before the locked door looking anxious and disheveled, he was too sleepy to ask questions. After buying a one-way ticket for Boston, Kathryn hurried into the ladies' room, where she washed her face and brushed her hair. She waited there until the train arrived and then scurried out onto the platform and into the nearest car. Rummaging in her bags, she pulled out a book. Although she dreaded seeing the gaunt black-and-white figure staring up at the train with hatred in his eyes, she had to know if Edward was looking for her. As the train pulled out, she peered over the top of the book at the rapidly disappearing station. The platform was empty. Even the automobile was gone.

The train rocked like a cradle, lulling Kathryn into an exhausted sleep, and the heat pouring into the car warmed her chilled flesh.

Had anyone else been in the car, he would have thought what a beauty she was, sleeping soundly with all the innocence of a child.

The loud cries of porters and the clatter of opening doors at the Boston station woke her. For a second she didn't know where she was; then she quickly gathered her coat and her bags and climbed down to the platform. Breakfast, she thought as she felt the tight knot in her stomach. The station restaurant was small and steamy, but after studying the fly-specked menu hanging in the window, she went in and asked the swarthy waiter for a cup of coffee and two slices of toast.

Her stomach full, she began planning. She hardly knew Boston except for Miss Fitch's and a few cultural landmarks that were considered proper and necessary to the education of young ladies. The idea of going back to Miss Fitch's was comforting. She had her own room and belongings, and if no friends, at least she would be surrounded by familiar faces. No, that would be playing right into Edward's hands. Miss Fitch would never believe her story. She'd be more willing to believe Edward's tale of insanity. Well-bred young women were known to suffer from nerves.

Amanda—the one person who would believe her story and help her would be Amanda. What was her address? Kathryn closed her eyes and tried to envision the blue envelope and the return address written in rounded script in the corner. She was jolted by a vision of her letter to Amanda—the letter that had unleashed this nightmare—lying addressed, but unstamped, on her dresser. Where Edward would find it. It would be the first place he'd look for her. She could not ask Amanda to lie to Edward. No, she had to go someplace the bloodhound would never think of looking for her or someplace he'd never find her.

"Could you please tell me when the next train leaves?" she asked the uniformed man at the ticket window.

"For where, miss?"

"Anywhere."

In his twenty-five years with the railroad nobody had ever asked him that question, and he scratched his graying hair for a few moments before answering. Finally he said, "New

York. Stopping at New London and New Haven. Leaving at seven thirty-seven from track thirteen."

"Yes, I suppose that's far enough away," she murmured to herself. "Fine, I'd like a ticket," she said, pushing a ten-dollar bill through the grille.

He looked at the bill suspiciously. "Round trip?"

"No," Kathryn said firmly, "one way only."

Gratefully she sank down into a corner seat in the train and pretended to stare out the window, hoping no one would sit down next to her. Not that she would have noticed if anyone had. By the time the train pulled out of the station, she was sleeping soundly.

She awoke refreshed and relieved. She had escaped to begin a new life, a life of her own so far away Edward would never find her. Far from the memories, the pain and the fear. Never again would anyone have the power to threaten her. Nor would she ever have to answer to anyone. It was her own life lying gloriously ahead of her, and she would live it exactly the way she chose. When the train pulled into Grand Central Station, she stepped off confidently. In the back of her head a little warning voice whispered, but if she concentrated hard enough on the future, she could not even hear it.

Her first task was to find a place to stay. At a newsstand she counted out her pennies for an evening paper and a map of the city. Neither gave a clue as to where a respectable woman could find lodgings. So she wandered and looked. Studying the people, houses, apartment buildings, stores, restaurants, hotels, museums, art galleries, streetcars and elevated trains. When it began to get dark, she found a small hotel that looked respectable but not too expensive.

The next morning she set off enthusiastically to find a place to stay. She rang the doorbell of every respectable-looking house that displayed a Room to Rent sign in the window. No one even admitted to having a room to show her. By the end of the day her feet were blistered and her shoulders and hands ached from carrying two heavy bags. Her spirits were sagging and she begrudged spending money for another night at a hotel. This time she chose one that looked shabbier, hoping it would be cheaper. It was, but when she glanced around the lobby, she realized that every chair was taken by a young woman dressed in evening clothes. Every time a man walked by the door, the women's heavily made-up eyes rose expectantly.

After she reached her room, she carefully locked the door behind her, then cast her eye around the small, shabby room for something to barricade the door with. The scuffed wardrobe and dresser were too heavy for her to move. The cane chair with the hole in the seat was too light to do any good. Finally she chose the washstand. It wouldn't keep anyone out, but if someone tried to get in, the sound of the china pitcher and bowl falling would warn her.

The grumbling sounds of her stomach told Kathryn that she was hungry, but she wouldn't have walked through that lobby and faced those staring women if she'd been starving. If she went to sleep she'd forget her hunger. Then she looked at the bed. It sagged in the middle and the bedspread was stained and filthy. Pulling it off, she discovered that the sheets were no cleaner and gave off the same sour odor. A greasy headprint lay in the middle of the pillowcase. Carefully she folded her own clean petticoat around the pillow and then lay down fully clothed, praying there weren't any bedbugs. Sleep refused to come. As soon as she drifted off she was awakened by the sound of squeaking bedsprings or by shrieks of laughter and slamming doors from the hallway. When the footsteps stopped at her door, she couldn't breathe, waiting to hear the pitcher shatter. The minute it was light, she packed her bag and made her way through the deserted lobby. The little voice in the back of her head was growing louder.

Seated at a grimy table in a cheap restaurant, she realized that she was no longer hungry. The thought of spending another night like the last made her stomach tighten. She had to find a room. Today.

As soon as she got to her feet everything started spinning. She forced herself to walk, concentrating on her feet rythmically hitting the pavement so she wouldn't collapse. In the moments when her mind was clearer, she was afraid the fog that surrounded her mind and body would grow thicker and cut her off completely. And then it would be only too easy to walk in front of an automobile or a streetcar.

When the bells began, she knew she had slipped into an unconscious dream world. The air seemed to vibrate with their clashing and clanging. It was as if her heart were pound-

ing along with them. The noise of shouting, screaming and
crying surrounded her, pressing against her body. Like ants
from an anthill, people poured out of every building onto the
streets, forming an overpowering wave and forcing her along
with them. She wanted to shout at them to stop. To be quiet.
But her mouth felt dry and soft as cotton, unable to move.

She couldn't remember falling, but suddenly she was lying
on something hard and strange faces were staring down at
her. She blinked, trying to force them into focus. They looked
familiar. Men. Like Edward. She closed her eyes again.
Something touched her arm, but her body lacked the strength
to pull away.

"Stop staring at her," a voice commanded. "She'll be all
right. It's just the excitement."

She felt a face next to hers. "Are you all right, miss?"

"I don't know," she said. She felt arms picking her up
and carrying her. At last she felt herself being set down and
heard a voice say, "Lean back against the steps. I'll get you
something to drink."

Gratefully she leaned back, trying to block out the noise.
She lost track of the time. All at once something was pressing
against her lips and a voice said, "Here, drink this."

She drank and felt the fog clearing. Gradually her body
lost its heaviness. She opened her eyes. He was staring at
her. "They're hazel, I see. And pretty."

Kathryn felt herself blush at the absurdity of the situation. She'd never fainted before. And to do it here in the
middle of the street and allow some strange man to take care
of her . . .

He saw her embarrassment. "It's all right. It's not every
day a war ends."

"War . . . what do you mean?" For the first time she saw
he was wearing a uniform."

"You mean you didn't know? All the bells and horns and
people—what do you think they're for? The Germans surren-
dered this morning. It's all over." His round face beamed
with joy.

Kathryn couldn't help smiling in return. "I'm sorry. I was
concentrating so hard on trying to find a room to rent that I
guess . . ."

"Is that the problem? Maybe I brought you to the right

place after all. Look up there.'' Kathryn turned and looked up. Right above her head in the bay window of the brownstone was a sign that announced, in bold black type, Room to Rent.

"Come on, Dick,'' a woman's voice shrilled. Kathryn turned to see a red-haired girl, her arm linked through a sailor's.

The young man looked regretfully at Kathryn. "I've got to go. I promised to join my friends. Are you sure you'll be all right?''

Kathryn nodded. Her first acquaintance in the city, and he was disappearing. "Of course. Thank you for rescuing me.''

With a reluctant wave of his hand he was off, part of the crowd of happy people holding hands and singing. She watched until she could no longer see him, then stared up at the sign in the window. Well, if I believed in omens, she said to herself, this would be a good one. As she gathered her bags, smoothed down her hair and suit and mounted the steps, she tried very hard to believe in them.

Chapter Three

"Now don't expect to get a meal every night," Rachel Aarons announced as she carried the steaming tray into Kathryn's room. "You understand that you are renting this room, not paying for full board?" Without waiting for an answer, she slid the tray onto the marble-topped dresser. "But since it is a special occasion . . ."

"You mean because the war is over?" Kathryn asked.

"I mean no such thing," Rachel snapped. "It's because you've just arrived. And because you look as if you've had a hard trip."

Kathryn watched her eyes—small, dark and oddly penetrating. It's almost as if she knows everything, Kathryn thought. As if she could tell it all by looking at me. She would have to be very careful of her new landlady. What if she thinks it's her moral duty to return me to my family? Kathryn thought with a shiver. Edward's dark eyes and whispered threats were as real as if he stood before her.

There was something else strange about Rachel Aarons. Why, when everyone in the city was going mad with joy over the end of the war, did she show no signs of happiness? If anything, she appeared annoyed by the armistice celebration.

"I'd appreciate it if you would take the tray to the kitchen when you are finished. The kitchen maid has already left for the night." Her voice was as steely gray as her hair.

"Of course," Kathryn murmured. "And, Mrs. Aarons, thank you. It was very kind."

"I hope you like lamb stew," she said with a sniff as she closed the door behind her.

Kathryn turned to the newspaper spread out on the bed.

She had intended to ask her new landlady for suggestions on where to start looking for a job, but the woman's brusqueness made her reconsider. *What if she tries to throw me out when she finds out I have no job? No, I'm on my own now.*

The idea half delighted her; she was poised on the edge of a new world, a world where anything could happen. Where she could make anything happen. The old Kathryn Townsend had been left behind. She was no longer a daughter, no longer a sister. She was anything she wanted to be—Kathryn Townsend, writer; Kathryn Townsend, shopkeeper; Kathryn Townsend, doctor. Perhaps even Kathryn Townsend, millionairess. She laughed aloud, remembering her long-ago vow.

Her life would not be tied to a man's. She wouldn't be tied to anyone ever again, she assured herself as she fought down the memories of Adam that overwhelmed her. She sat very still, staring at a late-season fly trying to walk up the windowpane to freedom. Her eyes prickled with tears and the fly and the window became a wet blur. She longed to throw herself on the bed and cry until her tears ran dry.

No, this is my new brand-new life. I won't ruin it by mourning over the old. Taking out a handkerchief, she blew her nose once and returned to the newspaper. *Well, Kathryn Townsend, millionairess, you'd better find yourself a job.*

Typewriter operators, waitresses, women to run machinery in clothing factories—that was all New York City seemed to require. But as she was leafing through the paper she couldn't help noticing the full-page ads for department stores: Bonwit Teller, Best and Company, B. Altman, Lord & Taylor and R. H. Macy's, which advertised itself as "the world's largest store." All these big stores, Kathryn decided, had to need employees. She was certain to find a job.

Her stomach felt hollow and sick. It was the first time Kathryn had ever ridden in a hydraulic elevator, and she wasn't sure she liked the sensation. At each floor the gold-braided attendant stopped the elevator, announced in a monotonous tone of voice the wares to be found on that floor, then opened the gates with a metallic clang. People got off, people got on and the gates clanged shut again. Slowly the car jerked upward, leaving her heart, it seemed to Kathryn, on the floor below. It was just one of the marvels of New York department stores.

They were big, bigger than Kathryn could have imagined. And more elegant, with mosaic floors and crystal chandeliers, mahogany staircases and big show windows filled with dresses in the very latest of styles. Kathryn walked around the stores, observing carefully. She studied the merchandise, the displays, the salesclerks, the customers each store attracted. Before applying for a job, she wanted to learn everything she could.

The quantity of merchandise awed her. There were endless rows of gloves of every color in the rainbow, all arranged neatly in wooden boxes; hundreds of hats decorated with bows and feathers, beads and fur; sealskin capes and coats and jackets and muffs; she couldn't even begin to count the bolts of silk, satin, wool, cotton and cambric. All the girls and women behind the counters seemed so competent as they ruled their little domains, measuring fabric, fitting gloves, advising customers on their choices of perfume or pearls. That could be me, Kathryn told herself as she felt a bubble of enthusiasm rise in her chest.

"Two days ago," the mustached man in the employment office told her, "I could have given you a job, but now, with the war over . . ." He looked at her disappointed expression and wished with all his heart that she had appeared in his office two days ago. She was beautiful; it would have been a pleasure just to know she was working in the same building. "The boys will be coming home, you see, and they'll want their jobs back. As it is, we may have to let some of our own women go. They were only filling the posts temporarily— until the war was over. It isn't as if they have families to support, like the men. I hope you understand."

Kathryn grasped her purse firmly and lied. "Yes, yes, I do." I wonder what he would say if I told him I had no family and only one hundred and forty-seven dollars left?

She tried her second choice, and her third and fourth. They all said the same thing—"The boys are coming home; we can't hire anybody new." After three days she'd exhausted all the large stores and tried some of the smaller ones. Bookshops and flower shops and linen shops and jewelry stores, stores specializing in furs and shoes and children's clothing.

There were no openings. With each refusal her spirits sank lower, but she kept trying, forcing her face into a smile, pretending her feet didn't ache. She tried different approaches. She tried being serious and being flirtatious. The answer was always the same. No one wanted a seventeen-year-old girl with no experience when fighting men would soon be flooding the market looking for jobs.

She'd been trying for four days and had decided she was too tired to try one more place. Her mind wasn't on where she was walking, and she found herself crashing into a large body in the middle of Fifth Avenue.

"You keep walking like that, miss, and you're going to get yourself hurt." His voice was deep and kind. So was his face. Round and florid, with twinkling blue eyes. He was wearing a uniform, a very smart uniform, scarlet with black braid.

"I'm so sorry. I wasn't thinking," she said, nervously re-adjusting her hat.

"And sure you didn't think I was so handsome you were looking for an excuse to run into me."

She blushed, then joined in his laughter. "No, my mind was on something else. Finding a job. I think I've applied at half the stores in the city."

"Why not try the hotels?" he asked, gesturing at the building behind them. The Lamont Hotel, it proclaimed in gold script. "Go see Mr. George—he's the manager—and tell him Kevin O'Hara, the doorman, sent you."

"Do you think there are any jobs?"

"If there are, I'm thinking you'll have a good chance of gettin' one. Mr. George, he likes a pretty colleen."

"Mr. O'Hara, how can I thank you?"

"Seein' that pretty smile on your face is thanks enough. Now go on in, and good luck to you."

He's right, Mr. George does like a pretty face, and that's not all, Kathryn thought as she felt the manager's eyes focusing on her ankles. "You understand," he said as his eyes rose slowly up her body and to her face, "that we have very few jobs available for a young woman of your . . . breeding. Of course, we do employ a great number of chambermaids, but . . . Let me see your hands." Reluctantly Kathryn held them out. He took them and turned them over to look at the palms. "As I thought, these really aren't the hands of a maid, are they? Much too pretty and too delicate." When Kathryn tried to pull her hands away, he held them tighter. "Perhaps you would have dinner with me and we could discuss what opening wc would have for a woman of your talents." He grinned a leering, toothy grin, and Kathryn made her decision.

"Mr. George, would you please let go of my hands? Obviously you and I don't have the same sort of job in mind, so I had better leave and not take up any more of your time."

"But, Miss Townsend, surely you don't think . . ." He was sputtering as she walked out of his office. Ashamed to see Kevin O'Hara, she slipped out a side door.

But, she told herself philosophically, the experience hadn't been a waste. Hotels were a good idea. At least she'd worked in the boardinghouse, so she could claim a little experience, more if she exaggerated.

This time she didn't start with the best hotels but tried smaller ones, making sure they were in respectable neighborhoods. She'd had enough of the other kind to last a lifetime.

Five days and only one offer—to work in a small, greasy kitchen washing dishes and doing other dirty chores the cook refused to do. For a moment she was tempted, but decided that she had to begin her new life doing something better than dishwashing.

When Saturday afternoon came and she had to pay Mrs. Aarons, she almost regretted her decision. The roll of bills was melting away. What would she do when it ran out? Mrs. Aarons was not likely to extend credit; she'd be afraid even to ask. Perhaps she should save enough for train fare back to Boston. If she could persuade Edward that his secret was safe . . .

A sharp rap on the door interrupted her agonies. "I've come for the rent," Mrs. Aarons announced.

Looking at Kathryn's pale, scared face, Rachel knew that something was wrong. The girl had been out every day looking for work, but obviously she hadn't found anything.

Jacob, forgive me for interfering, but she looks so lost. She turned her beady eyes on Kathryn. "Can't find a job, can you?"

How did this woman know, and what else had she found out? Kathryn debated showing her the rest of her money to ensure that she could keep the room for a few more weeks. Glumly Kathryn shook her head.

"Are you educated? Well educated?"

"Yes," Kathryn said, not sure why Mrs. Aarons was asking. Could her education matter if she was going to be thrown out on the street?

"Then," said Mrs. Aarons with an air of satisfaction and one of her rare smiles, "I have a suggestion."

Chapter Four

Would this day never end? Kathryn stared around the classroom. Sixteen vacant-looking sixteen-year-old faces stared back at her. The last thing in the world these girls wanted to hear about was past participles and parenthetical expressions, but that was what she was hired to teach them, and teach she would.

Not that it would make a dent. It hadn't in the three years she'd been teaching English composition and literature at The Abbott School. With a few exceptions, the girls attended class, pretended to listen, graduated, married wealthy young men and never gave another thought to grammar. And every year Kathryn found herself caring less. Not that she wasn't grateful for the job. The money assured her a comfortable life.

She was as relieved as her students when there was a knock on the door in the middle of her lecture. A uniformed figure stalked into the classroom and Kathryn's heart nearly stopped. The girls smiled eagerly, too young to remember the war days and the terror a Western Union deliveryman could evoke. Nonsense, Kathryn said, giving herself a mental shake, the war's been over for years. Besides, who would be sending me a telegram? It must be a mistake.

She studied the yellow envelope carefully. There was no mistake. Her fingers were stiff and cold and she opened it clumsily. The message read: "Regret to inform you of death of mother, Lily O'Donnell Townsend, in unfortunate accident. Please contact undersigned in regards deceased's estate."

It was signed by a Wendell Carruthers of Carruthers, Peabody and Carlyle.

Bile rose in Kathryn's throat and the room began to darken and sway around her. She leaned against the blackboard for support and protection. It was as if Edward were reaching out his clawed hand and dragging her back, back into his own warped and evil world.

Nervously Kathryn scanned the offices of Carruthers, Peabody and Carlyle, barely taking in the Oriental carpets and mahogany furniture. Her head ached; her eyes were gritty; everything felt strangely unreal, hazy, as if it were happening in a dream.

She had been up all night talking with Rachel. In a cold, emotionless tone, as if it had happened to someone else, she'd told Rachel everything. Until she spoke of Adam. Then she found herself overwhelmed by memories and emotions.

Rachel sat by her side, holding her hand, letting Kathryn's story flow, asking no questions, making no judgments. When it was all over, she said, "That's too much suffering for a young woman to have kept bottled up. But you're strong and you survived."

She paused for a moment as if making a decision. "We're survivors, the both of us. Like you, I ran away, but I ran away from my husband.

"I grew up in Vienna. My father was a merchant. Never a really successful one, but always claiming to be on the verge of success. Finally he came up with a scheme to curry favor with a more prosperous businessman. I was to be the incentive, the lure, the bait in the trap—whatever you call it.

"The man was not old. Only five or maybe six years older than my eighteen years. But he was fat, swollen up like a great balloon. He had beady little eyes that you could barely see because his face was so puffed up. What I remember most now are his eyes—mean, like little pig's eyes. And the way he sweated. Like any other young girl, I had dreams of my Prince Charming. But Heshy . . . I couldn't even bear to be in the same room with him.

"Naturally when my father announced that I was to marry him, I refused. My mother was much like yours," she said, giving Kathryn's hand a gentle squeeze. "Her willpower was so eroded that she had no mind of her own. I wasn't surprised when she refused to help me. For two days I locked myself in my room without food or water. Finally my father relented and promised that he would not force me to marry Heshy. Only after I'd unlocked the door did he reveal the conditions: I could no longer live in his house if I refused. He suggested that I might earn my living by prostitution and dragged me out onto the streets to watch the women at work while he explained to his innocent daughter in the most frighteningly graphic terms what men paid them to do. After three days I relented. The fourth day I married Heshy.

"During the ceremony, every time I looked at him I had to fight down the desire to vomit right there in the synagogue. The thought of his bloated hands touching me . . . it was more than I could bear. I think if I'd had the opportunity I would have killed myself rather than face the wedding night."

Kathryn felt nausea rise in her own throat.

"But nothing happened that night," Rachel continued. "Or in the weeks afterward. And Heshy never explained. Never apologized. I was relieved, but at the same time confused. I worried that it was I who had done something wrong. I couldn't confide in my parents. In their eyes a wealthy son-in-law could never be at fault." There was a glimmer of tears in Rachel's eyes as she remembered. "We'd been married two months when he began to beat me. It started with an occasional rough push or shove. Then he slapped me—for no reason or any excuse at all. One day I happened to see his face in a mirror as he beat my backside bloody. He never stopped smiling."

She looked at Kathryn hesitantly. "You know, in those days properly sheltered young ladies such as I was had no inkling that there were men who preferred the bodies of men. Now I suspect that Heshy was one of those. His closest friend was his private secretary, and somehow I always felt like the outcast when I was with them. There was some sort of bond. . . . I suppose he beat me because he couldn't have what he really wanted."

"How did you manage to escape?" Kathryn asked, so caught up in Rachel's nightmares that she could feel her own heart pounding.

"It's amazing what courage and abilities God grants us

when we most need them. I simply went to the railroad station, studied the timetables and bought a ticket. Then I went home and packed a bag. Heshy had a stupid habit of hiding money around the house. I tore the house apart and found what seemed to me a fortune. I was free, but for every moment of the seventeen-hour train ride to Naples, I was terrified that Heshy and the police would be waiting for me at the next station.

"In Naples, I bought steerage passage to Boston; I thought it would be harder to find me amidst the hordes of immigrants. Even in America, though I was thousands of miles away, I was still afraid—afraid to make friends, even afraid to go out on the street. I found a job in a pharmacy. The owner was a good man, a widower, and he wanted to marry me. I panicked, afraid to tell him I was already married. Afraid I'd be arrested and shipped home.

"So I ran away again. To Chicago. That's where I met my Jacob. But I fell in love with him and I couldn't run away. I told him everything. Bless him, he loved me so much that he was willing to give up his job and his home and move with me. So we came to New York as Mr. and Mrs. Jacob Aarons.

"In a way, I don't regret what happened because I had Jacob," she continued. "For twenty-two wonderful years." Her tone turned bitter. "The war was hard, though. It brought back memories. I had two baby brothers who would have been in the army. I don't even know if they are still alive."

She gave Kathryn a long, penetrating stare. "I've never told this to anyone but Jacob. Sometimes it helps to share."

"You're wise, Rachel Aarons. Obviously some kindly god was watching over me the day I came to your front door. I don't intend to spend the rest of my life hiding. I refuse to let Edward threaten or terrorize me again." She paused. "But there's one thing. . . . Why should my mother's estate affect me, unless . . . unless Edward is also dead?"

"Why, then it would be a blessing and you'd have nothing to fear, would you?" Rachel said, heaving her body out of the chair. "Go on, pack your bag and you can catch the early train. You won't rest easy until you find some answers. I'll prepare you breakfast. Some things are better faced on a full stomach. That's what I always told Jacob."

* * *

"Needless to say, I am saddened to have had to give you such tragic news, Miss Townsend." Wendell Carruthers passed his palm over his balding, dome-shaped head. "What happened to your mother was an unfortunate—shall we say freak?—accident." Kathryn nodded encouragingly, wondering if she should feign some emotion. "She was," he continued, "changing a light bulb—the house had recently had electricity installed and she wasn't familiar . . . Apparently she was electrocuted. A pity. It was your brother who discovered her."

Kathryn found herself drawing a deep breath. So Edward was alive. Which didn't explain . . . "I still don't understand why you contacted me about the estate. Surely my brother—or rather my half brother—inherits everything."

"On the contrary, Miss Townsend. With one small technical exception, you are the sole heir. We went to a great deal of trouble to locate you. Your brother was convinced that you were dead, and he tried to persuade us so."

"I'll bet he did," Kathryn whispered under her breath.

"Excuse me, Miss Townsend?"

"Nothing. Go on, Mr. Carruthers."

"The tragedy occurred four months ago. It has taken us all that time to locate you. It was a"—he glanced down at the papers in front of him—"a Bridget Costelloe McDermott who suggested we contact various private schools. I have informed Mr. Townsend that you are alive. But I must say that he did not seem happy about it. Not that I could have expected . . . He stood to inherit a great deal of money."

From the way his brows pinched together in distaste, Kathryn knew he disliked Edward. "Surely my mother's estate wasn't a large one," she protested.

"On the contrary. The family house was hers, of course." Kathryn's heart pounded. That could only mean her father was dead. "And there were two other establishments—operated, I believe, as boardinghouses—also in Lowell. There was a small hotel there and," he said, checking his papers, "one here in Boston, the Blackstone. As well as several bank accounts, some bonds and a few parcels of real estate." He massaged his head more vigorously and smiled. "You are a very wealthy woman, Miss Townsend."

"But how? My brother was the businessman in the family. My mother . . ."

"Two and a half years ago—I suspect it was shortly after you left home—your brother—against my advice, I might add—placed all of his assets in your mother's name. As he added new holdings, they were also put under her name. I tried to discourage it—I anticipated problems—but he refused to listen to me. He insisted that he had his reasons."

You bet he had his reasons, Kathryn said to herself. He didn't want to be accused of murder.

"Six months ago your mother came to me requesting that I draw up a new will for her," the lawyer went on. "She claimed to have some old debts to settle. She also gave me something for safekeeping for you." Reaching into his waistcoat pocket, he withdrew a small key and opened a desk drawer. He pulled out a small white envelope which he handed to Kathryn.

Her fingers trembled as she tore open the envelope and unfolded a thin sheet of paper. Would her mother at last explain why she had been so slavishly devoted to Edward? Kathryn was shocked to see only three words: "I'm sorry. Mother." But confession was not part of her mother's practical, no-nonsense character. The simple words and the message in her will proved she loved her daughter. All of a sudden Kathryn felt the prickle of tears.

Mr. Carruthers saw her furiously blinking back the tears and stood up abruptly.

"Perhaps you'd like a few minutes alone," he suggested. "Why don't you make yourself comfortable in the outer office while I prepare the necessary papers for your signature."

The secretary had tactfully left the room, and once alone, Kathryn fought the tears. Think of something else, anything else, she told herself as she focused on the print of a fox-hunting scene hanging on the wall in front of her. She pitied the poor fox. Running for its life. All those dogs and horses pounding after it.

When the door opened she didn't even recognize him. He'd lost weight. His cheeks were hollowed and lined. His clothes hung awkwardly on his skeletal limbs. But it was the eyes she remembered—dark and chilling. She met them without hesitation. "Edward, I didn't think I'd ever see you again."

"I'd hoped you were dead," he said dully.

"I admit that I had the same thought about you."

"You can't have it. It's my money. I made it." His voice was a snarl, like an angry dog's.

"No, you stole it," Kathryn said with satisfaction. "And then you outsmarted yourself."

"The bitch betrayed me." Suddenly his voice was less hostile. "And I thought she loved me."

"She did, once—and that was her mistake—but you pushed too hard and too far and you refused to let her love anyone else. Not me. Not my father."

"Your father, that poor excuse for a man. . . . Do you know that we had a party—just Lily and I—to celebrate, the day he died? The smell of death was finally out of the house. I fired Bridget, too." There was childish glee in his voice.

If only she could know her father had forgiven her for running away. . . . But she couldn't let Edward sense the chink in her emotional armor. "I'm sure Bridget would have gone anyway. Her loyalty was to my father, not to you."

He pretended not to hear her. "I rented his room the next day. The space was wasted on the cripple for years. All that money lost. . . ."

"Money. It always comes down to money with you, doesn't it? It certainly never occurred to me that I would have this inheritance, but believe me, I shall take great pleasure in spending it, knowing how badly you want it."

Edward's pale face suddenly flushed red with anger and his tall body hunched over her threateningly. "I'll get back every single penny. It's mine. I want it." His voice rose hysterically. "It's mine."

Wendell Carruthers came at a fast trot. "Calm yourself, Mr. Townsend. As I told you before, the money is now legally Miss Townsend's."

"I'll contest the will. It isn't right for a mother to disinherit her son. She loved me. It's my money."

"Please. I've explained to you before that the property was Mrs. Townsend's to dispose of as she chose. And she chose to will it to her daughter. She warned me that you might have objections, but I can assure you that you will not be able to overturn the document. Technically you were not disinherited. You were given the sum of one dollar, which," he said, reaching down into his pocket, "I am prepared to pay you immediately."

"Keep your damn pittance. I intend to have it all. She," Edward snarled, pointing a bony finger at Kathryn, "won't live to see a penny of it."

"Now, Mr. Townsend," Wendell Carruthers said, swelling up with professional and moral indignation, "I must warn you against making threats. If you say one more word I shall call the police. And you can be assured that Miss Townsend will press charges against you."

Edward suddenly realized he'd gone too far. As his anger defused, his face grew white and his arms fell limply to his sides. But there was still a frightening glimmer in his eyes and a coldness in his voice. "I will have it all—remember that. No matter how long it takes."

At the railroad station, Kathryn reclaimed her luggage and directed the taxi driver to the Blackstone Hotel. It was her hotel now—although that fact might take as much getting used to as the idea of being an heiress.

As the taxi pulled up to the narrow brick-fronted building, she noticed that the awning was torn and the gold lettering in "Blackstone" was fading. The doorman was a grayer and boozier version of Kevin O'Hara. In the small lobby, she took in the threadbare carpet and the dingy gray walls. Edward never was one to spend money on frills—like paint.

"I'll need a single room," she said to the desk clerk as she removed her gloves and prepared to sign the guest register. Mr. Carruthers had offered to make the arrangements, but Kathryn had said no. She would be an ordinary guest.

"Are you alone?" the clerk asked. He was an elderly man, and from the look on his face he found something surprising, if not downright scandalous, in her request.

"This is 1921, so I assume you are modern enough to accept single female guests?"

"Oh yes ma'am, I mean, miss." By the tone of his voice it was obvious that he also wasn't accustomed to modern women who talked back—and that he didn't approve of them.

Kathryn signed her name with a flourish, wondering what he'd think if he realized she was the new owner. Probably be bowing and scraping within seconds.

Her room was a disappointment. As small as it could possibly be—a narrow bed, a straight chair, a scarred table and barely enough room to walk around. The drapes emitted a cloud of dust. The window refused to open. That the panes were encrusted with dirt didn't matter; the only view was down an airshaft.

Kathryn examined every square inch of the room and made mental notes. There was a ring of scum around the sink. The lone towel was small and worn limp. The shelf in the closet was thick with dust and harbored a pair of dirty socks. The mattress sagged. The sheets were gray and patched. How could Edward have let his investment deteriorate so shamefully?

By the time she finished it was dinnertime, and knowing instinctively what the hotel dining room would be like—small, dark and dreary—she had no desire to face it. Instead she ordered a meal in her room. It was cold. The waiter was apologetic. "You see, miss, the staff elevator is broken—has been for the past two months—meals have to be carried up." Kathryn filed the information away.

The next morning she chatted with the maid who came to clean her room. Even under Kathryn's watchful eye the job was haphazard. The maid was a young woman with pasty skin and dark circles under her eyes. Her name was Grace, and she explained that she had a baby at home who kept her up half the night. "I don't mind, not really. What with working here from six in the morning till seven at night, I don't get much chance to be with him. At least when he cries in the middle of the night I get to hold him."

Suddenly Kathryn was overwhelmed by anger. Anger at Edward for all the people he'd hurt—her mother and father, Adam, Bridget, poor Grace and her baby. Rage boiled up inside her. It wasn't fair. Edward should be forced to pay for his crimes in kind. Money was not enough.

As she fought the tears of anger and hatred she remembered a saying of her father's: "The mills of God grind slowly, yet they grind exceedingly fine."

In time Edward would pay.

Chapter Five

Wendell Carruthers was nervous. He kept passing his palm over his balding head as if he were trying to massage his sluggish brain into solving a particularly knotty problem. Kathryn watched in silence, worried that he would wear out the few remaining strands of gray hair.

He'd been in the legal profession for thirty-one years and this was the first time he'd ever encountered such a problem. He'd dealt with spinsters who wanted to leave all their money to their cats and with young girls ready to hand over their fortunes to gigolos, but this . . . By comparison, those were simple problems. What Miss Townsend was proposing—why, it was unthinkable, for a woman.

Kathryn watched him anxiously. "Mr. Carruthers, is there any legal reason why you can't do as I've requested?"

His massaging became more vigorous and Kathryn wondered if he'd been struck dumb. Finally he spoke. "Now, Miss Townsend, let me make sure I have this straight. You want me to liquidate your assets—the houses, the hotels, the land—so that you can buy a hotel in New York City. Is that correct?"

Kathryn's heart sank. The way he said it, the plan didn't sound as sensible as she'd persuaded herself it was. She'd been awake half the night, thinking. She couldn't stop her mind from churning with ideas, schemes, innovations for her hotel; then suddenly fear and doubt would seize her. *Am I crazy? Risking everything when I could live comfortably on my inheritance? People will think I'm insane. A teacher— what preparation do I have for the business world? A little voice kept repeating, "None. Absolutely none at all."* But toward dawn another voice rose above it. It was the voice of David Jamison, drifting back across the years: "Sometime you have to follow your own heart and your own dream, if you want it badly enough." His voice was so real she could almost feel the gold piece, smooth and cool, in her hand. Then the memory of Lily's words came to her: "Your life is what you make it."

She met Wendell Carruthers' eyes. It was her decision, her life, her responsibility. "Yes," she said firmly, "that is correct. I don't want a large hotel, you understand. Nothing to compete with the Plaza or the Waldorf. Not yet." She saw the pained expression on his face. "My idea is to find a hotel like the Blackstone, small and respectable, but run-down. One that I could renovate into an elegant little hotel where ladies—and gentlemen, too—would find all the comforts of home."

"But, Miss Townsend, have you had any experience in the hotel business, or in any business at all?"

She shook her head. How could she explain how perfectly right this decision seemed to her, so right that it had to work? But lawyers were like bankers: when it came to money, one did not operate on instinct. "I intend to learn. To study the hotel business thoroughly. And meanwhile I will hire people with experience."

Wendell shook his head sadly, wondering if his beautiful client would prove as unstable as her brother. Perhaps it ran in the family. But no, this girl had a different fire in her eyes, a determination. If he ignored the facts, he could almost believe she would succeed, she sounded so sure of herself. But that was nonsense. His professional duty was to advise her against this crazy scheme.

"Why don't you keep the Blackstone and renovate it, if that's what you're so determined to do?"

"Mr. Carruthers, I'm sure that you've realized my family—what's left of it—isn't close. I have painful memories here and I have a new life in New York. I'd prefer to go back there."

"Fair enough, but you shouldn't make any hasty decisions. You must understand that you are taking a considerable risk. There is a great deal of money involved, and if you make an unwise investment you could lose it all. Why don't you give your plan a little thought while your mother's will is being probated? You may change your mind."

"Mr. Carruthers, I've considered all the risks. I promise you I won't change my mind. This is what I want to do. My dream."

Looking at the determined line of her chin, Wendell Carruthers knew arguing would be futile. He had a sudden feeling that Kathryn Townsend was destined to become his most challenging and successful client. It was a vision he would pride himself on in later years.

Kathryn marched into the threadbare lobby of the Blackstone Hotel with such hard-eyed determination that the elderly desk clerk considered ducking down behind the counter before she saw him. But he was still thinking about it when she demanded, "I want to see the manager of this hotel. What is his name?"

"Pennington, miss. Roger Pennington."

"Does he have an office, or should I voice my complaints out here in the middle of the lobby?"

He pointed to a door on the opposite side of the lobby, and before he could say anything she was striding in that direction.

Roger Pennington looked just like an English butler—or at least what the motion pictures want you to believe an English butler looks like, she decided as she stood in the doorway to his office. His face was pale and not too thin, not too fat. His features were regular and forgettable. His hair was light, not exactly blond and not exactly brown, but definitely thinning. He was neither tall nor short.

A practiced smile came to his lips. "May I help you, madam?" His voice was soft and solicitous, and Kathryn wasn't surprised to hear that he had a polished English accent. He looked too good to be true.

Without preamble she launched into her speech. "This hotel is a disgrace. The lobby's dingy and in disrepair. The rooms are ridiculously tiny and shamefully dirty. The fact that I found a pair of dirty socks in the back of my closet shows how well the maids clean, which isn't surprising since you make them work thirteen hours a day. The food from room service arrives cold. The linens should have been used for rags years ago and the furniture chopped into kindling. And it isn't as if this were some low class hotel; your rates are high and you have—or at least had—a good reputation."

"I must agree with you, madam," he said, sounding so sad that Kathryn felt sorry for him. "I'm afraid it's the owner . . . well, he isn't willing to spend any money on upkeep or improvements. Although there is a rumor that he is selling the hotel. . . . At the moment it's out of my hands, I'm afraid. But I'm sorry that you've had to suffer through our problems."

Kathryn looked at him. He sounded sincere and she sensed that he wasn't the sort to play games. "I'm afraid that it's my problem, too."

"Pardon me, madam?"

She reached her hand over his desk. "Let me introduce myself. I'm Kathryn Townsend—the new owner." Watching his eyes pop with surprise, Kathryn wondered, Aren't good butlers supposed to be unflappable?

"But—but—" he stammered.

"I'm not here to fire you. I need your help."

He seemed to regain his composure. "Anything, madam."

"First, don't madam me. It's Miss Townsend. And if you are free for the rest of the day, we can sit down and decide what's wrong with this hotel and how to fix it. I won't lie to you—I do intend to sell the hotel. But I will recommend that the new owner keep you on if everything works out."

They worked through the afternoon, ate dinner at his desk and finally, a little after midnight, completed the list of things to be done. Painters were to be brought in. The public rooms were to have new carpeting. Guest rooms were to be thoroughly cleaned. Every room would have new drapes, bedspreads and linens. The worst furniture would be replaced. The elevator was to be repaired.

As they worked they discovered they had a goal in common: to make the Blackstone Hotel perfect. They agreed that there were to be no halfhearted efforts; everything would be done the right way. The effect would be simple, yet elegant.

The following morning Kathryn called the staff together. Seeing the fear in their faces, she wanted to reassure them, but she knew that a little healthy fear would also keep them on their toes. And they would all have to stay on their toes.

"I'm going to need each and every one of you," she said, surveying the forty-two anxious faces, "to do his or her absolute best. Within six months I expect the Blackstone to be one of the finest small hotels in the city. It's going to be hard work—I won't lie to you about that. There will be painters and plumbers and carpenters and electricians all over the place, making your work even more difficult."

Watching their faces hanging on to her every word gave her a swelling sense of power, and a determination to win them over.

"I can hear you grumbling, asking, 'What am I going to get out of this?' First, if you work hard and well, you won't get fired." She was interrupted by an outbreak of nervous laughter. "And if you survive the next six months, you are assured that both Mr. Pennington and I will give you good references to the new owner. And," she said, feeling like Santa Claus about to hand over the presents, "there will be a bonus to every employee who gives his or her wholehearted cooperation. One hundred dollars."

When Kathryn finished the speech, her new employees all applauded loudly and enthusiastically. As she listened to them she felt her confidence growing.

"My congratulations, Miss Townsend. It was quite extraordinary the way you won them over." You won me over, too, Roger Pennington thought to himself. "But," he said as his practical nature asserted itself, "surely it wasn't necessary to promise such an extravagant bonus?"

"In the long run, I don't think it will prove an extravagance if we can make this hotel into the little gem I envision.

"Do you know what you remind me of?" she said suddenly. "A butler, a very proper English butler."

Roger chuckled. "That, milady, is because I was."

"Do you mean that the butlers in the motion pictures are authentic-looking?"

"Are you saying that I look like a film star?" They stared at each other for a moment and then burst out laughing.

"Yes, you are perfect for the role," Kathryn said with a delighted grin.

"The fact of the matter is that I was a butler for a mere two years, whereas my father was a butler for the same family for thirty years. I came to America as a young man."

"But," Kathryn protested, "you still have your accent."

A sheepish look came over his face and for a moment he hesitated. Finally he said, "That is because you Americans are such wretched snobs."

"We are?"

"You certainly are. Most Americans consider it the height of elegance to be served by an Englishman who they believe speaks as if he'd gone to Oxford. Actually," he drawled, "I can speak like any Bostonian."

"Why, you . . . you old phony," she exclaimed. "You keep your English accent polished up just to impress snobbish guests, don't you?"

His faced assumed a mock-somber expression. "Yes, milady, I daresay I do."

As soon as Rachel's brusque voice came across the line, Kathryn experienced an overwhelming sense of relief. Everything seemed so . . . so unreal, so far removed from the life she'd been living only three days ago. It was as if her whole world had been shaken up and spilled out like dice to form a brand-new pattern on the board. Rachel was a tie with the past, a tie she desperately needed right now.

With a "You'll never believe what happened," she launched into her story. Rachel was silent until Kathryn announced, "And now I know what I want to do with my life: I'm going into the hotel business. Edward turned the Blackstone into a disaster, but I know I can put it back on its feet and then buy a hotel of my own."

"Kathryn Townsend, are you wasting good money on a telephone call to tell me this nonsense?"

Her voice was indignant. "Rachel, it's hardly as if I've said I'm running off to wear pink-spangled tights and ride bareback in the circus. The hotel business is a perfectly respectable one." Then her voice fell, crushed. "I thought you'd understand."

"A perfectly respectable business maybe, but not for a single young lady."

"What difference does that make?"

"It will make a difference when you get married and have a family. Then you won't want to be tied down with a business."

"My plans don't include marriage."

"Not even if that nice Mr. Carroll were to ask you?"

Kathryn's mind flashed to John Carroll's round, fresh-scrubbed face. He was nice and polite and earnest, and she knew that he was more than a little in love with her. "Reverend Carroll's fondest dream is to be a missionary in China. Me a missionary's wife—now that's true nonsense."

"Well," Rachel said, and Kathryn knew her bosom was puffing up with indignation, "I've said my piece. If you're too stubborn to listen, you have my blessing. Go ahead, make your own mistakes."

Chapter Six

Kathryn was tired of hotels. She'd stayed in twenty-two of them in the past four months. Being a guest was, she had decided, the first step in learning the hotel business. If she could put herself into her guests' shoes, could know exactly what they wanted—maybe even before they did—then, given an experienced staff, she could run a successful hotel.

At first—against Wendell's nervous advice—she indulged herself in the best hotels. Two nights at the Plaza. A sinfully expensive suite at the Waldorf for three days followed by a small single at the Lamont for the weekend. To her dismay, she discovered that Manhattan's luxury hotels were not the flawless paradises she'd expected. But at the same time she couldn't help being awed by the marble lobbies, gilt furniture, massive bouquets of flowers, and battalions of waiters, busboys, maids, bellhops and elevator operators poised to cater to her every whim.

At the end of four months she had eight bulging notebooks and a very clear idea of how she would run her hotel. She had assessed everything—from the choice of desserts in the dining room to the condition of the towels in the bathroom. And she saw everything in a new way. No longer did the enormous crystal chandelier at the Lamont blind her with its radiance; instead she wondered how many men were required to clean the thousands of tiny pendants, and how often, and whether it was worth the time and expense.

She indulged shamelessly in eavesdropping on fellow guests. She also discovered that waiters, elevator operators and particularly chambermaids were usually eager to chat. That was how she found out about the Hotel Chambord.

"Dunna what's gonna happen to us," the aging blond maid had remarked glumly. "Mr. Gautier, he died last year, and Madame doesn't really like runnin' the hotel."

And it shows, Kathryn thought. The Hotel Chambord was small and in a good location on the Upper East Side, but it was verging on shabby. At best the staff seemed disinterested. Madame, whoever she was, was never in evidence. In fact, no one seemed to be in charge. So Kathryn extended her stay for another week.

At the end of that time she phoned Roger Pennington. "Remember I told you I'd give you a good reference for the new owners when I sell the Blackstone? Well, I've changed my mind." There was a stunned silence at the other end. "Instead I'd like you to come down to New York and look at a hotel I want to buy. If you agree that it's a good investment, I'd like you to manage it for me."

For another week Kathryn and Roger happily prowled the hotel together—observing, taking notes and talking to the guests and staff. In the end they didn't have to seek out "Madame." She came to them, a fiery red-haired, red-faced little French woman who descended at breakfast demanding, "Who are you and why are you questioning my employees? You're not from the unions, are you?"

"I'm here because I want to buy your hotel," Kathryn said, looking straight into her pinched little eyes. Madame Gautier was taken aback, but within seconds there was a shrewd glint in her eyes as she insisted that she did not want to sell "my beloved husband's hotel."

Two days later they agreed on a price.

"It's too much, too much," Wendell Carruthers insisted, rubbing his balding scalp. "I realize it's a valuable piece of property, but you can't afford it, Kathryn. I've liquidated your real estate, but you still need twenty thousand dollars more. You'll have to wait until I find a purchaser for the Blackstone."

"But that could take months." Kathryn felt like crying, a child deprived of a toy. She and Roger had such wonderful plans. "Why can't I borrow the money?"

"I'm afraid . . . well, a young woman with no business experience . . ."

"I won't know until I try," Kathryn insisted.

He paused, pitying the poor bankers forced to say no to her. She wouldn't make it easy. "I'll draw up a list of my banking contacts in New York."

Kathryn worked her way through the list. The answer was always the same. Some said no politely; others were incensed that an inexperienced woman with a harebrained scheme was wasting their time. There was only one name left on the list. Allan Jones. A simple, approachable name, Kathryn decided. Maybe he's the one.

That evening Wendell Carruthers phoned and announced, "I've found your investor." To Kathryn it was as if an enormous weight had been lifted from her weary shoulders. She was astonished that he'd managed to talk one of those cautious, prejudiced bankers into risking his money. "Who is it?" she asked.

At first he didn't speak, and Kathryn felt her dream fading again. Finally, in a small, nervous voice, he said, "It's me." What he didn't say was I must be insane, risking my own money, handing it over to a young woman with no experience. His instincts said she would be successful and that he was making a shrewd investment, but he didn't think an attorney should listen to instinct over the voice of reason.

Wendell Carruthers beamed like a proud father when, a year later, Kathryn took him on his first tour of the hotel. After the Blackstone had sold for almost twice as much as his cautious estimate, Kathryn had had money to invest in renovations. She'd spent it well. Walls had been pulled down and impossibly small rooms enlarged. Each of the sixty-five rooms now had its own sparkling white-tiled bathroom. All the old carpeting was ripped up, and the walls were painted in appealing pastel shades. She refused to hire an interior decorator and made all the decisions herself, from the brocade draperies in the suites to the blue-and-gold china in the dining room. For the lobby, with Roger's expert advice, she chose eighteenth-century English antiques—mahogany sideboards, overstuffed wing chairs, a Chippendale library table and brass buckets to be filled with fresh flowers.

"I want my hotel to look like an elegant English country house," Kathryn told the group of disgruntled reporters who'd been assigned to cover the opening of the small, virtually unknown hotel. But they were all won over by Kathryn's infectious enthusiasm, her obvious love for her creation, and not the least by her bobbed hair, delicate features and crackling hazel eyes. "An elegant little hotel has just reopened on East Fifty-eighth Street," wrote one reporter. "It's a gem, as is its owner, Kathryn Townsend. According to the lovely lady, this, the Townsend Manor, is just the first of many hotels she hopes to establish."

"I see you want to spend more of my money," Wendell said as he laid down his morning paper.

"Not yet, don't worry," she said, patting his hand. She knew his tendency to caution and worry and realized it was an effective brake against her own enthusiasm. "I promise I'll wait a year—until we're making money on this hotel—before I start looking for my next."

On his return to Boston, Wendell called with news that made her happiness complete. "It seems that fate is indeed smiling on you. Your brother is not going to contest your mother's will."

To Kathryn it was as if the massive sword that had been poised above her, threatening to fall and cut her success to shreds, had suddenly vanished. "That doesn't sound like him. What happened?"

"I'm not certain. According to his lawyer, he received a call from Mr. Townsend instructing him to stop proceedings, but with no reason given. Although Mr. Townsend did say that he was planning to go to California." He paused. "Perhaps he is resigned to his loss and is planning to start a new life?"

"I've never known Edward to forgive and certainly not to forget. Especially when it involves his pride or his money. I wonder . . . ?"

"Don't. I told you that the money is legally yours. He can't touch it. And even if he decides to return and contest the will, it would merely be an annoyance, that's all. Now I want you to think about something more important—making a profit on our hotel."

It took a little longer than a year before the Townsend Manor was firmly in the black. Business was good—people appreciated the quiet, elegant surroundings and impeccable service—but the renovations had been costly.

Kathryn relished her new role as hotel owner and general manager and threw herself into everything wholeheartedly, whether it was planning menus, finding the best and cheapest laundry or soothing the ruffled feathers of a difficult guest. Like the mother of a new baby, she found every task exciting and challenging and wanted to do it herself. Experienced and efficient as Roger was at hotel management, she felt happier when everything was under her control. "I'm not earning my keep," Roger would protest. But it was a lighthearted protest.

As she began looking for a new hotel, though, she realized there weren't enough hours in the day to do everything, and she called Rachel.

"Would you consider taking a job? As my assistant manager? I need someone I can rely on. And don't say you don't have any experience, because neither did I."

Rachel had missed Kathryn, who'd been so wrapped up in her work for the past two years that she'd seen little of her. Too wrapped up in her work. Maybe if she were there on the spot she could change that. What Kathryn was doing was certainly admirable, but was it the right life for a young woman? A beautiful young woman? "I accept," she said without hesitation.

"Don't you even want to know about the hours, salary, benefits?"

"I know you wouldn't cheat an old lady," Rachel said, the old brusqueness returning.

Two weeks after Rachel arrived, Kathryn started the search for a new hotel in earnest. The most likely candidate was an old-fashioned, genteel hotel in an elaborate baroque building on Central Park West. Its guests were mainly artists, writers and musicians. Which might explain, Kathryn thought, the faded, run-down look; perhaps creative people, their heads in the clouds, were less aware of their surroundings. As she looked around the dreary dining room her fingers itched to tear down the smoke-darkened paneling and redo the room in soft pink and gold.

She and Wendell did some careful figuring and prepared to meet the owner. It turned out that he wasn't interested in the hotel business anymore. "Radio, that's where it's at. The smart guys are putting all their money into this new Radio

Corporation of America. It's gonna be big. Take my word for it.''

Within a week he'd accepted their offer and Kathryn was ready to go to the banks again. "They can't turn me down this time," she told Wendell. "I've proved I can make money in this business.'' On a whim she chose to approach Allan Jones; he'd been the last banker on the list, the one who'd never gotten the chance to turn her down. He was a short, stocky young man who listened to her patiently, occasionally asking questions. Finally he agreed to study her books. A week later he called to congratulate her. She had the loan and, she knew, a valuable new ally.

"How long can she keep this up?" Rachel asked, looking across the table to where Roger sat toying with his appetizer. But she knew he wouldn't have the answer. It was an old conversation, and neither of them ever had the answer.

He shook his head glumly. "I can't say. Hardly human the way she goes on, is it? Never taking a day off. Never relaxing for an hour, even a minute. And now that she's started renovating the Townsend Park, it's worse. I assume she sleeps sometime, but I can't swear to it.''

"What she needs is a man—a husband. And children," Rachel pronounced.

Roger thought of the idle, pretentious society women he'd known in England. Kathryn could no more live that life than . . . than sprout wings and fly. "Rachel," he said tartly, "don't be so old-fashioned. What Kathryn is doing is admirable. It's just that she should do a little less of it. She must learn that work on the Townsend Park would not come to a grinding halt if she didn't stand over the carpenters all day.'' He paused, staring down at his half-empty plate for a moment. "Sometimes I wonder what demons drive her.''

When Kathryn rushed in red-cheeked and glowing, it was as if a whirlwind had swept through the dining room. She hadn't even bothered to stop in her suite, but gracefully and unconsciously shrugged off the beige fox-trimmed coat as she sat down. Rachel noted unhappily the traces of sawdust and plaster clinging to her stylish navy dress. "Sorry I'm late," she said as her eyes automatically traveled around the dining room. "We don't seem to be doing a good business tonight; there are eight empty tables."

Exasperated, Roger looked down at his watch. "Kathryn, it's late. Most people had their dinner hours ago."

For a moment Kathryn looked apologetic. "I lost track of the time. I was working on the decoration for the State Suite; you should see what I've done with the windows. . . ." Suddenly their grim expressions registered. "I'm sorry I kept you. I hope you didn't have other plans."

Rachel took a deep breath. "No, but *you* should have other plans."

Kathryn stared at her, a confused expression on her face.

"Kathryn, you're an attractive young woman. You should be out dancing, dining, going to the theater. Almost anything but cajoling carpenters and having dinner with a couple of old fogies like Roger and me." Rachel's voice suddenly became indignant. "There's more to life than worrying about whether the dining room is full and whether we'll need two hundred or two hundred and fifty new bath towels, you know. You should have a man—a husband and children to worry about."

People seldom saw Kathryn angry, but now her lips were pinched white, her jawline was stronger and more determined than ever and her eyes glowed dark and hard. She looked, Roger thought, like a volcano ready to explode. When Rachel reached out to her, she jerked her hand away.

"I'm sorry," Rachel said softly. "But doesn't a friend have responsibilities? I'm very fond of you, as is Roger, and we don't want to see you make a mistake. What sort of friends would we be if we didn't warn you?"

"Rachel, you of all people . . . you must see why I don't want another man in my life. Why I don't want to go through that pain again."

This time Kathryn let Rachel take her hand. "You had a bad experience, but that doesn't mean love is always painful, although you'll never find out if you bury yourself in business, will you?"

"Did it ever occur to you that maybe I don't want to find out? It's ridiculous to think that every woman in the world must have a husband and children. I know what I want to do with my life and I'm doing it—well. It's 1925. Women are showing their knees, bobbing their hair, voting, and sleeping with men they aren't married to. Why must I be conventional and marry? I'm happy with my life. And I don't want to have this conversation ever again.'' She glared at the two sheepish faces. "Rachel, Roger, is that understood?''

They nodded, Roger hoping he'd never see that side of Kathryn again and Rachel deciding she'd have to approach the subject more delicately in the future. After all, if Kathryn were entirely secure about her decision, would she have gotten so angry and defensive?

The headwaiter watched the table closely. Usually Miss Townsend, Mrs. Aarons and Mr. Pennington discussed hotel business through dinner. Miss Townsend always looked so intense, hardly noticing what she was eating. But then again, she had the reputation—to the dismay of the staff—of noticing everything. Tonight the trio was strangely quiet, eating as if their lives depended on it. And Miss Townsend looked angry, stabbing at the food on her plate. Maximilian hoped that nothing was wrong. He sighed; the news he had to give Miss Townsend wouldn't make her any happier.

Chapter Seven

The man in the Victoria Suite was oblivious to the eighteenth-century mahogany table, the wing chair in red-and-white silk and the marble fireplace. He was hunched over a desk, absorbed in an untidy pile of papers, but the Queen Anne desk was too delicate for his broad shoulders and thick arms.

Occasionally as he totaled figures on a sheet of yellow paper a "Damn" would erupt. Then he'd pull out a piece of paper from a file folder and start another column. Finally he circled a total and leaned back in the spindly-legged chair his body dwarfed. His black eyebrows were hunched over his dark eyes, but he was grinning. "This time I've caught him, really caught him," he announced to the empty room. "Damned Bertinelli thought he could pull the wool over my eyes with all those fancy dinners, cigars, bootleg whiskey. Thought I wouldn't do my homework." A scowl blackened his face. Bertinelli had even offered him a girl for the night. Anything to keep me away from the ledgers, he thought angrily. Is there no limit to what that man will stoop to?

Things were different where he came from. People in Welsh mining towns were so filled with the hellfire-and-damnation threats of the chapel preachers that they didn't dare. But money changed people. Maybe it wasn't the fear, just the fact that there wasn't enough money in those starving gray towns to make dishonesty pay. But here in New York . . . here there was lots of money to be made and lots of temptations.

Kathryn stood outside the door, her hand poised to knock. It was her policy to deal with complaints immediately. According to Maximilian, the guest in the Victoria Suite had complained about his dinner. She knocked. Silence. Someone was still up; she could see the yellow light pouring out from under the door. She tried again and finally heard heavy footsteps. The door flew open and she saw a dark, scowling face. For a moment she wished she'd waited until morning. He didn't look as if he'd be easy to pacify.

"Mr. Morgan, I'm—"

"I know exactly who you are and who sent you. Does Bertinelli really think I can be so easily bought?" As Owen Morgan stared out at the woman in the hallway, he couldn't help thinking that at least Bertinelli had good taste in women. She was a stunner, with that fox collar that framed her exquisite face and picked up the reddish highlights in her dark hair. But he knew that to accept a gift like this—tempting though she was—would tie him to Bertinelli and his crooked construction company forever. The nerve of that man! Owen could feel the angry blood rushing to his face. "I want nothing to do with you. Get out of here. Go back to Bertinelli. Make *him* happy."

As his voice rose, Kathryn glanced around her. "Please, Mr. Morgan. It's late. People are sleeping. Could I at least come in and discuss the problem?"

"I'm sure you would like to get in here," Owen said, stretching his arm across the doorway.

Kathryn stepped back, annoyed. "Mr. Morgan, I don't know what your problem is. After all, it was only a steak . . ."

"A steak?" The anger in his tone turned to confusion. "You mean Bertinelli didn't send you?"

"I don't even know a Mr. Bertinelli. Maximilian, the headwaiter, told me that you were dissatisfied with the steak you were served at dinner. I came to apologize. However, if you refuse to listen to me—"

"No, no, I'm sorry. Come in." He dropped his arm and Kathryn crossed the threshold.

"I'm afraid that I've made a rather stupid mistake," Owen said, feeling his face flush. He wasn't used to making apologies, and somehow he knew this beauty—whoever she was—would not make it easy. "Finding a beautiful young woman

knocking on my hotel door late at night, well, you see . . .
I thought you were . . .''

Angry realization flashed in Kathryn's mind. Why did men
refuse to accept women in the business world? ''You thought
I was a prostitute.''

It was the first time Owen had ever heard a woman use
that word. His chapel-going upbringing made him cringe.
''Well, shall we say that I didn't realize you were a lady. And
for that I apologize.''

''Maybe you were right—that I'm not a proper lady. But I
am a proper hostess,'' she added briskly, ''and I came to
apologize for the unsatisfactory meal and invite you to dine
again. Courtesy of the hotel.''

''To dine with you?'' he asked.

''No, I am afraid that is impossible,'' she announced automatically. But his invitation made her look at him more
closely. He radiated a certain strength, an appealing vitality.
He wasn't above medium height, but his limbs were thick
and powerful. His squared-off face was handsome. Not
smooth and perfect, but virile and rugged. There was a crisp
curl to his black hair. His alert dark eyes stared at her until
she looked away and repeated, ''Impossible. It's against hotel
rules to socialize with hotel guests.''

''Tell me who's in charge and why he won't permit the
rules to be changed in certain exceptional cases. I'll talk to
him.''

''Rules are not made to be altered.''

''Do you mean that if we had dinner together the whole
hotel would grind to a halt? Busboys would lure female guests
out dancing. And chambermaids would be so busy having
cocktails with male guests that the bathtubs would never be
scrubbed.''

For the first time Kathryn felt her anger dissipating and her
lips turning up in a smile. ''Not quite that bad. But it is a
hotel policy. To prevent . . . awkward situations.''

''And would having dinner with me be awkward?''

''Well, not exactly.''

''Good. At eight tomorrow.''

''But I didn't say—''

''Yes,'' Owen said, ''but your voice sounded less firm.
Think of it this way. You do want your guests to feel com-

fortable, don't you?'' Kathryn nodded. ''Well, I'm embarrassed about mistaking you for someone else earlier. And only you can relieve that embarrassment. It's your duty as an employee of the hotel.''

''Eight o'clock in the main dining room,'' Kathryn said, walking to the door.

She knew she should be annoyed—she was breaking her own hotel policy—but for some reason she was not unhappy about the thought of seeing Owen Morgan again. Remembering what a good-looking man he was, Kathryn decided that by dining with him she might kill two birds with one stone: pacify an angry guest and silence Rachel. She sighed as she stepped out of the elevator into the brightly lit lobby. Not that Rachel would let it begin and end with one dinner date. But, Kathryn decided, he doesn't even know who I am, so I can very easily slip out of his life again.

It was Maximilian who ruined her plan by announcing loudly, ''Good evening, Miss Townsend,'' as soon as they appeared in the dining room.

''Related to the owner?'' Owen asked, staring at Kathryn. She *was* full of surprises.

''Not exactly.'' He cocked his head inquisitively, and she said, ''I am the owner. Don't look so surprised and please don't say, 'But you're a woman.' I've heard it too many times before.''

Owen gazed across the table at her. She was so small and fragile-looking. Except for the strong line of her chin. And the determination in her eyes. They looked like fine-tempered steel. He pitied the poor man who didn't heed their message. ''You are an exceptional woman.''

''Why? Because I can do more than wear clothes, have babies and polish my nails?'' She paused. ''Do I threaten you?''

''You're defensive, aren't you? Honestly, I admire what you've done. You don't have to fight me.''

''Good. That should make the meal more tolerable. May I suggest the sliced steak with bordelaise sauce? It's the chef's specialty.''

As the dinner progressed, Kathryn's feelings toward Owen gradually thawed. By the time the dessert arrived, she had to admit to herself that not only was he good-looking, but he was also intelligent and entertaining. Most of all, she appreciated his lack of pretense. He seemed perfectly at ease wearing a tuxedo and eating in the elegant dining room. His manner never faltered. He knew which fork to use and treated the staff with the proper degree of cordial familiarity, but Kathryn sensed that none of it mattered to him.

By the time they drank their coffee, Kathryn was oblivious to Rachel staring across the dining room at them in delight and amazement. She found herself entranced by Owen's lilting voice. "I was born in Wales," he explained. "The south—coal-mining country. Beautiful green country except for the slag—mountains of it. And the towns. Pinched little gray stone houses. Gray streets. Gray people."

"You don't sound as if you liked it very much," Kathryn said.

"When I was growing up, it was all I knew. I knew that when I was old enough I'd go down into the mines like my father, his father, all his brothers and most of the men and the boys in town. I scarcely realized there was an alternative—none of us did. I have the war, bloody as it was, to thank for saving me from the mines. To a sixteen-year-old, the prospect of glory on the battlefield was infinitely preferable to a lifetime underground.

"Funny thing," he said with a bitter laugh, "there were times in the trenches, when I didn't know whether I was going to survive until morning, that the idea of stooping over in a mine with a crowbar and pick ten hours a day sounded good. But," he said more cheerfully, "I survived it with only a little piece of shrapnel buried in my arm."

Her tears took Kathryn by surprise. She didn't know why her eyes should well up listening to this stranger, but the image of him crouching in a cold, wet, rat-infested trench while the bombs sent shrapnel and dirt and bodies flying was sad and frightening. Why should it matter to her? She shook her head to free it of the irrational emotions and stared down at the table so he wouldn't see her tears. Rachel and Roger were right: she *was* overtired.

"In the last days of the war we got a new lieutenant. He was just out to the front and green as grass. The two of us ended up trapped in a trench behind enemy lines. A German stumbled on us and aimed his rifle at the sleeping lieutenant. I grabbed for it, but not in time. Poor bugger never woke up. Killing a sleeping man! You wouldn't do that to an animal. After the war I paid a duty call to the lieutenant's family and discovered they were a lord and lady and lived in a house bigger than our entire village. I told them how their son had died and tried to make it sound less futile. Two weeks later I received a letter from Lord Brattlesby. He wanted to send me to Cambridge. It's where his son would have gone. Don't know whether he was just grateful for my efforts or thought he'd do a spot of philanthropy for a coal miner's son. But I went.''

''And that's the last you ever saw of Wales?'' She didn't know why, but she was pleased to be unraveling the riddle of Owen Morgan.

''No, I never finished. After two years I went back to Wales. The mines were closed. The men were out of work. It seemed hopeless, but I wanted to help. I went to work for the unions—writing reports and letters and speeches, putting my education to use, trying to make the damned English politicians show a little compassion and take some action.''

''How did you happen to come to the United States?'' Kathryn asked.

He hesitated. ''That's a long story and for another day.''

Kathryn wouldn't admit it—even to herself—but she'd been slightly off kilter ever since having dinner with Owen Morgan. He kept slipping uninvited into her mind. His face appeared in the middle of ledger sheets. When she signed correspondence, his name instead of hers came to mind. She kept expecting to run into him, but she didn't, and she told herself that was good. Handsome and charming though he was, she simply didn't have time. She had a hotel—soon to be two hotels—to oversee. No time for friends or a lover. Kathryn blushed. Now what made her think of Owen Morgan as a lover? Ridiculous! He hadn't shown the least interest in her in that way. You couldn't even call him a friend. Still, her face felt hot with embarrassment.

A few nights after her dinner with him, she found an excuse to study the guest register. Owen hadn't checked out. She experienced a brief feeling of annoyance that he hadn't called her. No, she told herself sternly, you don't want to see him again. And you'd better stay out of his way until he leaves.

But the crisis of the next night made her advice impossible to keep.

Chapter Eight

The saxophone wailed. Couples circled the shadowy dance floor, clinging to each other. Moody music, clinking glasses and hushed whispers surrounded them like a cocoon.

"Will you think I'm naive if I admit that I've never been to a place like this before and I find it fascinating?" Kathryn said, recalling the unwavering fashion in which Owen had led her to the nondescript building off Sheridan Square in Greenwich Village. It looked no different from any of the other brownstones that lined the street, but he'd unhesitatingly rapped on that door. A small window slid open, and Owen flashed a red card in front of the eyes that peered out. The door opened and they followed a tall, dark-skinned man through a maze of dimly lit corridors and finally to another door—and another world. Gilt mirrors lined the mahogany-paneled walls. Hundreds of bottles of all shapes, sizes and colors lined the bar. Waiters in tails hovered amongst the small candlelit tables. Music and laughter filled the air.

"What, never sampled the pleasures of a speakeasy? You have been sheltered. Don't tell me you're a teetotaler," Owen said with a laugh.

"No, nothing like that. Just too busy." Kathryn was feeling warm and mellow and vaguely wondered if it was due to the pink gin or perhaps merely the forbidden, late-night atmosphere of the club.

Owen reached across the table and patted her hand. With a shock she discovered she liked the touch of his warm flesh against hers. "You really should have more fun. Go places. Do things. It isn't right for such a beautiful young woman to devote all her attention to business."

223

"That's what Rachel nags me about—constantly. I know all the arguments by heart."

"Who's Rachel?"

"Nominally, she's the assistant manager at the Townsend Manor. But she's also a dear friend."

"She sounds like a wise lady. You wouldn't be here tonight if it hadn't been for the overflowing bathtub, would you? Admit it."

Kathryn had to nod her agreement.

"See, it's fate that brought us together."

"No," she said, "it's architecture."

"Architecture?"

"Yes. The hotel was designed so that the two largest suites are one above the other. So Lord Dadleigh had the suite above yours."

"And," Owen said with another laugh, "he's an old souse who fell into a drunken stupor in the tub, letting the water overflow and bringing you to my suite at two o'clock in the morning. When I opened my door and saw you standing there—again—I thought I was dreaming."

His voice was soft and intimate and it scared Kathryn. I haven't had enough gin to let him get away with this, she thought. "Hardly a dream. I was standing there with two chambermaids and a plumber and announcing you had to get out."

Kathryn tried to forget how her heart had pounded at the prospect of seeing Owen again. How she'd assured the night manager that it was her responsibility to cope with the problem. And how handsome Owen had looked—his hair tousled, his eyes full of sleep—when he came to the door in his maroon silk dressing gown.

"Details, details. Don't you have any romance in your soul? No," he said, holding his hand up, "I expect I know what your answer will be: No time for it. Shall we dance instead?"

He guided her through the maze of candlelit tables to the dance floor. When he took her in his arms, she suddenly decided she must have had too much gin. Her body seemed soft and weak as she leaned against the solidity of his chest. Gradually the other dancers, the music, the tables, the room faded into the dimness, and she was aware only of Owen's arms around her.

"I see that Lord Dadleigh checked out yesterday," Kathryn said, looking at Roger. "Did he put up a fuss about those extra charges on his bill for plumbers and water damage?"

Sometimes Roger imagined he could see the wheels turning in Kathryn's head. From the first day she'd walked into his office, he'd known how exceptional she was. What he hadn't realized was how quickly and how brilliantly she would master all the complexities of running a hotel. He'd taught her the basics, but she'd taken them and sailed far beyond him. Always creative. Forever coming up with innovative solutions to tough problems. No challenge seemed too great for Kathryn. Occasionally Roger wondered if she didn't secretly relish the challenge of catering to especially difficult guests. Just to prove that she could.

"People, that's what's important," she would say. "You have to know what your guests like and how to provide it for them." To that end Kathryn kept in her office a card index listing the likes and dislikes of all her important guests. If the British ambassador liked Dover sole, she made sure it was available when he dined with them. If a certain society matron wanted to use the hotel for occasional solitary drinking binges, her privacy was assured. The hotel was always very discreet about its guests—for their sake as well as its own. Kathryn was determined that no scandal touch the Townsend Manor, not if they were to attract the right sort of guest. If guests proved not to be of the right sort, their names were put on her personal "No" list, and heaven help any poor clerk who ever gave them another reservation.

The hotel's guest list was impressive. Diplomats, businessmen, old New York money. They all liked the quiet, refined, elegant oasis Kathryn had created. "Let the flappers go jump in someone else's fountains," she said. "I want the people who will keep coming back year after year. I don't want to be in fashion this year, forgotten next."

Sometimes Roger wondered why the staff, with a few exceptions, was so loyal to Kathryn. She was demanding and could be ruthless when she discovered an employee who wasn't living up to her expectations. Perhaps it was because she'd managed to impart some of her enormous pride in the Townsend Manor to all of her employees. From the temperamental chef right down to the youngest, smooth-cheeked bellhop, they all shared her dream of making their hotel the best in New York. Perhaps it was also because she made it a point to know every employee by name and could inquire about sick mothers or new grandchildren.

"No, Lord Dadleigh paid his bill without a murmur. I should think he's rather used to that sort of thing," Roger said.

"Good. Any other problems?"

Rachel's voice was puzzled. "I have a rather strange one. One of the guests has been scaring the maids."

"What's he doing?" Kathryn demanded. If her employees were loyal to her, she was also fiercely protective of them.

"That's the problem: he isn't doing anything. He just sits in his room all day long. One of the girls says he looks like a corpse, but then she's Irish and her imagination tends to get the better of her sometimes. I haven't seen him myself. I did check with room service. They haven't heard from him. Since he never goes out, it's a mystery how he eats."

"Well, that's a new one, and I thought I'd heard them all," Kathryn said. "I'll check on our mystery guest myself when I have a minute. I won't have our girls being terrorized."

"At least he's quiet," Roger said with a chuckle. "Remember the old lady with the parrots?"

"Yes, I remember her. Now it seems funny, but it wasn't then. I remember we had to keep all the rooms on her corridor vacant so no one would complain about the squawking. And you, Roger, wouldn't ask her to leave because she claimed to be some remote relative of the Rockefellers. You really are a snob. But," she said, looking at Rachel and then fondly back to Roger, "I don't know what I'd do without the two of you."

Roger got up. "I will leave now before you change your mind."

Rachel stayed seated. As Roger closed the door behind him, Kathryn turned to her. "What happened? You look like the cat who swallowed a canary."

"I'm just pleased that you decided to take my advice," she said.

"What advice is that?"

"The advice you said you didn't want to hear . . . about having some fun. Your Mr. Morgan is a very handsome gentleman."

Kathryn's smile faded. "He is not my Mr. Morgan. And I've seen him only a couple of times. If you are keeping score, he's taken me to dinner twice, dancing once and to one concert. He prefers Beethoven, by the way. If you want to know any more, I suggest you interview him. And lest you get any ideas—"

"Do you like him?"

"I barely know him. We're acquaintances, that's all."

"Do you mind if I give you some more advice?"

"If I said I minded, would it stop you?"

"Kathryn, don't let him get away. Please."

"You make the man sound like some poor little animal to be trapped." Kathryn's eyes took on a gentler light as she looked over at Rachel. "I love you. You are my best friend. I sincerely don't know what I'd do without you—personally or professionally. But I have my own life to lead."

Her voice assumed a sharper tone, and Rachel could feel her pain. "Love is an indulgence, and I don't have the time or the emotional energy for it. I've only just begun to live my dream. I don't intend to stop at two hotels. I'll have the finest hotels in San Francisco, Chicago, Washington. And I'll take the Townsend name to London and Paris and Rome."

"Kathryn, do you ever stop to wonder why you're compelled to keep proving yourself? No matter how you might try to justify your obsessive love affair with success, I think I know the real reason: you want to prove to the brother you haven't seen hide nor hair of for years that you can do it. That women don't have to be weak and stupid and submissive. So you are trying to be a superwoman. But can't you see that you're still his victim now as much as if he'd locked you up in that asylum? If you keep on with this crazy pursuit of wealth and power just to prove something to a memory, you'll never be frce of the past. But if you can acknowledge he's the demon driving you, then maybe you can start acting more like a woman."

It was the first time Rachel had ever seen Kathryn speechless, and for a moment she was afraid she'd been too honest.

Standing up, she patted Kathryn's white-knuckled fist. "I'm sorry; I didn't mean to hurt you. Just promise me you'll do some honest thinking. And that you'll give Mr. Morgan a chance. Maybe you'll discover he has something to offer that a whole chain of hotels can't."

Chapter Nine

A light snow had begun to fall, coating the streets and sidewalks in white and muffling the noise of late-night traffic along Broadway. Snowflakes danced in the lights and fell on the crowds coming out of the theater.

"Confess," Owen said. "You loved it."

"Well," Kathryn said, "I'll admit that Charlie Chaplin *is* funny."

"Funny. There must be a word beyond funny for that man. I almost lost all the buttons off my shirt I laughed so hard. And don't tell me you didn't laugh. I heard you. Admit it, haven't you been missing something—like the fun and frivolous side of life?"

"Why do I get the feeling that you and Rachel are conspiring behind my back?"

"Maybe we should. For your own good." Owen grabbed her hand and stepped off the curb. As if by magic, a taxi glided to a halt in front of him. "I have a cure for your condition—ice cream. I know where they serve the most exotic varieties in the city. Kinds you've never even dreamed of." Sensing her reluctance, he said, "I know it's not exactly the right weather, but once in a while we all have to do something that defies common sense."

When they were seated at a round, marble-topped table in a small restaurant in Little Italy, Kathryn said, "They greeted you like a long-lost son; you must eat an awful lot of ice cream."

"I do. That's why I invested in the restaurant."

"Tell me, do you have interest in hotels, too? Is that why

you've been so attentive, trying to learn all my secrets? I must warn you: I'm not loose-lipped.''

Owen laughed. ''No, I'm not the competition. Restaurants. Stocks. Bonds. A partnership in a cosmetics company. Now that respectable women are wearing lipstick and rouge, it's a big business. But they all more or less support my real love.''

''That sounds intriguing. Who is the lady?''

''Actually, there are several. But mainly stallions and geldings.'' Seeing her puzzled expression, Owen explained, ''A stable of Thoroughbred racehorses. I have very high hopes for several of them. Kentucky Derby. Preakness. Who knows, maybe another Man o' War. Right now, though, they are strictly for pleasure.''

''An expensive pleasure.''

''Yes, but have you ever watched a Thoroughbred run? That grace and incredible strength and power. The way those slender legs support such a massive body. It's more thrilling than staring at a stock certificate.'' His eyes hovered over Kathryn's face. ''I can tell from the way you're trying not to frown that you don't approve.''

''It's none of my business,'' she said primly.

''But making money is only fun if you can enjoy spending it. I'm sure old John Jacob Astor enjoyed amassing his millions. It's his descendants who've had it so long they don't think it's proper to enjoy it.''

Kathryn held up her hands and said with a laugh, ''All right, I give up. No more lectures. You're making me feel very conservative and boring. If you promise to keep quiet, I'll promise to go out tomorrow and do something ridiculously . . . frivolous.''

Owen laughed. The sound was deep and manly and it delighted Kathryn. ''Your problem is so acute you can't even say the word, can you? I'll give you exactly twenty-four hours to buy something stunningly frivolous. To spend your money like a drunken sailor. It's your first assignment in Owen Morgan's How to Have Fun course. I have a feeling that you will become my best—and favorite—pupil.''

As his tone turned from light to serious, Kathryn watched him nervously and quickly redirected the conversation. ''With all your horses, you must have a home in the country.''

So the unflappable businesswoman is nervous about romance, Owen noted. "Actually, I have a town house in the city."

"Then why are you staying at the Townsend Manor?"

"Because my house is being painted."

"It must be an enormous house. You've been at the hotel for two weeks."

He smiled, pleased to know that she'd been counting. "No, it's not that big. The painting only took three days, but I met you and I couldn't leave."

"But that's . . . that's ridiculous. Extravagant. With our rates and a suite . . ."

"It was worth it," he said with a grin.

"Owen, I'm glad you like the hotel, but—"

"It wasn't the hotel I liked so much, it was you. I'm sure you realize that."

She glanced down at her watch. "It's late. I really should be going. We have a wedding breakfast scheduled for tomorrow and—"

"What? Before you've sampled the ice cream? What flavor do you like?"

It would be simpler to give in to him, eat her ice cream and go home. "Vanilla," she said without looking at the menu.

He gestured to the hovering waiter. "Giovanni, we are going to change this beautiful lady's life. Bring her a dish of your extraordinary pistachio ice cream and we'll show her what she's been missing."

Morning was Kathryn's favorite time of day. It was when her hotel was at its busiest best. Her office was right off the lobby, and she kept her door open to make sure everything was flowing smoothly and to jump in if it wasn't. This morning a steady stream of people flowed into the dining room, where starched yellow tablecloths, delicate blue-and-white china, silver urns of coffee and mounds of flaky pastry and fresh fruit awaited them. Bellhops, in immaculate, freshly pressed uniforms, stood at attention or carried a never-ending stream of luggage bearing labels from luxury steamships and the best hotels around the world. Behind the gold grillework of the cashier's desk a pale young man presided. Fashionably thin women in expensive fur coats stood by the front door waiting for the cars that would carry them off to buy yet more furs and hats and jewelry.

Kathryn also liked this time of day best because it was when she felt most organized. She'd had her meeting with Roger and Rachel and been briefed by the night manager. The mail had been read. She felt her finger was firmly planted on the pulse of the hotel. In front of her lay a yellow pad with her handwritten list of things to be done that day. She took great satisfaction in ticking off each item as it was accomplished. There was also the challenge of the unexpected. And with at least one hundred guests and forty-five employees, there was always plenty of that.

But this morning as Kathryn stared out her door at the bustle in the lobby, she suddenly realized she wasn't seeing it. All her senses were attuned to watching for Owen. It made her angry. He was taking up far too much of her time. She could not afford to drift off into daydreams like some lovestruck teenager. Besides, she felt strangely—what was the word?—disconcerted, off balance when she was with him. How dared he tell her how to live her life? What business was it of his if she wanted to eat vanilla ice cream?

She prided herself on understanding people, on her ability to analyze their strengths and weaknesses and to know instinctively where they were headed. But with Owen . . . She didn't know what he wanted. He'd obviously made his mark in the business world, but money and power and their trappings seemed to hold little appeal for him. He claimed he wanted to enjoy life, but he certainly wasn't like the wealthy, self-indulgent playboys who occasionally stayed at the hotel.

Owen Morgan unnerved her. He had an uncanny ability to penetrate her smooth, carefully constructed exterior and reach down to the woman beneath. Kathryn didn't know what to make of him; sometimes he scared her, but more often she had to fight down the warm feeling that arose in her chest every time she thought of him.

The telephone on her desk shrilled, making her jump.

It was Roger. "About our mystery man . . ." With a sinking heart Kathryn realized that she'd forgotten to check on him as she'd promised. "Perhaps you'd better come up here immediately and see for yourself. Room three-twelve."

The door was closed when she arrived. She knocked. It opened a few inches and Roger's face appeared. "Good. It's you. I thought we should keep this quiet," he said as he cautiously opened the door wider. His voice cracked nervously. Kathryn had never seen Roger's butlerlike calm so shattered. "Kathryn, I'm afraid it's bad."

The room was a shambles. Chairs, tables, lamps were overturned as if some powerful wild beast had been on the rampage. The silk brocade drapes had been torn down and lay in a red heap in the middle of the floor. The mirror over the dresser was covered with a black spiderweb of cracks as if something had been hurled at it—repeatedly. A Gideon Bible was splayed open beneath it. She turned to Roger.

He shook his head. His face was unnaturally pale. "I'm afraid you haven't seen the worst yet." He placed his hand gently on her arm and guided her over to the bed. The mattress, as if it were an animal, had been neatly eviscerated. An enormous black-handled butcher's knife was plunged through the pillow.

Kathryn looked at the knife and shuddered. This was one of the prettiest and lightest rooms in the hotel, but now a heavy, cold atmosphere seemed to hang over it. Suddenly Kathryn found it hard to breathe.

Roger sensed her distress. "Shouldn't we get out of here and call the police?"

"I don't want the police. The man undoubtedly registered under a false name; they could never track him down. And if we call them, the newspapers are bound to catch on and we don't need that sort of publicity. In fact, the fewer people who know about it here in the hotel the better, too. Rumors have a way of getting blown all out of proportion. Before we know it . . . Here, help me put all the furniture back. We'll fold the drapes up and send them out for dry cleaning. The broken mirror—well, accidents do happen."

She walked over to the bed and gingerly pulled out the knife. With a sigh of relief she turned to Roger. "It's crazy, but I almost expected to find blood on it. Tonight the two of us can carry the mattress down to some dark corner of the basement. And, Roger, let's not rent this room for a few weeks." She looked around, almost afraid of what she might see. "Give it a chance to . . . to get back to normal."

One thing Kathryn had learned in her career was to put things behind her and forget about them. She and Roger would hide the evidence from Room three-twelve; she'd made the decision not to call in the police; chances were the man would never return, so there was nothing more she could do. Tomorrow would bring different problems. In two weeks she would have completely forgotten about the mystery man.

If only she could forget about Owen Morgan. But he wouldn't let himself be forgotten. She would find herself thinking of his eyes. When he looked at her, his eyes were like smoldering coals so intense they sometimes scared her.

Finally she slapped her hand down on her desk—right where Owen's face had appeared unbidden moments before—and exclaimed, "Damn it, I've had enough."

Maude Willis, who had been Kathryn's personal secretary for three years, couldn't believe her eyes or ears when Kathryn walked out of her office at two o'clock and announced, "I'll see you tomorrow morning." Miss Willis polished her bifocals and looked again before she remembered to ask Kathryn where she could be reached.

"I can't be reached. Call Roger if you need anything," Kathryn said, turning on her heel and disappearing into the lobby.

She was nervous as a schoolgirl on her first date as she walked down the corridor to the Victoria Suite, but her mind was made up, her speech rehearsed.

Owen answered the door immediately. A smile lit up his face as soon as he saw Kathryn. "Are you going to invite me in this time?" she asked. Without waiting for an answer, she slipped in, careful not to let him see what she'd left in the corridor.

"I'm sorry," Owen said, reaching for his suit jacket. "I didn't know you were coming, but . . ." He smiled at her, and Kathryn felt her heart leap. "I am delighted to see you. You didn't bring any plumbers along this time, did you?"

"No, I just brought this." She thrust an elegantly wrapped box at him, then stopped and stared at it for a moment, as if it might explode. "Go ahead. Open it." As Owen untied the bow and rummaged through the tissue paper, her eyes never left his hands. For a second she felt exposed, vulnerable.

Then she shook off the feeling. When he extracted the object from the box, she let out a long, tension-releasing sigh. There was no turning back. "It was the most frivolous thing I could find. It's a gift. For you."

"Why, why, it's a swizzle stick, isn't it?" He sounded confused, not sure what reaction was expected. "A gold swizzle stick with a jade—what is this?—a Buddha on top. It's . . ."

"His eyes are diamond chips and it's ugly, that's what it is. But expensive and useless. I trust that it fits your definition of frivolous? No, wait a minute, there's more," she said, crossing to the door.

"I'm almost afraid to look. I really don't think I could use a mink umbrella stand."

Without a word Kathryn disappeared into the hall and reappeared with a room service cart. On the starched white cloth were arranged a bouquet of tiny pink orchids, two bowls of pistachio ice cream and a silvery ice bucket with a bottle of champagne nestled in it. Her nervousness was barely concealed as she announced, "I thought we should drink to the fate that brought us together." All of a sudden the perplexed expression that had darkened Owen's face turned into a smile, a wide smile that lit his whole face. As soon as she saw it, Kathryn's nervousness fled; she had made the right decision.

For a moment they stood on opposite sides of the table just staring at each other, trying to deal with the intensity of emotion that besieged them.

Finally Owen spoke. "Does this mean that you love me as much as I love you?" His heart stopped beating as he waited for her answer. Surely fate would not be so cruel as to bring her this close, then snatch her away. Kathryn had never looked so beautiful. He ached to take her in his arms and hold her—forever.

"Yes," she said, her voice strong and sure. "If being in love means that I can't get you out of my mind and I feel like my heart is on fire every time I look at you, then yes, I love you. Very much."

Chapter Ten

His sharp, eager eyes watched the scissors shear through the newsprint. The white dropped away along the razor-thin line, leaving only the photograph. The wedding photograph.

Edward smiled. His sister looked so pleased with herself. And her handsome new husband was grinning down so adoringly at her. Owen Morgan. Estimated to be worth two million dollars. How *did* the little bitch attract them?

He didn't really require the newspaper photo to remember. The acid of jealousy had etched every detail of the ceremony into his mind. She hadn't deprived him of that right. He had attended her wedding. And, he chided himself, lingered too long. The groom had caught sight of him slipping out the back of the church. Edward's thin white lips stretched as he thought of Kathryn. How he would have enjoyed watching her face when she saw him. He imagined the fear in her eyes—like those of a small, trapped animal—just like when she was a little girl and he'd caught her disobeying his orders. Too scared to defy him. Hating him for ruining her fun. White-faced. Her little head bowed. Her lips trembling, trying to hold in the sound of tears.

He turned to the leather-bound book. It was the sort of scrapbook a proud parent would keep. In each of the hundreds of clippings the name Kathryn Townsend was underlined in red ink which bled through the thin newsprint, leaving small marks, like wounds. Every article focused on her and her hotels. "Elegant," "fashionable," "sumptuous"—the words jumped out at him. Taunting him. She had stolen the success that was meant to be his, just as surely as she had stolen his money.

His bony white fingers flipped through the pages. He didn't need to read; he knew every word by heart. Every day he studied the scrapbook. Faithfully. To keep alive the memories. And the hatred.

He slipped the wedding photo into the album and closed it. The pleasure of pasting the photograph in he would save until tomorrow. Carefully he placed the scissors on top. Staring at the long, thin steel blades, he was reminded of something. The memory produced a sudden jolt of excitement but remained beyond his grasp. Ah, yes, that was it. His eyes took fire at the memory. A blade slashing through silk. Plunging into the softness of a pillow. The knife he'd used to destroy that perfect little hotel room of hers. Pity she couldn't know he was the culprit.

Book Three

Chapter One

Venice
January 1926

"Your eyes have the strange habit of changing color. Sometimes they're gold—or perhaps something more poetic, like amber. Sometimes they're hazel. Right now I could swear they were green, a bluish green. Must be the reflection of the sky."

Owen and Kathryn both laughed as they turned toward the rain-splattered window of the cafe. A leaden gray smudge in the distance was all they could see of the Grand Canal. The Church of San Marco was a vague domed shape blurred by the rain and sleet. The vast piazza was awash and empty. Even the hundreds of strutting and pecking pigeons were gone, sheltering under the massive colonnades which lined three sides of the square.

Kathryn didn't bother to disguise her shudder. "You don't like Venice, do you?" Owen asked.

"Well, perhaps if the sun were shining . . ." She wanted to like it for his sake. "But it's so old."

Owen laughed. A strong, solid laugh. "That's precisely what's so wonderful about it. Can't you just imagine what it was like being a seventeenth-century duchess living in a palazzo on the Grand Canal?"

"Probably cold, damp and smelly." Kathryn frowned. "Do you know, I counted three cabbages, two dead cats and I don't know how many wine bottles floating past the Doge's Palace. Don't these people have any idea of sanitation? Imagine algae growing on your front doorstep! And from the crumbling look of the outsides, I hate to think what the insides of those so-called palazzos are like."

"Kathryn, love, your soul is still suffering from a severe deficiency of romance. And here I was hoping that a honeymoon in Venice with an extraordinarily romantic Welshman would be the cure." He took her hand in his. "I expect that, given the chance, you'd have the whole city scrubbed down, repainted and renovated like one of your old hotels."

Her smile was sheepish. "You understand me too well." Her hand tingled under his. Loving Owen was . . . was more glorious than anything she could ever have imagined. It was extraordinarily exciting to feel his body inside hers, yet at the same time perfectly peaceful—as if it were meant to be. As if two integral parts of her own body and soul were finally coming together.

Making love with Owen was different from how it had been with Adam. Owen brought more experience with him, but if the thrill of newness was gone, so was the fumbling uncertainty. It was always as exciting as the first time and even more deeply satisfying. Instinctively each seemed to know what the other wanted, and they gave unselfishly as an expression of their love. Every time they came together they found their love immeasurably enriched and the bond between them strengthened.

Kathryn savored the last bite of her hazelnut ice cream—gelato, the Italians called it. It was delicious and quite unlike American ice cream. Perhaps she should introduce it into her menus. "I saw the artist today," she said, licking the last creamy drop from her lips, "that handsome young man I hired to paint a mural for the Townsend Manor. He's already booked his passage and will be arriving in New York at the end of February."

Seeing the light of enthusiasm in his wife's eyes, Owen asked, "Is that glimmer for the good-looking artist or for the prospect of going home and getting back to work?"

"Owen," she said, squeezing his hand, "it's been wonderful, a dream honeymoon, but—"

"But you're worried about your hotels. Even though you get a daily cable from Roger assuring you that he hasn't run them into the ground, you still don't believe things are done properly unless you're there supervising."

"I suppose you're right, but—"

"But you'll have to spend a bit less time at the hotels now that you have your own home to supervise."

"Home?" Her surprise showed.

"Don't worry. My Mrs. Blair is an excellent housekeeper. You won't have to play chatelaine unless you want to."

"But my suite at the hotel . . . I assumed we'd live there. It's perfectly adequate," Kathryn protested. How could he expect her to leave the hotel?

"For one person maybe, but we're two now," Owen reminded her.

"Well, it's big enough for the two of us."

"Kathryn, I have my own home, remember. I bought it for the wife I would someday have—and our children. We can't live in three impersonal rooms in a hotel. Of course, I want you to redecorate the house, replace every stick of furniture if that's what you'd like. It's yours now."

"Why didn't you tell me this before?" she said angrily, pushing her plate aside. "I must be at the hotel all the time to deal with problems. For instance, suppose something goes wrong in the middle of the night and—"

"Then the night manager will deal with it. I assume he's competent or you wouldn't have hired him. From now on, your place at night is next to me in bed—in our bed. Like any other wife." Owen's voice was firm.

It unnerved Owen the way Kathryn stared at him, as if she were seeing him for the first time and didn't like what she saw. Her eyes darkened.

"Owen, I told you, I am not some blushing young bride. I am a businesswoman with responsibilities."

Owen's tone was patient. "I understand. I have businesses to run, too, but you don't see me sleeping at the stables, or the factories, or the restaurants, do you? No. I hire good people to run them and let them do it. And I don't stand over their shoulders twenty-four hours a day. You are going to have to learn to do the same."

"I suppose you don't think it's seemly that your wife has a business. I suppose you want me to be there poised with your pipe and slippers in my little hands when you walk in the door." She paused, as her anger built. "And how dare you tell me how to run my business? I've been doing it on

my own for years. What I don't need is another man to tell
me how to run my life."

"Kathryn, I didn't mean . . . Come, love, let's not argue.
This is our honeymoon. I love you, and the last thing in the
world I want is to make you unhappy. But I do want to carry
my bride over my own threshold. Call me old-fashioned in
that respect, but it's hardly and unreasonable request, is it?"

"That's not all you're asking for. What you want is a devoted little slave, someone to make sure your shirts are ironed
and your meals are hot. Well, I refuse to iron and I don't
know how to cook. I'm not a homebody, which you knew
fully well when you married me."

"But I thought . . ." His tone was laced with hurt and
anger. "A home of her own—isn't that what every woman
wants?"

This is what proper little girls want . . . Nice young ladies
don't . . . Women can't . . . The familiar words rose out of
the past to taunt her. Only the voice had changed.

You're as bad as Edward, she almost spat out before she
remembered that as far as Owen knew, she was an only child.
For a moment she stared at him before springing out of her
chair, grabbing her coat and stalking to the door. There she
halted her steps and turned to him. "I'm not every woman,
Owen Morgan, remember that!"

Everything in Owen said, "Follow her," but by the time
he'd attracted the waiter's attention and asked for the check,
she was on the other side of the piazza—a small blue figure
running through the rain—and he was too angry. How dared
she refuse to live in her husband's house? Most husbands
wouldn't even permit their wives to work. Why couldn't she
understand that she was a wife now, as well as a hotel owner;
that marriage meant changes for both of them?

Damned if he'd try to find Kathryn. She could come to
him and apologize.

For hours Kathryn wandered in the rain. Through the dark,
dreary back streets, no bigger than alleyways. Across the open
squares, deserted and slick with puddles. Along the narrow
canals, black and bottomless beneath the driving rain. Once,
as she forced herself over yet another one of the humped little
bridges that crossed the small canals, a policeman inquired

in halting English if the signorina was unwell. She shook her head and hurried on, afraid that Owen had sent the police to find her.

Owen—there was no escaping him. Or her mistake. She shuddered, thinking of her mother and Jessica and what a man could do to a woman, remembering the vow never to let that happen to her. She had, and now she was trapped thousands of miles from home with a man she barely knew. Backing into the doorway of a small shop, she scrambled frantically through her purse, although she knew what she would find: Owen had her passport and money. All she had was a handful of lire.

She wandered aimlessly, staring into shop windows but not seeing the sparkling hand-blown glass, the spidery lace, the leather gloves in a rainbow of soft earth tones; oblivious to the rain, which dripped relentlessly from the roofs and ran over the cobblestones in small rivers. The stylish, high-heeled shoes she'd bought in Rome were so waterlogged they lost their shape and her feet slipped unstably from side to side. Her new silk stockings from Paris were mud-spattered and clung damply to her legs. Icy raindrops soaked into her coat, sending up the smell of wet wool to mingle with the ever-present odor of damp and decay.

Emerging from the maze of dark alleys like a mole from a tunnel, she found herself facing the open expanse of the Grand Canal. She continued walking. It didn't matter where she was. A few minutes later things began looking familiar—the blue-and-white awning of a cafe, the massive bronze doors of a church and finally the pink stucco front of her hotel. Because it seemed the easiest thing to do, she pushed through the revolving door. The concierge stared at her with amazement as she asked for her key and slowly trudged up the ancient staircase, leaving a trail of damp behind her. He shook his head and muttered to himself about people who didn't have the sense to carry umbrellas. He decided that she must be American. The English, they always carried umbrellas.

Peeling off her clothes, Kathryn dropped them in a wet heap on the marble floor of the cavernous bathroom and climbed into bed. The sheets were icy on her body as she slipped between them. Wet strands of hair clung coldly to her face, but the effort to brush them away seemed too great. She shivered—one of those awful internal shivers that made it seem as if all her organs were shaking. Burrowing her head into the pile of pillows, she drew the comforter up to her ears. The down sank around her, molding her body like a warm glove. She discovered that if she lay absolutely still and didn't move from the spot her body had warmed, she no longer felt cold—merely numb. And the shaking stopped.

If only her mind were numb. But it kept repeating the dreadful litany over and over again: I shouldn't have married him. I'm trapped. I shouldn't have married him. . . . The words circled round and round her mind, producing fear and anger. Primarily anger at herself for letting it happen. She'd risked so much to escape Edward; now she'd walked into another trap. Lured in by a handsome man with dark eyes and a dry sense of humor who claimed he loved her, but he wanted to control her, too. Love—she should have learned her lesson. Love brought pain and sorrow and entrapment.

Hearing a key in the lock, she burrowed deeper into the pillows, hoping it was the chambermaid. She waited. Heavy footsteps clicked against the tiles in the vestibule. She forced her eyes open.

A drowned rat. A little drowned rat, that's what she looks like, Owen thought. Her face sunken into the white linen looked pale and small. Hanks of hair hung wetly across her face. Her little hunched-up body dwarfed by the enormous antique bed. An adorable drowned rat. He wanted to take her in his arms, comfort her, protect her.

"You're home," she said. The tone was sharp and accusatory.

The moment was gone.

"Yes," he said. Giving the bed a wide berth, he crossed the room to the massive mahogany dresser. Kathryn's silver-backed brush lay there. He picked it up, turned it over and put it down again. He examined a bottle of perfume he'd bought her in Paris and fingered a pile of neatly wrapped packages. Outside, rain rattled against the shutters. Two stories below, waves lapped against the wall.

"Where were you?" she asked.

Without turning around, he said, "A museum." Why explain that he hadn't seen a single one of the paintings? "You?"

"Just walking."

"You forgot your umbrella, you know."

His broad back looked hostile, accusatory. "Yes, I do know, I got wet." She tossed it off as if it didn't matter.

"You should be more careful. You could get influenza."

"Why should you care about the state of my health?" she demanded.

He wheeled around and faced her. His eyes glowed dark and angry. "How dare you ask that? Because you are my wife and I love you, that's why."

Her heart leapt at his words. No matter how hard her mind tried to tell her she'd made a mistake, her heart refused to stop loving him. For a long time they looked at each other. The room reverberated with unspoken words. Finally she said, "I got soaked. It was silly, childish of me, running off like that. I'm sorry."

Owen looked at her for a long time. Apologies were not easy for her. "Why did you do it?" he asked softly.

The anger flooded back into her voice. "Because I don't want a man to tell me what to do. I refuse to be a subservient, obedient little wife."

"And do you think I would have married you if I'd wanted 'a subservient, obedient little wife'?" His own voice rose as he came over to her. "I'm not completely daft, you know. From the first moment I met you I knew you could never be that. Maybe that's why I fell in love with you." He sat down beside her on the bed. "I married you for what you are—a strong, independent, intelligent, high-spirited, successful woman. I don't want someone without a thought in her head. Without ambition. Without dreams. I want you and only you. Just the way you are."

"Owen, I love you, too." Her fingers caressed his cheek. "Please, can't you understand how important it is to me and my business that we live at the hotel?" Her eyes implored him.

"Wait a minute, you didn't hear the rest of my speech. I'm independent and successful, too. And I've been living my life the way I want to for far too many years to allow anyone—even someone I love—to tell me what to do. Ours isn't an ordinary marriage; it's going to require more than the normal amount of give-and-take. You're a very unique woman, Kathryn. But it's no longer just you and your hotels.

You've got to think of us. That's what is important. Our love.
Our life together.''

Kathryn's eyes softened. "I suppose that's what Rachel,
bless her heart, was trying to warn me about. She said that
marriage might surprise me, that there would be many
changes.'' She giggled. "I thought she was trying to tell me
about the birds and the bees.''

Owen smiled. "That's the easy part—at least for us," he
said, hugging her close. "You're frozen. What you need is a
nice, hot bath. Why didn't you have the sense to take one
right away? Especially since you claim to be so smart and
independent.''

"I don't know. I suppose I wasn't thinking straight.''

"Well, this once let me do the thinking for both of us. I'll
run the tub. Stay under the covers until it's ready.''

When he came back she looked up from her pillow. Her
eyes were dancing. "I've decided I will take a bath . . . on
one condition.''

"Exerting your independence again? I said I wanted a high-
spirited woman, not a stubborn one.''

"I promise you'll like this condition: you have to join me.''

"I'd be a fool to say no," he said with a smile, and without
taking his eyes off her he began unbuttoning his shirt.

"You know, you have a very hairy chest," Kathryn said as
she sat facing him in the bathtub, rubbing the bar of soap
over him. "Do you object to smelling of carnations?''

"No . . . feels good. Shall I reciprocate?''

Without a word she handed over the tiny bar of pink soap.
He lathered it up in his hand. Beginning with her throat, he
slowly and gently stroked. As he reached the top of her
breasts she gave a small moan of pleasure. With both hands
he circled her breasts, gently lubricating. Slowly and tanta-
lizingly he touched her, leaving a trail of sparks as if from
electric shocks. Gradually his circles became smaller and
smaller and finally his hands cupped her breasts. For a moment he held them and looked at them—beautiful pearly-white
orbs tipped with the most delicate of pinks. Perfect. Irresistible. With a moan he brought his lips down. Her nipples were
warm and slippery from the soap; they tasted of carnations
and her.

As she felt his tongue circling and teasing her breasts, her hands, in eager response, began caressing his broad back, feeling the hard muscles straining as he pulled her to him. His lips clamped onto hers and she wanted him more than anything in the world.

He stretched out his legs and pulled her soapy body on top of his. Every inch of her cried out her need. She forced her body closer to his until his skin was pressed everywhere against hers. Until her hipbones were resting within his. Until her thicket of hair was entwined with his. Suddenly all her feeling and awareness was directed toward one vital pulsating point. Raising her hips, she felt her body open moistly to receive him. He slid gently into her. Every instinct told her to move, to squirm closer and closer to him, to make their bodies meld together.

"No, don't move," he commanded. "Let's stay just like this. The reward will be sweeter for the waiting. I promise."

Silently Kathryn stared down into his eyes, wishing she could melt into their darkness, wanting with all her heart to become part of him, to make their flesh one. Their bodies slippery with soap were joined so firmly—one within the other. His broad hand was spread across the small of her back, pushing her closer and closer, forcing himself deeper and deeper.

Gradually and gently he began moving. Their bodies locked together, she moved with him, rising and falling in perfect harmony. Their rocking bodies sent waves against the marble walls of the tub. As they moved, their yearning for that one exquisite moment became unbearable. Their rhythm quickened, became more insistent, rose to a fevered pitch.

Faster and faster. Suddenly everything exploded and she wanted this instant to last forever.

As they drew apart she saw the white, half-moon indentations of her fingernails on his shoulder and she kissed them away. He buried his lips in her soft hair tenderly, all passion spent. "You're not cold, are you?" he asked.

"No. I don't think I've ever been so warm in all my life," she murmured, nestling closer to him.

"But we're lying in ice water."

"Are we? Then why do I feel warm and tingly like I never want the moment to end?" They were so close mentally and physically. How could she ever have imagined this man had trapped her? Memories of her frantic escape through the rain faded. This was Owen, her husband. He loved her and he would never hurt her.

Owen inhaled and said, "I don't think I'll ever smell carnations again without remembering this evening and wanting you." His eyes twinkled. "Which could be awkward. Especially if I dragged you off in the middle of a dinner party because the poor hostess made the mistake of arranging carnations on her table." He could already feel his body begin to yearn for her again. "I'm glad the Europeans have such enormous bathtubs. I don't think we could do that in mine."

She grinned. "You mean ours? And shouldn't we at least try?"

"We could keep at it until we can do it. That might be fun."

Kathryn's face took on a thoughtful look. "I'm sure we're not the only people who would enjoy oversized bathtubs. Maybe I should consider installing them in the suites. Enormous marble tubs"—she stretched out her hands—"set in great luxurious bathrooms like this. What do you think?"

Owen's eyebrows hunched down in warning. "I think that one of the changes you'll have to make is to stop talking about your confounded hotels when I'm making love to you."

Kathryn looked sheepish. "I'm sorry. I thought we'd finished."

Owen took her hands and gently pulled her soapy body up to cover his. "No, my love, we've just begun."

"Owen Reginald Morgan, you're—" she sputtered in surprise.

"Insatiable? I know. I'm afraid you have that effect on me."

Kathryn looked down on the traffic wallowing around the bus as it inched its way up Regent Street. The square black taxis. Open motorcars sputtering along. Bicyclists perilously weaving in and out. The occasional horse-drawn delivery van. She liked perching up on the open deck of the double-decker buses. It made her feel a part of the scene. "I think I'm falling in love with London," she said with a contented sigh.

The January thaw was upon the city, and she closed her eyes and held her face up to the gentle sun. But she couldn't keep her eyes closed for long; there was too much to see. Greedily she feasted her eyes on the sights as Regent Street curved north from Piccadilly Circus. The tall, elegantly proportioned eighteenth-century buildings. The expensive shops full of wools and tweeds and china. The fashionable restaurants. The crowds along the wide sidewalks bustling off to unknown destinations. The newsboys bleating out the headlines in unintelligible Cockney. She swiveled her head from side to side, trying to absorb it all.

"You said you didn't like Venice precisely because it was so old," Owen pointed out. "What makes London different?"

Kathryn thought for a moment. "I'm not sure. It's a different kind of old, I suppose. In Venice I had the feeling that the whole place was decaying before our eyes, but London is, well, London is venerable. It's a dignified old age. Like a well-preserved grande dame."

Owen smiled. "What you mean is that your fingers aren't itching to rebuild and repaint the whole city."

"Believe it or not, I don't want to change a thing." She paused and her eyes took on a faraway look. "I can almost imagine my ancestors walking down these same streets. Promenading in their elegant carriages through Hyde Park. Praying at St. Paul's. Doing the minuet in one of those great Georgian houses along Park Lane. Do you think that's silly?"

"Not at all. Who were these grand ancestors of yours?"

"A lord and lady somebody. According to my father, one of the sons did something dreadful—killed his brother in a duel—and fled to America. We are strictly the black sheep branch."

"Fancy that. Wouldn't my mother have been surprised to find her son married into the aristocracy?"

"Speaking of which," Kathryn said, "when are we going to Wales? It's only a few hours away by train. I know your parents are gone, but . . ."

"What, bored with London already? You know, a wise man—I think it was Samuel Johnson—once said that if a man is tired of London, he's tired of life. And we have so much more to see—the National Gallery, the Royal Academy, Harrod's, Kew Gardens, the Duke of Wellington's house. I even know about a pub with its own ghost, if you're tired of history."

"I don't care about the Duke of Wellington. I want to see where you were born and grew up." She couldn't explain, but she knew it would draw them even closer together if she understood what forces made him the complex man of many worlds he was.

"I'm afraid you'd be rather disappointed. It's a small, gray, wretchedly dull place. Insufferably cold and damp at this time of year. What about a trip to Stratford-upon-Avon instead?"

"Owen, you know you can't stand Shakespeare. Don't you want to go home?" Kathryn protested. "See your friends?"

"Home is East Seventy-third Street with you. Besides, there are hardly any of them left," Owen answered, his lips tight, his eyes focused straight ahead. "Mines are dangerous places to work in. And there was the war; most of my friends never came home. Then the influenza epidemic . . ." He wanted to protect Kathryn from the lines of unemployed men, hollow-eyed and hurt, their faces never quite scrubbed clean of coal dust. Or that was what he told himself. In his heart he knew he couldn't bear to see them because he'd escaped and they were still there. Because he had money and power and they had nothing.

What is he avoiding? Kathryn wondered. But she wouldn't push him now. After all, she had her own secrets. It was extraordinary how close she and Owen could be, and yet they knew so little about each other's lives before they met.

They sat silently, caught in their own webs of thought, until the bus lumbered into Oxford Street and Owen asked, "And what would your ladyship like to do this afternoon? Perhaps a spot of tea at Fortnum and Mason and then a bit of shopping at Harrod's?"

He was so eager to please her that it almost made her heart stop. "Definitely not another shopping spree. You bought out Paris for me." She paused. "What I would like to do is . . . is visit hotels. We're staying at the Connaught, we had dinner at Claridge's, but there are so many more. I just want to look around and take some notes. There is so much I can learn." She patted her handbag, which contained the notebook—the most recent in a whole series—that she carried around with her at all times. They were filled with details, written in her small, precise handwriting, of all the hotels they had stayed in—notes on decor, service, staff, food. She even recorded special recipes when she could coax them out of the surprised chefs, who suddenly found themselves confiding their secrets to the American lady with the irresistible smile.

"Sometimes I feel we've had a third person along on this honeymoon—you, me and those darned notebooks. They even go to bed with us."

"Don't you dare complain," Kathryn said, knowing he spoke only half in jest. "You've done business on this trip, too. What about the visits to the horse breeders in France? The factories? And boring old Olaf Swenson in Stockholm? If I never hear anyone mention steel mills again, it will be too soon."

"Truce," Owen said, throwing up his hands in surrender. "I guess we're two of a kind. You're dying to get back to your hotels, aren't you?"

"Actually," she said slowly, testing the waters, "I have an idea I'm anxious to get on with, a big idea. . . ."

"That I can see by the gleam in your eye," Owen said. One of the reasons he'd fallen in love with Kathryn was because of her enthusiasm—the wholehearted way she threw herself into life. The way her eyes sparkled when she talked about her dreams. He wondered about the lives of men with wives whose big ideas revolved around new dresses and dinner parties. Life with Kathryn would never be boring. He wasn't quite sure what it would be, but he knew it would never be boring.

"I have an idea for a marvelous new hotel." Her voice seemed to bubble.

Her words took Owen by surprise. "But, Kathryn, the Townsend Park—"

"I know," she said quickly, "the Townsend Park won't be open for another seven or eight months. But I won't start construction on the new one for years. Time enough to get the Townsend Park on the right track. But the moment is right to start making plans. To take the first steps."

With a sinking feeling Owen knew what she was going to say and he felt a sharp pain in his heart: Kathryn wanted a Townsend hotel in London. And that would mean months of separation—she in her English bed, he alone in New York.

They'd been married for less than two months. Certainly there were limits. . . .

The word came out in an enthusiastic burst, like air out of a balloon: "Florida." She paused, awaiting his reaction, oblivious to the stricken look on his face. "I know exactly what the hotel will look like. Remember those villas we saw on the coast near Naples? Pink. With red tile roofs. Built around courtyards. And flowers—masses of flowers and tropical plants, acres and acres of them. It won't be just a hotel, but a showplace. Even the people who can't afford to stay there will come to see it so they can tell the folks back home. A little piece of the Mediterranean on the Florida coast." She laughed. "It would be a perfect excuse to install those marvelous marble tubs, too. The time is right—now. Real estate is booming in Florida. Everyone is investing. It's the land of the future and I want to get in on it."

She read his expression and shook her head. "Owen, don't look so skeptical. Do you realize that in the past five years the population of Miami has more than doubled? Everyone is buying land. For investment. For homes. I've given it a lot of thought, and when I saw those villas it all came together. They'll need hotels. Luxury hotels for the very rich who want something very special. And I intend to cash in on the boom."

"Kathryn, did you hear what you just said?"

"What did I say?" she asked, her tone unmistakably defensive.

" 'Boom.' That's the way you described it. That's the way the papers are describing it. And you know what happens to booms: they invariably bust. It's an unhealthy situation. Too many people spending too much money, buying and selling land right and left at ridiculously inflated prices, all hoping to make their fortunes. You realize not many of them will?"

"Yes," Kathryn agreed, but her lips settled into a hard, stubborn line, "but I will. I'm not speculating in land. I'm buying a site for a hotel—a Townsend hotel."

"What happens when the bubble bursts? When land values fall and all those hundreds of developments go unbuilt? Who is going to be there to stay in your hotel? Elegant as it might be, if it's a ghost town . . ."

"Will you stop being a pessimist? I know what I'm doing.

And aren't you the person who claims that money is there to be spent?''

"Spent, yes. Or carefully invested. Not thrown away. And I wonder if you do know what you're doing.'' Seeing the determined set of her chin, he knew it was useless to argue, but he hated to see her make such an enormous mistake. So far she'd been lucky in her investments—very lucky. Failure would hit her hard, and he didn't relish being around the first time it happened.

Kathryn could feel the anger welling up in her chest and forced herself to be calm. "Remember that it's my money, my business, and I'll handle it the way I see fit. I don't tell you what horses to run or what to make in your factories, so I'll thank you not to tell me how to run my hotels.'' As if she'd run out of indignant steam, she turned from him and glued her eyes straight ahead. They were approaching Hyde Park Corner and the green expanses of the park. She could see small crowds gathered around half a dozen speakers who perched on soapboxes or stepladders, preaching their particular creeds, seeking converts amongst the spectators.

Owen stared at her rigid face, fighting down his annoyance. How could she be so stubborn? "I am not trying to interfere, but merely be helpful. I don't want to see you make a mistake—a costly mistake.''

She wheeled on him. "You can talk yourself blue in the face. I'm going to have my Florida hotel—no matter what you say. As soon as I get home I intend to see Allan Jones about a loan. I'm sure he'll realize that it's a wise move. And his bank will provide the money—with Townsend Manor as collateral. And if you—''

Her words were cut off. Her face grew white and her eyes widened in alarm. Drawing a gloved hand up to her mouth, she sprang from her seat.

Owen felt a surge of anger. "If you think you can run off every time we have a disagreement . . .'' he muttered under his breath. Then it finally registered how pale she had looked, and he dashed after her.

The open staircase tacked onto the back of the bus was steep and winding. As the bus lurched away from the curb Kathryn was thrown off balance. She grabbed out for the railing and hung on, but she didn't stop. The bus swayed out into traffic. Kathryn reached the open platform and stepped off. A car's brakes squealed, making Owen's heart stop, but she didn't even turn around.

"Sir, you aren't allowed to get off here. Against the rules, it is. Dangerous, too," the conductor protested.

Owen ignored him and leapt into the street. He hit the pavement hard enough to send a sharp pain knifing through his shin. Kathryn was standing on the sidewalk clutching a lamppost. He wanted to yell and scream and demand: What kind of dangerous stunt was that? You could have killed us both. But she looked as if her legs were about to give way under her, and instead he asked softly, "What's wrong, Kathryn?"

She managed a sickly smile. "I'm fine."

"Rubbish. Bloody rubbish." Owen exploded. "You're standing there clinging to that bloody lamppost for dear life. Your face is green and you have the gall to tell me that you're fine?"

"I am fine. Honestly. It's just that I've been awfully stupid. But I finally realized and . . ." She paused, and a sheepish grin spread over her face. "I'm saying this badly, but," she said with a giggle, "how do you feel about becoming a father?"

Chapter Two

An icy gale assaulted Edward as he stepped off the bus at Lexington Avenue and Fifty-ninth Street. The sidewalk was slush-coated and he walked slowly, occasionally pulling his coat more tightly around his thin body. He wasn't cold—he was too excited to feel the penetrating chill—but he didn't want anyone to see what he was wearing under his coat. Not that anyone would remember. Still, he could not afford to take chances.

Several blocks later he turned abruptly and disappeared into an alleyway. He threaded his way through the trash cans until he came to a door. It was open, and he could feel the sudden blast of hot, steamy air and smell the cloying odors of cooking. As he stepped through the door he unbuttoned his coat to reveal the uniform that would allow him to wander at will through the Townsend Manor Hotel. Of course, it would all be easier when he found someone on the inside to help him. Though that was proving more difficult than he'd anticipated. For some reason the staff was ridiculously loyal to his sister.

Quickly, before anyone caught sight of him, he concealed his overcoat behind a pile of cartons and hurried through a maze of behind-the-scenes hallways to the lobby. This was, he had to admit, a rather crude plan. There would be more subtle ones later. But now he wanted to take advantage of Kathryn's absence. She was on her honeymoon and . . . A vision of her slim, pale body assailed him. She was stretched out on a pristine white bed, open and waiting, and he found his own body responding. But he mustn't let emotions interfere with his plan. Later there would be time to immerse himself in delicious possibilities.

The grinning elevator operator asked no questions when Edward told him there was an attractive young lady waiting for him at the kitchen door. With a wink Edward said that he'd gladly fill in for him. Noting his uniform, which was the same as his own—well tailored in the Townsend blue and gray—the boy nodded his thanks and disappeared.

Edward assumed his post and waited. According to his plan, he had five minutes. It was a quiet time of day and the lobby was almost deserted. He took a group of women up to the third floor and a man to the sixth. Then he saw the right one. She was young and tall, with a long, horselike face and too many teeth. But her mousy brown suit was expensive and her manner self-assured. If he were lucky, she would be a screamer.

She played right into his hands, asking for the fifth floor and then staring at the ceiling as if he didn't exist. Slowly his finger inched out toward the red emergency-stop lever. He jerked it forward and the car came to a shuddering halt.

She glared at him. "What happened?"

"Nothing to worry about, miss," he said smoothly. "You must forgive me. I wanted to have you to myself. Just for a little while," he whined. "You are such a magnificent woman. Your body . . . I can't help myself."

It happened exactly as he'd planned. Smugly, he watched the fear dawn in her eyes. "What are you doing?" Her voice rose. "How dare you? Take this elevator down to the lobby immediately. I—" Seeing his bony fingers reaching toward her breasts, she stopped. They'd barely touched the nubby brown fabric of her suit before she let out the scream he'd been hoping for. Loud. Piercing. Bound to be heard.

Edward quickly withdrew his hand and pulled the operating lever. The car started upward and shuttered to a halt at the third floor. Pulling the gates open, he jumped out. The fire stairs were, he knew, six feet to his left. As he pounded down to the basement he could still hear her shrieks. "Silly cow," he muttered to himself. "That's probably the first and last time any man will ever try to touch you." How the newspapers would relish the story. He licked his lips in anticipation. He could see the headline now: "Young Society Woman

Assaulted in Exclusive Townsend Manor Hotel.'' A most delightful addition to his album.

Later that night Roger sat at his desk with his fountain pen poised over a yellow cablegram form. He hesitated. Every day for the last seven weeks he'd sent a cable to Kathryn. By agreement with Rachel, he'd reported only the good news. Not that there had been any bad news to relate—only a few minor problems—until now.

Roger sighed. It was ironic how quickly good news could turn to bad. And to the Townsend Manor, Mrs. Geoffrey Walmsly had been good news. With impeccable credentials extending back three generations, she was one of New York's social elite; one of the wealthy, the well-bred, the bejeweled society matrons Kathryn had worked hard to attract. For years they had held all their charity balls, wedding receptions and debutante parties at the Waldorf on Fifth Avenue at Thirty-fourth Street, but now they were drifting uptown, and Kathryn was determined they should drift in her direction. If only one of the high priestesses of this charmed circle gave her approval to the Townsend Manor, the rest would follow. And so when Mrs. Geoffrey Walmsly's secretary had phoned to set up an appointment to arrange a private party, Roger found it extremely difficult to pretend to consult his calendar and coolly set a date.

Mrs. Walmsly was an enormous woman swathed in a fur coat that made her look even larger. When she spoke, it was through her nose. ''Mr. Walmsly and I are planning to give a small party—two hundred or so—for my daughter. She will, incidentally, be joining us shortly. And I had heard, ah, interesting things about this little hotel. Although I am taking a chance. You are a new establishment, I believe?''

Roger quickly recognized her type, and smoothly and deferentially talked away her reservations.

Finally she drew herself up under her furs and announced, ''I have decided that I shall hold my daughter's little party here. I trust that the hotel—and you—will not disappoint me. The date is February sixth—mark it down—and I expect . . .''

But before Roger could find out what she expected, her words had been drowned out by a high-pitched scream. He shuddered at the memory. Dreadful that a young woman should be molested in a hotel elevator, but that it should be Mrs. Walmsly's daughter . . .

Fortunately, the lobby had been almost deserted, and he'd managed to usher her into Kathryn's office before anyone knew what had happened. But the girl, who had been on her way to the room of a school friend, insisted that the man was a hotel employee. "He was wearing a uniform," she sobbed. Roger racked his brains, but no one on the staff matched her description—"tall, thin and pale, very pale." Roger stared at her; she didn't seem the fragile, hysterical type, but could she have imagined the whole incident?

Finally, having calmed her daughter, Mrs. Walmsly said, "I want you to forget about trying to find this insane man, whoever he is." She enunciated each syllable carefully. "My daughter will be ruined, absolutely ruined, if anyone hears about this attack."

She fixed her eyes on him, daring him to object. "Needless to say, we shall not be holding our social event here. And I expect you to be discreet about this incident. If one word leaks out, I will see to it that nobody in our set ever patronizes your hotel."

"Certainly, Mrs. Walmsly," he assured her. An episode like this could ruin the Townsend Manor. In the hotel business reputations were fragile. Very fragile indeed.

Finally he put down his pen. No need to ruin Kathryn's glorious honeymoon. Better let the incident be forgotten. He had informed the house detective, naturally, but in all probability the man had disappeared forever.

Chapter Three

A pale sun fought its way through the early June haze. Over the racetrack the morning mist hung low, muffling the sound of hoofbeats. A sleek silver horse thundered past along the far rail, its black tail and mane streaming in the breeze, earth flying under its pounding hooves. Behind it, two long-legged chestnuts galloped neck and neck. Their riders, half crouching and half standing in the saddle, looked tiny, but their control over the huge Thoroughbreds was absolute.

Owen stood with one foot propped up on the near rail, a stopwatch in his hand. Without taking his eyes from the gray, he asked, "What do you think, Mack? Does he have a chance on Saturday?"

The short, bandy-legged man next to him grunted out of the side of his mouth and chewed on the stump of his cigar. "Competition's gonna be tough. That colt of Barrymore's can go like he's got buckshot in his ass when he wants to."

Kathryn, looking crisp and cool in navy and white, watched the little man with fascination. MacIntosh—no one knew his first name—was a racing legend. Owen had warned her about him. "He hates people—flies off the handle at the least excuse. He hates women especially. If he had his way, they'd be banned from the track altogether." Owen had chuckled. "The stories I've heard . . . but I put up with his temper tantrums because, fact is, the horses he trains win. You should see him—whispering to his horses, petting them, practically making love to them when he can't spare a civil word for his fellow humans."

Now Owen asked, "Mack, can't you sound more optimistic? This is Kathryn's first visit to Belmont and I'm trying to

261

impress her.'' He turned to Kathryn with a sly smile. ''I'm also trying to convince her that owning a horse like Dragon's Blood beats a vault full of stocks and bonds.''

Mack's eyes were glued to the barrel-chested bay nervously ambling by. ''Goddamned fool,'' he muttered, nodding at the rider. ''Pullin' him up too tight. Gonna ruin his mouth. Man should be taken out and shot.'' Then with one regretful look at the track, he said, ''Mr. Morgan,'' and headed for the stables.

As soon as he was out of earshot Owen and Kathryn burst out laughing. ''See,'' Owen said, ''I wasn't exaggerating. He's every bit as appalling as I said.''

''Worse,'' Kathryn said. ''And to think I wasted my charms on him. I smiled so much I thought my lips would break.''

''Poor man, if he's impervious to your charms he's hopeless. Condemned to lonely bachelorhood forever.''

Kathryn laughed. ''Perhaps he has high standards and is merely waiting for the right woman.''

Owen constantly marveled at how Kathryn managed to ignore her own beauty. Most women blessed with those chameleonlike eyes, mahogany hair and delicate skin would have had no choice but to become vain. But Kathryn wore her beauty unself-consciously and never seemed to notice how it affected other people.

As Owen turned his attention back to the horses on the exercise track, Kathryn thought how much her husband belonged here. Much more than he belonged in her elegant hotels. Everyone, from exercise riders to owners, knew and respected him. Kathryn was pleased to see how they all gravitated toward him to brag, to pass the time, to ask his advice. Physically, too, he belonged here. His skin was tanned, and she could see the little white lines radiating from his eyes from too much squinting into the sun. How handsome and at ease he looked with his white shirt open at the neck and his tan whipcord riding breeches tapering down to dusty leather boots. She smiled and resisted the urge to kiss his cheek. In this masculine world she sensed it was important to obey the rules.

''Confounded man,'' Owen said, ''Don't let Mack discourage you. You're always welcome here. Whenever you can tear yourself away. I'm still not sure how I lured you away from your office today. But I wanted you to see it while there's still time.''

"You mean before I'm too fat to move," Kathryn supplied, "and you're ashamed to be seen in public with your pregnant wife."

"Never," Owen said, and to her surprise, wrapped his arm around her thickening waist. "I love every inch of you. No matter how many extra ones there are. Besides, they'll be gone in eighty-five days."

As Kathryn watched Owen, an eager grin spread across his face until he looked like a child contemplating Christmas. "Are you really counting?" she asked.

"I certainly am. I'm very keen to meet our son or daughter."

Kathryn shook her head. How could she tell him that sometimes she forgot altogether that she was pregnant? After two weeks her morning sickness had disappeared. For months everything seemed exactly as it had been before. Now, of course, with her stomach large, it was harder to forget. She wondered if her feelings were normal. Her doctor was old and gruff and dealt in facts, not feelings. At times she felt that she was entirely alone in this brand-new and rather frightening world. A world of new experiences and sensations. A world in which she had no control over her body. Perhaps if her mother were still alive . . . Would the promise of a grandchild have drawn them closer, or was Edward's hold too strong?

I'll love the baby when it gets here, Kathryn assured herself. It's silly to get all worked up about it now, not with almost three months to go. And so many things to do. And the Townsend Park opening in July . . .

Kathryn's preoccupied silence worried Owen. "You are happy about the baby, aren't you, love?"

"Don't be silly. Of course I am. You just occasionally take me by surprise. Nobody ever warned me that men got so excited about babies."

His grin turned serious and the arm around her waist squeezed tighter. "I had no idea they did, either, and I'm not sure about all men. All I know is that with you and our baby, I can't think of anything else in this world I need or want.''

"Nor can I," Kathryn said, nestling her head against his chest. For a moment his heartbeats sounded as loud as the horses galloping past.

"That definitely does not sound like the Kathryn Townsend Morgan I know and love. What about the bigger and better hotels you plan to build all over the world? What about London and Paris and Milan? I thought they were waiting for your hotels."

Kathryn caught her breath as a dark cloud passed over, threatening to rain on their happiness. Owen was approaching what had become, by unspoken agreement, a taboo subject: her plans for a Florida hotel. She'd bought her land as soon as they returned from their honeymoon—five hundred acres on the Atlantic Ocean. Allan Jones had aproved the investment, and after he'd convinced his colleagues that "Kathryn Townsend is more clever than most men doing business in this city," the bank had authorized the loan. It was a very large loan, and it would be years before Kathryn could afford to start building, but that didn't stop her from drawing up her plans for the hotel and grounds. There would be the usual golf course and the requisite tennis courts, but she also wanted gardens, acres and acres of them, a tropical wilderness of color and texture and smell, for those who sought aesthetic beauty as well as physical exhaustion.

But whenever the Florida hotel was mentioned, Owen's eyes took on a hooded, angry look and he turned tight-lipped and silent. She learned never to mention it in his presence and again and again assured herself that it was only a very tiny blight on their happiness. Kathryn knew that it was better that she'd set the limits early: he must know she would not tolerate his interference in her business. She acknowledged that her husband was remarkably astute. That he coped with every situation calmly and competently. That he had many friends in high places and knew exactly what strings to pull to get what he wanted. And that at times it could be helpful to seek his advice and use his influence, but she refused to open the door even a crack. Cracks had a habit of widening. And Townsend hotels were her creation.

Now she refused to rise to his teasing bait. Keeping her

voice light, she replied, "I suppose I *could* survive without a whole *chain* of hotels."

"That's an admission I never thought I'd hear you make, and I expect I'd better quit while I'm ahead. Come back to the stables with me; there's someone I want you to meet."

"I warn you, I don't think I could take another Mack."

"I promise this will be a pleasant surprise."

It was a relief to leave the hot, dusty exercise track and stroll under the shade of the big old maple trees which sheltered the enormous green barns. Inside Owen's barn the air was cool and smelled of fresh earth and hay. Some of the horses were crunching on hay. Some watched with big, dark, wary eyes. Halfway down the line Owen stopped in front of a reddish-brown horse with a golden mane and alert eyes. He seemed to be waiting for Kathryn to say something.

She exhaled in approval. "He's beautiful."

Owen shook his head. "Not a he. She. She's a filly. Look." He pointed to the brass nameplate on the stall door. It said, "Miss Kathryn." "Her color rather reminded me of your hair. A sort of reddish gold."

Kathryn reached out and tentatively ran her hand over Miss Kathryn's velvety nose. The horse responded with a soft nicker of pleasure and a roll of its enormous dark eyes. "I don't know what to say, Owen, except thank you. I'm very flattered."

"Most women might not appreciate having a horse named after them."

"I've told you: I'm not most women," she replied. "Besides, it's not as though you named a cow after me. Or a pig. She's magnificent. It's absolutely the most wonderful gift you could have given me. Much better than stock certificates," she said with an embarrassed laugh.

She knew that Miss Kathryn would be a link between their two very different worlds. Despite the overwhelming love they felt for each other, a love that continued to grow, they were like planets coming close occasionally before spinning off on their separate orbits. She was constantly immersed in the thousands of details of running the hotels, details of which he was unaware; he was off at the racetrack or attending to his dozens of business interests. It wasn't until this morning that she knew what Owen actually did when he came out to the track. But, she told herself sternly, marriage is a long-term commitment. And we have time to learn and draw our worlds closer together.

"Miss Kathryn is running in the sixth race this afternoon. She's young—this is only her third race—so I'm afraid the odds are twenty to one, but I think she may have a chance. Especially if she has half the determination of her namesake."

Kathryn chuckled. "All right, Miss Kathryn, I'll see you after you win."

Coming out of the starting gate, Miss Kathryn was dead last, and Kathryn's knuckles were dead white from clutching at the railing. At the quarter pole the filly had moved halfway into the pack. At the half-mile pole she was neck and neck for third and Kathryn was screaming at the top of her lungs. "Come on, Miss Kathryn. Come on, my girl." As the horses approached the wire, Miss Kathryn gave a sudden leap forward and crossed the finish line two lengths ahead of the next horse.

"She won! My horse won!" Kathryn shouted, clutching her winning ticket and clapping wildly. When her stylish straw hat went sailing to the ground, she hardly noticed. "I won a hundred dollars. I won! Miss Kathryn did it. She did it for me." People in the nearby boxes stared, but she was oblivious. The men, Owen noted with pride, all watched her with admiration, while the women's smiles were tinged with envy. Owen thought his heart would burst with happiness. The cool, sophisticated Mrs. Kathryn Townsend Morgan had disappeared. In her place stood a little girl whose dream had just come true.

Owen smiled and wished he had known Kathryn as a girl. Giggling with her friends. Full of mischief. Naive. Wide-eyed. Vulnerable. But perhaps her childhood had not been the kind to permit easy gaiety. She said so little about her past. She was complex, but of one thing he was absolutely sure: he would love this fascinating girl/woman for the rest of his life.

Later she stood next to Miss Kathryn, her small shoulders proudly thrown back, a smile across her face for the pho-

tographers. She squeezed Owen's hand and whispered, "I
know I have everything in the world I want right at this
moment. And nothing is ever going to spoil our happiness."

Chapter Four

Would they never end? Yesterday's problems. Today's crises.

This morning two equally insistent mothers had each declared their intention to hold a wedding breakfast in the Venetian Room on the same day in July. The mysterious German who had reserved the Victoria Suite for a month had failed to appear, and the German consulate claimed that Baron von Friedrichstein of Freiburg didn't exist. Then two chambermaids claiming homesickness up and announced they were returning to Ireland.

"It's Mr. Jones. Shall I put him through or ask him to call back this afternoon when it's quieter?" For the tenth time that morning, Kathryn blessed Miss Willis, her efficient, unflappable secretary.

"It's all right, Miss Willis. I'll talk to Mr. Jones." There were several clicks before Kathryn said, "How nice to hear a friendly voice." Over the past few months her relationship with Allan had become a personal as well as a professional one. She liked his wife, Maureen, a bright, breezy Irish woman, and whenever they found the time, the two couples got together for dinner or an evening of bridge.

"Good morning, Kathryn."

"Allan, you sound glum; what's . . . ?" Kathryn bit down firmly on her tongue. "I'm sorry. How tactless of me. I heard that Maureen had another miscarriage, and I am awfully sorry."

"It's harder on her than me. I want to forget about trying to have children, but Maureen, good Irish wife that she is, refuses." His voice softened. "To her, motherhood is everything. Though I don't know how many more times she can survive the disappointment. But I won't burden you with our problems. You have a large one of your own looming on the horizon.''

"Problem? What problem?" she demanded, her mind scrambling.

"You do find time in your busy schedule to read the newspapers, don't you?"

"Of course I do." She paused, for a moment puzzled, then said, "You're referring to the articles about Florida, aren't you?"

"The situation is becoming serious."

Kathryn laughed. "Allan, do you always believe everything you read? If they didn't exaggerate, they wouldn't sell newspapers."

"Kathryn, don't forget that we are investment bankers. We do dig a bit deeper than the daily papers. And I'm afraid that the bubble has definitely been pricked." He paused. Kathryn said nothing, but he knew she was listening, listening hard. "Too many people are defaulting on their payments. The price of land is dropping. It looks bad."

"Every market has its ups and downs. It will come back." She tried to sound cheerful, but her mind was racing, juggling figures, weighing consequences. She had a great deal at stake.

"I'm afraid our experts don't think so. But I do have good news for you. We have an offer of seventy cents on the dollar for your property. As your banker—hard as it is for me to do—I'd advise you to take it. Immediately."

"Seventy cents. Never. You know that property is much too valuable."

"Not now it isn't. Believe me, I know how difficult it is, but sometimes it's better to admit defeat early, salvage what you can and bail out. Think about it and give me a call tomorrow. I'm sure you'll realize it's the only sensible course."

For a long while Kathryn sat at her desk staring at her calendar and trying to digest Allan's news. But it stuck in her throat like a large, painful lump. How could she have been so stupid? Every instinct had told her it was the right investment. Instinct. Maybe that was it. Maybe her instincts weren't to be trusted. Maybe she should make her decisions based on cold, hard facts. The way men did.

Her mind abruptly switched to the thousands of other investors caught in the boom. Most of them were men. And she *had* based her final decision on facts: Florida's warm climate, its beautiful beaches, its tropical scenery. She'd inspected the property herself, and knew that it was a good investment. But as Owen said, what good would her hotel be if it were in the middle of a ghost town?

Owen—how was she going to tell him? How could she admit that she'd been pigheaded and stubborn and he'd been right? He was such a clever businessman; what would he say when he heard she'd been so stupid, disregarding his advice and failing so spectacularly?

Over dinner, trying to sound calm and unfazed, she told Owen what Allan had said. The confession over, she let out a sigh of relief and prepared herself for the worst. But Owen was silent. "Well, aren't you going to gloat and say, 'I told you so'?" she demanded.

"Why? You took a risk. You have to when you're in business. It didn't pay off, that's all. Sometimes they don't. You've been lucky so far. Shall I tell you about the time I bought a lame horse?" But he could see by the crushed look on her face that she didn't believe him.

"Every paper in the city will have a field day," Kathryn said. "I'll be a laughingstock and so will you."

Owen grinned. "I have a thick skin. And a beautiful wife I'd love if she lost every penny. Relax, this is hardly the end of the world."

Kathryn dropped her fork with a loud clatter. "Relax! Don't you understand the Townsend Manor is my collateral? How can you be so calm? I could lose my hotel. Lose everything I've worked for." Her voice rose. "What would I be without my hotels?"

Her words hung ominously in the air. Owen's face hardened. "You'd be my wife and the mother of our child. Isn't that enough?" Kathryn was silent.

"You didn't answer my question. Isn't being a wife and mother enough for you? At the track you said it was, but maybe success is more important to you."

Kathryn stared at Owen's dark face and felt her own anger

ebbing when she saw how she'd hurt him. "I'm sorry. But pregnant women tend to get emotional, and I . . . I got carried away."

What she didn't say was: Edward was right; women have no place in the business world. How tempting it would be to turn her hotels over to Owen. Let his people cope with the problems of worthless land and missing barons while she sat peacefully awaiting their baby. Obviously she was putting unreasonable, unnatural demands on herself, just as Rachel had insisted. Why did she have to keep proving herself? To whom? Edward was long gone. Why couldn't she let go? Why couldn't she be content with life as a good wife and mother? Why did she want more? She felt a tear slide down her cheek.

Owen reached across the table and grasped her hand in his. "I won't let you lose the hotel, Kathryn. I know how much it means to you."

Despite the tears welling up in her eyes, she bristled in protest. "Owen Morgan, I told you once that I would not tolerate your interfering with my business, and that goes for bailing me out of trouble as well. I've got to do it on my own. I won't let you use your money to cover my mistakes. If I make mistakes I'll pay for them. Like everybody else." She looked at him, at the wealth of concern and love in his eyes, and said softly, "But thank you. It's not that I don't appreciate your generosity."

"Generosity! It's not generosity. I believe in you, Kathryn. No charity, just a loan, all very businesslike."

"Absolutely not." The line of her chin looked as if it were cast in bronze, and Owen knew it was useless to argue. Why couldn't she understand that he didn't want to control her damn hotels? All he wanted was to see her happy, and he'd do anything in the world to keep her from getting hurt.

They finished the meal in silence, the occasional clatter of silverware resounding in their enormous, formal dining room, emphasizing the silence. At last Kathryn spoke, "I've decided that no matter what Allan and his experts say, I still believe in the future of Florida. I have five hundred acres of waterfront property and I know there's money to be made. Call it ridiculous female intuition, but I'm sure of it. The bubble may be on the verge of bursting right now, but someday people will be flocking to Florida for the sun and the beaches, and I intend to be ready with the most beautiful and luxurious hotel they've ever seen."

"You are stubborn, aren't you?" Owen remarked. "But I expect that's why I love you, because you stick to your guns. And who knows? Maybe you're right. Maybe Florida does have a future."

But the fear of failure refused to leave Kathryn. Mercilessly it dogged her. It was with her constantly, sometimes hovering in the background, then leaping, without warning, into the forefront of her mind. It flashed through her head like an annoying neon sign, blotting out all else. Then came the inevitable question: What would I be without my hotels? There was never any answer, because she refused to put into words the message of her unconscious mind: my hotels are my identity. Without them I am nothing.

In July, what had been a smooth, problem-free operation at the new Townsend Park suddenly turned into a nightmare. By early August, on the eve of the grand opening, it seemed that everything that could go wrong had—or would.

"If I were superstitious, I'd swear it was jinxed," Kathryn complained to Wendell Carruthers. "Or at the very least ill-fated. The wallpaper in half the rooms is peeling off. The draperies for the executive suites were delivered and they're all the same color, a vile shade of . . . I suppose if you were kind you'd call it mustard. Then, as if that weren't enough, the hotel stationery arrived yesterday. Twenty thousand sheets of it, all with the wrong address. Instead of Central Park West, it says Central Park East. There is no such a place. What idiots!"

Wendell clucked sympathetically. Kathryn never was one to suffer fools gladly. There was a warm friendship as well as a strong professional bond between them. Wendell was fond of bragging to his colleagues how he'd discovered Kathryn Townsend. "I knew from the start that she'd make a success of herself. A petite young lady, but she had fire in her eyes." At this point in the story he'd harrumph slightly and add, "That's why I went against my own principles and invested in that first hotel of hers. A smart woman. Smarter than most men." Then he'd look around, daring anyone to contradict him. Except for the most conservative, they all would have been delighted to be able to say they'd had the foresight to back the famous Kathryn Townsend.

"But that's not what I'm calling you about," Kathryn continued. "I know draperies are hardly in your area of expertise. We have a contract with the window washers. For some inexplicable reason they refuse to work. They're unionized, but as far as I can figure out, this is not an official strike. Would you take a look at the contract, then talk to them and see what you can do?"

Wendell's tongue clicked again, this time not in sympathy. Kathryn, who had long experience reading him, demanded, "Something's wrong?"

"You may be in a difficult position here."

"Stop being so lawyerly cautious," Kathryn said impatiently. "Whatever it is, as my attorney as well as an investor in the hotel, you can straighten it out, I'm sure."

"It's going to be sticky. You see, this particular union is reputed . . . well . . . is involved with organized crime. They may be trying to extort money—realizing they have you over a barrel, so to speak. I'd advise you to be very careful. Please don't do anything to rile the workers. This is one time in your life to maintain a ladylike silence. They have a reputation for . . . ah . . . shall we say ruthlessness? And in your condition . . ."

"Don't worry about me. Just get them back to work."

"Do you want to pay them?" The question was straightforward; it was a practical, not a moral, issue.

Kathryn thought for a moment. "I'm not sure. Find out what you can. There are so many other things going on here—I'd really like to get this problem out of the way."

He could hear the exhaustion in her voice and quickly asked, "How are you feeling?"

She laughed and sounded more like herself. "Like a beached whale, thank you very much. And I imagine I look like one, too. I can't wait until this baby is born. Not that I want it to come early. As it is, the baby and the opening of the hotel seem to be on a collision course. I refuse to be carted away from my own party to the delivery room. I have the most magnificent celebration planned for the opening. It's going to be a party to set this city on its ear. I'll tell you all about it next time we talk. You are coming, aren't you?''

''Wouldn't miss it for the world, Kathryn. Remember, I knew you when.'' She laughed; this had become an old joke between them. ''And now when all the gossip columnists in New York are wagging their tongues speculating on the origins of the beautiful and rich Mrs. Kathryn Townsend Morgan, I could make a fortune selling your story.''

Or what little you know of it, Kathryn thought, wondering what the press would do to a woman who had a murderer and a thief for a brother. A woman who built the foundations of her business on stolen money and a lie. It wasn't something she thought of often. She'd trained herself not to. But the wounds were still there, unhealed. Perhaps they always would be unhealed, threatening to open at the slightest touch.

Bracing herself, Kathryn said, ''Speaking of which, have you heard from Edward or his lawyer?''

''Not a word. He seems to have vanished without a trace. And without, according to his lawyer, paying his bills.''

Kathryn felt her tension sloughing off. Was it too good to be true that Edward had finally disappeared from her life?

Chapter Five

The next morning when Kathryn opened the front door, it hit her—a wall of heat and humidity. Every brick, every stone, every stretch of asphalt had soaked up the sun and were now radiating it out on a city that even at seven o'clock was wilting. What a relief it was to see the huge black Packard waiting at the curb, its top down. The limousine had been Owen's idea. At first she'd protested, but now, hot and heavy and pregnant, she enjoyed every luxurious moment of it.

Owen was in Saratoga racing a trio of three-year-old geldings, and Kathryn was eagerly taking advantage of his absence by getting an early start in the mornings. She liked being at the Townsend Park long before any of the workmen or staff arrived, when there was only one watchman on duty and she could wander the hotel alone, enjoying her creation in solitude. She smiled to herself at the thought; maybe it was foolish to love an inanimate object, but she loved that hotel, every inch of it. Is this the way an artist feels about his paintings, or a composer about his music? she wondered. Her feelings were hard to put into words—a combination of love and pride and smug self-satisfaction. The joy of creation. Will this be the way I feel about my baby? she asked herself.

The car pulled to a halt in front of the Townsend Park with its wildly ornamented facade. Bow windows projected out over the sidewalks. At each corner was a rounded turret looking like something from a fairy-tale castle. Stone garlands and cupids and urns overflowing with flowers created a baroque fantasy which made the building one of the most extraordinary architectural landmarks in the area.

Expertly Emil, the chauffeur, slipped out of his side of the car and came around to Kathryn's. He opened the door and extended his gloved hand, which perfectly matched his dove-gray livery. She took it gratefully. Every day extracting herself from the car became a more awkward task.

Safely on the sidewalk, she stood for a few seconds staring up at her hotel. Instead of lettering on the awning, the hotel's presence was discreetly announced by a small brass plaque to the right of the door—"The Townsend Park"—and below it, in smaller script, "A Townsend Hotel." Kathryn reached up with her white-gloved hand and wiped an errant fingerprint off the brass.

A sudden desire flashed across her mind: I wish Edward could see me now. To see what a mere woman can do. All he had was one small hotel he allowed to slide downhill and a few boardinghouses that reeked of cabbage. She shivered. No, better that Edward didn't know. Let him scent money and success and he'd be at her door, demanding his share.

Taking a key from her purse, she unlocked the massive door. A filigree design of ironwork fronted the glass and made the doors extremely heavy. She wondered where the watchman was; Gus was usually waiting to open the door for her. The lobby was cool and silent. She imagined the sound of her high heels tapping against the marble floor, echoing throughout the empty building. At the far end of the dimly lit lobby one lone lamp was burning. It was part of her morning ritual to flip on the light switches, one by one, and watch with awe as her creation came to life.

This morning she gasped in horror, refusing to believe her eyes. The elaborate gilded table and the mirror above it were the focal point of the entire lobby. Golden nymphs reached up sinuous arms to support the black-veined marble tabletop. Golden cupids frolicked amongst flowers around the edge of the mirror. According to the antiques dealer in Paris, they had been made for Louis XIV's private chambers at Versailles, which was how he justified charging a fortune for them.

Now an ugly, jagged black crack ran down the middle of the smoky mirror. A sinister web of smaller cracks surrounded it. Kathryn wanted to cry. The cupids and flowers hadn't been damaged. She could replace the mirror, but it wouldn't be the same. It wouldn't be the mirror that had reflected the image of a king. The mirror that had seen the celebrated beauty of his royal mistresses.

She spent the morning trying to discover who was responsible for the damage. All she found were three staff members who swore that the mirror had been unbroken when the building was closed for the night. And Gus insisted that no one had entered the hotel while he was on duty. Finally she located an antiques dealer who promised to replace the mirror with something equally antique-looking. "I can't promise French glass. But no one will ever know," he assured her. "It will be our little secret." But Kathryn knew she could never forget. Her perfect creation was no longer perfect.

When Wendell called, she was not in the mood for his news. "I'm afraid that you're going to have to pay, Kathryn, if you want the hotel to open on time. The union man I spoke to claimed there was some sort of outside agitator stirring up the men—that's why they refused to work, but basically it seems that money is at the heart of the problem."

It usually is, Kathryn thought bitterly. "Then I'll pay whatever is required. I can't afford not to."

"Fine. I'll arrange for someone to handle it immediately. Someone who understands this situation," Wendell said.

"You mean someone accustomed to making payoffs. No, I think I'd prefer to handle this one myself."

That Kathryn refused to obey the rules he'd been brought up to believe governed a lady's behavior he'd accepted over the years—it was one of the things he enjoyed most about her—but this . . . this attitude was unthinkable.

"Kathryn, you don't know how to deal with people like this. And you don't want to. You are a lady."

"Nonsense. I'm a hotel owner first."

"Have you discussed this with Owen? I'm sure he'd agree with me."

"No, this is my business, not his, and I'll handle it the way I think best."

When she was at her most stubborn, Wendell knew better than to argue with her. Meekly he gave her the name and telephone number and wished her luck. But somehow he had the feeling that it might not be Kathryn who needed the luck. She had an uncanny ability to convince people to do exactly what she wanted. Still, she'd never run up against people like this before.

Kathryn made the call immediately. "Mr. DiFranco, this is Kathryn Townsend."

His voice grated on her ear like sandpaper. So did his words. "Yeah, little lady, what can I do fer you?"

"I am the owner of the Townsend Park Hotel. I understand that you don't approve of your contract with us."

"No, well, you see, Miz Townsend, it isn't exactly like that."

He's obviously not accustomed to dealing with women, Kathryn decided, realizing that fact could be turned to her advantage. "Then why aren't your men working? I have seven hundred and sixty-five windows. All of them need washing."

"Well, Miz Townsend, truth is it's hard work. The weather's been hot—really hot. It's dangerous, too . . . all them feet off the street." The longer he hemmed and hawed the more raspy his voice became.

"Perhaps your men should go into another line of work if they find window cleaning so difficult and unpleasant."

There was a long silence. "See, Miz Townsend, it's not that, but sometimes the men . . . well, you see, they need an incentive. A reason to go up there and risk gettin' killed. And if they don't have that incentive, well, then accidents happen, you know, things get broken. Windows. Other fragile items."

Kathryn thought of the antique mirror.

"Tell you what, Miz Townsend, why don't you get your husband to call me. I'm sure he'll understand"—he emphasized the "he"—"my . . . um . . . problem."

And take your head off at the suggestion of a bribe, she said to herself. "Mr. DiFranco, I understand your problem perfectly. You want to be paid a bribe before your men start work at my hotel, to ensure that there are no accidents. How much do you want?"

"Miz Townsend, I hear that you're a wealthy woman and—"

"How much, Mr. DiFranco?"

As she waited for his answer Kathryn became aware of a dull ache in her stomach. I'm not as calm about this confrontation as I thought, she realized.

"I'm waiting," she said coolly.

"One thousand dollars should keep my men in beer money."

And you too, she thought. "Tell you what, Mr. DiFranco, I'll give you five thousand dollars."

A strangled "What?" emerged.

The ache was becoming sharper, more insistent. She tried not to think about it. "My lawyer informs me that your men often require these . . . incentives. If I give you five thousand dollars this afternoon, I expect your men to work without any further incentives and without accidents for as long as I own this hotel. Is that understood? Nothing more. Ever again."

"I'll have to think about it," he whined.

"No. If you want this deal, you'll have to agree to my terms right now."

She could almost imagine him sweating, and the thought pleased her. Then all of a sudden she felt a sharp pain ripping through her body. It was as if someone had taken a knife to her. She gasped silently in surprise. The knife kept bearing down. She clutched the edge of the desk to stop herself from screaming out. A second later the attack was over, leaving her body cold and weak.

The voice on the phone seemed to come from a long way off. "Okay, Miz Townsend, you've got yourself a deal."

Pull yourself together, Kathryn told herself. She spoke, hoping her voice would sound normal. "You will have your money within the hour, and next time I look out my window I expect to see your men at work. Do we understand each other?"

She dropped the receiver back onto the hook. Exhausted by the attack, terrified that the pain would return, she sat frozen, not daring to move a muscle, almost afraid to breathe, terrified of bringing on another spasm.

After a quarter of an hour she decided that nothing was wrong. There was no need to call the doctor. At best he'd tell her to go to bed, at worst insist she be hospitalized. Nothing had happened. Just a few pains. And she couldn't afford to waste time with false alarms. She had a grand opening—the grandest one the city had ever seen—to orchestrate. Childbirth was perfectly natural. In China, didn't the women give birth in the fields and then go back to work? She would

not pamper herself no matter what Owen and Roger and that
foolish doctor said. They were men; what did they know
about having babies anyway?

The lavish gala opening of the Townsend Park was scheduled
for August 28. Only five days away, and Kathryn was afraid
half the rooms wouldn't be finished in time. But if no last-
minute problems raised their ugly heads, and if she could
keep to her schedule, and if the doctor was right . . . According to his calculations, the baby would arrive on the first
of September. The question that plagued her, making her
stomach churn with fear, was what to do if the baby arrived
early.

"First babies are never early," Rachel had pronounced
briskly. But she couldn't hide her worries and she threw all
her resources into trying to persuade Kathryn to cancel the
opening.

"Do you realize how lucky you are to be having a baby?
We tried for years. My Jacob would have given his right arm
for a son. Sometimes I think God was punishing me for my
past."

"I'm sorry, Rachel. But now that you're going to be an
honorary grandmother, shouldn't you be knitting little boo-
ties or something?"

"Don't be smart," she snapped. "If you won't consider
your own health, think of the baby's."

"Don't worry about that. My baby's a tough little one."
Kathryn thumped her stomach as if to prove it.

"Then what about Owen?" Rachel persisted. "He's so
excited about the baby, I'm sure he doesn't approve of your
taking risks." The way Kathryn's eyes darkened, Rachel knew
she had hit a sore point. "You've already had this out with
him, haven't you?" Kathryn nodded sheepishly, and Rachel
asked, "Who won?"

"He took his horses and went up to Saratoga for the races.
Said he always thought horses were the most 'pigheaded and
stubborn creatures in the world' until he met me. Those were
his exact words." She looked into Rachel's sharp eyes penetrating into hers. "Don't get excited. We've talked on the
telephone and everything is fine. He'll be home on Sunday."

"Remember when I told you to give Owen a chance? I was

right, wasn't I? What if you'd kept saying no? Where would you be now? Alone, that's where. No husband. No baby. I'm an interfering old woman, but believe me, I only do it because I love you and want you to be happy. I also realize that you don't listen to half of what I tell you and don't heed a quarter of what you do hear. But I want you to listen hard to what I'm going to tell you now.'' She looked at Kathryn, hoping and praying that she would understand.

"You know I'm fond of Owen, but he's no saint. No man is. Not even my Jacob. Owen adores you and right now he's willing to do just about anything to make you happy. But he has his breaking point. Don't push him too far, or someday . . . someday you might push him away forever. Then you'd realize what a wonderful man you'd lost for the sake of that damned hotel.''

Kathryn couldn't believe her ears. "You don't understand. I've worked too hard and too long on this hotel. New York has hundreds of hotels—dozens of fancy ones. Unless I can convince the right people that mine is the best—the most exclusive, the most luxurious, the most fashionable—I'll be one among the many, scrambling for every crumb of business.''

"Kathryn, dear, would it be so very terrible if the Townsend Park didn't turn out to be quite as grand and fashionable as you'd like?''

"I refuse to let that happen.''

"There's nothing so awful about failing, you know. It happens to everyone sooner or later.''

"Not to me.'' Kathryn's eyes blazed with indignation.

"Well, if you—'' Rachel stopped. In her mind she could hear Jacob's gruff voice. Stop being a meddling old woman. Can't you see the girl's terrified of failing?

Rachel's beady eyes peered out at Kathryn. Her chin was set, but as Rachel watched, she could see her chin tremble slightly, like a child on the verge of tears. Perhaps, Rachel thought, that's the burden of success. Kathryn has risen to such dizzying heights that a fall would be devastating. All her instincts told Rachel to comfort Kathryn, but instead she clamped her mouth shut and watched as Kathryn expertly forced her fears under control.

"You see, I know, I absolutely know, that this party will make the difference," Kathryn said, begging to be believed.

Her enthusiasm was dangerously contagious, and Rachel had to admit that Kathryn's plan for launching the hotel was brilliant and almost certain to ensure the Townsend Park a place in fashionable society. She had taken her theme from the baroque architecture of the building and the eighteenth-century antiques that filled the public rooms and suites; the party was to be a re-creation of a court ball at Versailles in the reign of Louis XIV. If they chose, guests could come dressed in period costumes, and the food and music, even the flowers, would all be of the appropriate period. "It won't be just another party, it will be the party of the decade," Kathryn promised her executive staff.

But New York society was jaded, and Kathryn knew that no idea, no matter how brilliant, would guarantee the attendance of all those who mattered. So with Machiavellian cleverness she began a whispering campaign. Select guests were told about the party in confidence and had to promise not to breathe a word to another soul. "Because this party will be terribly exclusive," Kathryn said, implying that only the most beautiful, the most fashionable, the brightest—like they—would be favored with invitations. Soon everyone was begging for invitations. They were sent out selectively.

Kathryn drew her guest list from everywhere, adding and subtracting, searching for the perfect mix that would make the party bubble and sparkle. There were members of New York high society—the Vanderbilts and Astors and Whitneys—and the nouveau riche, men who made their fortunes in manufacturing or retailing or the stock market. There were diplomats and politicians. Famous authors and artists and athletes. Actors and actresses whose names glittered nightly on Broadway. And movie stars—everyone seemed fascinated by them. Ruthlessly Kathryn exploited contacts and pulled strings to get the best. Her party would glitter like a ten-carat diamond, and they would talk about it for years. If only the baby didn't arrive early.

Chapter Six

Kathryn's eyes traveled around the ballroom. It had been worth all the planning and work and worry. Every surface glittered with painting and polishing. The hotel was perfect and she felt fine. Not a twinge of pain. Not a hint of a cramp. Nothing to spoil her triumph. The Townsend Park was being launched with all the star-studded fanfare it deserved. And deep down she knew it would be a success.

On the other side of the ballroom, Maureen Jones dropped a curtsy so deep that her carefully arranged tower of red curls almost swept the floor. The elegant silk gown nipped in her narrow waist and exposed the white, generously rounded tops of her breasts. Lace dripped from her sleeves, and behind her flowed three feet of peacock-blue brocade train embroidered in gold.

Owen bowed and graciously offered her his hand as she rose. "I see you are into the spirit of the evening." He didn't say what he was thinking: that it was a pleasant change to see a woman's natural figure. Nowadays women seemed obsessed with appearing boyish and angular.

Maureen laughed. "I suspect that your wife badgered Allan into wearing a costume, and then he insisted I wear one, too. After all, your wife is one of the bank's best customers."

"I sympathize. It isn't easy to stand up to Kathryn once she has an idea in her head."

"But you managed to." How handsome Owen looked in white tie and tails. Against the whiteness of his shirt, his hair stood out blacker and his eyes flashed even darker than usual. No one could mistake him for a man who spent his days behind a desk, not with that tanned skin. But Maureen couldn't help thinking he would be more comfortable astride a horse than at a fancy dress ball.

"I did. I put my foot down and refused to wear blue satin shoes," he said with a mischievous grin.

"I'm afraid," she said, "that Allan adores your wife and would do anything she asked of him, including wearing knee britches."

"Does that bother you?" Owen asked. She was an attractive woman, in a vigorous, wholesome way, but she couldn't hold a candle to Kathryn's delicate beauty.

For a moment she hesitated. "No, I don't think so. I have thought about it, but we can't all be Kathryn Townsends, and a woman like your wife requires an exceptionally strong man, which, bless him, I'm not sure Allan is."

Seeing a steely look come over Owen's face, Maureen knew she'd touched a nerve. Interesting, she thought; even a man like Owen Morgan, a man who seemed to exude raw power, found marriage to a woman like Kathryn difficult. Her voice was unnaturally cheerful as she quickly said, "Isn't this a magnificent room? Perfect for the occasion."

The Grand Ballroom of the Townsend Park was two hundred and fifty feet long and one hundred and twenty feet wide. But it looked even bigger. Mirrors lining one wall made it seem as if the golden room and the dancers were spinning on and on, ever smaller, into space. Under the dancers' feet an elaborate pattern of parquet glistened golden in the light of massive Bavarian crystal chandeliers. Above them on a vaulted ceiling, gods and goddesses and winged cherubs frolicked against a pastel-blue sky and pink-tinged clouds. The guests posed like fashion plates or perched on the delicate gilt chairs that lined one gold-and-white wall. Those who wore elaborate eighteenth-century costumes seemed to relish their roles as courtiers and their ladies. The ladies curtsied and flirted behind their lacy fans. The men in ruffles and satin bowed low and kissed the ladies' hands.

"The man in purple silk with the sword is the French ambassador. He's talking with the English ambassador and his wife," Owen explained. "Kathryn considers it quite a coup to have gotten them both here."

Maureen nodded, her eyes taking in all the glittering details. Finally they lit on a man and woman fox-trotting by.

She was thin as a twig and weighed down by rubies. "Isn't that a minor Vanderbilt? I think she's a client of Allan's." The man swung his partner around, turning to face them. Maureen's mouth dropped open. "And isn't that . . . ? I've seen him in the movies, but I never imagined he was so dashing in real life."

"It is," Owen said, helping himself to a drink from a passing waiter splendidly costumed as a footman in blue-and-gold satin livery. "He's stayed at the Townsend Manor several times. Incognito. I'm not sure how Kathryn persuaded him to be here tonight on display, though. My wife is a little like the Pied Piper." The pride in his voice was plainly evident.

"And isn't it all a bit much for a poor Irish farm girl?" Maureen said with wide eyes and an exaggerated brogue. She'd worked hard to banish the brogue that betrayed her County Cork origins, and it now appeared only in jest or when she was nervous.

"What would you have said if someone back in Ireland had told you what your life in New York would be like? That you'd marry a rising young banker and rub elbows with the stars."

"I'd have told them they'd been at the poteen. All this"— she gestured limply as if the excesses exhausted her—"would have been inconceivable. Why, I thought it was the height of luxury when we killed a pig in the fall and I knew there'd be bacon for the next six months. As far as I knew, not even the King and Queen of England lived this magnificently."

Owen nodded and surveyed the room. He felt a sympathetic bond with Maureen. They shared the same roots. Besides, she was unpretentious and easy to talk to. Squinting up at the crystal chandeliers, he said: "Do you know, I don't think there were that many lights in my whole little village— even on a winter night." He fell silent, trying to imagine what his life would have been like had he stayed in Wales. But he gave up; it was impossible to imagine a life without Kathryn. He thought of his mother and the other women in the village. Even the young girls were pale and sad-eyed, with little hope or ambition and certainly no dreams. Their goal was merely to survive.

"What about Kathryn? She seems to take all this in her stride," Maureen said.

"She does. But then she doesn't have her roots in Irish bogs or Welsh coal mines." He paused. "We don't talk about our pasts, but something, or someone, made her determined to prove herself."

"And tonight she certainly has," Maureen said. "Everybody who is anybody in this city must be here. And no matter how sophisticated, they all seem awed. Do you know that I could almost convince myself I'm at Versailles in the court of Louis the Fourteenth?"

"I expect it's your overactive Celtic imagination. But you know Kathryn—when she does something she plunges right in and does it right."

Maureen stared at the arched doorway where Kathryn stood laughing, talking, receiving her guests. "She looks radiant."

For a moment Owen was startled to see how greedily her eyes were fixed on his wife. As if she were torn between love and hate. Then he understood. Maureen desperately wanted a child, and seeing Kathryn looking so pregnant must be a heartbreaking reminder of her own failures.

"She certainly doesn't look at all like she's ready to give birth at any moment," Maureen said with a hint of wistfulness. Kathryn was wearing a long gown of pale green watered silk. It was low-cut but unbelted, falling gracefully about her body.

Kathryn felt Owen's eyes on her and flashed him a smile. She knew he was worrying, but she felt fine. For some miraculous reason, tonight even her body seemed lighter and less awkward. Everything was happening according to plan.

Buoyed up by the enthusiasm of her guests, Kathryn made her rounds tirelessly. She checked to make sure that the buffet tables were not picked over, that the chamber music drifting through the rose-colored lobby never stopped—conveniently forgetting that Rachel and Roger were checking the same details. This was her party, her responsibility, and she was determined that everything be perfect. She seemed to be everywhere—talking and laughing and sparkling, relishing her triumph.

Late in the evening she found Owen at her side. He kissed her gently on the forehead. "You look beautiful. And your party is a spectacular success. Everyone says so. But I have one complaint I want to register.'' She frowned and he quickly continued. ''I haven't danced with you.''

Kathryn patted her stomach and laughed. ''I'm afraid it wouldn't be much fun. We couldn't get close. At least we know one thing about our child—having timed his arrival for after the party, he, or she, has proved himself considerate.''

''Smart, too,'' Owen added, putting his arm around her thick waist. ''He knew he didn't dare spoil his mother's night of success.''

Outside on the street, the crowd had been gathering for hours. By the time the first limousine pulled up, there were barricades on either side of the entrance to the Townsend Park, and two burly policemen, beefy arms folded across their chests, dared the crowd to come within touching distance of the guest. But the people just wanted to look.

Every time a car drew up, a whisper of anticipation arose. ''Who is it? Looks like . . . Do you think?'' And as the guests climbed out of the cars, flashes popped and reporters poised like gundogs on the scent, waiting for the quotes that could make headlines.

Across the street, hidden in the entrance to a store, Edward waited in the shadows and wondered why he had come. He hadn't wanted to. Every day his hatred of Kathryn grew. The jealousy festered until it became a physical force. In his mind's eye he could see it: bricks, piled up one on top of another, resting on his chest. The pain was becoming unbearable. It pressed against him, threatening to crush him. To squeeze his windpipe. To collapse his lungs. Sometimes he could scarcely breathe, the pressure and fear were so great.

Kathryn, why was it Kathryn? Why should she be the darling of the press and that mob of riffraff? He'd be rich now with hotels all over the country if she hadn't stolen his money.

At three in the morning, when the last of the glittering guests had reluctantly departed, Kathryn and Owen finally emerged to find the street deserted. Only the faithful Emil waited in the Packard.

From his hiding place Edward watched with sharp, hawk-like eyes. Kathryn, he noted, was smiling, but great dark circles hung under her eyes and her movements were heavy,

as if she were forcing her swollen body forward with every
last ounce of strength. She never had known how a proper
lady should behave. He felt his anger rising. The pain in his
chest was growing sharper. If he concentrated on his pain,
then perhaps he'd be able to breathe. Tomorrow . . . tomorrow he would conceive the perfect plan. For revenge.

By the time the Packard pulled up in front of their house,
Kathryn was asleep with her head resting against Owen's
shoulder. When he helped her into the bedroom, she barely
opened her eyes. The next afternoon she was still in bed, but
wide awake and surrounded by newspapers all proclaiming
her triumph.

The social columnist for the *Tribune* pronounced: "Although the Townsend Park is smaller, I predict it will give
the famed Plaza and the Waldorf a run for their money." In
the *Telegram* the gossip columnist lauded: "The brilliant little hotelier Kathryn Townsend Morgan came up with a sen-
sationally innovative way to launch her newest hotel. Imagine
a re-creation of the court of Louis XIV. Amongst the sparkling ensemble of guests were . . ."

It was late afternoon before Kathryn reached her office.
There was a note in the middle of her desk marked "Urgent," and Miss Willis was fluttering around anxiously. "It's
Mr. Jones. He's called three times already and must talk to
you. It's extremely urgent, he says, but I wouldn't let him
disturb you at home."

"Thank you, Miss Willis. Get him on the phone immediately." Allan was not an alarmist. What could be so important?

"Kathryn, your party was magnificent. Maureen and I had
a wonderful time." Allan paused. "But unfortunately, that's
not why I'm calling. Damn it, I hate to rain on your parade,
but there's a time problem."

Kathryn's fingers drummed impatiently on her desk. "Go
on. Spit it out."

"I'm afraid the bubble has officially burst. The Florida
bubble, that is. You can barely give land away. Last night a
hurricane ripped up the coast. You lost a lot of shorefront,
and the three cottages . . . well, they're now piles of sticks.
However, the good news is that the gentleman who wants

your property phoned this morning and is willing to pay forty cents on the dollar. A very generous offer, considering. Problem is he has to have an answer by six o'clock today. I hope you won't insist on being stubborn, Kathryn. This may be your last chance to unload that white elephant and salvage some of your—and the bank's—investment.''

Kathryn's voice was thoughtful. ''Just who is this gentleman and why is he so interested in this supposedly worthless land? It seems odd. What does he know that I don't?''

''I have no idea. Never met him myself. We've only talked on the phone. But he's legitimate. Comes well recommended by Ralph P. Poindexter, the president of the bank.''

Kathryn took a deep breath. If she was going to change her mind, she'd have to do it now. If she accepted his offer, the Townsend Manor would be safe. After a few long moments, she said: ''Tell him to take his forty cents and— No, that would be rude. Just tell him that Mrs. Townsend has decided to be stubborn.'' Under her breath she added, ''She refuses to sell her dream cheap.''

Chapter Seven

She was in the arms of the French ambassador, whirling around the floor. She looked up. Pink-and-white cherubs grinned down at her. Thousands of crystal pendants winked and blinked. He spun her faster and faster. The cherubs disappeared. The painted ceiling dissolved into a pastel blur. Faster and faster. The chandelier was a golden ball of light. Her feet no longer reached the floor. She was flying, spinning up toward the angels and cherubs and light. Everything was a wheeling mass of color and light. He was holding her closer and closer, tighter and tighter.

All of a sudden the pressure became intolerable. Why was he hurting her? They'd been dancing and it had been wonderful. Then everything was dark and her body was falling, tumbling through an endless black void.

When Kathryn awoke she understood: it had been a dream. The party—she'd worked so hard, so long; now, three days later, it refused to let her go. She smiled. It had been wonderful. A triumph, just as the newspapers said.

When the second contraction tore through her, she knew that the pain hadn't been a dream. It seemed to send every nerve in her body into screaming agony. She gasped and pressed herself into the bed, trying to escape the pressure. But it dogged her. Torturing her. Leaving her shaking.

Finally she woke Owen. "It seems that our child is an early riser," she said between contractions. "I think you'd better get me to the hospital." When the next contraction gripped her, Owen held her, pulling her closer and closer to his own body, trying desperately to absorb her pain.

During one of the quiet, pain-free moments Kathryn found

herself staring up at him. With a start she realized she was trying to memorize his face—the dark, crisply curly hair, the thick expressive brows, the eyes black as coal, the tanned and rugged skin. In case she never saw him again.

She gave herself a mental shake. It wasn't the same as with Jessica. An expert medical staff would be attending her. But no matter how hard she tried, she couldn't erase the image of Jessica's gnawed, bloodstained lips.

She gripped his hand and tried to speak through the pain of an oncoming contraction. "Owen, I want you to know how . . . how much I love you." The pain was growing sharper, the knives cutting through her body, slicing away at her organs. She struggled for breath. "I know I haven't been . . . the sort of wife you deserve, but . . ."

He returned her squeeze. "Kathryn Townsend Morgan, are you getting sentimental?" His coallike eyes lit up with laughter, until he looked into her haunted eyes and realized that she was scared. Her fear unnerved him. She was always so strong; he'd never known her to be unsure or afraid of anything. His heart leapt into his throat. Should he be afraid, too? Women did die in childbirth. If he lost her . . .

He forced his voice to sound hearty and confident. "Nothing to it, you know. You told me yourself that in China women have babies right in the fields and then go back to work."

"That's fine for you to say. You don't have to go through it." He was relieved to hear the familiar teasing note in her voice.

"Yes, but don't make my part sound too easy. I'll be out there in the father's waiting room wearing a hole in the carpet. All that beastly pacing back and forth will be exhausting, you know."

A smile came to Kathryn's lips, but it was caught unawares by a spasm of pain worse than all those that had gone before. As agonizing waves assaulted her body, her mind kept reiterating the same thought—a thought that shook her by its unexpectedness. Mother. I want my mother. She could make the pain stop. She'd protect me. When the contraction finally faded, her whole body was weak and shivery from fear and exhaustion. Her unconscious, primitive response stunned her. Did every woman long for the comforting presence of her mother at this time? It wasn't as if Lily had ever been a normal, loving mother, yet something deep inside Kathryn called out for her.

As if he sensed her need, Owen hugged her closer, pressing her head to his comforting, solid shoulder. "Kathryn, I'm here. Everything will be all right, I promise you. Besides, I love you too much to lose you." Yet underneath his encouraging words he felt powerless to protect her.

Their son entered the world with a minimum of fuss at ten twenty-two a.m. on September 1, 1926. The doctor was pleased; he liked his predictions to be accurate. At two o'clock the nurse decided that Kathryn was awake enough to see her baby. "He's perfect," she whispered, handing her the blue bundle.

Kathryn was almost afraid to look down. When she felt the baby's weight in her arms and then saw his little red, scrunched-up face, the truth hit her with the power of a bolt of lightning: it was real. A living, breathing baby. An adorable, fat little nose. Wisps of dark hair peeping out from under the blanket. A tiny human being.

All the months she'd carried him she hadn't really believed in this life. It had moved and kicked and positioned itself uncomfortably on her bladder, but it hadn't been real. It had merely been it. Not a real baby with stubby eyelashes and ears that unfolded like rosebuds. A baby who would walk and talk and learn algebra and someday have children of his own. Stunned, she leaned back against the mountain of pillows.

For a long while she just lay there cradling him gently, staring down into his unfocused eyes, almost afraid of him. She could run a successful business, but holding this tiny life made her feel inadequate. He looked so small, so fragile. So heartbreakingly vulnerable. She was afraid to touch him. As if, like a fine piece of crystal, he could shatter at the slightest touch. He was asleep, but what if he should awaken? What if he squirmed out of her arms? Cautiously she pulled him closer to her.

Curiosity finally overcame her fears. The nurse claimed he was perfect, but had she looked carefully? Could she have confused him with another baby? If there was something wrong, would they tell her now or would they break the news gradually? She looked up. The nurse had tactfully disappeared, leaving the door ajar. Very slowly—almost afraid of what she would find—Kathryn peeled off the blanket. She examined every inch of his miniature body. It was perfect. Her son was perfect.

Years later she would be able to call back that moment with utter clarity. That moment when her awe and fear turned to love—an incredible, unexpected love that overwhelmed her. Her heart seemed to swell up within her chest and her whole body tingled. It was nothing like the love she had felt for Adam or experienced with Owen—that was a love between two independent people. This was the love she felt for a tiny, absolutely perfect creature that had come out of her body and was totally dependent on her, an infant whose every instinct told it to reach out toward her. "I love you and I'll take care of you forever. I promise." She brought her lips to his wrinkled forehead. "I'll make sure you have a perfect life."

When the nurse brought in a bottle, the baby grasped it immediately. Kathryn marveled at his cleverness, but the nurse said flatly, "They always do." Watching his miniature mouth seize the nipple, Kathryn felt her fears receding. He was a strong and tough little boy, her son. She didn't have to worry about him. He knew exactly what to do.

When Owen arrived, the sight of his wife holding their child rooted him in the doorway; for a moment he was paralyzed by the force of his precariously balanced emotions. He didn't know whether to laugh or cry. When he finally spoke, he knew the voice wasn't his own. "You know what you remind me of?" he said, coming over to her bed. "One of those madonnas in the paintings we saw in Italy. Only so very much more beautiful." Finally he dragged his eyes from Kathryn's palely radiant face to his son.

"He's perfect," she said. "I checked. All his fingers and toes. And you should see the tiny little fingernails and . . . ."

"Are you going to introduce us?" Owen asked. The armload of red carnations dropped onto the bed unnoticed.

"Mr. Morgan, I'd like you to meet your son, the handsomest and brightest baby in the hospital," she said, carefully turning the baby to face his father.

Against the baby's tiny cheek Owen's hand was enormous as he reached out to touch him. It was a long while before he spoke, and when he did his voice was thick with emotion. "We never did decide on a name."

Kathryn hesitated. "I'd like to call him . . . Adam."

"Adam." He repeated it slowly. "A good name. Solid. The first man. Our first son." His eyes were glued to the baby's face.

"You don't mind if he doesn't carry your name?"

Owen shook his head. "I would love him even if you wanted to call him Hortense."

Kathryn breathed a silent sigh of relief. She didn't know when the idea had first come to her, but the name kept hammering at her in the midst of the worst of her labor pains. Repay a debt. Because of you, Adam Elliott's life was cut short. Grant a new Adam a long and happy life. Her son would be as rich as his namesake, but he'd also, she vowed, have the support of two parents who would love him enough to let him lead his own life.

Edward sniffed. The aroma of flowers was cloying, overwhelming. Massive bouquets filled Kathryn's hospital room. Greedily his eyes surveyed the baskets of fruit and elegantly wrapped gifts, so many they spilled onto the floor. How pathetically anxious people were to curry favor with those in power. Edward stood in the doorway, wearing a white coat and looking like one of the doctors scurrying around the hospital on an errand of mercy. No one had questioned him. And Kathryn, the only person who would recognize him, couldn't see him; she was asleep, a peaceful smile resting lightly on her lips. So sweet. So innocent. For a moment he forgot she was the enemy.

The baby was also asleep, its round little eyes closed, its miniature fists tightly clenched. Edward stood transfixed, staring at it for as long as he dared.

His own child hadn't survived, but Jessica had produced a sickly female and Kathryn had given birth to a big, strong boy. But of course, Kathryn would produce a perfect heir. His sister did everything perfectly. He could feel his jaw tightening with hatred and he willed himself to be calm. He had to think. To plan.

Suddenly the child's eyes snapped open and stared straight into his. Mature and wise, they seemed to penetrate into his mind, reading his every thought. Feeling the baby's eyes fixed on him, he was gradually overcome by desire. Prickling his mind, tantalizing, then filling his mind and finally overwhelming his body. He wanted the baby dead. He wanted to see its tiny body stiff and cold. Its knowing little eyes forever closed.

No. Everything had gone his sister's way for too long. What he wanted to do was to break her spirit in the slowest, most painful way possible. His pink tongue emerged like a hungry lizard's and licked at his bloodless lips. What he wanted was to see her squirm in helpless agony as she watched her empire crumble, brick by precious brick.

Everyone said his sister was clever. But he would prove himself even more clever by engineering her downfall. He would see to it that she went down in the flames of public humiliation. No laws would be broken—only Kathryn's spirit. And he knew exactly how to do it—once he found the right women.

And the baby? It wasn't the boy's fault. He would give the infant a gift. The gift of a mother's love. When Kathryn no longer had her hotels, she could devote herself to the boy. A devoted mother. That was what every boy deserved, wasn't it?

Chapter Eight

Daisy knew what men liked. Men were her business. Not that she always understood why they wanted what they did. Like tonight. But it was a job. At least she'd get a free meal out of it.

She blotted her scarlet lips on a scrap of toilet paper and stared into the mirror again. Her friend Maddie would be going with her. Poor Maddie wasn't in the bloom of youth—forty-three compared to Daisy's thirty-eight—but Daisy figured she could use the meal.

Maddie teetered over to her in a pair of orange high-heeled sandals. A thin turquoise chiffon skirt ended above her knees and was thin enough to show most of her plump, dimpled thighs. Despite the warm September weather, she'd draped a wilted pink feather boa around her neck, taking care that it didn't cover any part of the rounded breasts that popped over the top of her dress. A bit overdone but, Daisy decided, just what her gentleman had ordered.

"How do I look?" Maddie asked nervously. "Am I okay?"

"You'll do," Daisy said. "But hurry up, we can't be late."

"I'm so excited," Maddie gushed. "I ain't never been to a place like that before." On the subway uptown Maddie bubbled over with questions. "What's his name? Where did you meet him? What's he like?"

Daisy slowly chewed on her gum. "Says his name's Edward. But ya can never tell, can ya? Sometimes they think they have to make up names fer girls like us. And fer Christ's sake, Maddie, don't get your hopes up. He's old. If you ask me, he's half in the grave already."

Maddie sat and sulked, wondering if the evening was going to be a dud after all. "I won't do anything weird, you know. Not even if that's the way he gets his kicks," she said as they got off the subway. Worry puckered her puffy lips. "He won't expect ta see us doin' it together, will he? I ain't never done it with another woman and I won't. Sorry, Daisy, it ain't nothin' personal, you know."

"Stop bein' silly, Maddie. You probably won't even have to take off your clothes tonight."

As they approached the front entrance Maddie's mouth dropped in surprise; then she balked. "They don't let girls like us in places like this, do they?"

"I told ya, my gentleman said he'd fix it. We just have to be there on time." But the same fear had been running through Daisy's head. Maybe it was all some sort of cruel joke. She clutched her purse. The man who called himself Edward had given her twenty dollars; that was no joke. So even if they were turned away at the door . . . Would she have to share the twenty with Maddie? "Just pretend ya know what yer doin'," she said, ignoring the doorman and pushing open the revolving door before anyone could stop her.

"Ya should've seen that headwaiter guy's face when he saw us," Daisy said later. "Looked like somebody hit 'im with a wet fish."

It was William's first night on duty, filling in for Maximilian in the Venetian Room, and he was bursting with pride as he escorted guests to their tables, presenting the menus with the flourish he'd been practicing in front of the mirror at home. He wished his mother and little brother were there to watch his triumph. The two women, however, caught him by surprise. He knew what they looked like, but they couldn't be, not in the dining room of the Townsend Manor. It was unthinkable. Not knowing what else to do, he led them to their table. The man had tipped him ten dollars on the way in and explained that he was expecting two guests. Was it, William wondered now, his way of assuring that the women would be seated without any problem? And since he'd taken the money . . .

Edward smiled when he saw the two women. He had made an excellent choice. No one but the most naive could doubt their calling. Old and fleshy and ridiculous-looking in their short skirts, which revealed too much of their fat little legs. Painted up as if they were Indians on the warpath and convinced they were still beautiful and desirable. Like Lily, who had believed herself young and beautiful until the day she died in that tragic accident.

To Edward's delight, the women made a great, noisy fuss about being seated. What he didn't like was the soft, fleshy feel of their lips puckering against his. He quickly wiped his mouth and then refolded his napkin to hide the bloody stains of their lipstick.

As William backed away from the table, he couldn't help noticing the women's plump legs and white flesh above the tops of their rolled stockings when they bent over to kiss the man.

"I think I'll have the filet mignon. It's the most expensive," Daisy said, licking her bow-shaped lips. "And tonight . . . why, anything goes, doesn't it, darling?"

The man muttered something which William couldn't hear, but he could sense an uneasy stirring around the dining room as people resumed their conversations rather more loudly than before, hoping to drown out the embarrassing party.

"Yer not gonna be sorry," the woman in blue promised. "We'll make sure of that, won't we, Daisy?"

"Damn tootin'," she shrieked, hoisting her glass.

That was the final straw for the gray-haired man at the adjoining table. He abruptly signaled the waiter for his check and hurried his pale-looking wife out of the dining room. William was in over his head. Perhaps if he just told the women to lower their voices. . . . How he wished that Maximilian hadn't chosen tonight to visit his sick sister-in-law. Maximilian would know exactly what to do. By now even William had to admit what the women were, but they were accompanied by a very respectable-looking old gentleman. Were they doing anything illegal? The police would know. He reached for the phone, but as he was about to dial, Mrs. Townsend's instructions came back to him: "Never call the police except in the most dire emergency. We must avoid bad publicity at all costs." Mrs. Townsend was always very kind and understanding, but when somebody deliberately disobeyed her orders . . .

He replaced the receiver and stared down hopelessly at his

reservations book. Perhaps he should call the night manager. But he didn't like the night manager. Rhcinhold had once unjustly accused him of being rude to a difficult guest. Now he was bound to blame the whole situation on him. William was fighting panic, feeling too young and inexperienced for the job and wishing with all his heart he were still a waiter.

"We're gonna have a great time." The voice was husky. "You want a free peek at the merchandise? Right now?"

From out of the corner of his eye Edward risked a look at the headwaiter. The boy's mouth was open in astonishment. The fool had no idea what to do. It was a sign: God was on his side. If He weren't, it wouldn't have been Maximilian's night off.

As the woman's scarlet-nailed hand reached down into her cleavage, the room fell silent. It was an ominous, embarrassed silence. Realizing what had happened, she laughed, a loud, braying laugh. "Guess that means everyone wants to see 'em." She pulled down the front of her dress slightly to reveal two mountains of crepelike white flesh sagging under the weight of two large brown nipples.

There was a collective, shocked intake of breath. Chairs were pushed out, one by one, as guests fled the dining room. Most of them were too stunned to say anything, but one man announced to a red-faced William, "If this is what the Townsend Manor has degenerated to, I certainly will not pay for my dinner. And if Mrs. Townsend has any objections, she can call my lawyer. Imagine exposing my wife to such lewd . . ." His protest ended in a sputter of indignation.

It's all my fault, William thought miserably. If only I'd done something. But he still didn't know what he should have done. He did know that this could destroy his career. He'd be lucky to be demoted to busboy. Or dishwasher. His head buzzing with fear and embarrassment, he stared glumly around the almost empty dining room. Only one other table was occupied—by a man in a tuxedo who appeared oblivious to the drama under his nose. He was bowed over a notebook. William decided to let both tables finish their meals. What else could he do?

But by three o'clock the next day, the evening edition of the *Tribune* hit the newsstands, and by seven o'clock almost everyone in New York knew.

An incredulous Roger reread the story before crumpling the paper in his fist. "That bloody bastard." Why hadn't he been told about the incident? He might have been able to hush it up, but now . . .

As soon as the word arrived for him to see Mr. Pennington, William knew: it was the end of his job.

"Why wasn't I informed about the scandalous incident in the Venetian Room?" Roger thundered as William opened the door.

Amongst the younger, more irreverent members of the staff, Roger Pennington was referred to, behind his back, as "Paleface." Winter or summer, his English pallor never varied, so now William was surprised to find his face bright with emotion.

"It . . . it didn't seem all that important, sir." William stumbled.

"Not important according to you, perhaps. Obviously someone was of a different opinion." He thrust the crumpled newspaper into William's shaking hand.

As he read, William could feel the bottom dropping out of his world. His shame was right there in black and white for everyone in New York to see. His mother. His brother. Their neighbors. His friends. Everyone to whom he'd bragged about his job. Why wouldn't the blue-carpeted floor open up and swallow him? What could he say? He'd failed. His first chance and he'd failed miserably. Worse still—he'd brought shame on Mrs. Townsend.

"I trust you agree now that it was rather more important, don't you?"

William managed to squeak out a "Yes, sir."

"Then tell me how it happened. I want to hear every detail of this beastly affair." Newspapers exaggerated. Perhaps it wasn't as awful as it sounded, Roger told himself.

After William had haltingly told his story, Roger could barely breathe. It was worse than he could have imagined. Finally he said, "I don't suppose you remember what the man looked like?"

"No . . . not—not really," William stammered. "I mean, he sat with his back to me and the rest of the room."

"Pull yourself together and try to remember. When he

came in. When he gave you the money. Do you remember anything at all about him?''

His voice was anxious, and William desperately wanted to tell him something. He screwed up his face in concentration. The harder he tried the more blank his mind became.

''Well, was he old or young? Fat? Thin? Dark or fair? You must remember something. You aren't a complete idiot, are you?''

''The man looked ordinary and I guess he was old. I know he was taller than me.'' He spoke more confidently. ''Not good-looking either. I understand why he had to have that kind of woman . . .'' His voice trailed off. Why should this matter? Suddenly he remembered what did matter. ''Mrs. Townsend, she won't have to hear about this, will she? Please, Mr. Pennington.''

Roger looked as if he were on the verge of explosion, and with all his heart William wished that he hadn't asked. ''I don't know how we can keep it from her,'' Roger said. ''By tomorrow everyone in the city who can read will know. We will be the laughingstock of the business. There won't be a respectable woman willing to be seen within blocks of us. I remember how a perfectly respectable hotel was once mentioned in a popular music-hall song. The hotel was ruined.'' Roger stared down at his desk. ''No one but out-of-towners who don't know any better will stay here. Midwest milkmaids. Pig farmers from Iowa. Cowboys who smell as bad as their horses.'' How on earth was he to explain this to Kathryn?

The next morning Roger lingered outside Kathryn's hospital doorway, embarrassed to be seeing such a private moment and at the same time deeply moved. Before him was a new Kathryn. A softer one without the quick, wary, watchful look in her eyes. She was a mother cradling her child like millions of other mothers had throughout the centuries. A far cry from the determined spitfire who'd marched into his office at the Blackstone five years ago.

Kathryn's sleek dark head was bent over the baby's small fuzzy one. His round eyes were wide, carefully moving around the room, trying to take it all in. ''You're curious, aren't you?'' she was saying. ''And you want to get out of this hospital and see what's going on in your new world. To tell the truth, so does your mother. Oh, Adam, there are so many things I want to show you. Such wonderful things I can teach you. Things we can do together. And you'll have an easier time than I did. Your father and I love you more than anything in the world and we always will.''

She stopped and looked up when she sensed another presence. Her smile was sheepish. ''I'm afraid it's a rather one-sided conversation at the moment.''

''I apologize for interrupting, but I have some news that can't wait.'' His eyes darted nervously around the flower-filled room.

''You sound as gloomy as you look. Come in and sit down.'' She patted the bed. ''Whatever it is, it can't be awful enough to justify that pallbearer expression.''

Roger positioned himself at the foot of her bed and told his story, quoting the newspaper column word for horrible word. He kept his eyes glued to Kathryn's face, waiting for signs of erupting anger. There were none, although the corners of her mouth did twitch slightly.

''You mean we had two . . . two hookers dining in our hotel?'' she asked.

''I'm afraid so.'' His tone was sepulchral. ''What I can't quite understand is how the newspapers picked up the story so quickly. Someone must have called them. But we are ruined. Ruined.''

''Nonsense. Of course we aren't ruined.''

''What do you mean? Don't you remember the story of that beastly music-hall song? It ruined that hotel. The damage . . .'' He shook his head, unable to finish the dismal thought.

''Roger, that was years ago. People think differently nowadays. They talk about sex in mixed company—frequently. They debate the virtues of free love over tea.''

''Kathryn, have you taken leave of your senses? I'm sorry to be so blunt, but you know how important it is to maintain a hotel's reputation. It's as sacred as . . .''

''As what—a virgin?'' Kathryn supplied with a light laugh. ''I don't think this incident will really harm us. No one was hurt. The two women got a good dinner out of it. Some people will find it amusing. It may even give us some momentary celebrity. Now what about young William?''

Roger's face flushed. "I must confess I was so angry that I forgot to fire him. I'll see to it this afternoon."

"Don't. He's young and inexperienced. He was in over his head in a delicate situation. But he's hardworking and loyal, and I have a hunch he'll be valuable to the hotel when he grows up. In the meantime, don't worry. It will all blow over."

She paused. Something did disturb her. "I can't help thinking, though, how peculiar this is. Why would any man in his right mind want to invite two common streetwalkers to dinner at a fine hotel? As a joke?" She stopped, and Roger could see the wheels in her mind turning. "No, it's almost as if he had a grudge against us."

Then her face lit up. "Have Miss Willis check my card file to see if we've had any disgruntled guests recently. Men who would fit the description William gave us."

"I can't help thinking this would be a great deal less worrisome if we understood why," Roger said glumly.

Kathryn nodded. Unanswered questions, like loose ends, bothered her, too. "I wonder if . . . Just before the Townsend Park opened, I had a problem with one of the unions, remember? Wendell claimed they're run by the mob." She paused, her face concentrated in a thoughtful frown. Finally she said, "No, I don't think it's Mr. DiFranco's style. Brass knuckles, yes, but this was a bit too clever and sophisticated."

"It's probably irrelevant," Roger said, "but what about the man who vandalized his room? Remember, the mystery guest."

"Interesting," she said slowly. "But that happened almost a year ago and that man was obviously crazy. This man is clever. Why don't you get that house detective you insisted on hiring to work on it?"

House detective—her words prodded Roger's memory. There was something . . . yes, the man on the elevator. The man who had attacked Mrs. Walmsly's daughter. Three unexplained incidents. Motiveless. Unsolved. Could there be a connection? Probably not. A hotel, any hotel, attracted queer characters occasionally. It was a fact of life in the business and impossible to guard against; hotels were too accessible and these people were too unpredictable.

* * *

Ralph P. Poindexter wasn't proud of the fact that he read the gossip columns—and would never admit it to anyone. But after plowing through *The Wall Street Journal* and *The New York Times,* he felt he deserved some light entertainment, and so he turned to the *Tribune.* Hilarious story, really—two prostitutes dining in style. Suddenly a bell rang in his mind. Townsend Manor. Kathryn Townsend. Hadn't his bank made a substantial loan recently? Some deal arranged by that young Allan Jones fellow. All at once the story seemed less amusing.

"Get Jones on the phone," he barked at his quivering secretary.

"Jones. Poindexter. Something's just been brought to my attention. One of the bank's clients—one of your clients—is sitting in the midst of a scandal." He stopped. Puffed on his cigar. Let him wonder. Let him sweat. Finally he said, "Kathryn Townsend."

From Allan's end came a relieved laugh. "I can't imagine that she's done anything too scandalous."

"You can't, huh? Look at today's *Tribune.* Page eighteen."

Allan scrambled through the newspapers on his desk. After a few moments he said, "I see it, Mr. Poindexter. Obviously someone is trying to manufacture a story. Probably the columnist himself, short of news. Silly, really. It will blow over soon enough."

"Tell me, Jones, how much of the bank's money did you loan her?" He gave a low whistle when he heard the figure. "Her collateral?"

"The Townsend Manor, sir."

"Won't be able to give that away when this scandal hits. And guess who'll be stuck holding a hotel no one will go near? The bank, that's who."

"Sir, Mr. Poindexter, aren't you overreacting?"

"Certainly not. Merely cautious with our investors' money. Must keep your ears and eyes open. Banking is not just figures, you know. Got to be able to spot people's weaknesses." He paused, and Allan prayed the tirade was at an end. "And that's not all," he began with renewed vigor. "This reminds me. Some unfavorable gossip about that woman floating around. Something unsavory about her past."

"Nonsense." Allan tried to hide his growing annoyance. Poindexter was barking up the wrong tree. "I will personally vouch for Kathryn Townsend. Her business instincts and abilities are as good as any man's."

Poindexter harrumphed. "Tell you one thing, they're certainly better than yours. Imagine a loan of that magnitude." Allan could see what was coming and dreaded it. "What did she use the money for? Another hotel?"

"No, sir. Land."

"Land? Where?" he barked.

"In Florida." There was no use trying to defend her purchase. He only hoped that Poindexter never found out that she had refused two good offers for the property.

"The stupid . . . Throwing money around. . . . Proves that women should leave business to us. Just don't have the brains for it."

Allan Jones could be pushed only so far. Poindexter might be the president of the bank, but he didn't have an original or creative bone in his conservative pin-striped body. "Wait a minute, sir. Kathryn Townsend is—"

"No, you wait a minute, Jones. I want a complete dossier on this Townsend woman and her finances. Everything— personally and professionally, past and present. Hire a private detective. I want it by Friday. Then I'll decide whether to call in her loan or not."

Chapter Nine

Kathryn leaned back on the overstuffed sofa, allowing her sore body to sink down among the cushions. Their living room had never looked more inviting with its cheerful beige-and-rose colors, graceful English antiques and tall French doors that opened onto a small balcony overlooking the street. Late afternoon sunshine flowed in through the open doors, filling the high-ceilinged room with warm light that turned the cream-colored walls to apricot. In the empty fireplace stood an enormous antique blue-and-white porcelain bowl filled with wine-red chrysanthemums. A gentle breeze wafted their tangy scent to every corner of the room.

What a relief it was to be home. No more bland food. No more antiseptic odors. And no more white-uniformed processions marching through her room telling her what to do.

Under Rachel's watchful eye, Mrs. Blair put down the tea tray, arranged the silver and set out the delicate, flowered cups. The sweet smell of freshly baked pastries rose temptingly.

"It's good to have you home," the housekeeper said. "Mr. Morgan asked you not to wait for him. He doesn't want tea. He's in the nursery."

"Where else?" Kathryn said with a laugh. "Rachel, did you know that men could be so crazy about babies? I thought they just wanted sons to play baseball and go fishing with, but Owen . . . he spends every moment he can with Adam. Sometimes just staring down into the crib. I don't think he can quite believe what we've created. Then, neither can I."

"And since when is your Owen like other men?" Rachel said with a sniff. "He's strong enough and confident enough to let his gentle side show. Like my Jacob was. Most men are afraid to."

"If I didn't know better, I'd think you were in love with my husband," Kathryn said with a fond smile.

Rachel's laugh seemed to resonate from her massive lace-covered bosom. "Believe me, if I were younger . . . well, I'd have given you a run for your money. But I'm afraid it would have been hopeless. That man would move heaven and earth for you if he thought that's what you wanted. And believe me, he just might be able to. Nothing, or nobody, seems beyond his power and charm. Did you notice how the whole hospital staff jumped to attention every time he appeared? Even that dried-up old nurse who was such a stickler for rules."

"He did win her over, didn't he? Although I think he did it just because she was such a challenge."

There was a knock at the door, and Mrs. Blair reentered carrying a stack of letters and packages. "I thought you might want to open these right away. They look like cards and baby presents."

"Please," Kathryn said, patting the sofa next to her, "just leave them here."

"Speaking of Owen," she said, turning to Rachel, "since you're one of his greatest fans you'll be interested to know that he had a phone call yesterday from the mayor, offering him a post." Kathryn didn't even try to keep the pride out of her voice.

"So what job is it and when does he start?"

"No idea," Kathryn said. "He didn't get that far before Owen turned him down."

She said it so matter-of-factly Rachel was amazed. "Turned him down! But it's an enormous honor."

"I suppose so, but you know Owen, he doesn't like politics. Considers it all corrupt and he doesn't want to get involved. He hates dishonesty with a passion. Could you imagine him as a politician? I don't think he could tell an outright lie to save himself. He's still the Welsh chapel-goer at heart. All that hellfire-and-damnation fear absorbed with his mother's milk, or so he claims."

"This city would be better off with some honest men like your husband," Rachel said tartly.

Eyeing the intriguing pile of packages, Kathryn could control her curiosity no longer and began tearing them open to find soft, woolly blankets, tiny pastel-colored sweaters, delicately embroidered pillowcases. Just as Kathryn was about to start opening the cards the doorbell sounded, bringing Mrs. Blair to the doorway a minute later.

"It's Mr. Jones. I told him that you'd just come home from the hospital, but he says it's urgent and—"

Kathryn held up her hand. "It's all right. I'm always home for Allan." When Allan appeared in the doorway, he looked ill at ease and surprised to see Rachel.

Rachel heaved herself out of the chair. "You two have business to discuss. I'll go visit my grandson."

"Tea?" Kathryn asked, gesturing to the teapot as Allan sat down in Rachel's chair. Then, noticing the paleness of his skin, she asked, "Or do you need a brandy?"

"No, thanks. I think we both need clear heads. Kathryn, I tried to stave this off as long as possible, but we have a problem."

"I told you I wasn't selling my Florida land, no matter what your prophets of doom predict."

"Actually, now I'm afraid it's a matter of what Ralph P. Poindexter says."

"Your bank president. The resident ogre, isn't that what you call him?" Kathryn asked.

"He called me a few days ago. He'd seen the column about the incident in your dining room."

"But that's all a tempest in a teapot. Surely you can convince him of that." Kathryn had all but forgotten the incident. It hadn't affected business one way or the other.

"You have to understand that once Poindexter gets the bit between his teeth . . ." He shrugged. "I spoke to him again this morning and he still insists we hire a private investigator to look into the Townsend Corporation."

"Well, he won't find anything," Kathryn snapped. "Except that it's making money."

Allan swallowed hard. "It's somewhat unorthodox, but he also wants to have your personal background investigated. Seems he heard . . ."

Kathryn didn't hear the rest of the sentence. She couldn't hear anything over the sound of the wave that roared into her head. *Her personal life.* He'd find out about Edward, Adam, the stolen money—everything that she'd worked so hard to bury and forget. It would all come out, and Owen . . . She felt a sob rising in her throat. And Owen would never forgive her. He could never accept being married to a woman whose brother was a murderer. A woman who had built her business on stolen money. The roar in her head grew louder and louder. What if Owen left her? Of course he'd leave her. Her own words rang in her ears: "He hates dishonesty with a passion." And for the past eight years his own wife had been living a lie.

". . . has lined up an excellent firm of private detectives." With a start Allan realized that Kathryn's eyes were hard and affixed to a point somewhere above his head. Her face looked as if it had been cast in stone, and obviously she was not listening to a word he said. "Kathryn, are you all right?"

His voice came from a distance, echoing through her head as if they were trapped at opposite ends of a tunnel. Under it another voice whispered sternly, "You've got to pull yourself together. You can't let him suspect anything is wrong."

With a great effort she opened her mouth—it felt as soft as cotton—and forced her numb lips to form words. "I'm sorry. It's just . . ." To her amazement, her voice began to sound surer. She continued briskly. "It's just the aftereffects of childbirth. Sometimes I find myself drifting off." From the quizzical look on Allan's face, she knew he barely believed her. "When you and Maureen finally have your baby, you'll learn all about postpartum depression."

He smiled, distracted. "Yes, I bet we will."

"Surely you can make Poindexter see that an investigation is totally ridiculous and a complete waste of money—and I thought that if there's anything you bankers hate, it's wasting money. All he has to know is that I took two old down-at-the-heels hotels and made them not only fashionable, but profitable. Three, if you count the old Blackstone in Boston. You've seen my books, and I suspect you had every bottom line memorized before you even considered making the loan."

Allan had to admit she was right. Kathryn had a talent for making money. But going up against Ralph P. Poindexter wasn't to be taken lightly. It could jeopardize his entire career. The career he'd planned so carefully. He wanted the walnut-paneled corner office. He wanted the efficient, well-groomed secretaries. He wanted the private luncheon clubs.

He stared at Kathryn. Could what Poindexter said have any truth to it? Poindexter had sat there at his massive desk puffing on his cigar and pontificating. "You can't be too careful. Some fellow at the club knew her family years ago. Seems your Mrs. Townsend was once institutionalized." He had savored the words. "Apparently some fellow jilted her. Drove her over the edge. She's also a pathological liar. Can't believe anything she says."

Ridiculous. Of course, it was Poindexter's friend who was the liar. Just gossip generated by someone jealous of her success. And this morning he'd told the ogre so in no uncertain terms. "If Kathryn Townsend isn't as honest and stable as you or I, I'll hand in my resignation."

"Don't worry, Kathryn," Allan said now. "I assured him you were an astute businesswoman and that his money was completely safe." He reached over and patted her hand. There was no need to worry her with speculation and gossip. Not that such outlandish lies would worry Kathryn. They'd just roll off her like water off a duck. Maybe he'd tell her someday when all this fuss died down; then they'd have a good laugh over it.

But the tightness didn't leave her lips. "And is he convinced?"

"Well, not exactly. He's still blustering about those detectives. You and I know this is all ridiculous, but I'm afraid he's threatening to call in your loan. He thinks you're no longer a good financial risk, what with the problem at the Townsend Manor and . . . Anyway, I called the fellow who had made the offer on the Florida property. The number's been disconnected and he seems to have disappeared."

The wave of fear crashed through her head again, threatening to overwhelm her.

"Poindexter may think better of it," Allan said, although in his heart he didn't really believe it. He just wanted to say something to drive out the panic he saw in her eyes. Why was Kathryn so terrified? Despite her insistence upon being independent, he knew, and she knew, that Owen could easily afford to bail her out. And would do it willingly. Surely under the circumstances she wouldn't be stubborn; she couldn't afford to be. "I'll tackle Poindexter again," he promised her. "Make him change his mind."

After Allan left, Kathryn had no idea how long she sat there clutching a cup of tea that had long ago grown cold. Finally Rachel's voice dragged her out of the nightmare. "I tell you, that grandson of mine . . ." There was a pause and a sharp intake of breath. "Kathryn, what in the world . . . ? You look as pale as a ghost. Maybe you should be in bed; after all, it's your first day—"

"Allan says the bank is threatening to call in my loan. I could lose my hotels."

"That's ridiculous; how can they do that? You're a very wealthy woman."

Kathryn laughed. "On paper maybe. Do you want to know how much I have in my bank account? One thousand six hundred and thirty-four dollars. And do you want to know how much money I owe the bank?" She looked at Rachel and shook her head. "No, you don't want to know. But they can call in the loan and apparently have every intention of doing so."

"But why? Certainly they had to give a reason."

"It was the article about what the papers are now calling 'the hookers in the dining room' that triggered it. Those damned conservative old bankers are convinced that the scandal will be the ruin of the hotel. But I suspect there's something else Allan's not telling me."

"Absurd. This is 1926. People aren't easily shocked. And if your bankers are so conservative, well, then, find another bank. One that isn't stuck in the Victorian era."

"I'm afraid you haven't heard the worst. The bank president intends to hire private detectives to investigate me." Kathryn sighed. "Of course, they'll find out everything, if they're any good. And I thought my past was well hidden and completely forgotten. Do you know," she said with a weak, bitter laugh, "sometimes I forget about Edward for months at a time. Now from three thousand miles away he's still going to destroy everything. Again."

Kathryn paused for a moment, trying to sort out her thoughts. "Maybe it's just an excuse—because I'm a woman. The bankers want to see me fail. It offends their precious male pride that I can be as smart and successful as they are. Just like Edward, they can't wait for me to fall on my face.''

All of a sudden she felt like a little girl. Edward had caught her climbing a tree, and she would be punished for breaking the rules of ladylike behavior. She could see him towering above her. Cruel lines etched into his face as he stared down at her—a great tomcat tormenting its tiny prey. Men had the power. Men always won in the end. She wondered if the little mouse ever managed to escape the cat's claws, no matter how hard it struggled.

Kathryn shook her head slowly. The faraway look in her usually clear, sharp eyes worried Rachel. ''Maybe it's time,'' Kathryn said, ''to give it all up. Admit I was living a dream. Devote myself from now on to raising my baby. Like a normal woman.''

''Kathryn, stop talking nonsense. Normal. Hah! You'd be bored within a week. Much as you love your son, you're not other women. You need wider frontiers to conquer than the nursery.''

Kathryn's rigid body relaxed slightly; the white balls of her fists unclenched. ''Allan promised to talk to them again, try to persuade them. But I borrowed that money to buy the site for the Florida hotel. Now the land's almost worthless.''

It hurt Rachel to see Kathryn like this, Kathryn who was always so strong and confident. ''Don't worry, I'm sure it will all turn out fine.''

Suddenly Kathryn's eyes blazed with tears and an angry golden fire. Her chin trembled. ''Don't you understand? I could lose my hotels. There's only one way to save the Townsend Manor: by selling the Townsend Park. And there's only one way to save the Townsend Park: sell the Townsend Manor.'' Kathryn's heart ached. ''I feel like a mother who's forced to choose between her children. How can I make a rational business decision? I put my heart, my life, my dreams into those hotels. They are a part of me. Just as much as Adam is.''

She couldn't talk about it any longer. Nervously she began sorting through her mail. ''Best wishes . . . congratulations . . . your new son''—the words ran together. Her mind kept returning to her hotels, her beloved hotels, and the awful realization that she could lose them.

The last envelope was gray. When she unfolded the note she saw that it was black-bordered Victorian mourning paper. Spidery black writing crawled across the page. Impossible to read. Her eye flashed to the bottom, searching for a signature. There was none. So she began laboriously deciphering the spindly lines.

Rachel watched as Kathryn's face faded from pale to deathly white. Her eyes glowed dark and haunted against the pallor. It frightened Rachel. "What is it, Kathryn? What's wrong?" she asked.

Kathryn's lips were still trembling, trying to form an answer, when the door from the hallway opened and Owen appeared, wearing tan jodhpurs and polished riding boots. Hands on his hips and a broad grin across his tanned face, he announced: "Do you know what my extraordinary son just did? He smiled at me. A big smile. It's quite plain he knows I'm his dad." He strode into the room, his boots clicking against the oak floor.

Kathryn forced a smile to her frozen lips. "Did you two have a pleasant conversation?"

"Don't make fun of me. Even I don't expect Adam to be talking for a least another few months. But he is clever, that I know." His chest seemed to swell with pride as he spoke. Fixing his eyes on Rachel, he said, "Tell the truth. Isn't he the most splendid baby you've ever seen?"

As they prattled on and on about the baby, Kathryn brimming over with counterfeit cheerfulness, Rachel grew more and more worried. Why didn't Kathryn tell Owen about the loan?

Darned pride, Rachel thought. Kathryn wanted to do everything herself. Why couldn't she share her problems with her husband? Rachel sometimes worried—and the idea scared her—that Kathryn, in her obsession with success, thought of herself in competition with Owen. That she believed she could truly prove herself only if she bested every man in her self-imposed arena. With all her heart Rachel hoped it wasn't so. Kathryn and Owen were so right for each other. It would take a powerful wedge to drive them apart, but Kathryn's obsession ran strong and deep.

Tenderly Owen bent down to kiss his wife's forehead. "Take care of yourself. Remember, you're just out of the hospital. What I mean is don't do anything idiotic—like go to work.'' His hand resting protectively on Kathryn's shoulder, he turned to Rachel with a conspiratorial wink. ''I'll be at the stables if you need me.''

''Give Miss Kathryn a carrot and a kiss for me,'' Kathryn called out after him.

As soon as she heard the front door close behind him, Rachel turned on Kathryn. ''You may be able to fool your husband with that cheerful chatter, but not me. That last letter . . . you looked like you'd seen a ghost. Was it something to do with the loan?''

Without a word Kathryn handed her the sheet of paper. Rachel frowned as she tried to decipher the writing. She adjusted her glasses. Finally she read it aloud. As she read, her voice became weaker and more horrified.

''Dear Kathryn. Congratulations on the birth of your son. I cannot help but wonder whether your adoring, trusting husband knows why you named him Adam, as I read in the newspaper announcement. I doubt that you have had the moral courage to tell him. There are so many things he could learn about your past, aren't there? Such as the fact that his wife is a thief.''

Rachel paused. The writing was becoming more and more erratic. She could almost feel the writer's tension in the tight, misshapen letters. ''Rest assured that your moment of glory along with your marriage will soon end. I am the instrument of justice and I will see to it that you and your hotels are destroyed. And that your precious little son does not live to spend his stolen inheritance. The flaming sword of justice will fall and the wicked shall . . .'' The last words fell off— unreadable.

For a moment Rachel sat stunned, unable to believe the words. Evil and insanity oozed from the paper. Instinctively her fingers pulled away, as if they'd touched something rotten, loathsome. As she stared in horror at the black words she felt the evil expanding, surrounding and chilling her body, penetrating into every corner of the room.

With an exaggerated calmness she faced Kathryn. ''It's just a nasty crank letter. You can't let it worry you. I'm sure whoever wrote it is harmless—sick, yes, but incapable of carrying out those absurd threats. You're in the public eye, so you have to expect this sort of unpleasantness occasionally.''

"Can't you see it's not just an ordinary crank letter? It's . . . Edward.'' Kathryn's voice was ragged with long-forgotten fears. "He's the only one who knows about Adam Elliott.''

Rachel stared at Kathryn, wanting to say something, not knowing what. As she studied her face she saw a transformation. The fire of determination was rekindled in her eyes. The line of her chin hardened. Her voice fell to a chilling whisper; her words held the solemnity of a vow. "Sometimes the mouse does escape. And sometimes she even lives to teach the cat a lesson.''

Chapter Ten

William was nervous; his hands were cold and refused to do what he wanted them to. It was the first time he'd seen Mrs. Townsend since the incident. Now she was sitting at one of the tables assigned to him. He clasped the menu to keep his hands from shaking and walked toward her.

"Mrs. Townsend, I just . . . wanted to say how sorry I am. About everything. I didn't mean to make any trouble for you. Or the hotel. You do believe that, don't you?"

His voice was so earnest, his face so scarlet with embarrassment, that her heart went out to him. "I believe you, William. It was a delicate situation—one you were not experienced enough to deal with, which makes it as much our fault as yours. So we'll put it behind us, shall we?"

"Oh, yes, thank you. Thank you. I'll never forget this. I won't."

She held up her hand. "Just bring me my lunch, please."

She opened the leather portfolio that rested on the chair next to her and took out an onionskin page. It was the preliminary report from the detective hired to look into the matter of the prostitutes. Another dead end. When William returned with her coffee, she asked, "Are you sure you can't remember anything more about the man with the prostitutes?"

"No, ma'am. It happened so fast. And when he came in, well, it didn't seem important then."

Kathryn's resigned sigh made William wish with all his heart he could help her. It was as he was preparing a selection of pastries that he felt a twinge of recollection. The long, narrow pastry tongs grasping the chocolate eclair stirred up the memory. The man's hands. At first he could see only the crisp ten-dollar bill held temptingly between two fingers. Then the fingers came into focus. Narrow and white; the nails long, like claws. He felt the hairs on the back of his neck prickle. In his memory his eyes traveled up from the hands to the face. He dug deeper into his mind. It was a thin face. Two lines etched into the cheeks. The features were sharp. And the skin? It was pale. Not just pale. White. Like marble. Or like a dead man's.

Should he tell Mrs. Townsend? He could imagine her laughing and saying he was overly imaginative. How could he tell her the man had hands like claws and looked like a corpse? Maybe he should just consider the matter closed and be glad he hadn't lost his job. He thought of the way his mother's face lit up when he told her about the rich and important people he waited on. How she pressed him for every last detail. He couldn't risk losing that.

Then he looked over at Mrs. Townsend. She was staring across the dining room, preoccupied, seeing nothing. Usually not even the smallest detail escaped her sharp eye. Now she was upset and it was his fault. He waited until she'd finished her coffee and then approached her table. Slowly, stammering, apologizing for the bizarre details, he told his story.

"I hope it helps," he said weakly as he finished.

Kathryn's heart was pounding, but she wasn't sure if it was from joy or fear. The mystery had been solved. Edward was not gone and forgotten, and his threats were no longer idle. He was on a very determined course to destroy her and her hotels. She knew him; he would keep his promise. Panic rose in her throat. He'd threatened to kill Adam. Adam—she must protect him. She jumped up from the table before she remembered: Adam was perfectly safe at home with his nurse and Mrs. Blair. Owen's valet, a tall, brawny Scotsman, was there. So were the cook and the maid.

She sank back into her chair. There was a detail in William's description that rang a bell. "He looked like a dead man." Where had she heard that before? Someone who looked like a corpse. Of course—the chambermaid who'd described the mystery man in Room 312. Edward. He had vandalized the room. The vivid image of the knife plunged into the pillow struck her. Had the pillow been only a substitute? Did he hate her that much? She felt her body turn cold and clammy. The hairs on the back of her neck bristled as the power of his hatred washed over her in ever stronger waves.

Her brother had declared himself her enemy, but where was he? How could she fight an unseen foe? He could be anywhere. A guest in one of the hundreds of rooms. Eating in her dining rooms. Maybe even working in one of the hotels under an assumed name. Or worse, lurking outside waiting to strike again. It was impossible to protect herself, not when her brother was so clever and held every advantage.

Her pounding heart suddenly stopped when she realized that it had to be Edward who was spreading rumors. If only she knew what he'd been saying. How close to the truth did he dare get? And whom had he been talking to? Was he working his way through the entire banking community, blackening her name with his foul lies? She might never get another loan, and without money, her dream of a chain of hotels would shrivel up and die.

But there was one way to beat her brother.

Two phone calls, and the appointment was set up.

"Mr. Poindexter, I am going to tell you a story," Kathryn said, trying to ignore his hostile look and project confidence.

As she spoke coolly about her mother and Edward and Adam, she could feel Poindexter's eyes traveling up her body. She thought of Mr. George at the Lamont Hotel and resisted the impulse to shudder. This time there was more than a job at stake; she couldn't afford to walk out in indignation. Desperate situations require desperate measures, she told herself, crossing her legs to reveal more of her silk-stockinged thigh.

The way his eyes widened ever so slightly, Kathryn knew she'd found the key to Ralph P. Poindexter. As she continued her story she blinked several times, as if she were forcing back tears. He handed her a monogrammed white linen handkerchief from his breast pocket and she dabbed at her dry eyes.

"And so you can see, Mr. Poindexter, what a dilemma I'm in. There was nothing else I could do but come to you and confess the truth. And hope that you would believe me." She stared at him. "You do, don't you?"

He tapped the ash off his cigar, watching as it dropped into the ashtray. He looked worried. "The money. You knew it was stolen. Yet you kept it."

"As I explained, at first I was too afraid. Then I realized that the longer I waited the more difficult—the more impossible—it had become to return the money without implicating myself. Two years ago I sent a check—a check for more than twice the amount my brother stole—to the Salvation Army. Adam was very concerned about the poor. I . . . I think he would have approved."

Poindexter looked thoughtful. "Perhaps," he said slowly, "the best solution in a difficult situation. However, the money didn't legally belong to your young man."

Kathryn shook her head. They were of the same class, the Poindexters and the Elliotts. He would never acknowledge the truth: that the money was a mere drop in Adam Elliott II's financial bucket. A drop he'd never miss.

"Well, Mrs. Townsend, yours is a rather fantastic tale, but I can't believe you would lie. Your brother, on the other hand . . . I should have suspected him immediately. Suspected that he didn't belong at the club. Not the right sort."

Kathryn held her breath for a moment. Now for the crucial test. As a man, he had sympathy for her, but as a banker . . . "Mr. Poindexter, I hope that means you'll reconsider calling in your loan now that you know the truth. As Mr. Jones will tell you, the Townsend Manor is operating at a profit and the Townsend Park is off to an excellent start. I expect it to be in the black within the year. As for the incident with the . . ." She stopped, sensing that he was old-fashioned enough to believe a lady wouldn't use certain words. ". . . women in the dining room, it has blown over. Several other newspapers picked up the story, but times are changing and it hasn't affected our business in the least."

Poindexter stared at her. This time not at her breasts, but at her face, as if he were judging her, trying to make up his mind. Finally he spoke. "Frankly, Mrs. Townsend, I find it difficult to believe that such a beautiful young woman as you are can also run a successful business. A woman's first duty is to her husband and children. That's what I was brought up to believe. But, as you said, times are changing. And as a banker, I must believe in facts and figures, and the facts and figures prove that you are an astute businesswoman. Although you did make an unsound investment in the Florida property. Very unsound." He puffed on his cigar. Kathryn watched the glowing ash, not daring to breathe.

"I don't like to be proved wrong. However, in this case I'll have to change my mind: the bank will honor our agreement."

It was hard for Kathryn not to show her enormous relief. "Thank you, Mr. Poindexter. I appreciate your confidence. I'll ask you to keep my story to yourself. Allan Jones knows nothing of it. It's something I've tried to put behind me. The past can become a burden if we let it."

He tapped the dead ash. "Your secret is safe with me."

"I'm sure it will be. We all have our secrets, don't we?"

From the way he looked at her, his nostrils slightly flared, Kathryn was certain of the nature of his secrets.

"Now," she said in her most businesslike manner, "I have one more favor to ask you. Obviously I must find my brother and stop him from doing any further damage. I'm afraid the only way of locating him is through your club. Would you mind if I send a private detective up there to ask some questions? I promise he'll be discreet. By the way, was Edward using his own name when you met him?"

"Definitely not. I would have remembered Townsend. No, he was calling himself Elliott. Elliott Turner."

They both stopped as they realized the significance of his choice. "Ironic, isn't it?" Kathryn said. "Can you remember anything else he might have said that would give any clues? About where he lives? His business? Friends?"

"No, he was vague about all that. I remember it struck me as odd at the time. Went out of his way not to reveal anything personal. Claimed he was a guest of Chuck Gordon. Later found out Chuck was abroad."

Kathryn rose and put out her hand. "Mr. Poindexter, I thank you."

He held her hand for a moment without saying anything, then gave it a damp squeeze. "Good luck, Mrs. Townsend. I hope you catch that man. If there's anything else I can do, let me know."

For the time being, her hotels were safe, and Kathryn had a plan for dealing with Edward.

She left a letter at the club addressed to Elliott Turner.

Although no one had seen him for weeks, the letter disappeared within two days.

In her brief letter she'd asked for a meeting "to settle our differences." She didn't know how she would settle them, but she knew she couldn't go on expecting to face Edward around every corner. It was like dealing with a ghost who could materialize at will, do his damage and disappear. A very real ghost from the past. Panic rose in her throat when she thought of it. Her stomach churned. If only she could meet him face-to-face, *then* she could deal with him.

Chapter Eleven

Kathryn sat at her desk, her head bent over a ledger. It was late. Miss Willis had left for the day and the outer office was dark. All of a sudden she sensed someone standing over her.

It was what she'd been dreading. Every time she scanned the crowds in the lobby. Every time the phone rang. But she couldn't live the rest of her life afraid of Edward's clawed hand reaching around every corner. She shivered and forced her eyes upward.

"Owen!" She almost sobbed with relief and jumped up from her desk and ran to him.

"If this is the welcome I get, I'll have to visit your office more often."

"Owen, hold me, please hold me." He squeezed her tighter and she could feel her fears evaporating, her body melting in the warmth of his. No one could hurt her if she stayed in his arms.

"Kathryn, what's wrong? You're shivering."

"No, I . . ."

"Are you sick?"

If she told him everything, he'd make it right. He'd find Edward and stop him. Her brother would never threaten her again. "No," she said. Her head was pressed so tightly to his chest that her voice was muffled.

"Then what's wrong, love? You've been acting nervous recently. And that's not like you. Whatever's wrong, you can tell me. Remember, I married you for better or worse."

Kathryn said nothing, and after a moment he continued. "Sometimes we seem so close, so very close—almost like one person. And then at other times . . ." He shrugged. "At other times I get the feeling that you don't see me as a partner in your life. That you're too busy proving yourself. Trying to be independent. Of me and everybody else."

She pulled away. "Oh, Owen, please . . . that's not true at all. I love you so much that—"

"I never said I doubted your love. I just occasionally get the feeling that there's a part of you I've never seen. Something you keep hidden. And I don't want any barriers, any secrets coming between us, spoiling what we have together. Our love is too special to risk." He pulled her closer and then asked, "Don't you trust me?"

At the sound of the hurt in his voice, Kathryn felt a lump grow in her throat. At last she said, "I know what's making me nervous. I'm worried about the man who brought the prostitutes into the dining room."

"Have you found out who he is?" Owen demanded. "He's obviously demented and should be locked up immediately, not allowed to go roaming the streets."

"I'm afraid . . . afraid that he's also responsible for some other incidents at the hotel."

"Did you find out who he is and why he chose your hotel?" Owen asked.

Because he's my brother. Because he's a thief and a murderer and because he hates me. How can I tell Owen that? And why should I allow Edward to poison another life? I probably shouldn't even have told Rachel.

"No," she said slowly, "I don't know who he is. But"— her voice sounded surer—"hotels are unfortunately vulnerable to this sort of craziness. Next week our man will probably be off creating problems for the Plaza. I'm sure we've seen the last of him."

At the embarrassed sound of a throat being cleared, Kathryn looked up. Rachel stood in the shadows of the outer office. Her dark, buttonlike eyes blazed with anger, and Kathryn knew she'd heard every word of the lie.

"I'm sorry," Kathryn said when they were alone.

"Don't apologize to me. It's not my marriage you're trying to ruin."

"Rachel, stop overreacting. I told that lie because it was necessary. To protect Owen from my brother's craziness."

"And you're lying to yourself if you think Owen needs to be protected. He's the strongest, most capable man I've ever met. And for once maybe you should let him protect you."

Kathryn turned her back and pretended to rummage through the papers on her desk. When she looked up and faced Rachel, her chin was set in a familiar line. "I'm perfectly capable of dealing with this myself. Owen never has to find out."

"Why?" Rachel asked with a sniff. "Because Edward will suddenly become cooperative and waltz out of your life? No, secrets like that never die. Believe me. They wait and then raise their ugly heads and threaten to destroy your life when you least expect it." She paused, then asked brusquely, "Exactly what do you think would happen if you told Owen about Edward?"

"No. . . ." Kathryn felt a lump rising in her throat at the thought of losing Owen.

"Kathryn, your husband adores you. He couldn't stop loving you even if he knew about Edward." Why does she have this blind spot? Rachel wondered. She's bright and beautiful—the kind of woman most men can only dream about—why is she so vulnerable?

"But how can I be sure? What Owen loves is the image of Kathryn Townsend."

"Image?" Rachel's beady eyes popped in anger. "Images are for newspapers. That's not what Owen fell in love with. He loves the real flesh-and-blood Kathryn Townsend, flaws and all. The one who eats too much when she's nervous. Who can be stubborn as a mule. And who works too hard for her own good and doesn't know why.

"Your brother doesn't have a prayer of shaking Owen's love for you. The only thing that could break up your marriage is if you continue to lie."

At times Edward thought of his scheme as a ballet with every step carefully choreographed. And now the dance was building to a crescendo. In his head he could hear the music. The tempo becoming faster and faster. Trumpets, drums, cymbals. Aching for release. Racing toward the climax. But was it merely the climax of the first act? Or was it the end of the entire dance?

That he had yet to decide. It would be tempting to play out the second and then the third act of his extraordinarily clever plan. To watch while his sister's world was destroyed one small, painful piece at a time. First he would see to it that she lost one of her precious hotels. Then the other. Then her husband. And, finally, her child. At last she would be alone and penniless.

On the other hand, perhaps there should be only one act. Once Kathryn was out of his way, he could get on with his own life. She'd been a thorn in his side since the day she was born. Over the years that wound had festered, spreading its poison throughout his body. Filling his mind and body with pain so agonizing it was often impossible for him to think of anything else.

Once he freed himself, he could concentrate on his own dreams. Dreams that would carry him farther than Kathryn's ever had. He was smarter than his sister and he would prove it by destroying her financial empire and constructing his own. He would be rich, richer than she had ever been. The press would proclaim his genius. People would fawn at his feet. Everything he'd wanted so desperately would at last be his.

His eyes scanned the harbor. Beneath him the ferry rocked on the wind-whipped waves. The Staten Island ferry—the symbol of all he'd lost. His sister lived in luxury, and he was forced to live in a cramped apartment on unfashionable Staten Island. He felt his jaw tightening. The pressure in his chest was building. The burden of bricks was once again intolerable. His fingers grasped at the rail. To his surprise, it moved slightly under their pressure. He looked down and saw that he was clutching a gate. A gate almost indistinguishable from the rest of the railing. He studied it more closely. A flimsy, rusty bolt was all that kept the gate from swinging open. A dangerous situation. He stared over the edge. Twenty feet below, the black waters churned angrily, slapping against the rusty hull of the boat.

Darkness. Kathryn had always been afraid of the dark. He remembered how he could make her little eyes widen with fear by threatening to lock her in the cellar. What terrors her young mind must have conjured up out of the looming shadows and musty smells. That particular punishment he'd used sparingly, always afraid she'd realize her terrors were imaginary.

This time the threat was real. He envisioned the waves closing over her head—cold and suffocating, condemning her to a perpetual darkness from which there would be no escape. But first she would struggle—his lips stretched into a satisfied smile—his sister was a fighter. She would not go down into the darkness easily. He imagined her head bobbing against the waves. Saw her face slapped by each oncoming onslaught. Her ripe mouth filling with vile, salty water. Her fingers reaching out for safety and finding none.

Would she cry? Or would she be stubborn the way she'd been as a little girl? No matter how her eyes had brimmed over with tears. No matter how her little chin had trembled, she'd refused to give in. No, this time she'd cry out when she realized she was going to die.

Her body—he wondered if they'd ever find it. After all, that young Elliott had never been found. Perhaps if enough time passed, a name would never even be given to the decomposed flesh that had been Kathryn Townsend.

His hawklike eyes scanned the bay. It was a tempting possibility. He would have to give it additional thought.

Chapter Twelve

The wind whipped at her skirt and sent icy shivers up and down her legs. Kathryn pulled her coat more tightly around her and wished she'd worn her fur, but she'd decided that it would only antagonize the situation to appear too prosperous. Struggling against the wind, she made a half turn and waved reassuringly at Emil, who put the car in gear and chugged off on an errand for Owen, no doubt wondering why she'd asked him to drop her off here. For a moment she felt very much alone; then she was quickly swallowed up by the throng of people hurrying aboard the ferry.

In the boat's main cabin, heat rose steamily and people began unwinding mufflers and unbuttoning coats. Harried last-minute Christmas shoppers juggled boxes and bags. A fractious child drooled over a candy cane and whined about not seeing Santa Claus. An elderly man with a white beard balanced a small Christmas tree in one hand and a red-bowed wreath in the other. In the middle of the room four young men—college students, probably—wearing bulky raccoon coats and full of seasonal spirits serenaded the passengers with Christmas carols.

It was the day of Christmas Eve, and Kathryn could feel the spirit of Christmas bubbling up in her chest. For the first time she had a real family to celebrate with. The thought delighted her and she knew that once this afternoon was behind her, she would do so with a free mind. Her troubles would be part of the past.

No more shadowboxing and starting at ghosts; she would deal with Edward face-to-face. And she would win. He had replied to her letter with a curt instruction to meet him at a quarter past noon on the twenty-fourth at a restaurant on Staten Island. Her private detective, a brawny young man named Beamish, would be waiting at the restaurant ready to follow Edward. And protect me from my brother, Kathryn thought with a flush of shame.

Beamish was the only one who knew about the meeting. Once she dealt with Edward satisfactorily, she'd share the good news with Rachel. Right now she knew that Rachel's fussing and fretting, well intentioned as it was, would only ignite her own anxieties.

As Kathryn sat reviewing her plan, a broad-beamed man came toward her. Before she could protest, he was wedging himself down into the small space beside her, jabbing into her with his elbows to make room. Comfortable at last, he blew smoke rings into the already blue air. The cigar smell reminded her of Ralph Poindexter, and suddenly the prospect of the open deck even with the cold and wind was appealing. As she pushed her way through the crowd and to the door, she heard the boys strike up "It Came Upon a Midnight Clear."

The wind whipped the door from her grasp and forced her to grab onto the railing. In the distance Manhattan looked like so many gray building blocks painstakingly piled one on top of the other. The sky was flat and dark, the air damp and bitter with the threat of snow. The harbor, like molten lead, peaked occasionally into whitecaps as the wind skimmed over it. She peered over the railing, watching the blunt bow of the ferry nosing its way through the waves, churning up the cold, angry wake.

"Greetings of the season." The voice came from behind her and cut through her mind like a knife. She turned slowly.

Edward was smiling. His thin, bloodless lips spread over too many large teeth. "I trust you are well, Kathryn. You'll forgive me if I don't kiss you hello. I have a slight cold." If he found it strange that she didn't reply, his face revealed nothing. "I must say that you are looking lovely. Motherhood obviously agrees with you."

Kathryn knew she should say something, but the words refused to come. Finally she managed, "I thought we were supposed to meet at the restaurant."

"Joy to the world . . ." The husky male voices rang out.

"True. But it's such a crowded, public place for a personal reunion. And I thought you might enjoy some company on the trip over. A lovely sight, isn't it?" he said, gesturing to the harbor.

Kathryn stared at him, trying to figure out what he was doing here acting as if nothing out of the ordinary had ever happened between them. Had his mind completely snapped? No; when that happened, she decided, he'd go with a bang, not a whimper. More likely this was his clever way to keep her off balance. She'd been prepared to deal with him over a restaurant table. Now she had no choice but to play along with him, to find out where his ridiculous charade of politeness was leading.

"May I suggest that we walk," he said. "It will keep us from getting cold." As if it were the most natural thing in the world, he took her arm; it required all of Kathryn's willpower not to wrench it out from under his bony fingers. Nausea rose in her throat as she looked down at his white hand with its long, curved, yellow nails digging into the sleeve of her blue coat. It was the hand of an old man.

He talked mainly of the weather. Did she think it would snow for Christmas? Did she remember the blizzards in Lowell? With each question Kathryn found herself making the proper, polite response. All of a sudden he dug his fingers into her arm, forcing her to stop. Her heart leapt into her throat. But he was quick to explain. "There's a patch of ice on the deck. I wouldn't want you to step on it and risk falling."

She forced a "Thank you" to her lips. Could this be the same man who had slashed a mattress and plunged a knife into a pillow in some insane fit of rage? Was this the brother who had killed a man and threatened to have her institutionalized? Who had vowed to destroy her and everything she loved? As they circled the deck arm in arm, she couldn't help thinking that they were like two volcanoes waiting to erupt.

How bizarre it all was. How civilized. They encountered other passengers and Edward nodded pleasantly. To the women he doffed his hat. To an old man he cheerfully offered a "Merry Christmas." Around and around the deck they went. Again and again and again.

"O little town of Bethlehem, how still we see thee
lie . . ."

When she thought she could stand his playacting no longer,
Kathryn began cautiously probing. If she could discover
something about him—anything . . . But he was evasive.
When she asked what he did, he explained tersely: "I have
business interests." The way he said it, it sounded vaguely
sinister, but perhaps that was her imagination. In her mind
everything Edward touched was evil.

Yet under all his evasions Kathryn could sense Edward
tightening up, and she decided to take the plunge before it
was too late.

"Edward, I think we should talk about what we came here
to discuss." She looked up at him; his white face betrayed
no emotion. "You believe you were treated unfairly. You
think that I took money that belonged to you. I want to end
our disagreement and I'm prepared to repay you the entire
amount"—she carefully refrained from adding the words
"that you stole from Adam"—"with interest." If only he'd
accept the money, she would be free. The debt repaid, the
feud ended. He was grimly silent. "You can use it to make
a fresh start. Once upon a time you were a dreamer like me;
you had plans and ideas. Remember? It's not too late. You
could go into the hotel business again. Or anything else you
want."

She wondered if it was her imagination, but all of a sudden
the temperature seemed to plunge and the wind intensified.
Her feet were growing heavy and numb. She looked around;
all the other passengers had the good sense to shelter inside.

She was glad when Edward stopped walking and drew her
over to the rail, out of sight of the cabin windows. Released
from his bony fingers, she grasped the rail, clinging to it like
a drowning swimmer to a life raft. She looked up at him,
hoping to see some sign of accord on his face, but as she
watched, his eyes darkened and the lines on his cheeks
seemed to dig deeper into his brittle, parchmentlike skin.

"Edward, for your own sake you can't continue to be obsessed by the past. It won't bring you any happiness, believe
me. I'm offering you the chance of a new life. Please take
it."

He said nothing and she pressed on. "If you take the money

we'll never see each other again. And I promise never to tell anyone about . . . about Adam. Your secrets are safe."

Out of the corner of her eye she was aware of his hands fumbling with something. Suddenly she felt the metal beneath her arm move slightly. It gave way an inch or so. At first she thought the wool of her coat was slipping along it. Then all at once the railing swayed outward. In horror she watched Edward's hand reach out toward her and his talonlike fingers push against her body, forcing it out over the water. She looked down to see an ever-widening gap between the deck and the gate she clung to. Twenty feet below, she could see the churning white foam roiled up by the boat. Her instinct was to grip the railing more tightly, but she knew that then she'd be left clinging to the gate as it swung farther and farther out over the water.

Slowly she forced her stiff fingers to relax their grip. It took all her courage and strength to let go and hurl her body backward over the chasm and onto the deck. A sharp pain shot through her ankle as she landed, but she righted herself immediately and faced him.

"O come, all ye faithful, joyful and triumphant . . ."

It had begun to snow—big, wet flakes. They settled on Edward's dark, pomaded hair. They sprinkled over his black coat. They fell on his pale skin and melted like teardrops. When he saw Kathryn rising unhurt from the deck, his face crumbled in disappointment. The two volcanoes were at last about to erupt.

"You cold-blooded, scheming bastard! Just tell me one thing, Edward, tell me why you hate me so much. So much that you are willing to kill me!"

She stared at him so long and hard that he found himself speaking. "Because you stole everything that was ever important to me."

"Stole! You're confused, Edward. *You're* the thief and destroyer in the family. *You're* the one who vandalized my property. Tried to ruin my reputation and the good name of my hotel. Why?" She grasped his arms and shook them, trying to shake an answer out of him, but his arms were thin and unyielding as sticks.

For the first time he smiled. "Ah, so you did unravel the

mystery. I thought you might. Yes, I did a pretty job on that room, didn't I?"

"But why, Edward, why?" she demanded in frustration.

"Because I took great pleasure in the insignificant little things that would spoil your success. Do you remember the Baron von Friedrichstein? The mysterious German who never arrived to use the suite he reserved?"

"You?" Her voice was incredulous. What else was he responsible for? Her mind flew from possibility to possibility. Sabotage, that's what it was. "The mirror, the antique mirror in the lobby of the Townsend Park, was that . . . ?" she asked.

"My dear sister, you give me too much credit. You can't blame me for all your mishaps; people will think you are paranoid. After all, I'm sure you have other enemies." He smiled broadly at the thought, a smile with no shred of humor or sanity. "There was, however, the horsey-looking young woman in the elevator with whom I . . . um . . . took liberties." Seeing the blank look on her face, he asked, "Hasn't your tame lapdog Roger told you about that incident? It happened while you were on your . . . honeymoon." His lips twisted strangely as he said the word. "And it did cost you a rather valuable customer, I believe."

"Lapdog—how dare you refer to Roger like that!" The wind whipped at her hair and tore at her coat, but she scarcely felt it.

"You must admit he does follow you around like a puppy, and with that adoring look in his eyes. But then you do inspire admiration and loyalty in your employees, don't you? It's made my job harder. Fewer disgruntled employees willing to do my little deeds for me. What would happen if all those devoted employees knew that Kathryn Townsend was a thief? How loyal would they be then?"

"I will not listen to any more of your lies. Confession is supposed to be good for the soul, but in your case I doubt if you even have one."

"My plan was really so brilliant I want you to hear it all. Of course, you already know that I was the one who planted those doubts in the mind of your fat, cigar-smoking banker. A dreadful man. Common. But what you don't know and what I think will surprise you is about that property in Florida. It really was an unwise investment. But I know how stubborn you are once you've made up your mind and I knew you would refuse my offers.''

"You . . . you were the anonymous buyer who disappeared?''

"Yes, and just when you needed me most. Just when the noose was tightening around your lovely white neck.'' He said the last words softly as he stared at her, his eyes taking in every detail of her face. Kathryn drew the collar of her coat up higher, but it didn't stop her shivering as she imagined his cold eyes penetrating through the wool.

"Ah, but my pièce de résistance,'' he said, waving his hand as if commanding some invisible orchestra to strike up, "that was the incident in your dining room with my lady friends. It was clever, as I'm sure you appreciate.''

"You still haven't answered my question. Why were you willing to go to all this trouble? Why do you hate me so much? Tell me.''

"You stole everything from me and you wonder why I hate you? You stole my mother's affections. She dressed you up and fussed over you. Then she tried to pretend she didn't love you. But I knew. I couldn't make her see that you were unworthy of her love—a scrawny little girl. A mere girl. Why did she want you when she had a son?''

His face looked so tired and tormented that Kathryn felt a twinge of pity.

"And that woman. You brought her into my life so she could be unfaithful to me. Did you two have it all planned? To hurt me. To humiliate me. You did, didn't you?'' Accusation burned in his eyes.

"Are you ashamed to say her name?'' Kathryn demanded. "Say it. Jessica. And she died giving birth to your child.''

He shook his head and stared off at the distant horizon. "I loved her, I really loved her. When she died . . .'' Then, as if realizing what he'd said, he added quickly, "And you mishandled that young man. You ruined my plan for an association with the Elliotts. It would have been the beginning. Just the beginning.''

"So you killed him and stole his money.'' She could feel the anger and hurt boiling up inside her, threatening to erupt. The pain assaulted her—raw and fresh.

"I was merely trying to make the best of a bad situation."
His voice assumed an angry whine.

"You certainly have a peculiar idea of the truth. In your
version you're always the victim. But you were cruel and cold
and manipulative. You loved abusing me, didn't you? And
you haven't changed one bit." She paused. "But I have. I
was crazy to think I could buy you off. As crazy as you are."

"Crazy. Yes, I suppose I might appear crazy to you. But
I can assure you that I am perfectly sane. The worst I could
be accused of is being overemotional." He put his hand up
to silence her protests. "You see, I am overwhelmed by an
emotion that gives me no peace. An emotion that torments
me constantly. Sometimes in my darker moments I even
imagine it might kill me. And that emotion which rules my
life is hatred. Hatred for you."

His fevered eyes stared so fiercely into hers that for a moment Kathryn imagined she could feel them physically penetrating her. "You are sick."

"No, I am no more sick than I am crazy. I know what my
problem is and I intend to do something about it. When the
star of your success is extinguished, when every newspaper I
read will no longer remind me of my hatred, then and only
then can I devote myself to my own future. Right now you
are the only obstacle to my success, and like any intelligent
person, I plan to remove that obstacle."

Kathryn laughed, a cold, hollow laugh. "In case you have
any second thoughts, my offer to buy you off no longer stands.
I shall stop you some other way. Some way that will be less
profitable and more painful for you."

"If you can find me." His voice rang triumphantly.

"Don't worry. I'll find you."

"I know all about your expensive lawyers and private detectives. But I'm smarter than they are. I'll disappear just like
before." He snapped his fingers, startling her. "But I won't
be gone. I'll be there every day. Watching. Waiting. You'll
never feel safe again. I'll be there plotting to destroy your
hotels piece by precious piece. And all the police and private
detectives in the world won't be able to protect you and your
baby, not to mention that handsome husband you seem so
fond of. Or perhaps I should merely tell him the truth and

watch how fast he abandons you. 'Mr. Morgan, are you aware that your wife . . .' "

She refused to rise to his bait. "I'll hunt you down." Her hard eyes challenged his. "And I'll have you charged with murder. As well as attempted murder—mine." The wind whistled past her ears.

"Proof, dear sister. Where is your proof?"

"Proof is no longer as important as it was when I was an eighteen-year-old girl all alone in the world. I no longer have to run away in the night. Now I'm a more dangerous enemy. I have money and money means power. I am wealthy and respected. I have influential friends. When it comes to believing Kathryn Townsend or some unknown with a shadowy past, who do you think would win? And don't fool yourself into thinking I won't pull every string and call in every favor to get you indicted and sent to prison where you belong. Remember," she said through clenched teeth, "I'll do anything in the world to protect my family and my hotels."

"Deck the halls with boughs of holly . . ." The voices rang out in the snow-filled air.

Unexpectedly Edward cocked his ear to the music. "Is that any way to treat your only brother—your only living relative—on Christmas Eve? Surely you can exhibit a trifle more Christian spirit."

"I've exhausted my Christian spirit, Edward. You'll live to regret not accepting my generous offer, I promise you. You chose revenge instead, but you always were greedy. Always wanted more. You demanded all of our mother's love. It galled you that there should be any left over for my father or me. And you were never as bright as you thought. Isn't it ironic that I, a mere woman, am the one fulfilling your dreams of wealth and success? I should thank you for that."

His face wilted in confusion. "What . . . what do you mean?"

"Surely you realize that you made me what I am today. That you goaded me into it with all your 'nice little girls don't climb trees,' 'proper little girls don't go swimming,' 'girls don't need an education,' 'women can't become millionaires' speeches." Her mimicking tone cut through the air cruelly. "I suppose in part I did everything to prove to myself, to the world and to you that women aren't dumb, inferior creatures only one step above barnyard animals. To prove that women can be as smart and powerful and successful as men. That they can play the same games as men and win. And I did, didn't I? I dared to dream.'' The wind whipped at her hair. "So in the spirit of the season, I'll thank you for helping me to achieve the success you will never enjoy. Thank you, Edward. And Merry Christmas.''

She turned and slowly, her head held high, walked down the deserted deck. As she opened the door to the main cabin, a carol poured out into the cold air. "Hark, the herald angels sing, glory to the newborn King. Peace on earth and mercy mild, God and sinners reconciled.''

Chapter Thirteen

Christmas, Kathryn had decided, would be a combined holiday celebration and a belated housewarming for their closest friends.

But Christmas Eve she saved for a private celebration with Owen. They ate supper in the living room, which was dark except for the fire and the flickering candles on the massive Christmas tree. Afterward they sat on the floor in front of the dying fire, sipping champagne and talking until long after midnight.

It should have been a perfect night, but every time Kathryn looked into Owen's face she couldn't help imagining it ravaged by grief. If Edward's plan had been successful . . . A lump rose in her throat. She knew that he could no more imagine a life without her than she could conceive of living without Owen.

Even in bed with his arms around her, his naked body pressed against hers, his lips seeking out her most sensitive places, she couldn't forget. Numbly she forced her body to respond the way she knew Owen expected.

Tomorrow, she told herself, tomorrow the fear will start to fade. The pain and the memory will no longer be raw. Time will begin its healing process, and I can begin my new life.

On Christmas Day, trying to forget, she busied herself with the details of dinner until Mrs. Blair tactfully ushered her out of the kitchen. After dinner the guests arranged themselves around the Douglas fir, which filled the bay window.

Every inch of the tree was covered with ornaments. Shiny glass balls in rich, jewellike colors. Golden-haired angels.

Flowers and trumpets and Santa Clauses. Mounds of silvery packages spilled out from under the tree.

After all the scarves and pens, perfume and books had been exchanged, Kathryn picked up five white envelopes. "What I have here are not really Christmas presents. They are not even gifts. They were all—except perhaps for one—earned." Everyone's eyes were on her.

"Rachel, Roger, Wendell and Allan," she said as she nodded to each. "You are my business associates and even more important, you are my friends. Dear, loyal friends who've helped me make my dream come true. And who will in the future, I know, help that dream to grow.

"As you know, the Townsend Manor and Townsend Park are now part of the newly created Townsend Corporation. Control of the corporation will always remain in the family, but it is only fair that you who've believed in me share in my success in more than a nominal way.

"So in each envelope you will find a certificate for shares in the Townsend Corporation. It comes with my thanks—my deepest, warmest, most sincere thanks and my love."

Her voice abruptly became businesslike. "In case you are wondering, the fifth envelope is for my son. I want him to get involved in the hotel business as early as possible."

There was a slight titter of laughter. "And what about my businesses?" Owen demanded with mock ferocity. "I expect the boy to be a horseman by the age of five."

Kathryn stared at the dear, familiar faces ranged around her. Wendell was nervously brushing back his remaining wisps of hair. Probably worrying if I can afford it, she decided. Allan's broad face was beaming with delight. Beside him sat Maureen, whose smile was even broader as she looked at him. Roger, more at home with etiquette than with emotion, blushed pink with embarrassment. Rachel looked so proud that she could burst.

Finally Owen broke the emotional silence. "I think this deserves another toast. To my wife and the woman who is destined to become the finest hotelier of the century. To Kathryn—the beautiful woman who shares my home and my entire life."

"To Kathryn, an extraordinary woman," they all echoed. "And to her success."

By nine o'clock the guests had left, but Rachel lingered, saying she wanted to see her grandson. Afterward she found Kathryn in the study. The room was cloaked in shadows. The fire had died; only a few embers still glowed orange in the grate. The only light came from the mullioned window that arched upward, silhouetting Kathryn's slender shape.

"Kathryn," Rachel said softly, "I was worried about you. You seemed nervous. Is anything wrong?"

For a few minutes they stood silently watching the enormous snowflakes drift past the window and melt on the street. Finally Kathryn turned and spoke. "I saw my brother yesterday. And I can't get the memory out of my head. All day I've had the feeling that he's here. Like some ghostly presence." She shuddered as Edward's words echoed through her head: I'll be there every day. Watching. Waiting.

"Kathryn, dear, I'm sorry. I can understand how awful it must have been. Did you get him to confess what he'd done to you?"

"Confess! Not exactly. He bragged. He boasted. He gloated about the problems he's caused."

"But why? Why does he want to destroy you? He must have given some reason."

Kathryn shook her head. "He's decided I'm responsible for all his losses—Jessica, the Elliott family fortune, Adam's money. His whole failed life, I suppose. I don't know if he honestly believes that or has made me the scapegoat, someone to take out all his hatred and frustration on. Or whether . . . or whether . . ." She licked her lips nervously. "Or whether he is truly deranged. It was frightening to watch his emotions jump back and forth. One moment he'd be gloating, then he'd get angry, and before I knew it he'd be acting as if nothing out of the ordinary were happening. What scares me is what if he's not crazy? What if he is truly evil and clever enough to pretend he's mentally deranged?"

The idea hung in the darkening air until Rachel said, "That would make him a very dangerous enemy." Her voice was heavy with fear. "Promise me you won't go near him again. For any reason."

"I won't have to. Edward will never threaten us again." Kathryn's heart pounded. This is what you must believe, believe, believe.

"And why not? You didn't do anything foolish, did you?"
Rachel demanded.

"No, but—" Kathryn broke off and went over to the fireplace and knelt down on the hearth. "But now he realizes
that at last I hold the trump card." She stared into the dying
fire and wondered if she should go on. If she knew the truth,
Rachel would worry and fuss over her, and Kathryn didn't
know if she could stand it right now. She felt as fragile as a
piece of crystal. Ready to break at the slightest touch. To
shatter at the wrong word. Her voice was dull as she said,
"Because if he ever comes near me again or I suspect he's
been in one of my hotels, I'll inform the police."

Rachel gave a loud harrumph. "Yes, and tell them what?
That he murdered a young man in Massachusetts ten years
ago, a murder for which you have no proof?"

Her hands felt like ice and she held them out to catch the
last heat from the dying fire. She had to tell someone. Her
voice was steady as she said, "I will inform the police exactly
how Edward tried to kill me yesterday. How he tried to push
me off the ferry. I would have drowned." She stopped, caught
by the import of her own words.

Rachel gasped. Suddenly Kathryn felt the carefully built
dam give way. It was as if by speaking of Edward's treachery
she breathed life into it. It grew so horrifyingly real she could
see the waves churning cold beneath her feet, and the tears
that had been prickling at the back of her eyes burst forth and
streamed down her face. She felt Rachel's arms pulling her
close. Felt the smooth, cool fabric of Rachel's dress growing
damp with her tears. She wanted to scream out her fear and
her anger, but she didn't dare. She bit her lip to hold back
the sobs. Please, please, her heart said. Let Edward be gone.
And let my secret be safe.

Chapter Fourteen

Joseph Henry Patrick Gallagher stared at his shoes. So perfectly spit-shined he could almost imagine his own reflection staring back at him. But something looked wrong; he supposed it was the floor beneath them. All shiny white with gray veins. Marble—that was what the rich always had.

After twelve years with the New York City police department, Gallagher sported sergeant's stripes and thirteen medals for bravery. Except for when drink loosened his tongue, he seldom spoke of them. One was for rescuing two children from a burning building. Another for stopping a bank robbery single-handedly. To be honest, facing a bank robber and a sawed-off shotgun would have been preferable right now. The rich made Gallagher nervous. Very nervous.

Out of the corner of his eye he glanced at the dragon manning the desk. She was pretending to type something, but her lips were pursed in disapproval. Directed at him, no doubt. She'd hustled him out of the lobby and public view fast enough. Obviously policemen had no place in the hallowed halls of the Townsend Manor Hotel.

She typed on. Interminably, it seemed. Click. Click. Clickety-click, click. With each click he grew more apprehensive. Finally a sharp buzzing interrupted the rhythm of the keys and she turned to him with a sniff: "Mrs. Townsend will see you now. May I remind you, however, that she is a very busy woman, and since you do not have an appointment . . ."

But he was already halfway through the door. He'd heard about Miss Townsend and her hotels. She was rich and powerful and very smart for a lady, so they said. But he wasn't prepared for the petite figure with the bright eyes and soft smile. She was so young. And attractive. She stood up, and the next thing he knew, her small, surprisingly powerful hand was clutching his.

"Sergeant Gallagher, what can I do for you? Don't tell me the hotel is harboring any notorious jewel thieves."

"No—no," he stammered. "It's not about the hotel, Miss Townsend. It's about you, that is . . ."

"Yes?" Kathryn said carefully, trying to remember what she could have done to attract the attention of the police. What if he was here to—what did they call it?—shake her down. She'd heard that some of the city's policemen were not above such temptations. She wondered how much he'd ask for "extra protection" and decided how much she'd be willing to pay. It wasn't an idea she liked, but it was a reality of doing business. "Yes, Sergeant Gallagher?"

The sudden frostiness of her tone made Gallagher realize he was taking too much of her time. She was, as the dragon had said, a busy woman. "Actually, it isn't so much about you as it is about your brother."

Kathryn's heart stopped beating for an instant, and when it started up again it roared in her head. When she said, "What about my brother?" her voice sounded unfamiliar and far away.

Gallagher pulled out a dog-eared notebook and flipped through a few pages. "You have a brother named Edward James Townsend?"

Kathryn nodded. Had he come to inform her of Edward's death? No, his manner seemed too businesslike for bad news.

"Miss Townsend, your brother is accused of stabbing a young lady." He paused, wondering if he should have approached the subject more delicately, but it was too late now and he plunged on. "Aboard the Staten Island ferry. Boat called the *President Roosevelt,* on the day before Christmas. At approximately eleven fifty-five a.m."

Kathryn felt her head and her emotions reeling. Was it her fault? Had Edward, so frustrated by his failure to kill her, found an innocent substitute? "I . . . I read about it in the newspaper. How is the girl?"

"Not expected to live, I'm afraid. But there were witnesses. They all described a tall man in black." He consulted his notes. "Very thin face—cavernous, one lady called it. Pale. Prominent nose. Probably in his mid-fifties. He was behaving strangely, they claim. Now, Miss Townsend, does that description fit your brother?"

"Yes, it does." Her voice was dull, and he worried that the shock had been too great for her. He hoped she wouldn't faint. She did look pale. "Miss Townsend, are you all right? Can I get you a glass of water?" he asked.

With a great effort she shook her head. For a moment she said nothing. Then gradually, as the fog of shock lifted, she began remembering. Suddenly it occurred to her that for some reason the pieces weren't fitting. Something was wrong. She went over it again in her head. She saw herself boarding the ferry. There was a name on the side. In her mind's eye she saw the letters in black: *The Manhattan.* Yet according to this policeman the attack took place on the *President Roosevelt.* Of course, Edward could have boarded another boat later. Later? Desperately she ransacked her memory. She was to have met Edward at the restaurant at a quarter past twelve. What time had she boarded the boat? She couldn't remember. But at five minutes to twelve, hadn't Edward been on the *Manhattan* with her? She couldn't be sure.

"Miss Townsend, I realize this has been a shock, but . . ."

"I'm fine, Sergeant Gallagher." She forced her voice to sound normal. "I appreciate your bringing me this news about my brother personally, but I don't see . . ."

"Miss Townsend, we are holding your brother on suspicion of what I expect will turn out to be murder. But he claims he has an alibi." He stared at her closely, ready to register her reaction. If she was going to lie, this was when she would do it. Strange, what families would say and do to protect each other under circumstances like these. Their lies were inevitably found out, but it made his job more difficult.

"According to Mr. Townsend, he was with you at the time of the attack."

Kathryn's eyes met the policeman's as she tried to ignore the emotions revolving around in her head. Could it merely be an extraordinary coincidence, or had Edward . . . ? Did it matter? "I'm afraid, Sergeant, that I can't help you. I haven't seen my brother in years."

Two minutes later Gallagher found himself walking across

the vast marble lobby trying to look inconspicuous. Kathryn
Townsend hadn't seemed rich at all. A nice lady. His wife
would enjoy hearing all about her—what she was wearing (it
was, he remembered, a purple suit, sort of plum-colored);
how she spoke; what her office looked like. Not that her
office had been terribly grand. He'd have to exaggerate that
a bit to please Nora.

Funny, though, how Miss Townsend's eyes had flickered
slightly when she said she hadn't seen her brother. In his
experience that usually meant a witness was lying. But why
should she lie? Besides, if he raised that possibility it would
mean not closing the case today. Tonight was New Year's
Eve, and if he played his cards right he could spend the afternoon at O'Shaughnessy's, start celebrating early. Besides,
he didn't really like Edward Townsend. Something strange
about that man—type that made your skin crawl. That would
explain why his sister wasn't close to him, Gallagher decided,
pushing his way through the revolving door to the street.

Why doesn't he turn around? Can't he hear it? To Kathryn's
ears her heart resounded through the room like a bass drum.
Sergeant Gallagher must hear it. But his footsteps continued
through Miss Willis's office, and a moment later she heard
his heels clicking against the marble of the lobby.

She leapt up. She had to tell him the truth. If she didn't
. . . if that girl died . . . if Edward were convicted of killing
her . . . if he were sent to the electric chair . . . then she,
Kathryn Townsend Morgan, would be guilty of murder, too.

But what if he weren't innocent? What if he had attacked
the girl? It was possible. Hard as she tried, she couldn't remember. It had all been so confusing. She'd never looked at
her watch and perhaps was wrong about the name of the boat.

If she told Sergeant Gallagher the truth, if the girl died, if
Edward was indicted for murder, then she'd be called to testify at the trial and it all would come spilling out. Kathryn
Townsend Morgan's name would be linked with a murderer's
and splashed all over the tabloids. And Owen would never
forgive her. Her reputation. Her marriage. Dead as that poor
girl. Victims of her brother's hatred and greed.

Every day—sometimes two or three times—Kathryn phoned
the hospital to inquire about the girl. The nurse sounded dour:

her condition was critical. After a week the nurse's tone lightened. The patient was in "stable condition." Kathryn felt as if an enormous weight had been lifted from her shoulders. She sneaked out of the hotel and walked across town to a florist's where she wasn't known to order two dozen roses to be sent to the girl's hospital room.

But finding out about Edward was trickier. She knew both the police commissioner and the district attorney, but there were bound to be questions if she called them up out of the blue to inquire about a brother she wasn't supposed to have. And calling Sergeant Gallagher was certain to arouse his suspicions. Some instinct told her he hadn't completely believed her story. But then, why hadn't he come back to question her?

She could only sit and wait for the news to come to her. After three weeks of combing the newspapers, she found what she was looking for:

"Edward Townsend, 46, of Staten Island, has been indicted on charges of attempted murder for the attack on Miss Priscilla Ames on December 24 of last year on the Staten Island ferry. No trial date has been set."

She waited, daily expecting to receive a subpoena. Surely Edward's lawyer would insist on her testifying. Wasn't she his only hope of establishing an alibi? But the weeks stretched on and she heard nothing.

When at last she began to feel safe, she spotted a small item in the gutter column: her brother had been convicted of assault with a deadly weapon and sentenced to six years in prison.

Edward was locked up. Let him plot and scheme to his evil heart's content, he couldn't touch her. Her hotels were safe. Adam was safe. Owen was safe. And her secret was safe.

Book Four

Chapter One

New York City
September 1929

"Mama, I want to see horses."

Adam stood rooted in front of Kathryn, wearing his sailor suit and a determined look. "All right," she agreed, "I'll put a chair by the window and you can watch for the ragman's horse—how will that be?"

"No," he said, sticking out his chin. "Daddy's horses."

Kathryn shot a pleading look across the living room at Rachel. "My smart little boy knows exactly what he wants, and sometimes I think he's going to drive me crazy."

A deep laugh erupted from the depths of Rachel's massive bosom. "He may look like a miniature version of his father," she said, "but see that stubborn line of his chin? Exactly like his mother's when she's bound and determined to have her own way. That child is going to give you a taste of your own medicine."

"You mean I'm getting my just deserts?" Kathryn asked with a laugh. "Adam's only three. I can't understand why he is so obsessed by Owen's horses. It's all he talks about. I thought little boys were supposed to live for trains and toy soldiers, but not Adam." What she didn't say, because she knew how unfair it was, was that he didn't show the same enthusiasm for her hotels. Even the prospect of eating in the main dining room with the grown-ups and ordering anything he wanted didn't make his eyes light up the way the promise of going to the stables did. It will be different when he gets older, Kathryn told herself. He's only a child; he'll have many

349

more passing fancies. He'll want to be a fireman and a policeman and a cowboy. In time he'll learn to love the hotels
as much as I do. Of course, she told herself guiltily, there's
no reason why he can't love both.

"Adam," she said sternly, "you saw the horses yesterday." He remained impassively silent, his chin frozen in a
familiar line. One hand was firmly planted on his hip and
from the other one hung Giddyup, the fuzzy brown horse
with the pink satin ears Rachel had made for him when he
was a baby. The two were seldom parted. "I know you like
to see the horses, but the stables are no place for little boys.
You could get hurt."

A spark of recognition lit his eyes. "Like Grandpa Roger?"
he asked.

Kathryn felt the tears well up in her eyes and she wondered
how long it would take her to get over Roger's death. "No,"
she said, "Grandpa Roger died peacefully."

"Peace . . . fully," he repeated. Adam collected words
the way some little boys collected rocks. Many times he didn't
know what they meant, but he picked them up quickly and
seemed to like the new sounds rolling off his tongue. Sometimes Kathryn teased Owen that their son was destined to be
a poet. "Peacefully," Adam said again, pleased that he'd
mastered the word.

Roger had died the way he'd lived—quietly, gracefully,
without causing any fuss. He'd faded gradually, becoming
thinner and whiter and weaker. Kathryn visited him often
once his illness condemned him to bed. They would discuss
hotel business, but as his strength ebbed, she often found
herself sitting silently by his bedside, trying to will her own
strength into her old friend. Sometimes she brought Adam
with her. Illness and death held no fear for him, and he would
eagerly clamber up onto the bed and gallop his pony over the
hill-like lumps in the bedclothes that were Roger's thin limbs.
Roger's eyes would light up with delight as Adam babbled on
and on with his imaginary games, and Kathryn felt free to
leave the two of them playing happily together.

One afternoon she returned to find an exhausted Adam
curled up like a small animal against Roger's body. Roger's
hand, the skin so palely transparent the veins showed through
in great gnarled blue ridges, was lying protectively over

Adam's dark, curly head. They were both asleep. Adam peacefully. Roger's breathing painful and halting. The sight brought tears to her eyes. The beginning and the end of life lying side by side in a narrow iron bed.

The next morning the nurse called to say that Roger had passed away during the night. . . .

"Horses?" Adam chimed in to remind her.

"We'll see. But right now why don't you look out the window." Kathryn picked up a chair and carried it to the bay window facing the street. Adam trotted after her on sturdy legs. He climbed up on the chair, positioned his elbows against the sill, his chin against the glass, and stared out intently as if he were willing a beloved horse to appear in front of him.

Suddenly there was a clatter of little feet as Adam threw himself off the chair and flew across the room as fast as his chunky legs could carry him. He threw his arms around Owen's knees and shrieked with joy. "Daddy here. I see my daddy's horses." Owen grabbed him up and raised him over his head. Adam shrieked louder and began to giggle. "Horses. Horses. See horses."

"Horses. Horses. Horses," Owen repeated, swinging him even higher. "Do you want to see my horses, is that it?" Owen asked, beaming up at his son. "Yes, of course you do. Right now?"

"Yes. Yes. Horses now," Adam chanted.

"Wait a minute," Kathryn interrupted. "You took him to the stables yesterday as a special treat for his birthday."

Owen grinned. "And he loved it. Don't worry, he knows enough to stay out of everybody's way."

"Owen, he may be a very bright boy, but he's also a very small boy and he has no idea how high-strung those Thoroughbreds can be."

"Don't fret, love. Our son has charmed everybody in the barn. The grooms. The hot-walkers. The exercise riders. I even think he's carving his niche in Mack's heart. They all keep a close eye on him."

Kathryn sighed with exasperation. Owen found it impossible to deny his son anything. He liked to take the boy to the racetrack and the stables to show him off and was thrilled that his son loved it all as much as he did. To Owen, Adam was perfect. Was that why, Kathryn wondered, he avoided discussing having more children? "Sure I'd like to have a daughter," he'd admit if she pressed him, "but let's wait a few years."

"I concede," Kathryn said. "He's probably safe from the horses, but what about the germs? All those fleas and whatever. Not to mention all the heaps of manure. Last time he came home reeking of it, and Miss Gobel raised a dickens of a fuss."

Owen grinned up conspiratorially at Adam. "I think your mother wants to make a sissy out of you. But we won't let her, will we? We'll tell her that you're a big, strong boy and a little dirt and some germs won't hurt you."

"Germs," Adam repeated happily. Then suddenly he stopped his delighted wriggling. His smile faded and he was silent. Solemnly he turned to Kathryn. "Mama, please?"

She smiled. Kathryn knew that she was putty in Adam's tiny hands just the way Owen was. She found it impossible to deny her son any reasonable request. "I suppose I'm outvoted," she said.

But Adam continued to stare at her pleadingly until Owen said, "I think she's just said yes, old man. Say thank you."

A smile broke like a sunrise all over Adam's face. "Thank you, Mama."

Owen hoisted Adam onto his shoulders and headed toward the kitchen.

"Let's ask Cook for some carrots, shall we? And you can tell me which horses you are going to feed."

Kathryn could hear Adam's reedy voice reciting: "Black Knight, Magic Man, Crusader, Red Chief, Kingdom Come . . ." all the way down the hall.

Looking at Rachel, Kathryn shrugged. "You're right. He's as stubborn as I am."

Rachel reluctantly heaved her increasingly stout body out of the chair. "I must go. I have a chambermaid to discipline." Seeing the question in Kathryn's eyes, she added quickly, "Nothing for you to worry about. Hardly a challenge, so don't feel you need to jump in to the rescue. One of the guests caught the girl trying on her favorite sable. The girl has dreams beyond her station."

Kathryn laughed. "So did I."

"I'm afraid this girl's dreams involve finding a rich husband, that's all. A bit of a tart, actually, but a hard worker." Rachel gathered up her gloves and handbag. "I'll see you here this evening."

"It won't be easy," Kathryn said with a sad sigh that seemed to come from her heart. "Why did Wendell insist on coming all the way down from Boston to read Roger's will?"

Rachel patted Kathryn's cheek. "Because Roger *was* a stickler for doing things the proper way."

"You know what this is like? The opening scene in a mystery novel," Owen said with a laugh. Kathryn looked pale and tense, and he was glad to see her flash a weak smile at him.

They were gathered in his study. Tension hung heavy in the air. Wendell sat behind the massive antique desk rubbing his bald head, shuffling a pile of papers and looking nervous. "I'm sorry," he said primly, "to take up your time, but it was my client's wish that there be a formal reading of the will. I'll spare you a verbatim reading. First, there are some small bequests to charity. Then, to you, Rachel," he said, nodding at her, "is bequeathed the sum of ten thousand dollars."

There was a sharp intake of breath. "He shouldn't have done that," Rachel said in a thick voice. Her dark, beady eyes were watery.

"And now we come to the major item," Wendell said nervously, rubbing his scalp. "Kathryn, my dear, Roger wanted you to understand that it was not his intention to slight you. You know how much he loved you, but—"

"I certainly don't expect anything. Roger, I'm sure, had his own family back in England."

"If he did," Wendell said, "they are not mentioned. It was Roger's wish that his entire fortune go to Adam."

"Adam?" both Kathryn and Owen repeated in surprised unison.

Her voice caught as she said, "I know he was fond of Adam, but this . . ."

"When I said fortune—" Wendell began.

Kathryn interrupted. "I know it's not really a fortune. The amount doesn't matter. What matters is that he treated Adam like a grandchild. Blood couldn't have made them any closer.''

"When I said fortune," Wendell continued, "I meant fortune. Adam is a very wealthy little boy. Or he will be once the will is probated. Roger Pennington left an estate of over two hundred thousand dollars.''

"But how . . . ?" Kathryn sputtered, echoing everyone else's thoughts.

"I gather he played the stock market. Rather successfully, too. Adam will inherit an impressive portfolio of some of the best stocks: General Motors, Radio Corporation of America, Woolworth, Union Carbide, Electric Bond and Share.''

"I don't understand," Kathryn protested. "Why did he stay on here, working so hard, when he didn't need the money? He could have retired and lived in luxury.''

"Kathryn," Wendell said, "you know that Roger wasn't the type to retire. He enjoyed his work too much.''

A look of worry crossed Kathryn's face. "I hope he didn't feel any obligation to me. That that's why he refused to retire.''

Wendell looked at her fondly. Kathryn really was remarkable, but sometimes she didn't have an inkling about the enormity of her own powers, her ability to infect others with her passions. Roger had been absolutely devoted to Kathryn Townsend and her dreams, and he would have done anything in the world for her. She had been his life. Wendell cleared his throat nervously. "I'm sure he did exactly what he wanted. And he wanted to leave the greater portion of his estate to your son.''

Kathryn flashed a smile at Owen, expecting to see his beaming face. But his brows were lowered, his eyes ominously dark. "Isn't it wonderful?" she asked.

"I'm not sure," Owen said slowly.

"But why?"

"Kathryn, you know how the stock market has been behaving.''

"Yes," she said impatiently. "Going up and up. Everyone is making his fortune.''

"That's just the problem: everyone is in it—whether they know anything about it or not. Take Roger, for instance. He was a knowledgeable hotel man, not a financier. My barber thinks he's an expert in the stock market. My garage mechanic is up to his eyeballs in debt, buying stocks on margin. My stenographer just plunged her whole life's savings into shares of American Telephone and Telegraph and is convinced that she'll be rich as Croesus within the year. It's not a healthy situation.'' His eyes flashed, and Kathryn knew he'd had his say. She didn't agree with him, but they'd discuss it later.

Later came that night as they were preparing for bed. Kathryn sat before her triple-mirror dressing table brushing her hair. She was wearing a long, slim pink nightgown, its low neck edged in handmade Chinese lace. It was Owen's favorite. As she did her one hundred strokes, until her hair gleamed like fine mahogany, she felt Owen's eyes on her. Glancing up at the mirror, she saw he was sitting up in bed watching her, his chest bare, only a sheet drawn up over his legs.

"About the stocks . . ." she said.

"Don't misunderstand me," Owen said. "I'm happy about the bequest. And pleased that Roger cared about Adam so much.''

Kathryn smiled into the mirror. "Imagine, while Adam is growing up, the money will be growing. After college he can do whatever he wants; money will be no object. He'll be independent." She paused, remembering her own struggles. "Don't take that away from him.''

"*If* the money continues to grow.''

"I know," Kathryn said, brushing her hair more vigorously. "I'll admit the market has had its downturns, but it always bounces back stronger than ever, despite what some of the experts predict. Besides," she said, putting down her brush, "there's only a handful of prophets of doom.''

"And what if they're right? It could all tumble down overnight. The economy of this country would be in chaos. Millions of people are heavily in debt, living off paper profits—what would happen to them? In fact, I've been seriously thinking of selling off all the rest of my stock holdings. I refuse to come crashing down with everyone else when this great American spending spree is over.''

Kathryn turned from the mirror to face him. "And you want to deprive our son of his inheritance because you think you know more than everybody else and insist upon being so damned cautious?''

"Don't get testy. I'm not depriving him of anything. All I'm suggesting is that we liquidate the stock and invest the money in something safer. Something that won't be affected when that tinderbox of a stock market goes up in flames.'' He smiled a pacifying smile. ''I'm not going to do anything without your agreement.'' He looked at her and could see the anger dying in her eyes. "Come here,'' he said, stretching his arms wide.

As Kathryn snuggled her head against Owen's bare chest, she wondered how she could have been mad at him. He only wanted to do what he thought best. And maybe he was right. She thought about her Florida investment and experienced a twinge of guilt. He'd warned her and she hadn't listened then. Maybe this time she should put aside her own feelings.

Every day their love grew, their relationship strengthened, as they watched their son develop into a real person. She wouldn't have thought it possible. Everyone talked about the honeymoon as if it were the most intense and loving time in a marriage. But, Kathryn thought, they are wrong. A honeymoon is like a baby's first step, exciting but feeble compared with the joy of walking strong and unaided. The longer she and Owen lived together the better they came to know each other, the more love they were capable of giving each other.

How wrong Rachel had been. There had been absolutely no reason to open that Pandora's box, to let the past wreak havoc on the present. Her lie was long forgotten.

Chapter Two

Indian summer had arrived. Just as New Yorkers were taking their woolens out of storage, the city was overwhelmed by a wave of heat and humidity. Kathryn sat in her office, a small black fan stirring up a warm circle of air around her. Unenthusiastically she flipped through a real estate listing, although she knew she would find nothing.

It was time to expand. Both hotels were operating smoothly and showing a healthy profit. The question was where to open her new hotel. This time she was determined to build from scratch. No renovations of someone else's mistakes. She would work with the architects and design her dream hotel. But where? Chicago was the logical choice. Chicago—big, gray, sprawling. She couldn't warm to the thought of putting her heart and soul into a city she didn't care for. Of course, she knew exactly where she would like her next hotel to be— Florida. Blue water. White sands. Pink hibiscus. Rows of stately palms. But the time wasn't right. She could not single-handedly make the state popular no matter how magnificent her hotel. But someday. Someday she'd prove to Allan Jones and to Owen that her instincts had been right.

"Daydreaming, and I've caught you red-handed."

Kathryn tore herself away from the images of pink stucco and palmettos and looked up. Her heart gave a startled leap of pleasure, as it always did when she saw Owen unexpectedly. His broad shoulders almost filled the doorway. A smile was spread across his face and his eyes danced with delight.

"You're up to something, aren't you?" Kathryn asked. "Don't bother to deny it, you're grinning like a Cheshire cat. What crazy thing have you done? Bought a yacht? Gone into the movie business? Or is it some pretty new filly in your stable?''

"Sorry to disappoint you. I'm here on a humble errand. To invite the most beautiful woman in the city to dinner on Friday night.''

"How can I refuse when you put it that way?'' Kathryn leaned back in her chair with a sigh. "Where are we eating?''

His grin broadened. "Nice little place I know. New Orleans.''

"I hope that's a new restaurant; otherwise it's an awfully long way to travel for a meal.'' She loved Owen's spontaneous little surprises, but sometimes they were overwhelming, and considering the way he was grinning . . . She'd better be prepared for anything.

"Actually, it's less a trip than a vacation. You do know what a vacation is, don't you? If only by hearsay.'' He held his hand up. "I know, you'll fuss, so that's why all the arrangements are set. No cancellations. No refunds. No matter what you have on your agenda. I have to go down to look at two horses I'm thinking of buying. We'll take Adam; he'll love the train. And I've invited Maureen and Allan. Do Maureen good to get away; she hasn't been herself lately. Depression, Allan says. And you know how she adores spending time with Adam.''

For the first three hours of the trip Adam sat miraculously quiet, entranced by the new world of the train and the scenery speeding by outside the window. He didn't know where to look next and then had a million questions, which he fired at them with the rapidity of a machine gun. "Where will we sleep? Will we eat real food? Why doesn't the train fall off the tracks? What makes it go clickety-clack?'' Even Giddyup, wedged next to him in the seat, went unnoticed. Finally, when dusk settled in and Adam could no longer see out the window, he gave in to his exhaustion. His thumb sought his mouth and he pulled Giddyup into his lap.

"Poor little tyke is tired,'' Maureen said. "I'll have the porter make up my berth and then I'll put him down to sleep and stay with him.''

"But what about your dinner?'' Owen protested.

"It doesn't matter. I'm not really hungry anyway. What

does matter is that this little boy gets his sleep.'' She brushed a few dark curls off Adam's forehead, but he was too sleepy to notice.

"Don't be silly, Maureen," Allan said. "You need your food, too. You're much too thin. Someday I'll put my arms around you, and all there'll be will be air." He tried to joke, but the tension in his voice was all too obvious.

Kathryn understood. She'd seen Maureen change over the past few years. She wanted a child so desperately, and after the first few miscarriages, now she couldn't even get pregnant. It was as if her life had no meaning without a child. Her sweet, easygoing temperament had taken on a brittle edge. Kathryn saw Allan's mouth harden. It was difficult for him, too.

The next morning Adam was up with the sun and determined to explore every inch of his new domain, with an anxious Maureen dragging at his heels. He couldn't stop talking about everything: "I slept in a berth. That's what Auntie Mo says they call a bed on a train. And there was a real table. And I ate two eggs for breakfast. But the toast was hard." He screwed up his little nose. "And this is a Pu—Pullman. And the wheels make the train go clickety-clack."

Owen smiled as he listened to Adam's monologue, wondering if all three-year-olds were this bright and energetic. Wait until Adam was older; then he could put that energy to good use, teach him about Thoroughbred racing. The boy had a head start already. When he was old enough, Owen would let him exercise the horses, let him know the feeling of speed and power between his legs, understand the jockey's job firsthand. Someday the whole racing world would know Owen Morgan and his son. They'd have the finest racing stable in the country; there would be no stopping them.

From the moment Kathryn stepped off the train in New Orleans, she had the feeling she was in an exotic new land. Even the air felt different—hot, humid, almost tropical. Sounds were different—soft, slow Cajun speech filled the air. The smells were new—the perfume of flowers and spices. The buildings with their elaborate iron grillwork, the homes with their flower-filled courtyards, looked peculiarly out of place in an American city.

The limousine dropped Maureen and Allan at their hotel

in the city, where Maureen parted with Adam amongst many hugs and kisses, and then they continued on to "The House," as the driver called it. Kathryn felt like a child, swiveling her head from side to side, afraid of missing anything. When she finally caught a glimpse of the Mississippi over the top of a levee, she gasped in astonishment. Vast, more like a sea than a river.

Adam momentarily turned his attention from trains and horses to boats, furiously jabbering questions at Owen and giving him no time to answer. The first time he saw Spanish moss swaying in the trees, he squealed with delight. "Look, the trees have beards!"

Every time Adam or Kathryn exclaimed over some new discovery, Owen smiled and said smugly, "Just you wait." What surprise did he have in store that could be even more fascinating and beautiful? Kathryn wondered.

They were staying with Claude Marchand, the wealthy and socially prominent owner of the horses Owen was considering buying. His home was upriver, an hour's ride from the city. Kathryn knew Owen had visited him several times before to purchase horses. Her beloved Miss Kathryn, now a prolific broodmare, came from his stable.

At last the chauffeur pulled off the main road onto a smaller road. On each side enormous trees arched over the road to form a cool tunnel. Each tree was festooned with silvery Spanish moss. "Big trees," Adam pronounced gravely, poking his head out the window so he could see their tops.

"They're very old," Owen said.

"Even older than my daddy?" he asked incredulously.

The double line of trees seemed to stretch on endlessly, when suddenly they ended and Kathryn felt her heart stop. Ahead of her was the plantation house, gleaming so white in the sunshine it made her eyes hurt. Nestled amongst huge oaks and magnolias, it looked like a giant wedding cake. A hipped roof covered it; galleries wrapped around it on all sides and were supported by dozens of slender columns. Under the shade of the galleries the tall, stately windows looked cool and welcoming.

As soon as their car drew up, two figures burst out of the front door. Claude Marchand was a leonine man with a soft, wrinkled face and a mane of silver hair. His wife was dark and diminutive with lively eyes.

"*Bienvenue*. Welcome," they both shouted.

When Adam leapt out of the car, Claude bent down and solemnly shook his hand. "*Bienvenue.*"

"*Bienvenue,*" Adam repeated carefully.

"Do you know what that means?" Adam shook his head. "It means 'welcome' in French. It is also the name of our plantation." He turned to Owen with a laugh. "Your son is going to be a linguist; he has a good accent."

When Kathryn stepped into the coolness of the front hallway, she felt as if she'd been transported into another century. Antique marble-topped tables alternated with delicate silk-covered side chairs along the walls. Elaborate gold-framed mirrors reflected the pure whiteness of the walls. The floor was a dark, flawless polished mahogany. Between the two fluted columns that supported an archway, a staircase spiraled gracefully up to the second floor.

Watching Kathryn's eyes widen with amazement, Virginie Marchand asked, "Would you like a tour? Most of our guests are intrigued because we try to preserve our home the way it was in the last century. I tell Claude it's because he's too cheap to invest in new furniture. But he insists he's keeping up a family tradition." She laughed indulgently. "The house has been in his family for one hundred and twenty years. But don't worry about your comfort. I put my foot down when it came to getting a modern kitchen and bathrooms."

After the tour of all twenty-two rooms was over, Virginie led Kathryn to her suite. "I'll send in our mammy. Her real name is Artemesia, but we call her Mammy, in the old Southern fashion. She took care of our daughters—they're all married now—and she'll look after Adam. It will do her good. I tell her she's getting lazy. I think she misses children. To tell you the truth, so do I. Take your time, my dear," she continued. "Have a rest if you'd like. Our heat can be exhausting if you're not used to it. We dine at nine o'clock. I'll see you then."

The next day, at Virginie's suggestion, the chauffeur drove Kathryn into the city. She saw all the sights—the magnificent houses of the Garden District, the French Quarter, Jackson

Square, the French Market, the Dueling Oaks, the sprawling, whitewashed cemeteries.

Returning in the evening to Bienvenue, she was bubbling over with excitement. Listening to her describe the city and seeing the gleam in her eye, Owen said, "Don't tell me, you've decided to open your next hotel in New Orleans."

"Yes, but not a new one. Not in such a wonderfully old city. What I want to do is find an old building and convert it into an intimate little hotel. Can't you see guests dining outdoors in a courtyard surrounded by flowers and fountains? Allan has promised to start looking around tomorrow for the right location."

"You sound as excited as your son, talking a mile a minute."

"I'm sorry. And I haven't even asked you how your day was."

"Almost as good as yours. Claude has two magnificent horses he's willing to sell—a bay and a roan. And then there's a chestnut I'm thinking of buying for stud."

"And Mack agrees?" Kathryn said, her brows arching in surprise. Mack had reluctantly traveled down several days in advance to visit other stables and advise Owen.

"Well, he didn't disagree. Looked over the horses as carefully as if he were choosing a wife and growled a 'Can't object,' which, coming from Mack, is high praise. I intend to make Claude an offer in the morning." He paused. "But first I have an idea to discuss with you."

"And I can tell by the hesitant tone of your voice that you don't think I'll like it."

"Well, you know we never did decide what to do about Adam's inheritance. I know it's rather a sore subject, but it's a decision we have to make sooner or later. What about using some of his money—just a small portion—to buy these horses? I think Adam would get a kick out of knowing they were his. And I do think they have moneymaking potential."

To Owen's astonishment, she smiled. "I think it's a wonderful idea. He'll love it. And I know Roger would want him to enjoy his inheritance. Why don't you wire Wendell and your broker first thing in the morning and tell them to sell the stock?"

"All of it?" Owen asked in amazement.

"Yes. This time I'm going to listen to your instincts. I think you're right: the stock market is headed for a crash."

That night at dinner all Claude Marchand could talk about was how high and how fast the stock market was going. "Do you know that some of my stocks have risen twenty percent in the last ten weeks? Twenty percent. Not one single stock down." Kathryn and Owen found it difficult to sit quietly and occasionally nod their heads.

Virginie, conscious of their silence, finally said, "Claude, not everyone is as interested in making money as you are. Stocks. A lot of foolish nonsense. Stick to what you know— horses. Your great-granddaddy didn't build this house with bits of paper. No, he planted. Rice. Sugar cane."

"And you don't have any gumption, Miss Virginie. Not like Miss Emilie." Claude nodded to the seven-foot-high oil painting of a sly-smiled young girl with pale skin, holding a white magnolia, that dominated the dining room. "My great-aunt. She saved the plantation from the Yankees."

Later that night when they were alone in their bedroom, Owen said, "Claude didn't say exactly how Emilie saved the plantation, did he?"

"Maybe that's not part of the family tradition."

"Looked a bit of a tart to me," Owen said. "I have a pretty good idea how she did it."

"Owen Reginald Morgan!" Kathryn said in feigned shock. "I'll bet all the Marchands are rolling over in their graves at the thought. And those graves are only a few hundred feet away." She paused. "You were dying to say something to Claude about the stock market, weren't you?"

"It was hard not to. But I doubt he would have believed me. He's too enamored of his paper profits. I only hope he isn't in too deeply. I'd hate to see him lose this place."

"I'm sure we made the right decision," Kathryn said. "I can't wait to tell Adam tomorrow. He's going to be so excited about having horses of his own."

"Is he having fun here, do you think?" Owen asked. "I've taken him down to the stables, but Claude and I have so much to discuss that it's hard to keep an eye on him, and I had to take him back to Mammy." He could see in his mind's eye the pathetic expression in Adam's eyes when he delivered him back into the old woman's hands.

"Mammy—what do you think of her?" Kathryn asked, trying to keep the uneasiness out of her voice.

"She's all right, I guess. Been with the family for years," Owen said.

Kathryn thought for a moment. "I don't like the way she looks at you. Actually, the problem is that she never really does look at you. She always seems to be looking out through slits." Realizing how silly she sounded, she laughed. "I guess I just expected a mammy to be fat and jovial. And she's so skinny. Dried up, as if there were no meat on her bones. But I'm sure Adam doesn't find anything odd about her. It's all in my imagination."

Chapter Three

Horses. He had two horses. And they belonged just to him. Papa said so. Adam stretched his arms out along the window-sill and leaned his chin on his fists and stared out. He could see the white steeple of the stable peeking out from behind the trees. Why did they keep the horses so far away from the house? Papa said it was because of the smell. He sniffed at the hot, humid air. Horses smelled nice.

He couldn't wait to see his horses. Papa had gone out right after breakfast, but he promised to take him to the stable soon. When was soon? he wondered. He couldn't wait to see what his horses looked like. A bay and a roan, Papa said. A bay was brown with a black tail and mane. He knew that. And a roan looked sort of red—if you shut your eyes a little. But he knew one thing: they'd be the most beautiful horses in the whole, entire stable. He stopped. Maybe he'd seen his horses already. In his mind he saw rows of horses staring out of their stalls. He wished he knew all their names, like he knew the names of Papa's horses. His horses were called Red Dancer and Ba—Bal. Bal something. He couldn't remember, except that the name was long and his tongue refused to move that way.

Why couldn't Papa come home and take him to the stable now? He wished he could tell time. It must be hours and hours that he'd been looking out the window. He turned to Mammy. Maybe she knew when "soon" was. She was sitting in a straight-backed chair next to his bed. Her eyes were half closed and he wondered if she was asleep. "Mammy"— why did he have to call her that? She wasn't at all like his own pretty mother. She was old and skinny had had funny

365

color skin. Lots of people had dark skin here; some of them
were black, black as the piano in Mama's hotel. Others were
a pretty brown. But Mammy was gray, like the ashes left in
the fireplace. He wasn't sure he liked her. And he didn't think
she liked him.

Why couldn't Miss Gobel be here? He liked her. Or better
still, why couldn't Aunt Mo take care of him? She loved him.
Sometimes she whispered to him when they were alone, saying she wished he were her little boy, asking him how he'd
like that. He knew he wouldn't like leaving Mama, but he
couldn't tell Aunt Mo that. Sometimes Aunt Mo hugged him
too hard, so hard he couldn't breathe. Once upon a time he
heard Mama telling Papa that Aunt Mo should have a little
boy of her own. Would that mean she wouldn't love him
anymore? Would she stop giving him candy? Maybe he should
hope she never had a little boy.

He thought about asking Mammy to take him to see his
horses. He didn't think she liked the stables, but if she knew
how important it was . . . But then he saw she was making
funny little sounds, like grown-ups sometimes make when
they're sleeping. He stared out of the window again. That
white steeple jutting into the sky seemed to dare him. He
knew he could find the stable by himself. Mammy liked to
sleep and he could run fast and she'd never know.

Holding his breath, he slipped past her and out of the room.
He tiptoed into the hall and down the stairs. The front door
looked very big; he'd never opened it himself before. There
was usually a very tall, very black man standing there to open
and close it. With one hand he reached out to the brass doorknob and turned it. He pulled and the door opened a little.
"Papa is right," he whispered to himself. "I am strong."
The door slammed behind him and he waited for someone to
appear and tell him to get back in the house. But everything
was quiet.

Resolutely he trudged toward the white steeple, stopping
every few yards to look around. He didn't want anyone to
see him. He almost walked right into a fat lady carrying a
basket of laundry, but he hid behind a tree and she didn't see
him. Mama said these people had been slaves. He wasn't sure
what slaves were, but from the way she said the words, he
knew she didn't approve. The funny little white houses all in

a row, she said, were slave cabins. They looked like doll-houses, they were so tiny. Still, it might be fun to live in one. The house Mr. and Mrs. Marchand lived in was so very, very big. But he liked the winding staircase. He bet the cabins didn't have those.

Suddenly a big green bug buzzed past his face, almost hitting his nose and startling him. There were lots of bugs here. Lots more than in the city. Black beetles that scurried away when you turned on the lights. And spiders, really big ones with fat, hairy legs, not like the tiny ones at home. He kept his eyes on the ground and saw a shiny green beetle and something brown that flew up with a lot of angry noise when he got near it. He liked it here. Maybe they could stay longer if he asked Papa. Mama would say no, that she had to get home to her hotels. He thought about going home; that would be fun, too. He liked trains.

He emerged from a grove of trees to find that the road was all of a sudden two roads. He stopped, trying to re-member which one Papa had taken. One way went to the stables and the other to the—he tried to remember what Mr. Marchand said; it was a funny word. Suddenly he remem-bered. "Bayou." The way Mr. Marchand said it, it didn't sound like a nice place at all. He stood, his eyes hopping from one road to the other. At last he saw that one road was wider. "That's it," he said aloud. "Lots of people go to the stable, so they make the road bigger. Nobody wants to go to the other place." With a sigh of relief he set off.

When the stable block rose up before him, he forgot that he was supposed to be hiding and set off at a run. Stalls lined three sides of an enormous cobblestone courtyard. Horses poked their heads out of every stall. He'd never seen so many horses in his life. Even more than in Papa's stable. For a moment he stood there struck with delight.

Next to each stall was a brass plate with the name of the horse printed on it. He wished he could read; then he could find his horses. He was halfway around the courtyard be-fore he realized he was all alone. When he'd come with Papa, there were always lots of people around. Feeding the horses. Cleaning out the stalls. Then as his stomach sent out a hunger pang he remembered: it was lunchtime, and

Papa said even grown-ups took naps here because it was so hot.

Never mind. He didn't need anybody else. He could look at the horses all by himself. He wished he had brought Giddyup; it was lonely having no one to talk to. Maybe one of the horses would like to talk to him. He looked up. They were so far away. Usually there was someone to hold him up so he could pat their great big noses.

One black horse looked down at him and gave a little nicker, and he remembered. Carrots. He should have brought carrots. But then he would have had to go to the kitchen, and someone would have told him not to go out alone. The horses would just have to understand.

If only he could reach them. Something to stand on—that was what he needed. His eyes swept the stable yard. There was a small wooden cart at one end, but he knew he couldn't move that. His eyes fixed on a bale of hay. He trotted over and grasped the wire that held it together. It would only move an inch or so, no matter how hard he tugged. He found himself getting very hot, and his whole body felt damp. Then he spied a metal pail. He grabbed it eagerly. Water sloshed out against his legs, but that didn't matter. Carefully he arranged the overturned bucket in front of a stall and climbed up. The horse's soft white nose remained temptingly beyond his fingers.

What he could reach was the bolt that locked the stall. His fingers grasped it. "No," he suddenly said, remembering how Papa had explained that horses were "nervous," which meant that they were easily scared. He'd find a horse that didn't look scared.

Solemnly he walked down the long rows, studying each horse. Some of them rolled their eyes, others twitched their nostrils. Those he walked past. Finally he stopped in front of a gray horse. The horse put down its head and looked at him. "Do you want to be friends?" Adam asked. The horse nodded. "Do you want to get out of there?" Again the horse seemed to nod. "I'll be right back," Adam said, toddling off for the pail.

In the distance he could hear voices, and he decided he'd better let his new friend out fast before someone came and spoiled everything. He pulled back the bolt, jumped off the pail and tugged open the stall door. To his surprise the horse just stood there, shifting nervously from one foot to the other as if deciding what to do. "Come out. It's okay. I won't hurt you. I'll let you have some nice grass," Adam cajoled. The gray rolled his eyes and Adam felt a flicker of fear. Maybe his new friend was scared after all. The horse lowered its head and shook it until its mane flew.

Adam was barely aware of the sound of footsteps on the cobblestones behind him. Then a voice exploded into the silence. "For Christ's sake, he's lettin' one of the god-dammed horses out!"

He knew it was Mack's voice and he expected his father to say, "Watch your language in front of the boy," the way he always did. But instead he heard his father say, "Back away, son. Slowly. You'll be all right. Don't be scared."

Hearing strange voices, the horse pricked up its ears. Then suddenly, as if he'd finally come to a decision, he leapt out of his stall. Owen, too far away to do anything, watched in horror as the huge animal jumped smoothly over his son as if he were no more an obstacle than a bale of straw. The front hooves landed clear of Adam by several yards, and Owen let out a sigh of relief. But before he could make his body move, he saw one of the horse's massive back hooves clip Adam's head.

The horse, experiencing an exhilarating taste of freedom, galloped around the courtyard like a madman, its hooves striking sparks against the cobblestones. Seeing a wall, it reared up in anger and confusion before changing direction. But Owen and Mack were oblivious to the horse's demented charge. Their attention was riveted to Adam's small body sprawled out on the cobblestones.

Owen shook off the paralysis of fear and raced toward his son. As he came closer he could see the bruise spreading across the boy's forehead where the hoof had hit him, and he watched for the reassuring rise and fall of the little chest. He came closer, but he couldn't see it. Adam lay absolutely still. Owen's body refused to move. He stood staring dumbly. It was Mack who went over to the boy, dropped on his knees and felt his neck with his fingertips.

Time seemed to stand still. Owen was acutely aware of everything that was going on around him. The sound of hooves on the cobbles. Excited whinnies from the horses. The shrill, mimicking call of a mockingbird. A fly buzzing around his face. The heat of the noon sun hitting his body.

And then Mack looked up.

Chapter Four

Kathryn was strong, Owen thought as he slowly opened the bedroom door. She would survive. But would he? He could feel his hand tremble. Yes, they would both survive. They had each other and their love; it would be their support and their reason to continue living.

If only he didn't have to say the words. If only that part were over and he didn't have to watch her beautiful face crumble in pain. Then they could hold each other, comfort each other. He closed his eyes; he couldn't look at her face.

"Owen, what is it? You look . . ."

"Adam is dead." The three words hung in the air.

"What?"

"He's dead. I saw it happen." His voice was cold and lifeless.

Gradually his words began to penetrate. Of course it wasn't true. Adam was a strong, healthy little boy—he was never sick, and Mammy was experienced and she was taking care of him. Why was Owen doing this to her? "Of course he's not," she said angrily. "He's up in the nursery with Mammy."

Owen shook his head. "It was an accident. A horrible accident." Before her eyes he began to disintegrate. His strong, square face was suddenly gaunt and haggard with pain. Silent tears began streaming down his cheeks.

All she could think was, Why doesn't he hold me? Take me in his arms and tell me it's going to be all right? The small part of her mind that was still functioning kept asking, Why does he just stand there looking broken? Owen is strong.

371

He always knows what to do. Now when I need him, how can he just stand there?

Her numb lips formed another question. "How . . . how did it happen?" She could imagine a hundred bloody and terrifying ways. It would be better to know the truth, better than letting her imagination . . .

"A horse . . . a horse kicked him in the head." His own head dropped.

Suddenly Kathryn's fear was transformed into anger. "What was he doing in the stables? I warned you again and again that it's dangerous. Why did you take him? Why?"

Owen's eyes refused to meet hers. "I didn't," he whispered. "I wasn't even there. I came back with Mack. We saw him. He was opening the door to a stall and . . ." He couldn't finish.

She flung herself out of her chair. It tipped over, leaving a deep white scar on the edge of the rosewood desk before crashing to the floor. "You insisted on taking him to the stables. You deliberately seduced him with your horses and your damned racing world. He was just a little boy. He didn't belong there."

Owen longed to comfort her. To take her in his arms. To be comforted by her. But he couldn't get past the hatred blazing in her eyes.

Her voice was hard and clear when she said, "You killed Adam. You killed my son."

"I . . . I . . ." he said and stopped. There was no excuse. If only he hadn't insisted on taking Adam to the stables. Of course a little boy would find it irresistible. What Kathryn said was true. He wanted to tell her he was sorry, but the words wouldn't come. He opened his mouth and tried again, but Kathryn turned her back on him.

There was nothing he could say. With a helpless shrug he turned on his heel and walked out the door. But her words followed him, flying through the air with deadly accuracy. "I never want to see you again. I hate you."

Kathryn heard the words, but it took time before she realized they were her own. Unconsciously she clutched the edge of the desk so hard she thought her fingers would break. But if she let go she knew she'd fall. Mentally and physically. Her mind wandered back and forth in time. She remembered

Adam, her son, and Adam, her lover. She'd lost both of them now. Why, her mind cried out in silent anguish, why must I lose everyone I love?

She was deaf to the sound of Owen's boots on the stairs and the slamming of a door. Seconds later an automobile coughed to life before roaring away. Then there was silence.

That was where Mack found her, hours later, staring out of the bedroom window. He knocked on the door and, hearing nothing, entered hesitantly. She didn't turn around. Didn't even appear to hear him. "Mrs. Morgan, are you all right?" She didn't move a muscle. "Shouldn't you be in bed or something?" Cautiously he moved toward her. "There are arrangements to be made and . . . Where is Mr. Morgan?"

To his surprise she whirled around to face him. "I don't know."

"But, Mrs. Morgan . . ." He damned Owen for running off. Damned the Marchands for being away. The servants were no help. Weeping and wailing as if the kid had been one of theirs. How was he expected to deal with a hysterical woman? "Maybe you should have a brandy. Or lie down."

"No," she said dully, turning back to the window as if the spirit had suddenly gone out of her. She wondered if she should tell someone. But who was there to tell? Saying the words—"Adam is dead: my son is dead"—would make it all too horrendously real. And she didn't have the strength to endure people's tears and sympathy.

Mack felt trapped. He couldn't leave her alone. Not when she was like this. But he didn't know what to say, to do. Women usually cried. Why didn't she? And where the bloody hell was Owen?

He inched back toward the door. It wasn't his problem. Owen's horses were his problem. Not his wife. Then he looked at her small figure silhouetted against the window. She looked so frail, her shoulders sagging under their burden of grief. He tried to imagine what she was thinking; he couldn't even imagine what having a child was like. But he could feel her pain. It radiated from her body and spread to every corner of the room, silent but more powerful than tears.

He backed into a small silk-covered chair and perched there awkwardly. "I'm gonna be right here, Mrs. Morgan, if you need me."

What seemed like hours later, her voice came out of the gathering dusk, startling him. It was surprisingly calm and clear. "Mack, has someone called a doctor and the police?"

"Yes, ma'am, that's been taken care of."

She nodded and walked over to the dressing table, where she began taking combs and brushes and bottles out of the drawers. Without turning around she said, "I want to take my son home. Will you please find out when trains leave for New York?"

She doesn't understand, Mack thought, that it may not be that simple, that there will be questions and legal formalities. But he didn't dare tell her. The Marchand name carried weight around here; there might be strings that could be pulled. Their trainer would know. Damn Owen, when was he planning on coming back anyway?

He rose stiffly from the little chair. "Anything else I can do for you?" She shook her head, engrossed in her task, and he left. On the way downstairs he decided to call the police. Someone had to find Owen. Wasn't safe for a man in a state of shock to be roaming around like that all by himself.

He found Kathryn waiting for him in the front hallway the next morning. Dressed in black and looking small, pale and fragile. She was alone. "Where is my son?" she asked in a brittle voice.

"He'll be at the station," he said, picking up her bags. They'd better have that tiny coffin stashed away in the baggage compartment before she arrived. He didn't know what would happen if she saw it.

He was turning to usher Kathryn out when he saw Mammy descending the staircase. Thin, gray and moving quietly as a wraith. The two women stared at each other. Emotion hung in the air like an unexploded bomb. "Better go; don't wanna miss our train," Mack said.

Kathryn ignored him. She felt all her hatred and anger being channeled toward the tiny gray figure. If it weren't for that ugly old woman, Adam would be alive, romping around the hallway, begging to be allowed to slide down the banister. The woman was stupid or crazy—it didn't seem important which—and she hated her. Every fiber of her body seemed to pulsate with hatred and anger. She could feel the blood pounding in her head.

"You were supposed to be watching him. You allowed him to wander off. A little, innocent child, and you let him go." Like a wounded animal, she cried out her pain.

Mammy's half-closed eyes suddenly flew open, and Mack could see they were black as coal and burning with emotion. But her voice was calm, her drawl languid. She stared straight at Kathryn. "You wuz runnin' off to do yore business in de city. Ain't proper for a woman to mess with men's affairs. God 'specs her to be home takin' care of her babies. I ain't never lost one of my babies before. Not ones that got proper mamas."

Mack dropped the suitcases and moved toward the old woman. "Why, you old—" He pulled himself up short. "How dare you say things like that to Mrs. Morgan?"

But Mammy ignored him, and as silently as she'd come, she turned and disappeared up the stairs, leaving Kathryn shaking with anger. "Don't pay no attention to what she said. People here think she's kinda crazy anyhow." Mack waited until Kathryn had stopped trembling, then added, "Now, let's go catch that train, get you home."

They rode into the city in silence. Every few minutes Mack looked nervously over at Kathryn. What worried him most was her stillness. Her white-gloved hands were folded in her lap, looking as if they were carved out of marble. Her shoulders, barely resting against the seat, were rigid. And her eyes never left the road in front of them. Mack couldn't help feeling that he was sitting next to a volcano that could explode at any moment.

It wasn't something he talked about, but Mack had a sixth sense. Sometimes he'd wake up in the middle of the night with the hairs on the back of his neck bristling, and he'd know one of his horses was sick or in trouble. And he was always right. But this was the first time he'd ever felt it about a person. As of seven o'clock this morning, the police still hadn't found Owen. Unfamiliar roads. Bayous where people could disappear without a trace. Just wasn't like Owen to do something crazy like this.

"Don't you worry 'bout Mr. Morgan," he said, more to reassure himself than Kathryn. "He'll turn up. And with some good explanation 'bout where he's been." But he couldn't help feeling that Owen was in trouble. He rubbed his hand over the back of his neck, wishing the sensation would go away.

Without taking her eyes off the road, Kathryn said, "Where Mr. Morgan is doesn't matter to me."

"But don't you . . . ?" Mack said. Then, seeing the way her chin was set in determination, he stopped, muttering in frustration to himself, "People, never could understand them. Ought to stick to horses."

Like a faithful shepherd, he guided her through the station, buying her ticket and escorting her to the proper track. Before she boarded he tried one more time. "Sure you don't wanna change your mind and wait for Mr. Morgan? Long train ride for a lady to make all by herself."

She looked at him with surprise. "But I'll be with my son."

"Yes, 'course you will," he said in embarrassment.

Kathryn followed him aboard the train and sat in the seat he indicated. "Nothin' else I can do for you?" he asked, wishing there were. Without thinking, he asked, "Like me to go with you?"

She managed a weak smile. A smile which to Mack seemed to light a small flame in his heart. "No, Mack, but thank you for everything. I don't know what I would have done without you."

Before he knew it, he was reaching down and patting her shoulder. "I'm sorry, ma'am," he said, his voice gruff with emotion. "Awfully sorry. He was a good little tyke." He turned and clumped down the passage on his bandy legs.

For a long time afterward Kathryn could still feel the warmth of his touch. She'd felt no human touch since . . . Where was Owen? She needed Owen to touch her, to hold her, to tell her that he loved her. But he was gone. They'd never been apart before. It felt so strange, like part of her was missing. But of course he was gone. He'd killed their son. How could she still love him?

She barely noticed when, amidst a blast of steam, the train pulled out of the station. Hour after hour the scenery rushed past her window in a blur of blues and greens. Clickety-clack, clickety-clack, the wheels repeated endlessly, reminding her of Adam, until she almost expected to see him stick his head around the door, grinning with excitement. She reached down into the small valise at her feet, rummaged around frantically for a moment and finally pulled out Giddyup. She'd found the little horse abandoned in the nursery. She held it up, and its chipped glassy eyes seemed to stare straight into hers. "You should be with him now. I bet he misses you." She sat the horse down in the seat next to her, and they sat silently side by side for hours as the train pushed farther and farther north.

Clickety-clack. Clickety-clack. Adam is dead, the wheels repeated. Owen's words kept echoing through her head. And Mammy's. Until she wanted to scream for mercy.

The porter went away shaking his head when she told him that she wanted no meals and it wasn't necessary to make up her berth. All night long she stared out the window into the black void, feeling small and lonely and hollow, not caring whether the train ride ever ended.

When they reached New York, she gathered up her bags mechanically. As she stepped off the train she was met by a tall, thin-faced man in black. "Mrs. Morgan?" he said, doffing his hat. "Let me offer my most sincere condolences. I am Mr. Corter from the funeral home. Mr. MacIntosh wired me to meet you and take care of arrangements. If it is convenient, I will call upon you and Mr. Morgan later in the day. To discuss the funeral."

Kathryn stared at him blankly. "I can see that you are exhausted," he said smoothly. "Let me escort you to a cab, and we can talk once you are rested." With a grateful nod she sank down into the back seat of the taxi and closed her eyes.

Minutes later she was jarred into consciousness by a rough voice.

"Don't mind me saying so, ma'am, but you look like you lost everything, too."

"What?" Kathryn asked blankly, wondering how he knew.

The cabdriver's eyes stared back at her in the mirror. "Well, at least you got company. Thousands of them. My brother-in-law, he's a contractor, ya know—thought he knew everything was to know about the stock market—lost his shirt." He paused, seeing her puzzled expression. "Ain't ya heard? The stock market, whole thing went bust yesterday. People ruined. Jumpin' out of windows. Thing's a mess. And they say it's gonna get worse. Guess nothin' will ever be the same, will it?''

"No," Kathryn said. What did it matter now that Adam's inheritance was safe? That Owen had been right? "Nothing will ever be the same."

Just as she closed her eyes again the car jerked to a stop. "We're here, lady."

"Where?" Kathryn asked dully.

"Where the gentleman said to take you," he answered. "Are you gettin' out or not?"

Kathryn looked out the window at the familiar facade. Home. She wanted to be home. But would it ever be home again? Without Adam. Without Owen. She dreaded opening the door. No one would be there. Mrs. Blair and the staff were off. The house would hold only memories. Memories too precious to endure. She stood on the steps with the key in her hand, wondering if she should go back to her old suite at the Townsend Manor. Back to her old life. She looked over her shoulder; the taxi had disappeared. No, she didn't have the energy to leave. She turned the key and the front door swung open.

Chapter Five

The devil rode at his heels. He drove faster and faster, but
still Owen couldn't shake him. Over the rutted country roads,
along the smooth black pavement, the devil clung to him.
Tormenting him. Never allowing him to forget.

Could he outrun the devil? He pressed his foot against the
accelerator. The speedometer shot up. Forty. Forty-five. The
needle hovered at fifty. He forced his foot toward the floor
and it jumped to sixty. Without warning, the road in front of
him faded, dissolving into the cobblestones of the stable
courtyard. The courtyard was vast, and Adam's body was so
small lying there. It was only a tiny bruise. How could he be
dead? Owen jammed his foot to the floor. Only the devil
could be so cruel.

The voice was clear. It was as if Kathryn were seated next
to him. "You killed Adam. You killed my son." Owen's head
swiveled around to face her. He had to tell her it wasn't his
fault. That he was sorry. That he'd give anything to have his
son back. Even his own life. The seat was empty, but her
voice hovered in the air. "You killed my son." With it came
the memory of the hatred that blazed in her eyes as she flung
out the accusation. The words that cut his heart into shreds.

He felt hollow, as if every emotion but guilt had been
drained from his body. Kathryn was gone. She'd never forgive him. How could she? And Adam, he'd never see his son
again. He closed his eyes to squeeze out the tears. Everything
was dark, and with the blackness came peace.

Little by little, he became aware of something blasting into
his hard-won peace. Why wouldn't the noise stop? Reluctantly he forced his eyes open. The two headlights bearing

down on him were less than sixty feet away. The road was
narrow and bordered by trees. His foot automatically reached
for the brake, but his brain told him it was useless. With all
his strength he whipped the wheel to the right. Massive, gray,
like the leg of an elephant, a tree trunk rose before him. He
felt the front of the car drop and his body pitch toward the
windshield.

Instinctively his fingers tightened on the steering wheel.
His head stopped only inches from the glass. He looked out.
The front of the car rested lightly against the trunk of the
tree. The front wheels, caught in a drainage ditch, spun fu-
tilely.

He barely registered the other car whooshing by, honking
its horn angrily. His heart was pounding like a drum, blocking out all other sounds. For a long time he sat staring at the
gray bark of the tree until every ridge and imperfection were
fixed in his mind. The devil had been shaken.

When he climbed out of the car, his legs felt like rubber
and he could barely stand. His mouth was dry and he was
panting like a thirsty dog. With startling clarity he realized
what had happened. "Goddamn it," he shouted into the
darkness, slamming his fist into the ancient tree trunk.
"You're a coward. You tried to kill yourself." Never before,
not even during the years in the trenches when he had watched
his friends dying, one by one, and had lain awake wondering
how long before he joined them, had he considered the ulti-
mate escape. He could have imagined life without limbs,
without sight, a victim of shell shock tied into a chair for the
rest of his life, but he could never imagine taking his own
life.

Kathryn needed him. He remembered the pain in her eyes
before it was replaced by anger. Even if he wanted to die, he
couldn't do that to Kathryn. She wasn't strong enough to lose
both of them. When the shock and horror faded, she would
forgive him. Then, together, they would grieve for their son.

For the first time he looked around. In the twilight all he
could see were fields. Flat, empty and stretching on forever.
He looked at the car. Its front wheels were firmly wedged
into the ditch. Nothing but a team of horses could get it back
on the road. He locked the doors and started walking. Half
a mile down the road he saw a small shack clumsily con-

structed of lumber scraps, but no light showed through the one tiny window, not one chicken scratched in the dirt outside and he didn't bother going to the door.

Kathryn had been alone for hours. He glanced at his watch. Why had he ever allowed his anger to drive him away when Kathryn needed him? He pushed on. It was getting darker. The only sign of life was a lone bat gliding across the sky, leaving a trail of high-pitched cries. He passed a grove of trees hung with Spanish moss and could hear Adam's voice squealing in delight, "Look, the trees have beards!" He wondered what Adam would think of the beards gleaming like silver ghosts in the moonlight. He stopped in his tracks. Why did his heart refuse to accept what his mind knew so well, that Adam was dead? His son would never talk, or laugh, or cry again.

Where was he? With each step Owen could be moving farther away from her. His heart cried out to be with Kathryn. To hold her. To comfort her. At last he saw light—two yellow pinpricks in the distance. They came closer. He stepped into the road and raised his hands. The car skidded to a halt at his feet. The driver stuck his head out of the window and asked, "Got yourself a problem, or you askin' to be run over?"

"Do you know Bienvenue Plantation? Please, I've got to get back there right away."

The driver, an old white-haired man, scratched his head. "Can't figure out what you're doin' out on this ole road. Nobody uses it no more. Not since the new highway gone in." He paused for Owen to explain, then went on. "Goin' into the city myself. Better come 'long. Never gonna find yourself 'nother ride here. Not this time a night."

Undeterred by his passenger's silence, the man chattered on until Owen thought his head would burst wide open. The trip was endless, bouncing through the darkness on worn springs with the slow, syrupy voice droning away at his side. When at last they reached the outskirts of the city, Owen asked to be let out at the hotel where Allan and Maureen were staying.

Maureen opened the door wearing a green silk dressing gown; the red hair she refused to bob hung loose around her shoulders. A small lamp burned in the distance, leaving her

face in shadow. In an instant her surprise gave way to a smile.
"Why, Owen, this is a pleasure. What are you . . . ?" Seeing his ravaged face, she asked, "What's wrong?"

He put his hand out and clasped hers. "I'm afraid . . ."
He cleared his throat nervously and then tried again. "I have
bad news." Her smile faded, leaving her pale and anxious.
"It's Adam, he's . . ."

"Is he sick? Is my baby sick?" Her voice rose hysterically.
He said nothing, but from the way he shook his head like a
broken man, she knew. "Oh, my God, he's dead, isn't he?"
she whispered. He nodded. She could feel her own heart
shattering, a sharp hollow pain piercing her breast, but her
aching heart went out to Owen and her arms went around
him and she pulled him to her. How could he stand it? His
son, the child he adored, was dead. She pulled him tighter,
as if the strength of her arms could hold him together, keep
him from breaking down completely.

For a long while they stood clinging to each other like
drowning swimmers. Gradually the tension left Owen's body
and he found his mind letting go, fading in and out of reality.
His arms reached for Maureen's waist, and in his confused
mind she became Kathryn. Like husband and wife, they stood
consoling each other wordlessly in the only way they knew
how. If they held each other long enough, squeezed each
other tightly enough, then perhaps they could survive the pain.

Adam is dead—the truth kept hammering away at Maureen's brain. How had it happened? She remembered the last
time she'd seen him, jumping up and down with excitement,
talking a mile a minute. The picture in her head was so vivid
she refused to believe it was only a memory.

Owen's head dropped to her shoulder and she felt his cheek
against her hair, his breath warm on her neck. Kathryn, she
almost said, why aren't you with Kathryn? She lost her child,
she needs you. Then the bitterness that floated just below the
surface of her mind rose. Kathryn had everything. What did
a child mean to her? She had her hotels; she was famous and
successful. A child was just the icing on the great big cake
that was Kathryn's life.

Maureen loved Adam more than his busy mother ever
could. She baked him cookies, played pony with him for
hours on end, bandaged his real and imaginary hurts and

never tired of reading his favorite bedtime stories to him. It was right that she and Owen mourn together. If Kathryn were a true wife, she'd never let Owen out of her arms. But here he was, in *her* hotel room, his body pressed against hers, his hands circling her waist.

Before he knew what was happening, Owen found his body responding. He wanted Kathryn more than he'd ever wanted her before. He felt her unconfined body moving under her thin dressing gown and longed to cup her round white breasts in the roundness of his hands. His fingertips touched the cool softness of silk and the warm softness of flesh. She cried out, a moan of surprise and pleasure that made him realize that her desires matched his own. They would blot out death by affirming life.

Maureen felt Owen's fingers untying the sash of her gown. With a soft rustle it fell open, and her nipples were suddenly thrust against the roughness of his shirt. It had been so long since lovemaking with Allan had been about love. Now they made love to make babies. Maureen could never abandon herself to pure physical pleasure, to satisfy her needs and Allan's, for always at the back of her mind was one thought: maybe this is the time. Maybe this time we are conceiving our child.

Now her body responded automatically, free from the longings of her mind. She wanted only to feel his flesh against hers. To feel his fingers, his lips, his tongue searching out her most secret, sensitive places. To feel his maleness thrusting hard inside her until she screamed out with pleasure.

Her eager fingers unbuttoned his shirt, fumbling slightly in their haste, and spread it wide to expose his chest. Then her hands dropped to his waist.

His body was inflamed. He couldn't shed his clothes fast enough. When at last he was naked she led him into the dimly lit bedroom. They were too anxious even to pull down the bedspread, and like two young animals, they fell onto the wide four-poster bed, their bodies entwined.

She wants me as much as I want her, Owen thought, feeling her wetness. There was no reason to wait. His body was ready to burst with desire. Her body opened to meet him and then closed around him like a soft, warm cave.

Maureen couldn't help crying out when he entered her; he

filled every inch of her empty, barren body. It was impossible
to control herself. She plunged and rocked with him, pushing
herself closer to him, forcing him into her, screaming out
with pleasure. The harder he stabbed into her the more she
believed her fantasy: I am Adam's mother. I am truly Adam's
mother. We are together, his father and I.

A pure animal instinct drove Owen, telling him, Harder,
faster, further. Faster and faster. Aching for release. At last
it came and he cried out like a wounded animal: "Kathryn!"

The cry came to Maureen as if from the distant end of a
tunnel. Kathryn. Kathryn. Echoing over and over again. It
was Kathryn who was Adam's mother. She, Maureen, was
barren. She would always be barren. Allan wanted a child,
but she couldn't give him one. She was a miserable failure.
Kathryn Towsend Morgan had everything, while she had
nothing, absolutely nothing, not even the right to grieve.

For a long minute Owen was quiet, lying heavily on her
body, breathing deeply. Finally his eyes opened and focused
on her. They seemed to leap out of their sockets. "My God,
Maureen, how could I ever . . ." He closed his eyes tightly,
as if he couldn't bear to see her face.

When he tried to break away, she held him. "Don't go.
Please don't go."

He looked down at her naked body. "But we can't . . .
What we did, it was wrong."

"It was natural," she said, her voice strong.

"For animals maybe. But we are civilized people. With
marriage vows to believe in and obey." He rolled off her
body and perched on the edge of the bed, his back toward
her.

When she put her hand on his shoulder, he shook it off.
"We were both in pain," she said. "Incredible pain. Wasn't
our only sin comforting each other?" What she couldn't tell
him was that she had been caught up in a miraculous fantasy.
"It's all right."

"How can you dare say it's all right? What we did was
against everything we believe in." His voice carried an angry
edge.

"But maybe not under the circumstances."

"It was wrong under any circumstances. My God, what if
Allan . . . ? Where is he?" he asked hurriedly as he rose

and began collecting the clothing strewn around the living room floor.

"At some bankers' meeting. He rushed out of here as if the hotel were on fire. Something about a crisis on the stock exchange."

Suddenly Maureen felt very lonely. "Please stay. I need you."

Owen pulled on his riding boots. "I can't," he said, his voice tense. "Kathryn needs me. She just lost her child."

His words were a slap in the face. Maureen's fantasy burst like a pricked balloon.

"She needs me, and what am I doing?" Self-disgust filled his voice. "I'm in bed with another woman. Her best friend. God, how could I be so bloody stupid?"

"Owen . . ."

"Maureen, I don't know what to say. I'm sorry. I would give anything in the world for this not to have happened. Anything. I must have been . . ." His voice fell. "Crazy."

He buttoned his shirt and stood before her fully dressed, stiffly, like someone she barely knew. "Please accept my deepest apologies. You have my word of honor that I will never refer to this unfortunate incident again. Either to you or anyone else." He nodded curtly and backed out of the room.

When Maureen heard the door to the suite click closed, she fell back on the bed laughing. She shrieked with laughter until the tears flowed from her eyes. "Don't be such a bloody gentleman, Owen. I enjoyed it. I enjoyed it! What does that make me? Do you hear me? What does that make me?" But he was long gone.

She buried her face in the pillow. It smelled poignantly of warm bodies, hot, wet sex and the musky odor of Owen's hair. "He walked out on me," she sobbed. "Just like I was nothing. To go back to her. Bloody Kathryn Morgan, why do you have to get everything?"

When she'd run out of tears, she reached down and patted her stomach. Wouldn't it be ironic if this were the night she finally conceived a healthy child? With an effort she pulled herself off the bed and stumbled into the living room. There was a bottle of brandy somewhere. Where had Allan put it? She needed something to numb the pain.

Gradually the bitterness of the drink eroded the bitterness

of the memories. She knew that something had happened, something awful, and that she should be sad, but she couldn't remember what, or why.

As morning light crept into the room, she awoke cramped and fuzzy-headed. Gradually the memory returned. Sharp. Painful. Insistent.

The telephone suddenly shrilling through the stillness set off an explosion in her head, and she felt her stomach lurch as she heaved her body out of the chair.

"It's Owen calling to apologize," she told herself. But the voice on the other end was not Owen's soft, lilting one. It was gruff, almost a growl. "It's Mack. Mr. Morgan's trainer. Have you seen him?"

Maureen's heart stopped. What should she do? If she told him that Owen had been here, then there would be questions, and she wasn't a good liar. She stopped. Why wasn't Owen home with Kathryn right now? Had something happened to him? She forced her voice to sound calm. "Owen, no, I'm afraid I haven't seen him."

Chapter Six

Balancing the breakfast tray with one hand, Rachel opened the bedroom door with the other. In her mind was the same prayer she repeated every morning: Please let this be the day Kathryn comes back to us.

"Kathryn's retreated into her own private world," she complained to Jacob. The day Kathryn returned she'd collapsed into Rachel's arms and sobbed out her story. Since then she'd barely spoken. "And she doesn't eat enough to keep a bird alive." Rachel seldom needed to talk to Jacob nowadays. After Kathryn had swept her up into the world of hotel management, the emptiness in her life was filled and she was able to release Jacob. "Kathryn Townsend gave me a new life," she explained to him. "That's why I have to bring her back to live hers."

Taking a deep breath, she pushed open the door. Kathryn was sitting up in the vast bed, propped up against a pile of pillows. Her bedclothes were undisturbed, as if she lacked the strength even to toss and turn. Great bluish circles hung under her eyes.

"Here's your breakfast," Rachel announced cheerfully. Slowly Kathryn turned to look at her, but her eyes were somewhere else. "You'd better be hungry this morning," Rachel chirped, settling the tray onto Kathryn's lap.

Inside Kathryn's head a voice was raging: "My God, how can you ask me to eat as if nothing had happened? As if my son were still safe and alive. As if my husband hadn't disappeared. My world has fallen apart, and you're trying to force toast and strawberry jam down my throat as if that's all that mattered."

387

Kathryn stared down at the plate and shook her head.

"Kathryn, dear, I know it's difficult, but you must pull yourself together. You've been like this for days, and there are things that must be done at times like these." Rachel paused. She hadn't dared to mention it to Kathryn before, afraid that it might drive her over the edge, but it could wait no longer. "Have you thought about what kind of funeral you'd like for Adam?"

"Funeral?" Kathryn repeated. Her voice came from a great, echoing distance. But she felt as if the dense fog surrounding her, muffling the world, were parting. Slightly.

"Yes, that Mr. Corter has called every day to discuss the details with you. I've told him you're too ill, but you must deal with it sometime. Why not today?"

Kathryn stared at Rachel, watching her lips move for a moment before she understood. "I will not have a funeral." She enunciated each word clearly, as if she were explaining something simple to a child.

"But, Kathryn, it's the expected thing."

"I don't care what people expect." What did it matter what other people thought? What did anything matter? Adam was dead.

Rachel reached down and patted Kathryn's hand. There was no use arguing with her. At least she was showing some emotion. "Whatever you want. But perhaps a memorial service in church?"

Her cheeks flushed, her eyes dark, Kathryn turned on Rachel. How could she expect her to . . . ? "You don't understand, do you? How can I believe in God after this? A cruel monster, that's what He is. Murdering a little boy. An innocent child."

She pushed away her tray. The milk spilled and ran in a rivulet down into the bedclothes, but she didn't notice. She felt a wild anger replacing the sorrow that weighed down her heart. "And don't preach to me about God's plan. I've already had that speech from Miss Gobel. Fine for her to say. Adam wasn't her child. She was being paid to take care of him."

Rachel bit her lip. Couldn't Kathryn see how much Miss Gobel loved Adam? If only she could see the poor woman moping around with red, watery eyes that threatened tears at any moment. Kathryn was too caught up in her grief to realize that everyone else who loved Adam was suffering. Poor Maureen Jones—according to Allan, she was too upset even to phone—Rachel could only imagine how she felt. Adam was the child she couldn't have, and she'd lost him just as surely as Kathryn had.

"He could have been anything he wanted," Kathryn said. "But he had only three years. Three lousy years. And now he's gone." She stared defiantly at Rachel. "And don't try to tell me he's up there sitting with God. I know where my son is. He's rotting away in a small wooden box."

The truth stunned them into silence. For a long while they sat there, Rachel clasping Kathryn's hand tightly in hers, forcing herself not to cry while she watched the silent tears streaming down Kathryn's pale cheeks. At last, when she was able to speak, Rachel said, "I'll tell Mr. Corter that there won't be a funeral or a memorial service, but I think we should send a notice to the newspapers, don't you? People must be told."

"Fine," Kathryn said briskly. "Go ahead and do it. Get this all over so we can get back to normal."

Rachel shook her head sadly. "Kathryn, dear, nothing can get back to normal. Not yet."

"Why not?" she demanded, showing a flash of her old spirit. What does Rachel want? she wondered angrily. She's the one who keeps telling me to pull myself together.

Rachel swallowed hard. She'd broached the difficult subject of the funeral, so she might as well tackle the next one. "Nothing will be normal until Owen comes home."

"I don't want him here. He killed my son." Kathryn's body slumped against the pillows, her eyes took on their glazed look and Rachel cursed herself for sending Kathryn back into hiding, back to her own private, pain-filled world.

"Come back, Kathryn, and face the problem. You owe it to your husband to see him again, to talk about what happened. You two have problems to resolve. I've never known you to be a coward; don't start now."

Kathryn's face was as immobile as a marble statue's, but Rachel went on. "Can't you see his side? He lost his son. He loved little Adam every bit as much as you did. Don't you think he's in pain, too? Suffering just the way you are?"

"I don't give a damn how he feels. The accident was his fault. If it weren't for him, I'd have my son." Why can't you understand? she wanted to cry out. But inside, a little voice was pecking away. What if Mammy was right? it asked. What if Adam is dead because you were greedy and wanted too much from life?

"Owen's been missing for four days. Aren't you worried?" Rachel was. She'd called his office; they were baffled; they hadn't heard a word from him. She spoke to Mack on the telephone several times a day. He'd stayed on in New Orleans to work with the police. He'd even hired a private detective. But no one had seen Owen since he sped away from Bienvenue. It was as if he'd vanished from the face of the earth.

"Why should I care?" Kathryn asked. "He left me." That would silence the little voice.

Rachel's bosom heaved in anger. "Left you? Face the truth—you drove him off. Blaming the poor man for killing the son he would have given his life for. It was an accident. A horrible accident. Blame God or Fate, or childish curiosity, but don't blame Owen. You need each other at a time like this. To love and comfort each other. And in time—though it won't bring Adam back—to make another baby."

Kathryn couldn't believe her ears. What was Rachel suggesting? There would never be another child. She would never betray Adam. He was her son, her only child, and she would love him till the day she died. How could Rachel dare . . . ? It wasn't as if Adam were a dog that died, a mongrel that could easily be replaced by another one from the pound. "I shall never have another child," she said with steely determination.

Once upon a time she had vowed never to love again. Why had she allowed herself to be so easily seduced by pair of dark eyes and an easy smile? When would she learn her lesson? Love hurt.

She paused and took a deep breath. "I'll never see Owen Morgan again. I hate him."

Something inside Rachel snapped, making her crepelike neck pulsate with anger. Her hand rose—Kathryn couldn't believe her eyes—and landed hard across Kathryn's cheek.

Kathryn recoiled in surprise and horror. Her eyes locked into Rachel's as she drew her hand up to her stinging face.

Like a bull too long tormented by the matador's jabs, Rachel attacked. "Maybe Owen never wants to see you again either. Have you considered that? When the man came to you in pain and sorrow seeking comfort, what did you do? You could only think of yourself. Remember I once warned you that you could push Owen only so far? That although he adored you and had the patience of a saint with you, he also had a breaking point?" She paused, her angry charge almost, but not quite, exhausted. "With a wife as self-centered as you, frankly I wouldn't blame him if he never came home."

Without waiting for Kathryn's rebuttal, Rachel stormed out of the room in a cloud of anger. Halfway down the hall she heard Kathryn's voice. It quavered slightly. "Wait, please wait." Ignore it, common sense told her. Then she turned around slowly.

The anger and hostility that contorted Kathryn's face was gone. Her features were relaxed, but her expression was one of unspeakably poignant, heartbreaking sadness.

"Rachel, I'm sorry. I've been a . . . a beast. Mean. Selfish. To you. To everyone. And especially to Owen. I was wrong." Tears streaked her cheeks. Her voice was as thin and reedy as a child's when she said, "I want my husband back. I need him and I love him more than anything in the world."

Chapter Seven

It was the boredom that was the worst. The same routine day after day. The day, the month, the seasons. It no longer mattered. It was always the same gray faces, the same dirty green walls, the same impenetrable bars.

Edward knew he was lucky to be assigned to the prison laundry. Despite the blasting heat, the constant stench of chemicals, it was, at least, clean.

By choice he was a loner. Fellow inmates—did they recognize the evil that burned in his eyes?—left him alone. He fought against sinking to their unthinking, animal level and spent all his free time at the scarred table in the prison library, reading everything he could get his hands on. In less than three years he'd read his way through the meager library.

He absorbed every single word—even the advertisements—in the daily papers. The last few days he'd fallen upon the papers like a ravenous animal. The stock market had crashed. Millions of people were ruined. All over the country banks were failing. Men were jumping out of windows. Widows and orphans were destitute. A smile spread across his thin lips. Had his sister been wiped out, too? His money, he knew, was safe. Cash. Hidden away in a vault, waiting for him to get out.

Getting out—it wouldn't be long. The red-faced judge in his abominable lower-class accent had sentenced him to six years, but from the day Edward had disappeared behind these ten-foot-high concrete walls, he'd devoted himself to becoming a model prisoner, going out of his way to cause no trouble and occasionally, when it could be done safely, providing tidbits of information to the authorities about other prisoners.

In six months he was eligible for parole, and he was determined to get out. He had plans.

At first he felt no remorse. It was Kathryn, he told himself through clenched teeth as he lay awake at night in his hard bunk that smelled of other men's sweat, who put me in here. But gradually be began to realize the fault was his own. A childish desire for revenge had driven him to the convoluted schemes for ruining his sister. Schemes that had sapped his energy and drained his emotion. And ultimately failed.

He'd even refused to allow Kathryn to testify at his trial, despite his lawyer's insistence. But the thought of Kathryn—elegant, poised and rich—smugly staring down at him from the witness box, as if he were some wild animal finally trapped, made the bile rise in his throat. She'd vowed to see him in prison. How could he bear the look of triumph on her face when he was convicted? So he refused her the satisfaction, accepting the judge's sentence without a murmur.

"When I was sick" was how he referred to that period when he occasionally delved back into the painful memories of his past. He would, he resolved, never be sick again. The future—he would concentrate on the future. He would strike out on his own, win his own fame and fortune. The festering hatred had been driven out of his body; he was healed and ready to go on with his new life.

Ironically, it was in prison that he'd found the means to reach his goal. He'd met some people he'd never have come in contact with in the outside world. They weren't, of course, his type, but they had power and money. Too much money, money from illegal bootlegging activities, money they were anxious to invest in legitimate businesses.

They'd expressed cautious interest in his idea for a chain of hotels to run from coast to coast. But their eyes lit up with greed when he mentioned how the two operations could go hand in hand: his hotels as outlets for their liquor. Not that Edward wanted to serve their watered-down Scotch in his hotels, but if that was what it took to get the money to compete . . .

And compete with Kathryn he would. In every city she built a hotel, he would give her a run for her money. They'd soon see who was the clever businessman in the family. No more ridiculous idea of ruining her for the sheer pleasure of the act. Now they would compete as equals, each striving to be the finest and most successful hotelier in the world. And once his new "business associates" had served their purpose, they would be dispensed with. Gravel-voiced men like Carmine Patrizzo would be terribly out of place in his elegant hotels.

His head spun with the visions—golden ballrooms, marble lobbies, palm courts, fountains of champagne—the visions that had kept him alive for the past three years. Reluctantly he shut them off and returned to his newspaper. In precisely ten minutes he would be sent back to the cell he shared with a hulking safecracker who could barely speak English and never washed. The lights would be turned off and then he could dream.

He was turning the page when a familiar name caught his trained eye. Townsend. He thought of his album of clippings. He scanned the article. Adam Townsend had been killed in an accident. He remembered him as a baby. A beautiful child. Now he was dead. Once upon a time, knowing that Kathryn was suffering would have made his body throb with excitement. Now he felt nothing. Except perhaps for the little boy. Another of Kathryn's innocent victims.

Chapter Eight

The telephone shrilling through the dark house awakened Maureen. It took her a few seconds to shake herself awake. Telephone calls in the middle of the night could only bring bad news. "Holy Mother, what could have happened now?" she whispered, feeling a lump in her throat and a fluttering in her stomach.

There was no sound from the next room, but hadn't she always told Allan that it would take a banshee wailing in his ear to wake him? Reluctantly she slipped on a robe and, without turning on the lights, made her way down to the parlor. If she walked slowly enough, perhaps the caller would give up.

But the phone kept ringing. Taking a deep breath, she picked up the receiver and said a nervous hello. Nothing. If it was someone playing a prank and scaring her out of her wits, she would . . . Finally she heard a weak voice, so low she barely recognized it. "Maureen? It's Owen." For a second silence hung between them as memories she'd tried so hard to forget filled Maureen's mind.

"I . . . I know I don't have any right to call, but there was no one else and . . ."

Maureen took a firm grasp on her runaway emotions. "Where are you? It's been four days. Everyone is frantic. They're afraid you're—" She stopped suddenly, unable to say the word.

"Dead?" Owen asked. "Believe me, sometimes I wish I were. But I've had time to think. And, Maureen, I need your help. I know that after what happened"— he paused awkwardly—"that's a lot to ask."

Maureen swallowed hard and then said, "What about Kathryn? Shouldn't you call her and let her know you're safe?"

"No." His voice was strong and sure. "And please don't tell her you've heard from me until we have a chance to talk. Will you meet me tomorrow? I'm staying at the . . ." It was a hotel she'd never heard of.

The next morning Maureen found herself staring at the slip of paper with the address she'd scribbled down. Surely this couldn't be the place. The hotel name painted on the glass door was peeling off. And the glass was opaque with dirt. As she stood there in confusion an old man with boozy breath staggered out and asked if he could help her. That made up her mind. She opened the door and disappeared inside, hoping he wouldn't follow her. The lobby was dark, dingy and barely bigger than a cloakroom. She approached the swarthy desk clerk hesitantly. "Do you have a Mr. Morgan staying here?" she asked, praying he'd say no.

"Room two-oh-one. And he's in. Don't go out. Say, you a friend of his? Is he sick or something?"

Maureen shook her head and hurried toward the dark, narrow staircase, ignoring the clerk's "First door on your right. And watch out for the holes in the carpet."

The nail on the top of the number two on the door was missing, and it dangled upside down. She knocked softly, and a strange voice told her to come in. Forcing aside all the horror stories she'd ever heard about young women being lured into white slavery, she opened the door.

She barely recognized him. He sat propped up on the sagging bed which filled the tiny gray room. His face was gaunt and gray, his cheeks stubbly with a half-grown beard. But she recognized his clothes. They were the ones he'd been wearing that night, the ones she'd helped him strip off. But now they were wrinkled and covered with stains.

"Hello, Maureen. Thank you for coming. I have no right to ask you for any favors, I know that, but I believe I can trust you. We're a lot alike."

Maureen's aching heart seemed to cross the room to him. She wanted to hold him in her arms and comfort him like a small child. To bathe him, shave him, dress him in fine clean

clothes and make him the strong, handsome man he had been.
"Owen, I . . ."

"I've been driving around. At first it didn't seem to matter
where I went. But somehow I gravitated north. Around
Washington I made up my mind. It was late at night, no one
else was on the road and all of a sudden my future seemed
so clear." For the first time he managed a weak smile. "I'm
leaving."

Knowing what she was going to say, he held up his hand.
"There's no sense in trying to see Kathryn again. She'll never
forget that I killed Adam and never forgive. She warned me
time and time again. But I so wanted my son to love what I
love that I refused to consider the danger."

"That's a load of bloody rubbish. Of course you didn't kill
Adam. Rachel told Allan how it happened. If anyone should
be blamed, it's that lazy mammy. Any person with an ounce
of brains could see it wasn't your fault. And so will Kathryn,
once she calms down." She paused. "Owen, I think you
should go see her. Allan says she's in a dreadful state. Refuses to talk to anyone, barely eats, never sleeps. You're the
only one who can help. Rachel is at her wit's end. Please
try."

His dark eyes were soft as he said, "Maureen, thank you
for caring, but I've had to face a great many unpleasant facts
over the past few days. The first is that I'll never see my son
again. The second is that my marriage is over and that . . ."
He paused for a moment, unable to say the words. "That my
wife hates me."

Maureen looked at Owen. Under the grimy beard he still
looked handsome. Memories of their lovemaking set her heart
pounding. But she knew what she had to say. "You still love
Kathryn. Love doesn't die that easily. Not the sort of love
you two share. I refuse to believe that Kathryn hates you.
You must believe, too."

"Even if she doesn't hate me, every time she looks at me
she'll remember the accident, and she'll grow to hate me. It
will be best for everyone if I disappear now."

Maureen smiled in spite of herself. "A bit melodramatic,
isn't it?"

Owen managed a weak answering smile. "I suppose it is,
but I don't know what else to do. My pain. Her anger. I can't

handle them both at the same time. And without me there to remind her, she'll forget in time."

"And what about you?" Maureen demanded. It took all her willpower to remain with her feet planted firmly in the doorway and not rush over to him.

"I'll be fine," he said. "I have a plan—that's why I called you. I need your help." He paused and she held her breath. "You see, I've decided to go home—to Wales. Pick up the pieces of my old life."

"And what would the grand Mr. Owen Morgan do back in Wales?"

His brow hunched down over his dark eyes and he gave a bitter chuckle. "Life is ironic, isn't it? I thought fate had stepped in to keep me out of the mines because she had something better planned for me. But maybe they're inescapable. My father was a miner. My grandfather was a miner. And I'll end my days a miner, too. It all comes full circle, doesn't it?"

"Mary Mother of God, you are talking tommyrot, Owen Morgan. You could no more be a miner than you could be a—an Indian chief, hunt buffalo and live in a tepee. I know how those people live. Neither of us could go back now, not after the life we've grown accustomed to. Do you really believe you could spend ten hours a day underground, fighting with a wall of rock? Then come home and collapse in some dark, damp, two-up/two-down cottage with outdoor plumbing and no running water? You have plenty of money. Take it and go off to some tropical island if you must, but this . . . this is crazy!"

His eyes were black as coal, his voice hard as steel. "It's what I must do." Why couldn't Maureen understand? Of all people, she knew how important children were.

"You're punishing yourself, that's all you're doing. Playing the martyr. Tell me, does it give you any satisfaction staying here in this filthy hotel, looking like something the cat would refuse to drag in?" A sudden feeling of hatred rose in Maureen's breast. "Let me tell you, Kathryn's not worth it. If she was stupid enough to lash out at you and blame you for Adam's death, she got what she deserves."

Owen's voice was calm. "It was a natural reaction. She was in pain."

Maureen was so angry she thought she'd explode. "What about *your* pain? The high-and-mighty Miss Townsend of the Townsend Corporation doesn't think of anyone else, does she? She's too wrapped up in her own success story to care about her own husband and child."

Seeing the hurt in his eyes, she realized she'd gone too far. "I'm sorry. I shouldn't have . . . It's just that I can't bear to watch you throw your life away." With all her heart she wanted to hold him, kiss away his pain, make him a whole, strong man again. Instead she said, "There was something you wanted me to do?"

He nodded. "I'll need money. Not a lot. Just something to get me started."

"That's no problem. I have some of my own I've saved."

"No, not yours. I couldn't do that." He pulled a key ring from his pocket and took off a small brass key. "This opens the top drawer of my desk at home. In an envelope in the back you'll find four or five hundred dollars. Call on Kathryn, then find some excuse to go into my study."

"But what about your bank accounts?"

"I want all my money to go to Kathryn. They'll assume I'm dead, and it will all be hers eventually. It's the least I can do. Besides, I don't want to leave any traces."

He looked up at her, his eyes pleading. "Will you do it?" he asked. She nodded and he stretched out his hand. She reached toward him and carefully took the key without touching him.

Owen felt like a criminal with his cloth cap pulled low over his face. Not that he was likely to be recognized. In a city of millions the odds were stacked in his favor—at least that was what he told himself. But he deliberately chose uncrowded streets and crossed to the other side if he saw anyone approaching him.

Who would recognize me? he wondered. The Owen Morgan the world knows does not skulk about sporting a scruffy beard and a cheap, ill-fitting tweed suit. Still, he carefully skirted the block where a brick-faced building bore the discreet sign: Morgan Enterprises.

Deep in his heart there burned a fear and a hope: What if Kathryn has hired someone to find me? What if she still cares? His heart seesawed between two emotions. At one moment he dreaded discovery on the eve of his escape. The next moment his heart pounded with joy at the possibility of seeing her again.

In a perverse way he relished his new, rootless freedom. He hadn't walked the city streets for years; time was too valuable, taxis and limousines too convenient. Back then he'd had no choice. A newcomer, young and penniless, he'd walked the leather off his shoes looking for a job. He'd been escaping then, too. From the poverty. The hopelessness. But then he'd had to escape—to survive. Now he had to escape so Kathryn could survive.

Ironic, wasn't it? All over town desperate men ruined by the stock market crash were flinging themselves out of windows. Yet he'd had the foresight to pull out in time. His money was safe for the moment, though he was as impoverished as any of those fools on their wild, speculative sprees. What did it matter if his son had died a very rich little boy? What mattered was that he had died. But at least Kathryn would be well provided for. Even without her hotels she'd be a wealthy lady. Not that he could imagine her without her hotels. They would, he realized sadly, soon become her sole reason for living.

He tried to imagine her new life, but he couldn't, and his feet plodded resolutely forward. Downtown. To the shipping offices. With a little luck he'd find a ship leaving tomorrow for Britain and a new life on the opposite side of the world from Kathryn.

Chapter Nine

How can I face Kathryn after . . . ? Maureen wondered as she forced her rubbery legs up the front steps. Don't worry, she told herself, there's no way Kathryn could know. Besides, you have something important to do for Owen.

Theirs was a formal condolence call, but she and Allan both found themselves stumbling over the inadequate words of sympathy. Then Allan asked softly, "Is there anything we can do . . . to help you find Owen?"

Like the face of a china doll, the calm Kathryn had been maintaining with an enormous force of willpower shattered. She squeezed her eyes tightly shut, but not quickly enough to catch the tears that seeped out from under her dark lashes and ran down her pale, powdered cheeks. In her lap her hands clenched into tight balls. She swallowed several times before she was able to speak, and then her voice was a small, scared whisper.

"He's just . . . just disappeared." The words seemed to clog her throat for a second. "We've hired private detectives, but they haven't found a trace. Not in New Orleans. Not in New York. I just don't know what to do. It's been five days now, and I'm afraid something awful has happened."

Kathryn looked so fragile, as if she might break at any second. Maureen could bear it no longer. "Kathryn, there's something you should know . . ."

Her words went unheeded as Allan leapt up and went over to the love seat where Kathryn sat, her head bowed. He sank down next to her and drew her to him with a fierce intensity. Kathryn seemed to melt into his arms; her tense body relaxed, and her head came to rest gratefully on his shoulder.

His arm tightened around her as if he were willing his strength into her body. His voice was soft and warm as he said, "Kathryn, don't worry. We'll find Owen, I promise you. He loves you; he won't stay away much longer." His strong, broad hands made soothing circles against the smooth fabric of her back.

Maureen sat transfixed, feeling like an intruder, as if she were spying on an intimate scene. Suddenly a wave of emotion swept over her, washing away her guilt and pity, leaving only an all-consuming jealousy that made her face flush hot and chilled her body. Memories flooded back. The pain of losing her own children when they'd barely been conceived. The emptiness when she'd discovered each month that once again she had failed. Where had Allan been then? Had he held her the way he now held Kathryn? Had he comforted her with strong arms and soft words? The flame of anger grew. No, he'd been so damned sensible. Telling her that there would be other times, and finally, impatiently, that it didn't matter. But he had refused to share her tears and pain the way he was doing with Kathryn.

"Excuse me," she said, getting up. "I'm going to powder my nose."

Neither of them looked up, and she made her way unseen out to the hallway and Owen's study. The envelope was stuffed in the back of the drawer, just as he'd said.

Quietly she closed the drawer and allowed her eyes to drift over the room. Her eyes fell to the desk in front of her. Two familiar faces stared up from a sepia photograph. Kathryn and Owen on their honeymoon, nestled together in a gondola, the towers of Venice rising behind them. They were smiling as if their joy was too great to be contained.

After Maureen and Allan left, Kathryn sat in the darkening room, silent and still, not bothering to turn on the lights. Time, she thought. Too much time has gone by. It's been almost a week. If . . . if Owen is alive, why doesn't he come home? Doesn't he know how much I love him? How much I want him? That I can't live without him? Sadly she shook her head. How could he, when the last words she'd said to him were "I hate you"?

The next day when Maureen called and asked to see her,

Kathryn sensed a desperate need in her voice. It was a plea, not an invitation.

In panic Kathryn's mind fought against the idea of leaving the house, but she knew she couldn't allow herself to drown in her own sorrow forever. Maureen was grieving, too; she was a friend and she needed her.

Kathryn closed her eyes. Her body felt bruised and beaten. She'd never in her life been so tired. Except after Adam was born. Adam. For a moment her mind wandered, and then she firmly clicked the box of memories shut. For Maureen's sake, she had to hold herself together.

Amidst great fluttering and nervous stammering, a young, rosy-cheeked maid answered the door. The sight brought a smile to Kathryn's lips. Kindhearted Maureen was forever bringing over Irish farm girls and training them for a better life. The new girl showed her into the drawing room, as if Kathryn didn't know the way. The room was comfortingly familiar. Kathryn knew the cozy, chintz-filled room almost as well as her own.

For a moment she didn't see the man standing at the far end of the room, his back toward her, studying the books that covered one wall. His figure was slumped and he wore a cheap tweed suit: not the sort of person Kathryn would expect to find in Maureen's drawing room. Perhaps an Irish relation down on his luck.

Since she could hardly sit down without saying anything, Kathryn coughed quietly to attract the man's attention. It took several seconds before he turned around, and then she refused to believe her eyes. Why hadn't she recognized him? But his shoulders sagged and his face was gray and gaunt.

"Owen?" she said, her voice barely a whisper. Relief washed over her. He was safe. Emotion told her to rush to him and throw her arms around him, but her feet remained rooted to the floor. Everything she longed to tell him flooded her mind. How sorry she was. How much she missed him. How worried she'd been. But her mouth was dry and her lips refused to move.

Owen felt his face flush with embarrassment and then anger. Damn Maureen. What sort of perverse game was the woman playing?

Time after time he'd planned out in his head the words he'd

say to Kathryn if he ever saw her again. But what was the use of apology and explanation now? Why had he sought out Maureen? He could have gotten the money some other way and quietly disappeared. In panic his eyes darted around the room. He had the absurd sensation that the lace curtains and flowered chairs were closing in on him. "I'm trapped," his mind shouted. But what choice had he? Maureen's drama would be played out on her stage.

He had to say something, stop staring. "Kathryn," he acknowledged with a curt nod.

"I . . . I was worried about you." But her tone was cool. "I'm sorry."

He seemed as cold and hard as a bronze statue. His voice was like ice. Like Edward's. Kathryn fought down a flicker of anger. Why couldn't he show some emotion? Even if he yelled and screamed at her. Told her she'd been hysterical and unfair. What was he thinking? His impassive face gave no clue. Did he hate her? Was that how he'd spent the past week, learning to hate her? She shuddered. His coldness was seeping into her own body. More than anything in the world, she wanted to escape this room. Seeing him here like this, consumed with hatred, was killing her.

But running away would be cowardly. You have to face him sooner or later, she told herself. There are decisions about the future to be made. You can't live in this limbo any longer. You must know if he ever intends to come home.

"Were you thinking about what I said to you?" she asked, trying to make her voice sound calm.

He nodded. "Among other things."

She forced the lump out of her throat. What did she have to gain by postponing the inevitable? The question had to be asked. "Did you make any decisions?"

"Yes," he said, but for an instant his hard, angry mask slipped, and Kathryn glimpsed the hurt and pain in his eyes. And she knew she couldn't bear to lose him without a fight. If she could fight to save her Florida land and fight Edward to save her hotels, then she must fight to save her marriage.

"Owen, you always said I was pigheaded and stubborn and you were right. I am. I know what I want, and when I make up my mind . . ."

He patted the pocket of his coat. The ticket was still there.

One way, second class, to Liverpool. Sailing at six tomorrow morning. "I can understand why you never want to see me again." The words were forced out between clenched teeth. "And I will respect your wishes." Why was this happening to them? A moment's inattention on the part of one old woman and a child was dead, a marriage ended. A marriage that he'd believed would last forever.

Her words surprised him.

"Owen, do you love me?"

What should he say? Did it matter? Did anything matter? Next week he'd be home in Wales, all the memories behind him. His tongue was thick as he said, "I do love you, and that is why I am respecting your wishes."

Was this man speaking with such exaggerated politeness her husband? "How do you know what my wishes are?"

Why is she taunting me? he wondered. "Surely you made your feelings perfectly clear."

He looks, Kathryn thought, as if he were ready to turn on his heel and walk out at any moment. He can't even bear to be in the same room with me.

Owen couldn't take his eyes off Kathryn. Her jaw was set and there was an angry fire raging in her eyes. "Owen Morgan, obviously I'm not the only pigheaded person in this marriage. You're the one who's incapable of forgiving and forgetting."

"Forgiving and forgetting what?"

"The awful things I said to you. I've been trying to understand why I did it. I was angry because you broke down when I needed you. You've always been so strong. I know I'm not the clinging-vine type, and I've fought you tooth and nail every time I imagined you were trying to interfere in my business life, but I still needed you. Knowing you were there, being my emotional support, patting me on the back and holding my hand, was important. More important than I ever realized. I expected you to make everything all right—the way you always did—but instead you were broken yourself and I was furious at you for failing me."

"But I couldn't make it all right."

Kathryn shook her head, and tears began to roll down her cheeks. "Do you still love me?" she asked again, her voice small and weak through her tears.

Their eyes locked. "Of course I do. Nothing could stop me from loving you. Although I tried, by God, I tried. For days I drove around, through some of the most godforsaken towns in the South, trying to convince myself that making a clean break would be best for both of us. That our love was dead."

"I tried, too."

"Did it work?" he asked.

"No."

"Shall we stop trying?" Owen was almost afraid to hear her answer.

As she walked toward him a ray of late afternoon sunlight hit her, turning her golden. It seemed strange taking her in his arms again—such a simple action that he'd performed so many times before, the desire for which had haunted him for days. He dreamed about the feel of her body in his arms, and when he awoke, the pain was fresh and unbearable.

"Yes, oh, yes," Kathryn murmured as Owen stroked her hair. "We'll pick up the pieces and try to pretend all this never happened. It will be like before."

"No," Owen said. "Let's make a new beginning. I refuse to lose you again, and sometimes I used to have the feeling that there was a lot more going on in your head than you ever told me. Can't we work on creating a marriage of equals, being partners who share everything—including their problems and fears no matter how terrible they may seem?"

As he spoke he felt her body stiffen against his. "Kathryn, what's wrong? Is that idea so terrible?"

She pulled away and looked up at him. "If we have a new beginning to our marriage, then there's something I have to tell you. Something I should have told you years ago."

When Kathryn finished her confession Owen said, "Your evil brother has nothing to do with us and how I feel about you. As long as you're always open and honest with me. Can't you get it into your thick head that I love you no matter what? Stop trying to prove yourself. Kathryn, my love is nonnegotiable. I don't need or want a wife who's perfect. I want you, and I'd love you even if you couldn't balance a checkbook and had Satan for a brother."

"Honestly?"

"Are you calling me a liar?" Owen asked with a grin.

"No," she said firmly. "You are the most honest, moral person I've ever met."

Her words struck unexpectedly at his heart. Did an honest man commit adultery—even the word stuck in his craw—with his wife's best friend? How could he have done that to Kathryn? The memory would haunt him until his dying day. Did he have the strength to tell her? She'd confessed her secrets. Didn't she deserve the truth, too?

"Kathryn, there's something . . ."

Maureen's ear was pressed to the door. The meeting had been of her making. Kathryn and Owen belonged together. She'd have to live with her jealousy. Like any good director, she knew enough to step in at the proper moment, and so now she tapped on the door and entered without waiting for an answer.

Owen looked pale, as if he'd seen a ghost, but Kathryn was grinning from ear to ear. She jumped up and threw her arms around her friend. "Maureen, you planned the whole thing, didn't you? How can I ever thank you? Did you know where Owen was the whole time, and why didn't you tell anyone?"

"I only found out yesterday. Your husband had some crazy notion about returning to Wales as a coal miner. He needed money and," she said with a laugh, "I guess he knew I'd be a soft touch."

"I'm glad you didn't give it to him," Kathryn said, her eyes never leaving Owen's face. "You are a rare friend."

Maureen hid her feelings with a smile. "You two belong together, even if you forgot it for a bit."

An enormous sense of relief washed over Owen. Maureen's message was loud and clear, and she was right. He wouldn't endanger his happiness with Kathryn by telling her the truth. The incident meant nothing. No one ever need know. Nothing would ever threaten the bond that made him one with Kathryn.

"Now," Maureen said briskly, "I'm going to chase you two lovebirds out. You have a lot of lost time to catch up on."

On the way out Kathryn caught a glimpse of herself and Owen in the hall mirror. What a handsome couple we make, she thought. Maureen's right: we do belong together. Then with a start she demanded, "Owen Morgan, where did you get that suit?"

He put his arm around her and squeezed tight. "I was dressing to fit my new life. It's a coal miner's Sunday go-to-chapel suit. Don't tell me you don't like it?"

Kathryn laughed. It was a young, carefree laugh that reminded Owen of bells. "It's . . . it's indescribable." She cocked her head as she assessed the suit. "No, since we promised to be honest with each other, I must say it's perfectly ghastly."

Owen turned to Maureen and clasped both her hands in his. "Thank you from both of us." He grinned. "I don't know what I would have done without your kind heart and good sense."

"Become a coal miner, I suppose," Maureen said with a dry chuckle, sounding almost like herself.

Kathryn kissed her on the cheek. "Thank you for bringing my husband back to me."

As they walked down the steps Owen said with a mischievous grin, "You know, coal miners are a passionate lot. You might have enjoyed being married to one."

Kathryn's eyes sparkled. "I think you should know my husband provides me with quite enough passion, sir." She paused. "But if you want to try to convince me . . ."

"Is that an invitation?"

"Most certainly. And I think, Mr. Morgan, you'll find that we hotel owners are a passionate lot also. And not only about our hotels. After all, there are more important things. . . ."

Owen knew what she was trying to say. It was a new beginning. "Is that a promise?" he asked, his voice suddenly solemn.

"It is," Kathryn said, slipping her hand into his.

Maureen stood in the doorway watching their car drive off. She wished she could have grand and glorious dreams like Kathryn Townsend Morgan. But some women's dreams just didn't soar as far or as high. It was a rare woman who dared to dream as Kathryn did. And whose dreams all seemed to come true.